JUN - 2006

also by r. garcia y robertson from tom doherty associates

American Woman

Knight Errant

Lady Robyn

White Rose

A TOM DOHERTY ASSOCIATES BOOK

New York

Firebird

R. GARCIA Y ROBERTSON

FIREBIRD

Copyright © 2006 by R. Garcia y Robertson

A Tor Book
Published by Tom Doherty Associates, LLC
175 Fifth Avenue
New York, NY 10010

www.tor.com

Tor® is a registered trademark of Tom Doherty Associates, LLC.

Library of Congress Cataloging-in-Publication Data

Garcia y Robertson, Rodrigo, 1949–
Firebird / R. Garcia y Robertson.—1st ed.
p. cm.
ISBN 0-765-31356-1 (alk. paper)
EAN 978-0-765-31356-0
I. Title.

PS3557.A71125F57 2006
813'.54—dc22   2006040363

First Edition: May 2006

Printed in the United States of America

0 9 8 7 6 5 4 3 2 1

for betsy

PART ONE

tales of the iron wood

Markovy is bordered on the west by Transylvania,
Hungary, Poland, and the Balts, and on the east by
Far Barbary and the Iron Wood. . . .

—JOURNALS OF BARON DE ROYE

I

prince sergey and the witch-girl

Once upon a time, deep in the north woods that circle the world, a witch-girl gathered fungus for the Bone Witch's supper, when she heard the fire jay call her name. *"Ahrr-ee-haa, ahrr-ee-haa, ahrr-ee-haa . . ."*

Brushing tangled black hair from sea-green eyes, Aria searched for the bird, seeing only tall pine trunks and blue bars of sky. Somewhere in her teens, Aria knew neither her age nor her birthday, but was otherwise quick-witted, as well as lithe and strong from living in the woods. Her strange name was given her by her mother, and it meant "song" in the forbidden language of the opera. Aria called back to the fire jay, "Here I am, silly bird. Come tell what you see."

She listened. Insects hummed in hot pine-scented air. Farther off, Aria heard a woodpecker knocking. Her bright homespun dress had the red-orange firebird embroidered on the bodice, done in silk from Black Cathay and the Barbary cloth called crimson. Aria had stitched it herself on sunless winter days, sitting by the Bone Witch's cold hearth with just the sleeping rats to warm her bare toes.

Now that she was fully grown, Aria never feared the woods by daylight. Leopards, troll-bears, lycanthropes, and forest sprites lurked among the trees, waiting to make a meal of the unwary. But by day, the boreal woods had a hundred eyes alert for any suspicious movement. No lynx or leopard could stir a foot without birds calling and squirrels chattering. All Aria need do was listen.

Night was another matter. But the Bone Witch never let Aria out at night.

Nor could she leave the hut without her slave collar and protective rune, showing she was valuable property. Each morning, the Bone Witch made Aria repeat her invisibility spell, saying, "I have not raised you to feed a hungry troll-bear. Not when you are finally becoming useful."

Aria did not argue, though she had found every moment of her short life thoroughly useful—no matter what others might think. She began as a girl-child thrown away in time of civil war and famine, but she had lived to become a prized slave of the Bone Witch. Survival taught Aria to make the best of today, for tomorrow was often worse, and not to shit where she meant to sleep, and never to tell the truth unless under duress. Most of all, it taught her to trust to her luck, which had saved her when hundreds of girls like her were taken by the Killer of Children. Lady Death had ample chance to find her, yet Aria was happily gathering fungus in the forest, making her think the Killer of Children had spared her for something special.

At puberty she was given to the Bone Witch for two handfuls of salt and a cattle pox cure. Her foster family figured they were doing everyone a favor. "The witch can better provide for you. We are poor," the father informed her—as if Aria had not noticed, sleeping between the hearth and the hogs, "while you are stubborn and willful."

His wife hastily agreed. "Making you obey is like trying to teach a cat to fetch." Had Aria been a boy, it would have been different, but she was a girl, naturally wanton, unruly, frivolous, and amoral, a growing threat to their son's virtue. They were duty-bound to keep her chaste and ignorant, then give her to some man in marriage—a dead loss to the family. Better by far to give her to the Bone Witch.

Only their lazy son objected. Not the least threatened, he wanted Aria around. Without her, who would do his chores? Who would he spy on in the bath? He had promised to rape her when they got bigger.

Aria herself had said nothing. Raised as a slave to serfs, she retained a stubborn sense of self-worth that regularly got her whipped. People called her *changeling* and worse, with her pert ways and wicked green eyes—a girl switched at birth for a defiant demon-child. Bundling up her straw doll and wooden spoon, she took a seat in the father's cart, and they lurched off, crossing the Dys at Byeli Zamak, headed for the Iron Wood. All she could think was that she was to become a witch-girl. And witches were burned.

That was years ago, and she had not been burnt—not yet. By now Aria had spent half her life in the woods, and she knew which mushrooms were food, and which were for flights of fancy, what berries were sweet, and which herbs cured, and which ones killed. Having nothing of her own, Aria happily appropriated all of nature. These were her trees, her flowers, her birds and beasts in the branches above. Every screech and cry in the foliage spoke to her. When it was safe, she spoke back.

"*Aarr-ee-haa, aar-ee-ha, aar-ee-ha . . .*" The call came closer. Like her, the fire jay was a curious soul, and could be coaxed with low, soft calls. Nothing could happen in his woods without him telling the world about it.

Picking up her bark basket, Aria set out after the sound, fording a shallow stream to enter a fern-choked glade ringed by stands of slim silver birch. Birches loved the light and fought to fill any sort of clearing. At the far end of the glade was a pond frequented by red deer and herons, and on the bare bank Aria saw pugmarks.

She knelt amid the bracken, feeling the tracks, finding the claw prints worn and splayed with age. Three nights ago, after the rain when the moon was full, an old female leopard came from the same direction she had, stopped to drink, and then headed up the ridge, aiming for the thickly wooded crest separating the woods from the settled lands beyond. Any leopard with business beyond the ridge could easily be a stock thief or man-eater.

Not a cat Aria cared to meet. Stomach tensing, she looked about. Mossy patches shone like polished jade. The protective rune on her armlet shielded Aria from magic—but not from fang or claw. Straightening up, she set out again, keeping the breeze at her back. Leopards did not know humans have no sense of smell, and so they never stalked from upwind—she need only worry about what lay ahead. These were her woods. Let some old leopard scare her, and she would never go out at all.

"*Arr-ee-ah, arr-ee-ah . . .*" She spotted a flash of orange among the pine trunks. The bird awaited her at the crest of the ridge.

And not just the fire jay, but a fire as well. Black oily smoke billowed from beyond the ridge crest, smearing the clear blue sky. Hairs rose at the nape of Aria's neck. She had not smelled the smoke, because the wind was behind her—but she knew where it came from. Byeli Zamak was burning.

Topping the ridge, Aria stared in awe. This was as far as the slave collar let her go. Below her the forest ended, and rolling steppe spread out from the foot of the ridge, broken by loops of river, dark patches of fallow, and the onion domes of village churches. Between her and the plowlands, guarding the fords of the Dys, stood a round white-stone tower seven stories tall, with walls twenty feet thick—Byeli Zamak, the White Castle. Smoke poured from the tower. Aria pictured the inferno inside, fed by grain and oil stored in the basement, burning up through the wooden floors, feeding on gilt furniture, Barbary tapestries, Italian paintings, and canopied beds. A cornerstone of Aria's world was consumed in flames.

She came from these settled lands. Somewhere out there, Aria had been born. Somewhere out there, her family was slaughtered—for the black earth beyond the woods was sown with bones and watered by blood. Constant strife consumed her family, and almost made an end to her. She had begged in those villages, and slept in the painted doorways of those churches, waking to find crows and ravens hoping to make a meal of her.

When she was given to the Bone Witch, all that changed. Her slave collar kept her penned in the woods—where the worst she need fear was leopards and troll-bears. Even when old King Demitri died, Byeli Zamak remained, towering over the fords of the Dys—the gatehouse to the Iron Wood. King Demitri and gold-domed Markov were the stuff of faerie tales, but Byeli Zamak was a solid part of Aria's landscape, built by earth giants from native stone. And now it burned. Her first thought was to tell the Bone Witch.

"Arr-ee-aah . . . ," the fire jay called again, this time from right overhead. Looking up, she saw the flame-colored jay perched on the limb of a tall larch, scoffing and chuckling. Clown prince of the bird clan, the fire-orange jay was a wicked trickster, a merciless nest-robber and accomplished mimic. Aria had heard him perfectly imitate the screaming whistle of a hawk, just to see what havoc he could wreak.

"Is this what you saw?" Aria tilted her head toward the inferno below. How like a jay to revel in someone else's misfortune. He squawked back at her, this time giving the man call. Jays greeted every predator with a different call, since warnings were useless if you did not know whether to look out for a leopard or a hawk. The man call was totally distinct—jays never used it for her or the Bone Witch.

Hearing brush rattle, Aria turned to see a roe deer bound up the slope and disappear over the ridge. Something alarming was coming, startling enough to flush a doe from cover. The fire jay flew off, still making the man call.

From below came the weighty clump of slow hoofbeats climbing the ridge.

A horse was coming up from the fords, carrying something heavy and clanking. Aria whispered her invisibility spell. So long as she remained still and silent, no one could see her. Or so the Bone Witch said. So far, it had never failed.

Aria watched the armored rider top the ridge. Bareheaded, he rode slumped forward, eyes half-shut, his soot-stained blue-and-white surcoat covering fire-blackened steel—a dark-haired man-at-arms, maybe even a knight, just managing to stay atop a big gray charger. Her heart went out to him. He looked so hurt and handsome, his long elegant eyelashes wet with tears. Bloody clots in his fashionable pudding-basin haircut dripped red streaks past proud cheekbones. His beardless face made him look young, marking him as a foreigner. Or a eunuch.

Here was her storm petrel, strong and beautiful, but a sure sign of the whirlwind to come. So long as Byeli Zamak had held for the King, only unarmed serfs crossed the fords into the forest, to gather sticks and snare squirrels, stripping bark for their shoes and stealing honey from the bees. On May Day they came singing, their arms full of flowers, celebrating the return of spring, slipping off in pairs to make love upon the forest floor—while Aria watched, invisible and intrigued. In summer the forest rang with their axes—the nearest thing they had to weapons. It was a flogging offense for a serf to have a bow, or a boar spear. Death to be caught with a sword.

But this stranger had a huge sword slung across his back, and his torn surcoat bore the embattled blue bend of the King's horse guards. His crested helm hung from his saddle bow, alongside an ugly sawtooth war ax, topped by a wicked spike. Hunched forward, he carried something heavy in the crook of his shield arm, wrapped in silk embroidery, tucked against his armored breast. She stood stock-still, letting him rattle past, just out of reach.

When he had gotten far enough ahead of her, she set off after him, slipping silently from tree to tree, following the birdcalls down the ridge and onto the forest floor. Tiny red flecks of blood shone on green fern fronds, marking his trail for her.

Now the breeze was full in her face, which Aria did not like. A leopard could come up behind her, stalking her as easily as she trailed this knight. Worse yet, the breeze brought the foul scent of a troll-bear's lair, faint but growing stronger. The rotting-corpse smell of discarded carcasses mixed with the rank odor of the troll-bear's droppings was unmistakable, like smelling a long-dead lizard on a hot day. Only the image of the knight's hurt face and elegant curved lips kept her going.

She caught up with her knight beneath a cool coppice of oaks. Leaves rustled like water overhead, and the rattle of armor had ceased—but the smell of horse droppings, and a nervous whinny, warned her she was getting too close. Sinking to all fours, she wriggled through the undergrowth, curious to see why he had stopped. Had he smelled the troll-bear?

Her knight had dismounted. Kneeling in the bracken, he attacked the ground with a big saxe knife, digging a hole in the dark earth. She watched patiently. When he had dug down the length of his arm, he sheathed the knife and picked up an embroidered bundle from the ground beside him. Gently he lowered the bundle into the hole. It had to be something precious from the way he handled it. A gold icon perhaps. Or a great crystal goblet. Or a dead baby.

He covered over the hole, hiding his work with fallen leaves. Then he looked up, straight at her, sensing he was watched. Aria stayed still as a fawn, and the spell held.

Drained by the simple act of digging, her knight heaved himself back onto his horse, no mean feat in plate and mail. Then he lurched off upwind, headed for the troll-bear's lair. Unless Aria did something, the troll-bear would savage both horse and rider, cracking her knight's armor like a badger breaking open a snail.

When the carrion odor got unbearable, his horse stopped again, refusing to go on. Aria waited for her knight to turn or dismount, but he stayed slumped in his saddle, eyes closed, his handsome gray mount nervously cropping the bracken.

Warning calls died away, and the woods grew still. A good sign. Either the troll-bear was gorged senseless, or away from the den.

Shrugging off her spell, Aria stepped out from between the trees, walking warily toward her knight. His horse saw her first, snorting and shying. Speaking softly, she reached out and took the reins. "Have no fear. I will take you to good grass and water."

Her knight opened his eyes, which were blue and alert. He smiled at her, saying, "*Mon Dieu,* I am dead." He did·not look very dead, clinging stubbornly to his saddle. "And here is an angel to bear me to Heaven."

"I am no angel," she told him. She was a witch-child—willful, disobedient, and hopelessly damned.

His smile widened. "Then a forest sprite, young and beautiful. The perfect Valkyrie for a vagabond." He spoke with a funny foreign accent, but his tone told her he was friendly. Gently turning the tired horse's head, she led him slowly downwind, away from the troll-bear's lair. Her knight swayed alarmingly in the saddle. "Fair nymph," he called down to her. "Where are you taking us?"

Aria grinned over her shoulder. "To water." He was by far the most marvelous thing she had ever found in the woods, and she wanted to see him with his face washed.

After leading the horse back to the base of the ridge—to where a spring burst from beneath tall triangular rocks—she helped her knight dismount. Sitting him down, Aria wet a cloth and wiped his wincing face, noting he cleaned up very nicely. His handsome, beardless face felt firm and manly, yet smooth to the touch. His head wound was bloody, though not deep, and it merely needed to be cleaned, then sewn shut. Luckily, she had been gathering bitter herbs for the Bone Witch, natural poisons used to cleanse wounds.

He watched as she worked, smiling ruefully. "Just when you wonder what you are fighting for, Heaven sends a reminder."

"What reminder is that?" She searched through her bark basket for the right leaves.

His smile widened. "You really do not know, do you?"

"No. That is why I asked." Her knight had a funny way of talking, even for a foreigner. She crushed the leaves with a rock, mixing them with water from the spring.

"I have had a most damnable day," he told her, "trying to hold Byeli Zamak for your infant Prince Ivan. Besieged by the boy's own uncle, upholding the honor of your dead king, and being badly beaten for my pains. Just when I think I cannot go on—that there is nothing in this benighted land worth saving—you come along. Proving me completely wrong."

"This will hurt," she warned him, parting his hair to expose the wound.

"*Certainement.* So far today, everything has." Taking that as assent, Aria poured her makeshift potion onto the bloody gash. He shouted in protest, raising a steel-gloved hand to shield his head. "*Merde!* Does Mademoiselle mean to murder me too?"

She grabbed his gauntlet to keep it away from the wound. "Do not worry—it is just poison."

He grimaced. "That I can tell."

"No. This will clean the wound, I swear." She found her embroidery needle with her free hand.

Her knight relaxed. "*C'est bien, c'est bien.* Mademoiselle merely took me by surprise." He sat stoically while she poured more potion on the needle, then began sewing his scalp back together, wincing when Aria tightened a stitch, but otherwise acting as if she were clipping his curls. He asked, "What may I call Mademoiselle?"

"Aria," she replied shyly, resisting the impulse to invent. She wanted him to know her name.

"*Enchanté.* Sir Roye de Roye, Chevalier de l'Étoile, *et le* Baron de Roye. At your service." He winced again as her needle went in. "What does Mademoiselle do when not torturing wounded gentlemen?"

She pulled the stitch tight, saying softly, "I serve the Bone Witch."

"A witch? But of course. And a wicked one too, from the way that potion burned . . ."

"But she is merely my foster mother. My real mother was a queen. And I am a princess." Not knowing who her parents were, Aria felt free to invent royal ones.

Baron de Roye arched an eyebrow. "Princess in disguise, I presume?"

"Of course," she replied scornfully. "Why else would I be dressed like a peasant?"

"Your Majesty carries off her masquerade effortlessly."

"Shush!" she whispered. From atop the ridge came the fire jay's man call. She listened harder. The call came again, fading as the bright orange bird took flight. Someone was coming. She asked, "Are there men after you?"

"There are," he admitted. "Though not for any good reason."

She hastily finished her stitching, saying, "I must hide you." Aria had no fear for herself, but the thought of seeing her newfound knight hurt or killed was too much to bear. Helping him to his feet, she guided him up the rocks to a protruding shelf, where two boulders formed a tiny cave between them, too high up to be seen from the spring. She shoved him inside, saying, "Stay here."

"Only if Your Majesty promises to come for me," he replied.

"I will." She truly wanted to see more of him, only not right now. Not with more men coming.

"Promise?"

"I swear." She pushed him farther into the cave, where her knight would not be seen from below.

"Bring food," he begged.

"I will," she agreed hastily.

"And wine."

Aria did not bother to answer, scrambling back down the rocks to the spring. Taking his mount's reins, she turned the horse away from the spring.

"Good wine. If Your Highness has it."

Still thirsty, the horse balked at being led off by a stranger. Aria had to heave on the reins to get him pointed back the way she must go. Her knight called down to her, "And what about my horse?"

"I will hide him too," she promised, pulling harder, hauling the unwilling animal away from the spring.

"Au revoir," he called out.

"Silence, please!" she shouted back, mortified to be making so much noise with strangers in the woods. Dragging the weary charger away from rest and water, she doubled back on their tracks. Anyone seeing the return prints would have no reason to search out the cave, and would follow her trail instead.

When she had put distance between herself and the spring, Aria found a swift brook leading into Long Lake and splashed along it, letting running water hide their trail. Spotting a good place to leave the stream—a rock shelf that would not take hoofprints—she deliberately passed it by. Downstream from the rock shelf, she let the horse stray, making tracks on the bank, then leading him back into the water and up onto the opposite bank. When she was satisfied with her false trail, she carefully retreated upstream, leading the horse out over the rocks, trying her utmost not to leave tracks.

She stayed on hard ground until she was well out of sight of the stream and could no longer hear its rippling. Then she tied the horse to a tree and went back alone. Walking as lightly as she could, Aria covered up any sign of the horse's passing, smoothing over stray prints and sprinkling dust where they had wet the rocks. When she reached the stream, she whispered her spell, lying down to watch.

Aria waited, her heart beating against hard stone. Stretching on the far side of the stream was a splendid spiderweb, shot with rainbows, well worth returning for when things were not so busy. In the meantime, she thought about her knight, with his funny foreign way of talking, and his warm smile. He had a good heart as well; Aria could tell by the way he laughed and joked about his troubles. He even seemed to like her too, though that was a lot to hope for.

First she heard warning calls—the indignant chatter of a red squirrel, the rasping cry of a frightened pine tit. Followed by the voices of men and the neighing of their horses. They came slowly downstream, searching both banks, looking for the spot where she left the water.

One huge fellow in half-armor and big bucket-topped riding boots urged his mount up onto the rock shelf, coming so close, she could count the flanges on the heavy steel mace hanging from his saddle bow. Matted hair and flecks of blood clung to the sharp steel. He wore his sallet tipped back, searching the ground for tracks, and his hard bearded face could not compare to the clean elegant features of Sir Roye de Roye, Chevalier de l'Étoile. But his surcoat bore the same embattled blue bend as her knight's—charged with the lightning-strike badge of Prince Sergey Mikhailovich, Grand Duke of Ikstra. Crown Prince Ivan's belligerent uncle, who had burned Byeli Zamak and was now hunting her.

She held her breath as he studied the spot where she led the charger out of the stream. Did he see something? A crushed leaf or overturned stone? The scrape mark of a steel shoe?

Calls came from downstream. They had found her false trail. Prince Sergey's ugly hulking man-at-arms turned his horse about, splashing back into the stream.

As the calls faded into the forest, Aria slid back off the rocks and carefully made her way back to the tethered horse. The Bone Witch would scold her if she did not return soon with her bark basket full of herbs and fungus.

As she set out, clouds of little white butterflies whirled up from patches of sunlight, fluttering among the horse's legs and then darting off into the trees. The deeper she went into the woods, the less she worried about hiding her trail. The only warning calls were for her. At the head of Long Lake, she saw wild swans swimming on clear water fringed by pines.

Beyond the lake, the pine wood ended. On the far side stood a forest of black iron trunks with stark metal branches—the Iron Wood—a cold dark barrier reeking of magic, stretching over the hills to the east, lifeless and forbidding. She led the reluctant horse into the black leafless wood. Spiked branches closed around her, and forest sounds faded. No woodpeckers beat at the hard metal bark. No squirrels ran along bladelike limbs. No living beasts made their home in the Iron Wood—just trolls and siren spirits, witches and the walking dead.

Happy to be nearly home, Aria threaded through the thorny metal maze. Finally a clearing appeared ahead, a white patch amid the black tangle. She led the big warhorse up to a tall white hut made entirely of bones, long white thighbones as big as a man, stacked one atop the other like grisly logs. Serfs called them dragon bones, but Aria knew better. They came from a long-haired elephant-trunked monster that once roamed the tundra, bigger by far than any Barbary elephant. She had seen their great curved tusks in a forest bone pit, along with bits of hairy hide.

Huge antlers from an ancient giant elk hung above the Bone Hut's leather door. Swallows nested in nooks beneath the eaves. Little chestnut-throated birds peered out of the mud nests at her. Their parents flew back and forth, chattering together, then streaking off in the direction of Long Lake, coming back with ants, gnats, wasps, and assassin bugs to feed their young.

Slowly the skin door swung open, and the Bone Witch emerged. Older than sin, and grim as death, the witch wore a necklace of child bones and a linen winding sheet. White hair hung down to her bare skeletal feet. Around her thin waist was a wormwood belt, supporting her thief-skin charm bag.

Sir Roye's gray stallion backed and snorted at the sight of the witch, but the Bone Witch muttered a charm and the shying charger relaxed. "A beautiful beast," the witch declared. "Where did you find him?"

"In the woods." Aria had always brought lost or stray animals out of the woods. Fallen eagle chicks. Little lame squirrels. Orphaned leopard cubs. This tall stallion was by far her most impressive find. She made no mention of his master, for the Bone Witch had warned her not to bring men into the Iron Wood. Abandoned cubs and a warhorse were one thing—but no stray knights, no matter how handsome and helpless.

Aria held out her basket to show she had not wasted the whole morning, saying, "Byeli Zamak has been burned."

The crone nodded. "I smelled it on the wind." It was impossible to surprise the Bone Witch.

"And a leopard drank from the pond beneath the ridge."

The witch nodded again. "Three nights ago, when the moon was full." Accepting the fungus, the witch told Aria to give the gray charger a rubdown. "And see he has grass and water. You cannot bring things home unless you care for them."

"I will, I will," she assured her mistress, taking the horse around to the paddock behind the Bone Hut, rubbing him down, giving him water and barley.

After filling a bark basket with food, Aria got out the witch's steel sickle, saying she would go cut grass at Long Lake. Nothing a horse could live on grew in the Iron Wood.

The Bone Witch sniffed her basket. "And you will take food to the knight hiding in the cave by the spring?"

She gave a guilty nod.

"You are free to play with whatever you find in the woods, so long as your chores do not go wanting."

"Oh, no!" Aria protested. "I gathered more fungus, and spied webs for spinning. See, I am taking my spindle."

The old witch shook her head. "You will be the death of me. Always rushing life along."

"No! Never." Aria kissed the crone's cold wrinkled lips. "You will always be here." The Bone Witch had been in the Iron Wood forever.

"Of course, but what has that to do with it?" The witch shooed her out of the hut.

As the witch predicted, Aria went straight to the cave, fearing she would find it empty, and that she would never see her knight again. Nearing the spring, she stopped to listen. And heard nothing. Maybe he had obeyed her and stayed in the cave. More likely, he was long gone.

She was thrilled to find herself wrong. *"Bonjour,"* he greeted her with a grin when she stuck her head into the cave. Wearing just his suit of mail, wool hose, and padded arming doublet, Sir Roye heaved himself upright, peering into her basket. "What is this? Food, how wonderful! Did you bring wine as well?" She admitted she had not, having never so much as seen a grape. "Alas, too bad. But this is magic enough. Is there meat?"

"Kolbasa." She doled out a length of smoked sausage.

"Excellent, good old kolbasa, and bread too. What a wonderful wood sprite." He gave her a happy pat on the hip, asking, "Would there be caviar to go with it?"

"There is." She liked the firm feel of his hand on her, and wished she had the nerve to kiss him. Instead she showed her knight the gleaming fish roe wrapped in a cool leaf. Long Lake teemed with sturgeon.

"Caviar! Fantastic. What a feast!"

"And myot also." Aria handed him the comb.

"Honey. How delightful." He gave her another pat, this time on the thigh.

"And yogurt." She shifted closer, enjoying the feel of his big strong body beside her.

"Ah yes." He looked in the little pot she held up. "Markovy's answer to sour milk."

"And diynya," Aria added.

"Diynya?" He looked puzzled.

She lifted the melon from the bottom of the basket, holding it out to him. "Diynya."

"Of course. Diynya. How utterly delicious." Taking the melon, he kissed her in gratitude. "*Merci beaucoup*, Mademoiselle Wood Sprite."

Her lips tingled from her first kiss by a grown man. The lumpish son from her foster family once held her down and tried to kiss her, but she bit his tongue. This was utterly different. Delicious shivers shot through her, raising goose bumps from nipples to groin. That he kissed her quickly and casually did not matter. Nor did it matter that he had clearly forgotten her name. It was enough that she remembered his: Sir Roye de Roye, Chevalier de l'Étoile, *et le* Baron de Roye. She felt utterly ecstatic, having her first real kiss come from someone so special—not just a knight, but a foreign lord. All hers to feed and care for, and hopefully kiss again.

Which made her worry even more for him. "Why do those men aim to harm you?"

"Rank prejudice," Sir Roye de Roye replied, spreading caviar with his thumb. "Silly baseless superstition."

She broke open the melon, sipped the juice, and passed it to him. "But why would Prince Ivan's own uncle attack Byeli Zamak?"

Sir Roye heaved a sigh. "Mademoiselle does not live in a nation. Markovy is a patchwork of family quarrels with disputed boundaries, ruled by civil war. Being a foreign heretic, I give not a lead sou who wins—but I swore an oath to your King Demitri to uphold his honor and his heir. Not that noble oaths mean much when your head is being beaten in."

Still beset by goose bumps, Aria took out her spindle and started spinning spider's silk, relaxing her nervous fingers—all the while wondering how to get him to kiss her again.

"Markovites are the most superstitious folk in creation," Sir Roye complained between bites. "Believing in all manner of faeries, imps, djinn, witches, and whatnot. Byeli Zamak supposedly held a secret treasure—the Firebird's

Egg, a marvelous magic egg that will hatch a huge fire-breathing phoenix. Your Prince Sergey is a grotesquely gullible grand duke, who thinks this mythical egg will make him master of Markovy—but I held Byeli Zamak for Prince Ivan, and King Demitri before him. As castellan, I would know if Byeli Zamak held such an egg, and it certainly does not."

Aria herself absolutely believed in the Firebird's Egg. King Demitri had stolen the Egg from the Firebird's Nest atop Burning Mountain, deep in the Iron Wood, and kept it locked in a cool deep vault beneath Byeli Zamak—where it would not hatch and would always be his. It had been King Demitri's greatest treasure, and his greatest curse, making his life tragic and miserable. The curse cost him both his wives and all his children, except for Ivan, his heir. Why Ivan's uncle would ever want the ill-fated Egg was totally beyond Aria—but that did not make it a myth.

Her knight told more stories, of far-off Gascony, where he was born, and how he had lost everything and ended up in exile. "I possess an astounding ability to choose the losing side. Counting this latest debacle at Byeli Zamak, I have been in half a dozen pitched fights—and have always come out a loser. A remarkable record, not easily achieved. When I sided with the English, they lost to the King of France. When I switched my allegiance to the King, he lost to the English. Scots in the French service call me Tyneman, in tribute to my many defeats. An honor, really. Any lout with a bit of ability can run off a string of victories. But to lose every time—that requires not just talent, but uncanny luck as well."

"I cannot believe your luck could be so bad." She did not want to think anything bad about Sir Roye. His stories were amusing, and she ached to have him take her in his arms and kiss and talk to her all day, and on into the night.

"Bad luck?" Sir Roye de Roye laughed. "Not in the least—my luck is excellent. Could not be better."

"Really? But is it not better to win than lose?"

"Better, perhaps—but not always easier. Anyone can survive a victory: just stay to the back and shout loudly. But surviving six defeats is a rare feat. Requiring more than a swift horse. Twice, I was the only one on the losing side not killed or captured. That takes phenomenal luck."

"I mean, I do not believe you must always lose."

He scoffed at her innocence. "Tell it to the Swiss, who were near unbeatable until I sided with them."

By now, dusk was settling outside the cave. Shafts of golden light slanted between the trees, slicing deep into the forest. Having seen her knight fed and cared for, Aria needed to get back and cut grass for his horse, then see to the witch's supper, making the most of the spring twilight. Sadly she took her leave, fairly sure he would not wander off, and meaning to be back by morning.

Sir Roye declared himself devastated to see her go, cheering Aria immensely. She finally had her knight in armor. Who cared if he was a foreigner, and somewhat the worse for wear—a footloose loser from some far-off land? He was the most wonderful thing she had ever found in the woods, and Aria could feel herself falling hopelessly in love.

His kiss good-bye made her ache between the legs. Only fear of the Bone Witch kept Aria from giving in totally to her feelings.

Before returning to the Iron Wood, Aria gathered more bitter herbs and spider's silk; then she sneaked up on the troll-bear's lair, hoping her own scent would be hidden by the carrion stink. When she found the spot she sought, Aria dug down into the deep forest loam, using the witch's steel sickle. She glanced repeatedly over her shoulder, uncomfortably aware that she had watched her knight dig in this exact spot without him knowing it.

Setting aside the sickle, she dug the last few inches with her hands, not wanting to harm what lay hidden in the hole. Finally she felt something soft and warm beneath her fingers. Brushing aside the last of the dirt, Aria recognized the embroidered tapestry her knight had kept next to his armored breast. Unwrapping the tapestry, she felt the smooth hard surface underneath, the warm living Firebird's Egg.

She folded the tapestry back over the Egg, then refilled the hole, happy her knight had not lied to her. He claimed that as castellan, he would have known if Byeli Zamak held such a magical egg—and it did not. But that was because he had escaped Byeli Zamak with it, and buried it here by the troll-bear's lair. Being a born romancer herself, Aria took such truthful misdirection as a sign of true love.

That night, the Bone Witch tucked Aria into her spider's-silk hammock and told her a tale from Far Barbary, about Sindbad the Sailor's second voyage, when the Muslim mariner was marooned on Roc Island, but made his escape by tying his turban to the leg of a giant roc. He flew off to the Diamond Wadi, "which swarmed with vipers and pythons as thick as a palm trunk, able to swallow an elephant whole."

"That sounds worse than rocs." Aria had never seen a python or a palm tree, but she lived in a hut made of elephant bones, and greatly feared any snake that could gulp it down.

"Much worse," the Bone Witch agreed, "but the serpents only came out at night, for fear that the rocs and eagles would eat them. That night Sindbad hid in a hole, and at dawn he was giddy from hunger and thirst, thinking that he had doomed himself to a hideous death. Then thanks to Allah, he remembered hearing that gem merchants harvested diamonds from this wadi, by slaughtering sheep and tossing their bloody carcasses into the valley, so that jewels would stick to the meat. Rocs and eagles would seize the meat, carrying the diamonds out of the deep canyon to their nests, where the merchants would gather up the gems. . . ."

The Bone Witch's stories of Far Barbary all ended the same way, with the witch saying, "Then Shahrazad saw the first light of day break over the edge of the world, and ceased her story, saying her husband could hear the rest of the tale the next night—if he did not cut off her head. Thus ended the Five Hundred and Forty-fourth Night, in the *Tale of the Thousand Nights and a Night*."

Shahrazad was an empress of Persia, whose husband so despised the sinfulness of women that he executed his brides after their wedding night to keep them from ever being unfaithful—until Shahrazad reformed her bloodthirsty spouse by telling an endless string of entertaining stories.

That night, Aria dreamed of flying off with her knight on the back of a huge roc, to honeymoon in Far Barbary. They flew south and east together, landing in the high harem of an exotic fortress-palace set on an island in a flat blue sea. Finding the harem empty and a warm perfumed bath already drawn for them, Sir Roye turned to her with a smile, saying, "May I assist Mademoiselle?"

Without giving her a chance to answer, he started undoing the ties on her dress. Forgetting that this was a dream, Aria thrilled to the feel of his fingers against her skin, stripping off her embroidered bodice and then dropping her skirts. Aria stood before her knight wearing only a linen shift and knowing she would soon be naked. Sir Roye's hands were bare, and he smiled at her, but his body was still encased in steel, coldly powerful and immune to her touch. His disembodied hands seized her shift at the waist, pulling the fabric up over her head.

Now she was totally bare. Her knight's smile widened as he told her, "Mademoiselle is most fetching, indeed. Now if she will allow—"

Sir Roye's big strong hands closed around her ribs, thumbs pressing against her breasts. He lifted her up, kissed her lovingly on the lips, then lowered her into the bath. A flood of warm wet sensation flowed up from her toes, through her ankles and calves, then finally immersing her thighs in hot wetness, making her squirm in her sleep.

And Sir Roye was in the water with her, his armor magically gone, replaced by firm thrilling flesh. Aria moaned aloud, and the Bone Witch visited her dream to get a better look at this Baron de Roye. Liking what she saw, the Bone Witch left Aria alone, just removing any unnecessary fears and an inhibition or two, replacing them with eager anticipation, and some unusual new desires.

Which Aria instantly acted on, twisting her legs around a pillow and rocking gently until she climaxed in her sleep. The Bone Witch closed the dream with pleasant thoughts about death.

Aria awoke excited and happy, laughing aloud at the sunlight streaming into the Bone Hut. She meant to see her knight again right after morning chores, before he could wander away from the cave—but the Bone Witch had a dozen extra things for her to do today. For no apparent reason, the witch wanted the swallows' nests taken from under the eaves and her pet rats turned loose, then her favorite fetishes hung on branches in the Iron Wood. So many pointless tasks that Aria suspected the old woman of trying to keep her from seeing Baron de Roye. The Bone Witch's motives were always as obscure as her methods.

The rats were at best moderately happy to be set free, and the swallows complained bitterly, chattering shrilly and darting at her head. It was useless to tell them that the Bone Witch ordered the mass removal. While she battled indignant swallows, the Bone Witch sat at her rib cage table, writing on thin strips of Cathayan paper in her little cramped script. After tying these tiny messages to the feet of her carrier pigeons, the crone released the pigeons one by one, sending them off into the broad blue sky.

Aria asked what was so important that they must tell the world. The Bone Witch shushed her. "Be patient, child. Time makes all things clear."

So the Bone Witch always said. Aria returned to her tasks, working until the Bone Hut looked positively bare. Since the day she arrived, her new home's chaos had fascinated her—fetishes decorated white rafters, swallows darted in and out, pigeons cooed in the eaves, rats peered from wicker cages, while rib-bone shelves held seashells, raven's claws, bloodred rubies, and big tulip-shaped paper lanterns. Such amazing clutter had taken her mind off the terror of be-longing to Death's grandmother—fully expecting to be cooked and eaten, un-less the witch preferred her raw. Aria soon discovered that she had to do the cooking, as well as feed the rats and dust off the Bone Hut's treasures.

Now it chilled Aria to see her home so neat. All the animals were gone, ex-cept for her knight's horse in the paddock out back. She hoped this latest mad impulse did not last.

Finally the Bone Witch let her go. "There is nothing else for you to do here. Now go and make your way in the world. Be smart. Be brave. Live in the mo-ment, but think of me now and again. And if you ever need help, call on me. No matter how far you go or what you become, I will be with you."

Aria rolled her eyes in protest, explaining that she was only taking breakfast to her knight, not running off to France. Her slave collar kept her from leav-ing the woods—but the Bone Witch had a way of seeing grand drama in mun-dane things, like the song of a lark or the first buds of spring. "Fear not," Aria assured her. "I will be back by afternoon."

"No, you won't." The Bone Witch shook her head at such a childish notion. "Remember, I tried to care for you and teach you trollcraft. Now recite your spell." Aria recited her invisibility spell, grabbed up her basket, and headed for the Iron Wood, happy to be free of the old witch—if only for a while.

She did not get far. There are no warning cries in the Iron Wood. No birds or squirrels to keep watch. Aria was winding her way through metal trunks when she caught a whiff of horses on the wind. That meant men were coming, since no horse would be silly enough to come here on its own. She froze, whis-pered her spell, and waited—hoping her heart was not banging too loud.

Hearing the clip-clop of iron-shod hooves on flinty rock, Aria realized that horsemen were riding down the crooked trail toward the Bone Witch's hut—in column of twos, to save getting slashed by spiked branches. In a moment they would be riding right over her, invisible or not.

She turned and dashed back the way she had come. Byeli Zamak had been gone for only a day, and already men were coming farther than she ever thought possible. At the clearing in the metal wood, the Bone Witch stood waiting by her skin door, a grim smile on her wrinkled face.

Aria told the sorceress she had heard horsemen coming, but the crone merely nodded. Had the Bone Witch known about these horsemen? Probably. The Bone Witch had sent her off with her basket and spell, knowing full well that Aria would not get far.

Hoofbeats grew louder as the column of riders neared the clearing. Aria stood close to the witch, curious to see what sort of horsemen dared come into the Iron Wood. But the first figure to appear was not on horseback—and was only half a man. Man-shaped and naked, he strolled lithely into the clearing, covered head to foot with soft brown hair. His eyes were wolf's eyes. Canine fangs protruded from thin smiling lips.

Lycanthrope. Aria had never seen one like this before—few had and lived. He was not the harmless sort who totally shed human form to run with the wolves and mate with the bitches. He was a soulless demon from deep in the Iron Wood—the absolute worst of wolf and man. Or so the Bone Witch always told her.

Behind him rode an incongruous pair. The taller of the two was a steel-helmeted horse archer wearing a blue horse guard's brigandine studded with silver nailheads. He had a huge dead swan hanging from his high saddle. Riding at his side was a dwarf mounted on a pony, wearing a particolored tunic and a foolscap.

More horsemen filed into the clearing behind the mismatched pair, spreading out from their column of twos—horse archers, knights, and men-at-arms, followed by squires and valets, even a steward and a butler in their uniforms of office. And an ensign, holding up a grand duke's banner, bearing the silver lightning stroke of Ikstra.

Beneath the banner rode Grand Duke Sergey himself, a prince of the blood from the bootheels up, wearing silver-chased armor and a gold coronet on his old-fashioned great helmet. He had his visor tipped back, and Aria could see the hard cold sheen in his pale blue eyes, glinting like dangerous ice in the spring.

He stared evenly at the aged witch—two of the most feared people in Markovy were meeting for the first time. Totally different, yet each in their own way absolutely terrifying. Crown Prince Sergey, Grand Duke of Ikstra, broke the frosty silence. "Good morrow, Grandmother. We are trailing a mounted knight, riding a gray warhorse and wearing a blue-and-white surcoat. He is most likely wounded. Have you seen him?"

"No, my lord," replied the Bone Witch. "Not him, nor anyone like him." Aria did her best to seen totally mute, and deaf as well.

"Strange," mused Prince Sergey, "our wolfman trailed his horse straight to this clearing." The lycanthrope stood waiting, a hideous look on his fanged face, clearly hoping to make a meal out of someone. "He was Castellan of Byeli Zamak, and claims to be a baron from a foreign land."

"And yet I have not seen him," the Bone Witch insisted. Aria gave a feeble-minded smile of agreement, letting the witch speak for both of them.

Prince Sergey looked to the dwarf sitting on his pony. Rising in his saddle, the dwarf took a deep breath through his nose. Two more sniffs, and the dwarf settled back in the saddle, saying, "She is telling the truth."

Prince Sergey nodded. Then his gaze turned to Aria, staring at her like she had failed to pay her squirrel tax. "What about the girl? Has she seen him?"

The "girl" gulped, then shook her head vigorously, shrinking back against the Bone Witch.

Prince Sergey looked again at the dwarf. This time the little man swung off his pony and walked over to her. His head came up to Aria's waist. Lifting his nose, he sniffed her belly and then ran his nostrils down her thigh. He stepped back, saying, "She is lying."

Sergey raised an eyebrow. "Has she seen the castellan?" His dwarf shrugged. The little man was a lie sniffer, not a mind reader. His Majesty turned back to her. "Have you seen a knight wearing blue and white?"

Aria had no good answer, caught between her need to lie, and knowing the dwarf would sniff her out. Anything she said would put her at the mercy of these men. The wolfman leered at her. He was the one who had found her. Without him, this clumsy crowd of horsemen could not have trailed her from the stream—but a lycanthrope can track a mouse on a moonless night.

"Well, have you seen him?" the Grand Duke demanded.

Before she could think of some truthful misdirection, a shout of triumph came from the back of the Bone Hut. A couple of squires came around the corner, proudly leading her knight's horse. Someone called out, "That's him, the castellan's big gray."

Prince Sergey looked hard at the horse, then back at her. "Have you seen the knight who rode this charger?"

Aria nodded dumbly, unable to come up with anything but the truth, though she knew it would doom her.

"Good," the Grand Duke concluded, "we are finally getting somewhere. Do you know where he is?"

"Not for certain." He could be long gone from the cave. In fact, she fervently hoped he was.

Prince Sergey smiled, a chilling and terrible sight. "Nothing in life is certain—but I wager you can find him." He turned to his ensign, saying, "Pay the crone for the girl."

Taking his reins in his banner hand, the ensign fished a gold coin out of his purse, tossing it at the naked feet of the Bone Witch, who made no move to pick up the coin. "That is for the girl," the ensign explained.

"She is not for sale," the witch replied, as Aria shrank back, putting the Bone Witch between her and the men.

"Give her the whole purse," the Grand Duke ordered impatiently. His ensign tossed the purse down beside the coin—but the crone ignored it as well.

"What do you want, Grandmother?" Grand Duke Sergey seemed astonished that the old woman refused his generosity.

"For you to leave." There was a hint of warning in the witch's answer.

"We will," Sergey agreed, "when we have the girl."

"She is under my protection," the Bone Witch insisted.

Grand Duke Sergey glared at her. Tension filled the clearing. Two dozen armed men sat loafing in the saddle, backed by valets, pages, a steward and butler. Horses looked on with equine curiosity. The lycanthrope stood waiting, aching to use his fangs and claws. "By rights, I could have you burned," Prince Sergey pointed out.

"Do it if you dare," replied the Bone Witch, unworried by the prince's power.

Sergey motioned for his archers to dismount, saying, "Seize the girl."

Horrified, Aria stepped back toward the skin door. This was all her fault. She had brought the horse to the Bone Hut. She had assumed she could easily lose a score of armed men.

A bowman tried to brush past the old woman, but the Bone Witch shoved him sideways, landing him in a heap. He did not get up.

Two wary archers seized the witch's arms, but she whirled about, faster than the eye could follow, sending the armored pair flying to opposite ends of the clearing.

Another archer tried to draw his sword, but the crone reached out and grabbed his wrist, twisting it until it snapped. His blade dropped from limp fingers. Bowmen fell back, hardened professional murderers looking completely appalled by the old woman's strength. The lycanthrope dropped to a crouch, prepared to spring.

Prince Sergey rose in the saddle, shouting, "Use your bows—but do not hit the girl. I will flay the man that misses."

A half-dozen arrows leaped from their bows, striking the Bone Witch in the chest and hip. She hardly even winced, standing stiff and tall between Aria and the men. Aria clung to the skin door, her fist jammed in her mouth, stifling a scream, aghast at what she had done.

More arrows thudded into the Bone Witch. Painfully the crone turned to face Aria, her chest looking like a bloody pincushion. Arrows continued to hit the Bone Witch from behind. Staggering from the impact, the old woman opened her mouth to speak. All that came out was a horrible gargling sound, followed by a great gout of blood. Shocked and sickened, Aria watched the witch sink slowly to her knees.

"Stop shooting! Stop shooting!" Prince Sergey cried. "You will hit the girl."

Silence settled over the clearing as tears poured down Aria's cheeks. Half a dozen bows were pointed at her, arrows nocked and ready. She could see their gleaming chiseled steel points aimed at her chest. The Bone Witch lay at her feet, feathered with arrows. Aria too expected to die—if not now, then soon.

Prince Sergey broke the silence, spurring his mount to put himself between her and the archers, shouting, "Down bows! Damn you! Down bows!"

Hurriedly his men obeyed. Wiping her tears away, Aria seized the prince's stirrup. "Why did you kill her?" she wailed. "I am the one who lied."

Startled, Prince Sergey stared down in disbelief, as if astonished she could speak. "The witch did not know where he was. You did." So the witch died, and Aria lived—for now. "You do know where the castellan is?" Sergey wanted to be sure.

Aria nodded. Any other answer would be her death warrant.

"And you can take us to him?"

She nodded again.

"Good." Prince Sergey pulled his boot from his stirrup, planted the heel on her shoulder, and shoved, sending her sprawling. He waved to his men. "Burn the place. Burn the witch's body. Burn it all."

Prince Sergey cantered off. For a moment Aria lay looking up at a blue sky framed by iron treetops. Her breath came in long ragged gasps, as if the whole weight of the Heavens rested on her breast.

Without warning, a big bearded archer took the prince's place. Looking down at her, he laughed. "Here's a cute little case of the clap. Already flat on her back."

"Give your middle leg a rest," another archer advised.

"What do you mean?" the man asked indignantly. "I've not been fucked in a fortnight."

"Small wonder." The second archer helped her to her feet, brushing the dirt off her dress, which was spattered with the Bone Witch's blood.

Someone called out, "Does she have a name?"

"Do you?" asked the archer.

Of course, she thought—but all she said was, "Aria."

"She calls herself Aria." The horse archer was speaking to a huge man in an oversize suit of plate armor. Mounted on a big black Friesian, he towered over everything, seeming to reach right to the ridgepole of the Bone Hut. He wore the same blue-and-white surcoat as her knight, but many times bigger, and marked with the sword-and-shield badge of a master-at-arms. Tipping back the visor on his German sallet, he asked her in a big booming voice, "Where do you come from, girl?"

Scared senseless, Aria still had the presence of mind to lie. "I am the daughter of a Kazakh hetman, Kaffa Khan. Harm me, and he will come with a toman of horse archers to hunt you all to death."

He laughed, saying, "Have Knee-High give her a sniff."

She had forgotten about the dwarf. Too much had happened since Aria last saw the little man. He walked over and took a deep sniff, then turned to the master-at-arms. "She lies."

The master-at-arms did not look surprised, her lie being feeble at best. "Come, my cute young khanum, give us the truth. Or I will see you suffer."

Aria admitted she did not know who her parents were, saying, "I was raised here, by the witch." Mentioning the Bone Witch made her want to cry, but she stopped herself.

"Are you virtuous?" asked the master-at-arms.

She stared dumbly up at him. What a stupid question to ask a witch-child. How could anyone be both damned and virtuous?

"There's your answer," the lecherous horse archer chuckled. "She does not even know what you are asking."

The master-at-arms grinned. "Well, it is bad luck to execute a virgin. . . ."

"Especially for the virgin," a horse archer added, getting a chuckle from his fellow troopers.

The master-at-arms signaled for silence. "But in your case, we will risk it. Stop your lying, and lead us to the castellan. Otherwise we will have you flayed and left to fry in the sun. Unlucky or not. Do you understand?"

She understood.

He turned to the squires and archers, telling them to get busy. "Drag the witch into the hut, and set it on fire." None too happy with their task, archers dragged the witch's body into the Bone Hut. Aria watched them pile the straw beds atop the dead crone, then throw on firewood, furniture, and the contents of the clothes chests. Dousing the pile with cooking oil, they set it alight. Soon the Bone Hut was blazing away. Aria saw her life going up in smoke and flames—just like Byeli Zamak.

"Mount up," the master-at-arms ordered. Squires hoisted her aboard de Roye's gray charger. One of them handed her the reins, and something to go with them. Looking down, she saw it was her straw doll—the one she had brought with her when she first came to live with the witch. The young squire who had given it to her looked embarrassed. Of all these men—from Grand Duke Sergey down to the lowest valet—this boy alone seemed ashamed for what they had done.

The master-at-arms gave her a grin that was all beard and teeth, saying, "Now lead us to the castellan."

She nodded, clutching the straw doll to her belly. Somehow, some way, Aria meant to come out of this alive and whole. But how that would happen, Heaven alone knew.

2

prince sergey finds the firebird's egg

Mounted on her knight's gray charger, Aria led the whole cavalcade along the winding trail out of the Iron Wood. The master-at-arms rode beside her, with the dwarf mounted pillion behind him, and the lycanthrope loping on ahead. Boxed in by armed ruthless men, she could neither lose them nor lie to them— not so long as they had the wolfman to track her, and the dwarf to sniff out her lies. Only a stroke of monumental good fortune could save her, and Aria had long ago learned she must make her own luck.

Whenever the master-at-arms questioned her directions, the dwarf made her tell the truth, a heavy burden for someone who relied on lies. Only the Lord's honest truth could save her.

At the head of Long Lake, hot pine scent replaced the cold metal odor of the Iron Wood. Swans clumped at the center of the lake, already learning to be wary of the archers. She turned west, heading straight for the ridgeline separating the forest from the steppe.

The master-at-arms looked askance. "You are leading us back toward Byeli Zamak?"

Aria shrugged. "That is where I left him, in a cave by the spring at the base of the ridge."

"Is that so?" he asked the dwarf riding behind him.

"She is telling the truth," replied the dwarf, looking pleased that she had learned not to lie.

The master-at-arms turned back to her. "And this is the shortest way there?"

"Absolutely." She nodded, and the dwarf confirmed her. An east wind had blown all morning, and she meant to lead them straight downwind, avoiding the roundabout way she came the day before. For once, she need not hide her tracks. "If I take you straight to him, will you let me go?"

"Of course, of course," the big man answered affably. "Who would want to keep you?"

But Aria was looking behind him at the dwarf, who glanced sharply up, saying nothing. Having a lie-sniffer riding on your horse's rump worked both ways. She had seen that same look of contempt on the dwarf's face when she tried to lie. The master-at-arms did not mean to let her go. None of them did. Once she had served her purpose, they would burn her as a witch—unless they had already promised her to the lycanthrope.

As they plunged into the living wood, with its green trees and countless eyes, she heard a squirrel chatter at them, followed by the fire jay's cry—but it was not the flame jay's man call. She kept her eyes fixed on the path ahead, so the master-at-arms got no warning from her. As the fire jay's cry faded behind her, she strained to hear what was happening at the back of the column. Horse archers laughed and joked behind her, sharing an endless stock of sacrilegious stories to keep their spirits up. "Did you hear about the Kipchak who went to hell?"

"How would a Kipchak even know?" Kipchaks lived in the cold deserts, the closest thing to hell this side of the Iron Wood.

"Satan met him at the gates and bade him be at home, offering up an oasis with sweet springs, fruit trees, scented blossoms, koumiss by the barrel—"

"And goats to screw."

"That too." The storyteller nodded eagerly. "Not just compliant young nannies, but milk-white maidens as well, and Cathayan concubines—as many as he wished. Only he had to listen to hideous screams and fearful cries coming from a fiery pit, where forlorn souls writhed in torment. So the Kipchak asked Satan, who had been put in that awful pit?"

"What did the Father of Lies say?" Satan had as many names as God.

"You know how Christians are, always wanting things done their way." Pagan Kazakhs convulsed in laughter.

Suddenly a scream rang out. The master-at-arms grabbed her reins, looking back down the column. They waited. The storytellers stopped laughing. She watched little white butterflies dance in the sunlight. Presently a horse archer on a bay mare came galloping up. "What happened?" demanded the master-at-arms.

"A leopard," the horse archer gasped.

"A leopard?" the master-at-arms looked shocked.

"Yes. It dropped out of a tree on the last man in the column—Vasily, from Suzdal. He stopped to tighten his stirrup and take a piss. Before he could get his cock out, the cat was on him. When we got there, he was dead, and the beast gone."

"That makes no sense," complained the master-at-arms. "A leopard attacking an armed man in daylight?" And from upwind, Aria added to herself, carefully searching the trees. A wood tit stared back at her. "No cat could be that hungry," insisted the master-at-arms.

The horse archer shrugged. "The cat did not act hungry. Or even angry. It silently broke Vasily's neck, then went on its way."

The master-at-arms snorted. "Which makes even less sense. Sling his body over a horse, and tell Prince Sergey we are ready to move." The archer turned his bay mare about and went trotting back down the column.

Again they waited. Aria sat listening to the pines murmuring overhead. A woodpecker started to hammer, then stopped suddenly. Had it seen something?

Slowly the profane stories reappeared: "A nun, a bishop, and a brothel-keeper are in a boat, and there is only one bottle. The bishop says to the nun . . ."

Aria kept her ears tuned to the trees, listening for the woodpecker, and wondering why he was silent, and why it was taking so long for the troop to get started again.

Prince Sergey's ensign trotted up, asking the same question, "Are you ready to move on? His Highness must be back at Byeli Zamak by supper."

Rolling his eyes, the master-at-arms told him, "I sent a man back saying we were ready to ride."

"What man?" asked the ensign.

This provoked another commotion. A search failed to find the messenger, but did discover his bay mare in a nearby clearing. Fresh blood shone on her saddle.

"This is absurd," the master-at-arms exploded. "We cannot sit here like dinner on horseback, waiting to be eaten. Tell His Highness we are setting out—unless the leopard gets you first."

Aria started up again at a brisk trot. No one complained about her abruptness or direction, not with phantom leopards stalking the column. Men twisted in their saddles and glanced over their shoulders, looking everywhere but ahead. Normally, Aria would have been properly terrified, blundering through the forest, dragged from one danger to the next by brainless oafs, but she was beyond fear. She was determined to see these men dead for what they did to the Bone Witch—if she destroyed herself too, so be it. They meant to kill her anyway.

Seeing a familiar break in the pines, backed by a tall stand of oaks, Aria braced herself. Since they were headed downwind, the only warning was a waxwing's whistle, which the men ignored. Looking uneasy, the lycanthrope padded silently along, ears cocked forward, claws extended.

Suddenly the werewolf froze, hairs quivering, supersenses fully alert. Aria swallowed dryly, thinking the next seconds would decide if she lived or died. The lycanthrope spun about and vanished into the undergrowth. An archer called out, "What scared the wolfman? Why has he scampered off?"

As if to answer him, the troll-bear burst from his hidden lair, bellowing defiance at the intruders. Twice the size of a normal bear, with steel-hard hide and razor claws, the beast roared into the column, scattering men and horses. Rolling out of her saddle, Aria dropped to a crouch and whispered her spell. Instantly she vanished.

From her invisible crouch, she got a close-up view of the swift horrific conflict. The troll-bear's forepaws flailed about, mace-headed battering rams that slashed through plate armor like parchment. The master-at-arms seized a lance from a squire, slapped down his visor, and charged the monster full tilt. His lance shattered on the troll-bear's hornlike hide. The enraged beast backhanded him out of the saddle, crushed him with a hind foot, then bit off his horse's head.

Of the heroes who captured her, he alone tried to stop the troll-bear. The whole column—six lances of horse guards, with their attendant squires, valets, and archers, along with Prince Sergey's entourage of pages, ensign, steward, and butler—evaporated in an eyeblink, as if they too knew an invisibility spell. The troll-bear went howling after them, snapping pine saplings and up-ending boulders.

Which is why sensible woods creatures avoided a troll-bear's lair, treating the carrion stink like a viper's hiss, a warning to the unwary.

Silence settled on the forest. Clutching her straw doll, Aria surveyed the new-made clearing out of the corner of her eyes. The biggest difficulty with being invisible was not being able to turn her head, which was incredibly maddening when she needed to know if it was safe to be seen. She was bent over, frozen in place, staring at the armored leg of the master-at-arms, sticking out from beneath a headless horse. Aria saw no sign of the dwarf who had been riding behind him.

Shutting her eyes, she let her other senses take over. Nothing. No warning cries, no rustle of leaves. No smell but the stink of troll-bear from somewhere upwind. She was free.

And alive. From the moment the Bone Witch died, Aria had counted herself dead too. She had let herself be tracked, and caught by men who meant to dispose of her in some grotesque fashion, and she had gotten the Bone Witch killed. Now her life was saved by a troll-bear—something awfully few people could say.

So what to do with her newfound freedom? Her first thought was for her knight, who was at the heart of this, along with the Firebird's Egg. Prince Sergey would never risk entering the Iron Wood just to put an end to some foreign-born castellan of Byeli Zamak. Love did not make Aria blind. She knew her handsome baron was not nearly as important as the Egg he had carried.

Moving stealthily downwind, ears tuned to the slightest sound, she crept up on the spring. Having gotten her life back, Aria did not mean to let down her guard. Hot afternoon air hung heavy and expectant, and unnaturally quiet. Beyond the high rocks and bubbling spring, the forest seemed to hold its breath.

Suddenly she heard the fire jay's shrill cry. Aria froze against a big boulder speckled with bird lime, whispering her spell. This was the second time today she had heard the bird's warning, as though the jay were watching over her— but this cry was different from any she had heard before, the man call mixed with an unfamiliar trill.

As Aria strained to survey the rocks without moving her head, a heavy form dropped on her from atop the boulder. Hairy arms circled Aria's waist, and vise-hard thighs gripped her hips. Her struggles broke the invisibility spell, which had been no match for the lycanthrope's senses.

Horrified, she fought to free herself. And got nowhere. Pinning her arms, the lycanthrope dragged Aria away from the spring—but did nothing else to harm her. No clawing. No fangs in the neck. Hardly reassuring, with his steel-like erection digging into the small of her back.

Forced into a shadowy forest glade, Aria felt the lycanthrope relax, and she looked up to see horsemen staring down at her. Prince Sergey sat bareheaded on his charger, having lost his gold-crowned helmet. His ensign was beside him, along with a single horse archer, several frightened squires, and a bedraggled-looking butler—all that was left of the proud cavalcade that had ridden boldly into the Iron Wood. The lycanthrope must have been stalking ahead of them. Coming on her scent trail, he had gone up the backside of the boulder and dropped down onto her.

Prince Sergey trotted over to where she stood, glaring down at her. "Did you know we were riding into a troll-bear's lair?"

Her immediate impulse to lie died on her lips when she spotted the dwarf riding behind the butler. She shook her head instead. "I will not tell you anything unless you let me go."

"Be cooperative," Prince Sergey warned. "I have only to say the word, and this man-beast will savage you on the spot."

"You will not learn much from that," she pointed out.

"Yes," Sergey admitted, "but I would enjoy your screams immensely." Nonetheless he waved to the wolfman, saying, "Let her go."

The lycanthrope let go of her, a little victory that was likely her last. Aria took a deep breath, wishing she could just disappear right here. What had she done to deserve all this? Not a thing so far as she could see. Prince Sergey leaned forward in the saddle. "Now, tell us what we want to know."

"If I do, will you let me go?" She stared past the Prince at the dwarf seated behind his butler.

"Simply tell the truth," Sergey commanded, "and you have naught to fear."

The dwarf's nose wrinkled as if he whiffed something foul. So much for honesty. Prince Sergey had no intention of freeing her. She closed her eyes, taking another slow breath, prolonging the inevitable. "What do you wish to know?"

"Tell us where the castellan is." Prince Sergey sounded royally impatient.

"Right here," came the cheerful reply.

Aria's eyes flew open. There was her knight, Sir Roye de Roye, standing tall and nonchalant, sword in hand, a wry smile on his handsome face. Seeing him appear out of nowhere was like suddenly getting her life back. He made a mocking bow to Prince Sergey. "Baron Roye de Roye, Chevalier de l'Étoile, and until late, Castellan of Byeli Zamak. At your service."

Sergey sat up in the saddle. "Satan be damned! You! Why did you not open Byeli Zamak to me?"

Sir Roye de Roye shrugged his armored shoulders. "You did not say 's'il vous plaît.' King Demitri gave me Byeli Zamak to hold for his heir."

"I am Prince Ivan's uncle," the grand duke replied. "Byeli Zamak should have come to me."

"And it has," Baron de Roye reminded him, smiling at his own latest defeat. Prince Sergey leaned forward again. "But not the Firebird's Egg."

"That is what brings us here." Her knight looked smug.

"So you have the Egg?"

"Not on me. But I know where it is," de Roye declared.

"Where?" Sergey demanded.

"What will you pay to know?"

"Half my kingdom?" Sergey suggested sarcastically.

"I will give it to you cheaper." Her knight smiled at her. "Set this wood sprite free. Her and me, alive and ahorsed—that is all I ask."

Aria fought back tears. Her knight had given up his hiding place, and the precious Egg he protected, all to save her. A foolish impetuous gesture that would probably get them both killed. Yet she felt ridiculously touched.

"Almost too cheap," Sergey mused. "Generosity from an enemy is always suspect—but perhaps you are merely a fool."

"Obviously." Baron de Roye politely conceded the point. "Pray indulge me nonetheless."

"You, the girl, and two horses—easy enough." Sergey lifted a steel-gloved finger. "After I have the Egg."

"As you wish." Keeping his big two-handed sword drawn, her knight turned to her. "Mademoiselle, I must go with these men—hopefully I will be returning with a pair of horses."

"She comes with us," Sergey insisted.

Baron de Roye rolled his eyes apologetically. "Alas, Mademoiselle, I fear this grand duke means it. Fortunately, it is but a short way into the woods."

"By a stand of big oaks," she reminded him.

His eyes lit up. "I see you know the spot."

She nodded excitedly. She knew better than he did. And the deeper they got into her woods, the safer they would be. Get far enough into the forest, and she and her knight were more than a match for any number of killers on horse-back. But Aria did not say that aloud, for fear the killers would hear. She had to rely on him reading it in her smile.

He seemed to understand, setting out happily, not the least worried by the armed men around them, laughing and making light of things. She wanted to tell him about the Bone Witch and all that had happened in the Iron Wood, but that too must wait. Instead, she listened to stories about France, and all the wonders he had seen between the Western Sea and Markovy. "Folks in France think they are the most worldly people on earth, but have no notion what is happening at the other end of Europe."

"Are we that strange?" Aria asked.

"Passing strange," Sir Roye assured her. "But passing lovely, as well."

"Really?" Most Markovites were raised to think that strange was bad, but the Bone Witch had wrung that out of her, taking *strange* to totally unforseen levels.

"*Absolument.*" He grinned at her amazement. "Here the blond serf girls all have engaging smiles, and even simple forest sprites are beautiful beyond be-lief."

Spoken like a Frenchman. This time they approached the troll-bear's lair from downwind—by far the safest direction. So long as you stayed out of the beast's hearing, you had little to fear. But as soon as they whiffed the carrion scent, Prince Sergey's men revolted, none of them wanting a rematch with the monster. Their horses too refused to go any farther, shying and whinnying at the fearful stench.

Sergey immediately demanded that the dwarf sniff her knight for false-hood. Baron de Roye submitted with good grace, for once having nothing to hide, and the dwarf went right up to him, sniffing vigorously. Aria guessed why. The little man desperately hoped to smell a lie. If her knight was telling the truth, they would have to march straight back toward the troll-bear's lair.

Finally, the dwarf admitted that Baron de Roye smelled sincere. Sergey was forced to leave the horses and squires behind, but he bullied the ensign, horse archer, and butler into accompanying him on foot. Aria did not fear any of these men half so much as she feared the lycanthrope.

The dwarf did not get a choice. Like her, he was too valuable to leave behind, and would come whether he willed it or not. Aria went out of her way to comfort the little man, whose sole concern was for the truth. He and the Bone Witch were the only ones she had never been able to lie to, something Aria very much respected. "Stay close to me," she told him, "and I will try to see you are safe."

He looked warily up at her. "Is that so?"

"I thought you would know?" He was the one with the educated nose. As they set out walking, she slid her hand inside her dress, stroking the straw doll hidden next to her breast, just for luck.

When they got to the oak grove, the butler had to go down on beribboned knees to dig with his bare hands, since Prince Sergey would not let him use so much as a toothpick, for fear of harming the Firebird's Egg. Her knight stood watching calmly, leaning on his big two-handed sword.

Aria motioned for the dwarf to get behind her, which he did at once, backing warily toward the bushes—a bad omen, since the little man knew best what his master's promises were worth.

Reaching his hands into the hole, the butler drew forth the Firebird's Egg. As he unwrapped the dirty tapestry, everyone stared in awe at Markovy's greatest wonder—except for the lycanthrope, who kept his hungry eyes fixed on Aria. What had he been promised when Prince Sergey had the Egg?

Baron de Roye spoke first. "*Excusez-moi*, this may be exceptionally foolish of me, but I beg you to listen to the advice of the late King, your brother."

"What advice?" Sergey looked suspiciously at her knight, as if the Frenchman were an insect with an especially annoying hum.

"King Demitri sent a deathbed message to me, ordering that this Egg be returned safely to its Nest on Burning Mountain. No easy task, yet one I heartily endorse. There is a terrible curse on this Egg. How many lives has that damned thing cost in the last two days alone?" Her knight was right, Byeli Zamak had been burned. And so had the Bone Hut. Prince Sergey's proud company had been reduced to a scared handful, standing around the magical Egg.

Prince Sergey gave a snort of contempt. "We need no lessons from the loser."

"There are worse things than losing," Baron de Roye pointed out. "My own fortunes have improved mightily since I put that ill-fated Egg in the ground."

"Is that so?" Prince Sergey arched an eyebrow.

"I stake my life on it." Her knight smiled at her. "As my lord well knows, I was beaten and bleeding, fleeing yet another defeat, hunted by both men and beasts. But as soon as I parted from that infamous Egg, this delightful forest nymph appeared, to stitch my wounds, then give me caviar and sweet kisses. Fate could hardly speak more plainly."

"How lucky for you," Sergey laughed. "My own ambitions are a bit higher."

Her knight shrugged. "To each their own. Hopefully, King Demitri will know I tried. Now if I may depart with my own prize." He reached a steel-gloved hand out to her.

"You may inform Demitri in person." Prince Sergey nodded to the lycanthrope, saying, "Kill him, and the girl is yours."

Faster than thought, the lycanthrope leaped at Baron de Roye's throat, fangs bared, claws extended. But her knight had expected treachery. His blade came up in a terrific backhand swipe. Only the wolfman's supernatural agility saved him from being sliced in half. Twisting in midair, the beast managed to evade the blade, landing on all fours.

All eyes were on the fight, so Aria stepped back against a tree trunk, whispering her spell. The dwarf had already vanished into the undergrowth. Holding her breath, she stood rigid, smelling sap sweating from the pine behind her, watching the fight and wanting to help, but not knowing how.

Sir Roye de Roye kept his sword between himself and the werewolf, feinting and slashing. Despite his speed and cunning, the lycanthrope could not get past the flashing blade. Twice he tried to duck under the sword, and got nicked in the shoulder and the ear. But the wolfman moved too fast for de Roye to land a killing blow. Stalking sideways, the glaring ghoul searched for an opening, flexing his claws.

"Help the beast," Prince Sergey cried. "Take the foreigner from behind."

His butler just stood there, stupidly holding the Egg—but the ensign and horse archer obeyed, drawing their swords and trying to slide around behind Sir Roye de Roye. So long as the lycanthrope kept him busy in front, it would only be a matter of time before one of the others got at her knight's back.

Being the bolder of the two, the ensign was first in position. As Sir Roye aimed a slash at the werewolf, the ensign raised his own sword, stepping in to strike.

Seeing the ensign lunge past her, Aria leaped forward, seizing the man's sword arm. Coming from out of nowhere, she took the ensign by surprise. As he struggled to shake her off, Baron de Roye spun about, hitting him a wicked two-handed blow just beneath the breastplate. Groaning, the ensign went down, rattling like a pile of dropped pans.

Instantly the lycanthrope bounded at the baron. But her knight seemed to know what was coming next. Ignoring the downed ensign, Sir Roye let his momentum spin him completely about. This time his backhand caught the lycanthrope between the neck and collarbone, severing the beast's jugular in a hideous spray of blood. The werewolf landed in a gory heap at his feet.

Strong arms seized her from behind. The horse archer had not dared to take on Sir Roye, but he grabbed her to use as a shield. Prince Sergey whipped his sword out, and she felt the sharp point at her throat. "Stop," the grand duke commanded. "Drop your sword or I will kill her."

Her knight let his point drop, saying, "Come now, Your Highness, that is hardly sporting. All we want is to be on our way."

"Drop your sword," Prince Sergey demanded. "Or I swear by Satan, I shall slit her throat."

With a sigh, de Roye jammed his sword point-first into the ground beside the dead lycanthrope. Then he stepped back, away from the blade, folding his arms. "I warn you—this will bring nothing but grief."

"Perhaps," Sergey admitted with a grin. "But you will not be there to see it." Aria's heart sank. Her knight would die—merely for showing mercy—and she would have to watch. Sergey stepped toward Sir Roye de Roye, hefting his sword.

As he did, an amber-and-black body dropped from the branches above, landing atop the grand duke. Prince Sergey gasped in surprise as the leopard sank her fangs into his neck. Staggering beneath the weight of the hunting cat, the royal duke dropped to his knees, then pitched forward onto his face. Aria watched in astonishment as the big cat continued to bite down on Prince Sergey, making sure he never got up.

Sir Roye jerked his sword out of the ground, saying to the horse archer holding her, "Let the girl go, if you want to live."

Without a word, the bowman obeyed. The arms around Aria vanished, and she heard footfalls behind her as the bowman disappeared into the forest. Her knight turned to Prince Sergey's butler, who still held the Firebird's Egg, a sick look on his horrified face. "Carefully set down that Egg, and you, too, may go."

Placing the Egg gently on the ground, the butler backed slowly through the bracken, bumped into a tree, then turned and fled for his life.

All that remained of Prince Sergey's expedition into the Iron Wood was a trio of bodies lying around the Firebird's Egg. *"Mon Dieu,"* Baron de Roye muttered, "that went far better than I could ever have imagined."

Slowly the leopard rose up, changing as she did, becoming a withered, naked old woman with wrinkled skin and bone-white hair. And not a single arrow mark on her. The Bone Witch smiled at Aria. "I told you I would be here if you needed me."

Her knight lowered his point and looked over at Aria. "This, I suppose, is your witch?"

She hastened to introduce the Bone Witch to her knight, proud of the way he went down on one knee before the withered old woman, saying, "Madame Witch, Baron Sir Roye de Roye, Chevalier de l'Étoile, at your service."

"Is that just a gallantry," asked the old woman, "or are you really at my service?"

"Without a doubt. Madame saved my life, and I owe her anything that honor allows."

"Good," the Bone Witch declared. "I have need of your honor." Then the Bone Witch turned to Aria. "Come here, my daughter."

She walked happily over, grateful to be free of Prince Sergey's killers and glad to see the Bone Witch alive—but utterly ecstatic to have someone finally call her *daughter.*

Giving Aria a wrinkled kiss, the witch took the slave collar from around her neck. "Now I have a one last chore for you."

"Whatever you wish." For once, she truly meant it.

"Return the Firebird's Egg to its proper Nest, so it may hatch and the curse on Markovy can be lifted."

"But how will I get there?" She felt surprised the Bone Witch would give her a task so important, and so seemingly impossible.

"These will start you on your way." The witch snapped her bony fingers, and a trio of horses ambled into the clearing—the knight's warhorse, a black mare with a horse archer's bow and quiver hanging from her saddle, and a big bay palfrey laden with supplies. Sir Roye's eyes lit up, seeing the gray charger he had clearly given up for lost.

"I mean, how will I find the Nest?" All Aria knew of the Firebird's Nest was that it lay atop Burning Mountain, deep within the most trackless part of the Iron Wood.

The Bone Witch gave a low call, holding out her finger, and the flame jay flew down to land on it. Stroking the bird's breast, the crone cooed, "You can take her there, can you not?"

Throwing back his head, the jay gave a confident raucous reply, flying over to land on the black mare's saddle. "See," the witch told her, "he is more than ready. Are you?"

Aria nodded solemnly, realizing this is what the witch had been training her for—how she would finally be "useful."

When she had the Egg safely tucked into the palfrey's pack saddle, Aria kissed the Bone Witch good-bye and climbed onto the black mare. She watched her knight bow good-bye to the witch, then mount his gray charger, grinning merrily. Her whole life had led her to this point. Drawing her straw doll out of her dress, she tucked it in the black mare's saddlebag.

One thing made her uneasy: her knight was a foreigner, not required to care if there was a curse on Markovy. And he a real baron to boot, who did not need her wild dreams and extravagant lies. She asked softly and sincerely, "Are you sure you want to do this? You are free to go your own way if you want."

"Heavens no, Mademoiselle." He grinned happily. "Not when my lady has at long last landed me on the winning side."

3

the witch-girl and the woodcutters

Woodmen's axes rang between tall straight pine trunks, sounding sharp and clear in the hot noontide. Aria could hear the axes even before she smelled the horse droppings or tasted woodsmoke in the air. Moving cautiously as civilization neared, she slid from tree to tree, stopping now and again to freeze against a mossy pine trunk, whispering her invisibility spell. When visible, she wore her dress with the firebird stitched on it in crimson silk.

Silent as a shadow, Aria slid softly between the tree trunks, stopping only to disappear. Here she knew every bird cry and animal call, but the settled lands were another matter. She had bad memories of the land beyond the trees, and now she must cross the settled lands—not their whole length, which stretched from Finland to Far Barbary—just the narrow part lying before her, the valley of the Upper Zog leading into the Rift.

And she had to get a mounted knight, three horses, and a national treasure across as well—all clearly visible. No easy task, but better than trying to brave the Rift. Axes rang louder as she spotted the first stands of stumps marking the end of the wilds, and the beginning of civilization.

"*Chi-chi-chi-chi,*" the red squirrel's high, staccato warning came from downwind. Turning to look and listen, she tensed, stiffening into immobility while whispering the Bone Witch's spell. The squirrel's high-pitched chatter was not the man cry; instead, it said wolf—which puzzled Aria. What wolf would be silly enough to come within the sound of axes?

Straining her ears, Aria listened for the soft pad of wolves; instead, she heard berry bushes rattle, followed by a hollow clop-clop, growing louder.

Ponies, coming from downwind or she would have smelled them. Whoever rode them was headed for the settled lands, just as she was, but Aria did not mean to wait and let them catch up—having problems enough already. Turning visible, she slipped off toward the settlement, threading through the stands of stumps, heading for the ring of axes.

Trees parted, and she came on a great cleared swath dotted with jagged stumps pointed at a broad blue band of sky—as if a giant scythe had sliced through the boreal forest, felling trees like ripe wheat. Aria froze and vanished, having forest folk's fear of open sky. She had heard of wild rocs that would take her as easily as a hawk hitting a mouse.

On the far side of the cleared space, she saw a tangled abatis of sharpened stumps and cross-felled trees, rearing high over her head, civilization's defense against fire, foes, and plague.

"Chi-chi-chi," the red squirrel's wolf cry sounded again, even closer, and Aria took off, hiking up her skirts and dashing into the cleared space, sprinting toward the tall tangle of trunks and stumps. Any roc that got her had to work quick.

Crossing the cleared space, she went straight up the pile of trunks, climbing with her skirt rolled around her waist—no easy task, since the trunks were tightly interlaced, with their branches trimmed to sharp wicked points. Scrambling up the barricade without so much as tearing her dress, Aria turned at the top, lying down along a log to look back, curious to know who was behind her.

Though she tried to be a friend to the world, Aria had enemies aplenty. Everyone seemed set on capturing her, or making her into a meal. Not just wild rocs or wereleopards, but two-legged foes more deadly than a troll-bear. Whispering her spell, she waited, hearing woodsmen's axes in the distance and warning cries from the far side of the cleared space.

Dire wolves broke cover behind her, big and black with bone-crushing jaws and bright white teeth. Aria silently thanked the sharp-eyed squirrel. Coming from downwind, the pack would have been on her without warning. Shooting across the cleared space, the wolves headed straight to the base of the barricade, showing they had her scent.

Horsemen came next, nomads carrying tufted lances and mounted on tough shaggy ponies, with short powerful recurve bows tucked into red-leather

Cathayan saddles. Tartars, savage nomads from the Land Beyond the Wall. Aria had never seen them before, but she recognized them from the Bone Witch's descriptions. Like Kazakhs or Kipchaks, they had lacquered armor and terrifying weather-beaten faces—but their curiously shaped caps, Cathayan saddles, and sky-blue trousers marked them as Tartars.

And they rode piebald Tartar ponies, stocky big-headed mares with stiff manes, that looked like the horses painted on the cave walls alongside woolly rhinos and saber-toothed cats. Crossing the clearing, the horsemen reined in when they reached the tree-trunk barricade.

Heart hammering, Aria lay atop the tall abatis, trying to imagine why these Tartars had come so far from home, and what they hoped to gain by trailing her. Aria was not about to climb down and find out what these nomads wanted. The witch's rune around her neck protected her from magic, but not from fang and claw, or horse archer's arrows.

Mounted bowmen inspected the base of the barricade, probing the sharp tangle with tufted lances. Their wolves ran back and forth a bit, casting for her scent, then clumped right below Aria and began howling at her, smelling what they could not see.

She held her breath, fearing the wolves would come climbing up the tree trunks after her. Attracted by the commotion, the horsemen trotted over, scanning the top of the abatis and peering between the trunks. Seeing nothing, the Tartars talked for a bit in their unintelligible heathen tongue, then turned and followed the line of the barricade northward, calling their wolves to heel. After moment's hesitation, the pack took off too, hurrying to catch up with the horses.

Breathing out, Aria broke her spell, sliding back along the log, then climbing down the far side of the abatis, glad to have it between her and the Tartars. And their wolves. Heaven knew what such murderous nomads were doing west of the Iron Wood, but it would be nothing good. Beyond the barricade, the pine forest thinned, broken by stump stands and leafy groves of second growth beeches and poplars. Slipping swiftly away from the abatis, Aria ran right into the big rough hands of a woodcutter.

"Where did you come from?" the woodsman demanded, looking big as a haystack, with a sooty straw-colored beard, and wearing a smoke-stained smock over trousers roped at the waist. He stank of sweat and onions, and his right ear was missing, cut off for failing to heed his boyar. Had she not been fleeing dire wolves, she would never have blundered into something so huge and smelly, and half-deaf. He demanded again, "Where are you from?"

"A convent." Lying instinctively, she picked the safest, most irreproachable place imaginable. "The Sisterhood of Perpetual Suffering, by the shores of the White Sea."

"Your head is not shaved." Rightly suspicious, the woodsman would not let go of her. His free hand held the peasant's all-purpose ax, able to frame a cottage or carve a spoon—the only weapon a serf could own. "Who ever heard of a long-haired nun?"

"Not a nun," Aria scoffed at the woodsman's ignorance, "a novice only, on my way to take holy orders. If you will pray let me on my way, the nuns will not like the delay—"

"But the White Sea lies hundreds of leagues away, in the land of the Finns, far beyond the headwaters of the Great Mother River." The interfering woodsman did not swallow her tale of a nonexistent nunnery.

"That is why I must hurry," she insisted. How could he stand in the way of her becoming a nun? What would the Sisters of Eternal Suffering say?

Keeping a tight grip on her, the woodman cocked his head to listen. "I heard wolves just now. What are you doing here?"

"Visiting my poor mother." Aria had no mother, rich or poor, but she would cheerfully invent a whole family to satisfy this big busybody. "I cannot become a nun without Mother's permission. But now that I have it, nothing needs keep me—"

"Your mother lives in the wild woods?" His head was still cocked, listening for sounds from beyond the abatis.

"Lives in the woods?" She scoffed at that foolish thought. "Of course not—but this is now mushroom season, and mother is a pious fungus gatherer."

"Who is her lord?" the woodsman demanded. "Who is yours?"

"As I said, the Sisters of Perpetual Servility."

"You said 'suffering' before." He continued to eye her suspiciously.

"Same thing. Servility. Suffering." Any serf should see that—but this one merely snorted, dragging Aria off toward the sound of the axes. Unable to vanish, she had to stumble along behind the huge woodsman, trying to avoid being clipped by his steel ax. Sooty hands left sweaty black marks on her skin.

Ahead of her, two dozen serfs were busy felling a tall stand of pines, sending one of the biggest crashing down as she arrived. With a cheer, the serfs swarmed over the forest titan, trimming off branches with axes and attacking the fallen trunk with giant two-handed saws.

Her captor called to his fellows, "Look what I found in the forest." Having hoped to see without being seen, Aria now found herself in the hands of the town crier.

"What is it?" Grimy-faced men called down from atop the log, "A wayward nymph? A wood sprite? A new young wife?"

"What will your old one say?" asked an axman.

"Good riddance." They all laughed good-naturedly, looking her over and smiling, glad to have an excuse to take a break and gawk at a helpless girl. She told her story again, including her imaginary mother and her invented nunnery. None of them bought a bit of it, leering and saying, "See her green eyes. She's a godless witch-girl. Totally wild. Bet she mates like a mink." Every woodman's dream.

"No, I am not," Aria insisted. "I am going to be a nun." By now she almost believed it.

"Or a nomad spy," someone suggested. "Horsemen have been lurking in the woods."

Her captor glanced back toward the tall trees. "I saw no nomads, but I heard wolves howl beyond the abatis."

"Maybe she is a werewolf." No one saw her as a nun.

"Whatever she is, the bailiff needs to see her," Aria's captor concluded. His fellows agreed and, having decided her fate, went cheerfully back to work. But her captor had found his way out of woodcutting, and he dragged her down the footpath toward town, past fat docile animals that would not last a day in the woods, grazing on stubble or pecking at sooty garbage.

Like most forest villages, Diymgorat had a single wooden plank street lined with log huts and lean-tos, and leading to a dock on the Upper Zog. *Diymgorat* meant "Smoketown," and the village lived under a black pall from charcoal burning for the ironworks upriver. Summer air tasted of soot and iron, and children's smiles shone against black-smudged cheeks. Even the tall wooden church, with its wide gables, carved birds, and troll faces, had a layer of dark ash on its onion dome.

Her captor sat her down on a log beside the bailiff's leather door, telling

Aria, "Do not move." Then he called for the bailiff. When the bailiff came, the woodsman pointed back to where she sat and swore. Aria was gone.

Sitting still and invisible, staring into the street, Aria watched civilization go lurching by—finding it about as bad as she remembered. Soot-black charcoal burners sloshed through the mud, making for an open vat of beer set up before a lean-to tavern, where ironworkers stood drinking with serf women wearing lilac kerchiefs, ruddy-faced from bathing naked in the Zog. Some of them had pawned coats and trousers for beer; several were passed out bare-assed in the mud. Aria listened to the woodsman swear she had been right here, telling the bored bailiff all the theories about her, from wood sprite to Tartar spy, making no mention of her brief career as a novice nun.

Men at the beer tub toasted the death of the Bone Witch, whom they had held in great fear. Then they drank to "His Highness the brave Prince Sergey, who earned his seat in Heaven, killing the gruesome witch in her white bone lair."

What a fine batch of fools. Bad enough to be serfs, but did they have to be bootlickers too? Serfs heartily toasted the lie, then praised the saints and damned Satan, downing yet more beer. Sitting motionless in the sun, Aria envied them, growing thirstier by the minute.

Crossing the settled lands would be harder than she had imagined. She had barely taken two steps before getting grabbed, dragged into town, and stranded on the doorstep of the local law. She would almost rather be in the Rift. How would she ever get through the settlements and across the Upper Zog with her noisy knight and horses? It would be hard enough getting off this bailiff's doorstep and back into the woods.

Bells tolled in the tall wooden church as the great carved churchyard gates swung wide. Out trotted a column of armored riders in horse guards white and blue, with black pennants on their lances, followed by white-robed priests swinging smoking censers. Behind the chanting priests lurched a gold-draped funeral carriage, with a lord's charger trailing behind, his silver-studded saddle empty.

Trailing after the warhorse was Prince Sergey's personal butler holding the prince's banner, bearing the lightning stroke of Ikstra—the sole surviving member of Sergey's original entourage. Behind the butler came the local boyar, Baron Boris of Zazog, a well-fed warrior aboard a gray charger, wearing blackened armor beneath a green silk surcoat. After the boyar came mounted retainers in Zazog black and green.

Serfs fell to their knees in the mud, abasing themselves before Prince Sergey's funeral cortege. Sensing the need for a speech, Baron Boris rode forward to address his awed inferiors. He rose in the saddle, shouting over their bent heads, "Be penitent, be humbled—the prince who defeated the Bone Witch was felled in his hour of triumph, sent by a lowly leopard to join the Almighty."

Baron Boris let his lie sink in, then added in shocked tones, "Alas, not everyone has your simpleminded devotion. Foreign traitors mean to profit from Markovy's misfortune. At the very moment that beloved Prince Sergey was struck down, the dastardly Castellan of Byeli Zamak, Sir Roye de Roye, so-called baron of France, stole the sacred Firebird's Egg. Whosoever sees this foreign devil must report him at once, or share in his evil deed and burn beside him."

Bad as that sounded, Baron Boris added, "This vile heretic has an accomplice, a godless witch-girl with dark hair and green eyes, who escaped with this false knight into the forest. . . ."

That brought up heads all around her. Diymgorat's bailiff hastily announced that such a girl was seen that very morning. Her woodcutter captor told how he had hauled her into town. Several drunken serfs spoke up as well, saying they saw the girl the woodcutter dragged in from the forest.

Delighted to hear they almost had her, Baron Boris ordered townsfolk to search their log hovels and tiny gardens at once. Serfs rushed to obey their boyar while the object of their search sat and watched.

Aria could not believe the commotion around her, and could not guess how she would get out of it. Her throat was parched, and she could not sit forever in the heat, watching people down beer and search for her. To take her mind off her thirst, she thought of her knight, hoping he had stayed where she left him. He was a foreigner, and likely to get lost without warning. Several half-starved dogs came up to her, sniffing suspiciously, but that was the closest they came to finding her.

Serfs returned to fall facedown before the boyar's stirrup, confessing failure. Rising higher in his saddle, their master sternly admonished them, "Wretched worthless oafs, the witch-girl was here this morning. Find her and bring her to me. Until you do, all hearths are extinguished. And find me the Castellan of

Byeli Zamak. Burn no fires. Bake no bread. And eat your porridge cold, until you bring them both to me."

Here the prince's butler announced that he had seen the fabulous Firebird's Egg, holding it in his hands. "I felt the Firebird Egg's living warmth. The Egg is no legend. It is the hope of Markovy, and the luck of her kings—it must not stay in the hands of witches and heretics."

Aria remembered how gladly this fellow had given that precious national treasure to a French baron and a wereleopard. Now he cavalierly urged these hapless villagers to get it back.

Groveling in the mud, grateful serfs blessed the baron's lenience, kissing his boot, swearing on their base souls to do better, vowing not to eat or sleep until they had obeyed their boyar. Baron Boris cheerfully accepted their apology, promising real punishments if they failed him again. Then he signaled for the funeral cortege to proceed. Horse guards escorted the gold-draped wagon toward the river dock, where a barge waited to take the body down the Zog to the Dys, which would bear it to a family crypt in Ikstra.

Glad to see the last of Prince Sergey, Aria did not follow the funeral's progress, since turning her head would have made her visible. Instead she waited like a bird in hiding, hoping the street would empty out, and she could somehow get away.

Bit by bit, the street did empty. Baron Boris's retainers closed down the log tavern, sending the clientele staggering off. Women came out to bemoan the boyar's ban on fires, asking how they were supposed to cook and wash, telling their men to scour the woods for her, "Or there will be no porridge tonight, and small beer for breakfast."

By and large the men obeyed, trooping off into the woods, leaving only some women behind, industriously using up the last of the hot water to wash themselves and their clothes, letting their bare bodies dry in the hot sun.

As people returned to their hovels, a two-wheeled wagon came jolting along, headed for the forest road, carrying a butt of beer and a big bag of bread. Seeing no one looking her way, Aria braced herself. When the cart came between her and the women, she jumped up and leaped aboard, dropping down between the beer butt and the wagon's side. Freezing again, she whispered her spell. So far, so good.

Staring straight back over the wagon bed, she saw a big woman in a berry-dyed skirt come running out of the bailiff's log house, followed by a pair of wide-eyed naked toddlers. Shouting and waving, the woman called after the wagon, but the driver did not even slow.

More women joined the chase, some throwing down their washing and picking up their skirts, others dashing naked after the wagon, trailing yapping dogs and grimy children. Quickly catching up with the uninterested driver, they demanded he stop, yelling that, "The bailiff's wife saw that witch-girl leap onto your wagon."

Unable to see the driver's reaction, Aria stayed stock-still, staring out the back of the wagon at the ring of women's faces. All of them looked worried and tired, some outright fearful, wanting to satisfy their boyar before he devised new torments. Hard to blame them, but Aria was not about to leap up and turn herself in. She heard the driver's seat creak as he looked about and then announced blandly, "There is nothing there but bread and beer. Go back to your babies."

"She must have jumped out," the bailiff's wife declared. "Did you see which way she went?"

"I saw nothing at all," the driver insisted, proudly proclaiming his ignorance. "Absolutely nothing."

"Useless fool!" the bailiff's wife shouted at his back as the wagon ambled away.

Aria watched the women disperse and saw Diymgorat's single wooden street disappear as greenery closed in. Ahead she again heard the ring of axes. Breaking the spell, she looked to see that it was safe, then reached into the bread bag and took two braided loaves. Sliding back the top of the beer barrel, she took a deep drink that went straight to her head, making it swim in the heat.

Another drink, and her problems did not seem so bad. This cart would take her back to the woods, where she had naught to fear but wolves and Tartars. There she would find her knight and devise some scheme for crossing the settled lands. Or so she hoped.

Without warning, the wagon jolted to a stop, and Aria just had time to replace the top on the beer before shrinking back into a corner to disappear. Men jumped aboard the bed of the wagon, big sooty charcoal burners, wearing smudged smocks and blackened leggings. Tossing the bread bag down to the ground, they wrestled the beer out of the wagon, nearly squashing her with the barrel. Luckily, none touched her.

Then to her horror, they began heaving big balks of wood into the wagon. Here was where she had to get off.

Leaping over the wagon rail, Aria nearly landed atop a surprised charcoal burner, who gave a startled cry and dropped his chunk of timber on a black bare toe, producing an astonished oath. Hitting the ground running, she shot off, holding her skirt about her waist, with the bread loaves tucked inside.

Shouts rang out behind her, followed by curses and running feet. Dodging between stands of stumps and leafy second-growth trees, she heard heavy footsteps gaining on her.

Aria dropped down behind a stump and disappeared. Frozen in place, she watched the charcoal burners go charging past, rattling the brush with their bulk. She kept to her crouch, hands pressed to the ground, feeling their huge footsteps fading. But by now Diymgorat had awoken to the uproar with church bells ringing and dogs yapping. Worse yet, the tall log barricade loomed ahead of her. She could never climb the spiked abatis and cross the cleared space beyond without getting caught, not with dogs and woodsmen at her heels. Her only chance was to head upriver toward the Rift, hoping for a break in the barricade.

Aria set out running, drawing more shouts from downriver. Ground rose up ahead of her, forming a sheer amphitheater of steep hills crowned with dark pines. To her right, the forest barricade curved to meet the base of the hills, and to her left lay the smoky ironworks lining the Upper Zog. There was a single sharp notch in the hills, where the Zog broke through the frowning heights, cutting a steep-sided cleft leading up to the Rift. Unless she found a gap in the barricade, her only escape would be up that narrow canyon.

Hearing dogs getting closer, she redoubled her efforts, knowing her favorite trick of running and vanishing would not work with dogs. Dogs would track her by scent and be all over her, forcing her to move and be seen. Finding no gap in the barricade, she looked hastily back, seeing her pursuers gaining fast.

Aria heard the firebird call her name. *"Arr-ee-haa, Arr-ee-haa."* Looking to her left, she saw the little flame-colored jay flitting between the birches, heading toward the notch in the hills, calling for her to follow, *"Arr-ee-haa . . ."*

She instantly obeyed the bird, breaking left, crashing through the birch thicket, heading for the steep slope at the opening of the canyon. This flame jay was the only bird that called to her by name, and so far he had never betrayed her.

Bursting out of the birch thicket, she heard the roar of rapids ahead, where the swift-running Zog tumbled out of the Rift, to power trip-hammers in the iron mills below. She hated to be heading into the Rift, which she had hoped to avoid completely. As bad as the settled lands might be, Aria feared the Rift even more. Much more. But now she had no choice.

"Arr-ee-ha, Arr-ee-ha," the bird called back to her, from somewhere farther up-river. Scrambling over rocks and gravel, Aria scanned the steep ravine ahead. Sheer walls rose up on one side, and on the other a vertical cliff dropped straight down to the roaring river, hundreds of feet below. Winding between the cliff edge and the canyon walls was a narrow trail, no more than a dozen yards across. She started up it, desperate to stay ahead of the men and dogs, even if it meant braving the Rift.

She did not get far. Blocking the narrowest part of the trail was a tight knot of thick-armed men in stained leather, holding huge hammers. Blacksmiths from the ironworks, some wearing slit-eyed welding masks and carrying big iron bars, were waiting to waylay her. Her heart sank. Woodsmen, dogs, and charcoal bunners were crashing through the birches behind her, and brawny ironworkers blocked the way ahead, warned by the church bells that something was amiss. Several of them saw her, and were shouting and pointing.

Moments like this made Aria wish she could really disappear. Sinking to her knees, she wanted to just lie down and cry, unable to believe her ill luck. Despite being a notorious trickster, mimic, and nest-robber, the flame-colored jay had never betrayed her before. How utterly unfair. What had she done? She was not hurting anyone, or taking anything. Aria wanted only to cross the little valley and go on her way.

Being down on her knees, she did not see the armored rider until he burst in among the blacksmiths, wearing Horse Guards blue-and-white over steel plate and whirling a great jagged war hammer, shouting a hearty *"Bonjour!"*

Terrified blacksmiths broke and ran, taken from behind by a mounted madman. Big blunt welding hammers were no match for his Lucerne hammer, a four-foot shaft with a steel head that had a hook on one side and three wicked curved blades on the other, made to inflict ugly jagged wounds. None of the ironworkers waited to test it.

Leaping up, Aria threw herself against the canyon wall, clinging to the rock and vanishing. Blacksmiths galloped past, tossing aside their heavy hammers and bellowing in fright, their instinctive fear of trained men-at-arms making them helpless against a mounted knight. Behind them came Sir Roye de Roye, swinging his gruesome hammer to shoo the ironsmiths along—not trying to kill, just encouraging their flight.

All the while, the firebird wheeled overhead, crying in ecstatic triumph at the havoc he helped create.

Reining in, Sir Roye de Roye pushed back the visor on his crested helmet, revealing his handsome face and fashionable bowl-cut bangs. His Lucerne hammer swung idly at his side. "Mademoiselle," he called to her, "I know you must be here somewhere."

Aria stepped happily away from the rock wall, glad to see her knight had not stayed on the hilltop where she left him, and had come looking for her instead. "How did you find me?"

"*Mon Dieu,* how could I not?" He extended a steel-clad arm to her. "The whole valley is an uproar, with bells ringing and dogs barking. And birds making a horrible racket—including this persistent jay, who absolutely insisted I come take a look. When I saw the ironsmiths blocking the pass, I decided to ride down and see why."

Seizing his hard mail wrist, she felt his gloved hand close on her bare forearm. Whenever they touched was special, but this time more than ever. After her exhausting chase and helpless terror, his firm gloved fingers felt tremendously reassuring, and exciting—even though it was not flesh to flesh. Scrambling up onto his charger's leather-armored crupper, she looped her arms about his steel waist, hugging his strong body to her, while laying her head against his armored back. "Thank you," she whispered. "Thank you so very much."

"You are most welcome, Mademoiselle." He could not turn to look at her because of his helmet, but she could hear the smile in his voice. "Pray see if our gentlemen friends are returning."

She laughed and shook her head. "Do not worry. They will not stop running until they get to Diymgorat."

4

prince sergey and the tartars

Hugging her knight's hard armored sides, Aria rested her head on his steel back, exhausted but happy, feeling the comforting sway of the horse beneath her. Safe again. She had hardly ever felt safe since the day the Bone Witch died—and when she did, it was almost always with her knight, who was smart, gallant, and a French baron to boot. True, he treated her nonchalantly, calling her Mademoiselle, but she could tell he loved her, even if he was too shy to show it.

"Where are we going?" she asked, glad to leave that grimy settlement behind, but wary of going deeper into the Rift.

"To where I left the horses." He turned his gray charger up a side canyon carved by a swift streamlet descending the pine hills bordering the Rift. The firebird flew ahead of them, calling raucously, making for the stunted pines above.

When they got to the tethered horses, the flame jay was sitting on the palfrey's pack saddle preening his red-orange plumage. From the hilltop, Aria got a sweeping view of the valley below, flanked on the east by the forest barricade, with the Upper Zog winding through the steep canyon, then flowing past smoking ironworks and dirty Diymgorat, headed for the flatlands and the Dys. No wonder her knight found her so easily; the hill looked straight down on the trail where the blacksmiths had stood. Behind her, the hills rose even higher, and the canyon widened, merging with the Rift. Somewhere up there was the Iron Wood and beyond that Burning Mountain, where they needed to go.

Dismounting, she helped her knight down, then offered him braided bread, being ravenously hungry herself—not having eaten since dawn. She did not like to sneak on a full stomach, which dulled her senses, but she was done with sneaking through the valley below—too many dogs and people. "Much too difficult," she decided.

"What is too difficult, Mademoiselle?" asked her knight, doffing his helmet and accepting the bread.

She sighed and sat down on soft pine needles, taking a bite of bread, savoring the fresh warm taste. "Trying to make it through the settled lands without being seen—it is impossible. I thought they would be stupid and unsuspecting, but there is a boyar down there setting the serfs to search for us."

"Which boyar?" Baron de Roye asked, working his words around a mouthful of bread.

She shrugged, the only noble Aria cared about being the one sitting next to her. "A big one in green silk and black armor."

"Baron Boris of Zazog," Sir Roye de Roye declared between bites. "He betrayed Byeli Zamak to Prince Sergey. Baron Boris is treacherous, brutal, has vile taste in wine, and never uses a fork except to pick his teeth."

Aria had never even seen a fork, but took her knight at his word. "And Tartars as well."

He looked at her quizzically. "As in steak tartare?"

"Tartars from Black Cathay, with wicked bows and worse-looking wolves." She shivered at the thought them. "They nearly got me."

Having taken off his gloves to eat, de Roye reached over and touched her cheek. "Mademoiselle is scared?"

"Terrified, actually." Tartars scared her more than all the boyars in Markovy, but that hardly mattered at the moment. Turning her head, she softly kissed his hand.

Baron de Roye grinned. "Mademoiselle is the bravest lady I have ever met."

Sometimes. Right now she felt incredibly nervous, just sitting and sharing braided bread with her knight. Now that they were alone and relatively safe, depraved ideas danced in her head. Women were silly sinful creatures, morally void and naturally promiscuous, best kept under lock and key. And being a soulless witch-girl made Aria more wanton that most.

That was why boyars imprisoned their wives and daughters in harems and convents, making it more likely to meet a unicorn than a lady on the loose. Serfs could not afford such luxuries, and their wives drank and bathed with men, their innate wantonness kept in check by the husband's whip hand. Markovite marriage custom required the bride to kneel and kiss the groom's dog whip, begging him to use it on her whenever she strayed—one of the many reasons Aria was in no rush to marry.

But her knight was a foreigner, full of foolish chivalry and silly delusions of feminine purity. Aside from a few chaste kisses, he treated her like a little sister, or niece, totally ignoring her incorrigible depravity. Until she saw him bathing and shaving, she thought he might be a eunuch. Now she knew he was "protecting" her from his own base male instincts. Charmingly absurd, even for a Frenchman.

"We will have to go through the Rift," she warned him. "Which frightens me a lot. But if we cannot get through the settled lands, that is the only way to the Firebird's Nest."

His hand went from her cheek to her shoulder, then slid down her arm, coming to rest on her hip—the first time he ever let himself be so familiar. "What is so bad about the Rift?"

"Everything." She shuddered at the horrors of the Rift, glad to feel his comforting hand on her hip. "Troll-bear lairs, ghosts, ghouls and lycanthropes, renegades and outlaws. Wild rocs and nine-foot cobras that can spit venom in your eye. And wereleopards, not the nice ones either." And the Rift had no trees, not even metal ones, no overhead cover at all.

"What about witch-girls?" He was not taking the terrors of the Rift seriously, using his hand to bring the two of them closer. "Would pretty witch-girls go into the Rift?"

"Reluctantly." She let him pull her nearer, her heart hammering harder than when she lay atop the barricade looking down on tufted Tartar lances. "Though not one with a bit of sense."

"Then I will go as well." He meant it. She had seen him cheerfully take on two armed men and a werewolf—all at the same time, and all for her. "For I would be with you, whatever the danger." Leaning closer still, he kissed her, letting their lips linger, not at all the way he would kiss a niece, or even a cousin. The hand on her hip squeezed harder, and he whispered, "Let me show you how the French do it."

His free hand cupped her head, and he kissed her again, deeper and more passionately, doing surprising things with his tongue. Unbelievably thrilling, but all they did was kiss; his other hand never left her hip. When he was done, he asked, "Do you like it?"

"Very much." Aria had seen drunken serfs lying with their mouths together, never suspecting this gross act was the most thrilling thing on earth.

Her knight smelled of sweat and leather mixed with the man-smell that all sane forest creatures knew and feared, but that she alone found incredibly compelling. She wanted to feel that sweat pressed against her bare skin, to have him fill her senses with warm fleshy pleasure. Luckily a couple of layers of armor lay between them; otherwise, there would have been no stopping her. She asked shyly, "Have you known many women?"

Sir Roye de Roye looked taken aback. "Some few. I am French, after all."

"Are you married?" Horrible thought.

"Not anymore." That question made Baron de Roye even less comfortable.

"What do you mean?" It never occurred to her that her knight might have a wife—or a family. Showing how new she was to romance.

"My parents betrothed me as a boy," de Roye confessed, "to an heiress whose lands adjoined ours. We were married when I was sixteen—but that was long ago and far away."

"Is she dead?" Aria asked hopefully.

"*Mon Dieu*, no!" Sir Roye de Roye hastily crossed himself. "Her name is Marie, and she is quite well, thank heaven. But when I was exiled, she moved back in with her parents and had our marriage annulled, on the grounds that I was a notorious traitor."

"Did you love her?" This was the question she feared most, but had to ask.

"Absolutely not." He looked aghast at the notion. "She is pious and arrogant as the pox, with a mean and pinched disposition, the perfect wife for Baron Boris. We disliked each other even as children, but our lands matched, and marriage is mainly business. For love, you must look elsewhere."

"Any children?" Marriage did not sound much like she imagined.

"No, not by me, anyway." He heaved a rueful sigh. "Marriage killed what little attraction we could muster."

"Good!" Aria kissed him happily. "Annulled or not, the marriage is meaningless."

"How so?" Sir Roye sounded intrigued.

"All marriages performed by schismatics on foreign heretics are meaningless." According to Mother Church, everyone outside of Markovy was living in sin, and all their children bastards.

De Roye sounded doubtful. "His Holiness Pope Pius might disagree."

"Only because he is a heretic too," she pointed out. Markovite patriarchs and Roman popes had lived under mutual excommunication since the tenth century. "He is the antipope, a lying castrated schismatic, whom you mistakenly worship. . . ."

"Celibate," Sir Roye corrected her. "Not castrated. And we do not worship him—it just seems that way sometimes."

"Either way, he never had a woman," Aria noted. "So what could he know about marriage?" Markovite clergy could at least marry, and learn about females firsthand.

Baron Roye de Roye laughed, giving her hip another squeeze. "Fear not, Mademoiselle. However many women I have been with, married, maiden, or crone—none were the least like you. You are unique, utterly and completely special."

That sounded much better, as if all the other women merely prepared him for her. She asked coyly, "How am I special?"

He looked her over. "You are the first female of any sort that I ever saw disappear—unless you count visitations by the Virgin."

She pooh-poohed the miracle of invisibility. "That is nothing, just a spell the Bone Witch taught me when I was a child."

Sir Roye smiled at her easy modesty, which made the miraculous into a matter of course. Such selflessness was as much an attraction as her youth and beauty. "You found me wounded and friendless in the woods, with a hefty reward on my head, and yet you have been feeding and caring for me ever since, without a thought for yourself. Or for what you might make by turning me in to my enemies. You are incredibly resourceful and loving."

To show her, he kissed her again, artfully guiding Aria's lips to his with one hand, making her feel her youthful awkwardness was incredibly precious, a treasure to be cherished, as magical as the Firebird's Egg. Closing her eyes, Aria gave herself totally to the kiss, hoping her knight would do with her what he willed. His hand on her hip moved to her lap, and his fingers pressed through the fabric, moving back and forth in a heavenly rolling motion. Her heart told her this was just the beginning.

While his tongue did marvelous things in her mouth, deft fingers kept massaging her groin, moving faster, and pressing harder. His firm rhythmic pressure sent waves of pleasure surging through her thighs, waves that broke deep inside her, shaking her whole being. Without lifting her dress or doffing his armor, her knight artfully brought Aria to orgasm, while sunlight poured down on them and birds called back and forth above.

When she came down to earth, Aria looked about shyly. No one was coming up the trail, but it was dangerous to tarry too long. Woodland instinct told her they needed a safer place to do this, a nice sheltered nest where she could abandon caution, and open up completely.

She whispered to her knight, "That was utterly unbelievable, but we must be gone. We must go deeper into the Rift to stay ahead of pursuit." And find a spot for love.

Baron de Roye acceded to her forest expertise, helping her up and mounting her back aboard the black mare. Handing her the lead rope for the bay palfrey that served as a sumpter horse, he led his charger to a sandy spot by the streambed. There Sir Roye knelt down and dug with his big double-edged saxe knife.

Eventually he set aside the knife, digging the last few inches with his hands; then he reached in and withdrew the Firebird's Egg, which was still wrapped in an embroidered tapestry. In his arms was all that remained of the legendary firebirds, giant flying guardians of Markovy, the living Egg that King Demitri had made his talisman. Every day since Sir Roye took it from the cold vaults of Byeli Zamak, the Egg's leathery skin had grown warmer and livelier, pulsing like a hard round heart.

Aria led the sumpter horse over, and Sir Roye slid the precious Egg into the bay's packsaddle. Baron Boris was only half-right, the Egg was the luck of the Markovite kings, but it was their curse as well. And now the Firebird's Egg had brought another catastrophe to its current owner—her. Only the absolute need to get the Egg back to Burning Mountain could tempt Aria into the Rift, one of earth's truly terrible places.

Descending the steep streambed, they worked their way along the cliffside trail overlooking the deep canyon of the Upper Zog. Spotting horse droppings, she reined in and dismounted, kneeling over the pony turds, sniffing and poking them, finding them fresh and moist—not a good sign. Picking up the largest, she broke it open, showing her find to Sir Roye. "Horse nomads came through here this morning, maybe the same Tartars I saw by the forest barricade."

"How can you tell?" asked her knight, wrinkling his nose, which was plainly unused to reading feces.

"Here, see these grains among the grass—" She sorted through the broken dropping. "—that is millet. Boyar's horses are fed on barley. And here is a pol-ished rice grain—we do not eat such things."

"Happy to hear it," her knight declared. "Personally, I will not touch any dish made from horse turds."

"It could be from Kazakhs or Kipchaks," she added hopefully, "but I doubt it." That stray kernel most likely meant some Tartar had given his favored mare a rice-ball reward. She held up the turd for her knight to inspect. "See how it is still warm at the center."

He vowed to take her word for it. Brushing off her hands, Aria washed them in a little stream tumbling down the rocks toward the Zog; then they set out again, headed deeper into the Rift.

As they rode, Aria kept looking over her shoulder at the cliff tops behind them. Everything was too still and silent. She missed having the wood's hun-dreds of eyes watching over her. Troll-bears you could smell, but wereleopards and lycanthropes could be stalking through the rocks above, waiting to catch them unawares. At the head of the canyon, the Rift widened and flattened out, and the Upper Zog sank to a trickle in a big sandy bed dotted with boulders. There they saw the first sign of how terrible a place they were entering.

Sitting in the middle of the trail was a woman's head, whose owner had been pretty, with long blond braids and good teeth; there was a black bruise under one eye, and the head had been in the sun for some time. Long lines of ants stretched away from the mouth and nostrils.

Her knight was aghast and started to get down, but she stopped him. This was just the sort of spot a lycanthrope would pick to lie in wait. He told her, "I was only going to give her a decent burial. She was young and fair, and I can-not just leave her head to the ants."

"She is buried," Aria explained, ignoring the head, looking up at the boul-ders instead. "There is a body attached to that head. Being buried to the neck and left to die in the sun is the penalty for killing your husband." Another rea-son not to wed.

"But we must at least bury her the rest of the way," Sir Roye de Roye in-sisted, unable to pass up even a dead woman in distress without doing some-thing for her. So Aria stood watch while her knight heaped sand onto the head, covering the mound with rocks, turning the horrid sight into a neat little mon-ument for the murderess.

Setting out again, Aria felt a warm wind spring up out of nowhere, blowing slow but steady at her back. Sand and grit gave way to hard flat shale as the Rift widened, its steep walls sinking down to bare white bluffs. After a time, Sir Roye asked, "What if a man kills his wife?"

"You mean like if he beats her to death?" Aria relaxed, glad to see frowning cliffs replaced by clear open views. Anything could be lurking at the base of the bluffs, but they were safe for the moment. "He gets a new one."

Her knight looked back toward where he had buried the head. "Hardly seems fair."

"But only up to three," she warned, least he think men could do anything in Markovy. "Mother Church allows a man only three marriages. Any man who whips two wives to death must be careful with his third."

"Or do his own washing." Baron de Roye could see the wisdom of setting a definite limit.

"Do they do things differently in France?" she asked, eyeing the ground ahead for sign of trouble.

"Somewhat," her knight admitted, still sounding shaken by what he had seen.

Aria was also shaken, but not surprised. Being unhallowed ground, the Rift was where the law did its worst deeds. "What happens in France if a wife kills her husband?

"We burn her alive." Sir Roye had thought that penalty harsh until he came to Markovy.

"How much more civilized," Aria exclaimed. "We are, alas, a very backward people, burning only witches and Catholics."

"Sensible policy," Her knight declared, being a Catholic in love with a witch-girl.

"So if we married, you would not beat me?" Strange customs could prove useful.

"I am married to someone else," he reminded her, "a baroness in France named Marie de Roye."

"Only according to the pope," Aria protested. "And what would he know?"

"What indeed," de Roye agreed, "he is just God's voice on earth. But I would not beat you, even if the pope ordered it."

"How would you ever hope to control me?" Aria considered herself a hand-ful, being wanton, willful, and raised by a witch.

Sir Roye laughed, saying, "I would have scant hope of that. Mademoiselle is a wild wood nymph, who will never be tamed." He looked her over with a grin. "Except, perhaps, by love."

She smiled back at her noble admirer, who risked his life to bury dead strangers but would not touch a pony turd. A black line appeared on the bluffs ahead, growing thicker and blacker as they proceeded. Sir Roye de Roye asked, "What is that?"

Aria wondered at his innocence. Her knight, who knew so much about kissing and killing, was naïve about the simplest things. "That is the Iron Wood."

"Truly?" He rose in his saddle, scanning the bluffs. "I have never actually seen it, even from this distance."

"It is closer than you think." She pointed out a dark patch growing nearby, slim black saplings poking up out of the ground, topped by curled iron leaves, looking like fireplace pokers stuck upright in the sand. "The Rift has only a sprinkling of iron trees, and is heavily logged to supply the ironworks on the Zog. See those stalks chiseled off at the base?" Black stubs dotted the ground around the stand of saplings.

Her knight stared past the black patch at the huge metal forest covering the bluffs. "Why does the Iron Wood not grow into the Rift?"

She shrugged. "No one knows why it grows at all." Nothing grew well in the Rift, and the bareness frightened Aria—with no berries to pick, or game to hunt, food would soon be a problem. The Rift felt like a giant funnel flanked on both sides by the Iron Wood, narrowing as they went deeper, reminding Aria of a carnivorous plant the Bone Witch used to have in her hut. Flies would crawl down the tall funnel-shaped stalk, drawn by the smell of nectar, then fall into the sticky trap below—she used to hear them buzzing angrily inside the stalk until they drowned in nectar and were digested by the plant.

"Arr-ee-haa!" the firebird called out a warning, and Aria glanced frantically around, seeing nothing.

"Look, up there." Her knight pointed a gloved finger at the wide open sky.

Aria looked up, expecting to see a wild roc diving down at her. Instead, a dark object drifted overhead, a big black inflated parasail with a boat-shaped hull hanging beneath it, complete with a dangling anchor and an incongruous set of wagon wheels. She identified the flying object immediately, from the Bone Witch's description. "It is a Tartar sky-boat."

"Something else I have heard of but never seen." Sir Roye sat in the saddle, staring up at the sky-boat, watching it slowly catch up with them. "What propels it?"

"Wind and magic," she replied, wishing it had been a wild roc. "Light gases fill the sail, keeping it aloft, and Tartar shamans are wizards at calling on the right winds."

"What are the wheels for?" Four spoked wheels made the boat hull look like a child's pull toy flying high overhead.

"Sometimes shamans fail." They were wizards, not miracle workers. "Then the sky-boats lower their sails and become steppe wagons, until the wind shifts." The warm breeze blowing at their backs sent the sky-boat drifting ahead of them, sinking steadily as it dwindled in size. Finally the wind died and the sky-boat sank down, disappearing between the Rift's ironbound bluffs.

Dismounting, they dined on braided bread and the last of the pickled meat given to them by the Bone Witch. She told her knight, "I must go on ahead, to see what the Tartars are doing."

"We should both go," Sir Roye suggested, loath to see her leave on her own.

She shook her head. "They have seen us from above, and know we are coming. There will be scouts lying in wait, making it hard for me to get close. With you and the horses, there will be no chance at all." Aria hated being so blunt, but this was life or death.

"Am I that useless?" asked Baron Roye de Roye, Chevalier de l'Étoile and former Castellan of Byeli Zamak.

"No, no," she assured her injured knight. "This very morning you saved me from dogs, woodsmen, and ironworkers. I would not be here but for you." Aria meant it with all her heart, but right now she needed to see what these Tartars were up to, and hopefully steal some food. She could not cater to knightly honor. "And you must guard the Egg while I am gone."

"Ah, yes, the Egg. The fabulous Firebird's Egg." From the way he said it, she could tell Baron de Roye cared far more for her than for the magical Egg and the future of Markovy. "How could I forget?"

"Please, my love. I will be back as quick as I can." She had no intention of leaving her knight alone in the Rift—not for long anyway. "Just watch over the Egg while I am away."

He looked at her intently, no longer insulted, grinning instead, saying, "You really do love me."

"Of course," she replied. "I never tried to hide it. You were merely slow to notice."

Sir Roye de Roye shook his head ruefully. "Mademoiselle must be wary, for love is a very dangerous thing."

Again she was Mademoiselle—he never called her Aria. "As dangerous as sneaking up on Tartars?"

"Easily," Sir Roye laughed.

"How so?" To her, love seemed nothing but good. Her only heartache came from the fear he might not love her.

Drawing her closer, he stroked her cheek with his finger. "Because you love with all your heart."

"Is that wrong?" she asked, kissing his finger.

"No," he told her, "love is never wrong, but it is dangerous. For that is how we are hurt." He guided her lips to his and kissed her, a long lingering kiss that turned her mouth inside out.

At the same time, his fingers undid the ties on her dress, and his hand slid inside her bodice, cupping her breast. Aria thrust herself against his hand, excited by the warm pressure, and the feel of his fingers playing with her stiff nipple through her thin silk shift. Too bad she had a flying boat full of Tartars to stalk. But tonight would be different. Tonight it would just be her and her knight.

As the kiss ended, he started to draw his hand back, but she would not let him. Seizing his wrist, she pulled his hand in deeper, saying, "Wait, do not stop. Do the other one."

Without hesitation, he seized both breasts at once, at the same time kissing her harder, more passionately, until Aria thought she would burst with joy. When she could take it no more, Aria whispered, "Now I am done."

His hands stayed where they were. "Really?"

"Only for the moment." She smiled wickedly, thinking of the night ahead. "Wait here. I will be back as soon as I can—maybe with food."

He let go, adding, "And wine—if Mademoiselle can find it."

She nodded, undoing the last laces on her dress and stripping down to her silk shift to move easier. Tartars drank fermented mare's milk—but she had not the heart to tell Sir Roye that. After one last, long look at her knight, Aria took off.

Following the Zog upstream over pebbles and bare rock, she walked in the water when she came to dirt or sand, to keep from leaving tracks. Luckily there was no wind now—trying to sneak up on dire wolves with a wind at your back was sheer suicide. Flitting ahead of her was the firebird, giving her some hope of warning. She moved as fast as she dared, anxious to get back to her knight.

At a patch of big boulders, the flame jay left the stream, flying from rock to rock, headed toward the far bluffs. Aria decided to follow the bird, rather than blunder on alone upstream, where thirsty and hungry things might be waiting. Moving quick as she could, she leaped from one boulder to the next, running along their backs.

Topping a low ridge, she caught sight of the Tartar parasail and froze, whispering her spell. All Aria saw was the parasail, and not the sky-boat beneath it, but she knew it marked the Tartar camp. Dropping down behind the nearest rock, she wormed between the boulders, stopping every so often to vanish and listen. Nothing. Without birds and squirrels, the Rift could be deathly quiet. Then as the rock field thinned, she spotted the Tartar sentry, lying prone atop an outcropping. She would not have seen him at all, but the firebird flew close by him, and he looked up.

She froze. He wore that weird Tartar cap with big ear flaps, and he followed the firebird's flight with his eyes, then turned back to slowly sweeping the area downstream, looking from one line of bluffs to the other, then back again. His gaze passed over her.

As soon as he was looking away, she moved, running lightly forward, then freezing when his head turned back toward her.

This was like a game Aria played as a girl, a rare happy memory from her childhood in the settled lands. One of the bigger boys would turn his back and let the little kids try to sneak up on him. Whenever he spun about, you had to freeze, or get a swat if he caught you moving. She nearly always won, but had never expected to play the game against a sharp-eyed archer who would shoot her if she slipped.

Flitting from stone to boulder, the firebird caught the Tartar's attention, drawing his gaze away from the deadly game of dare base.

Aria ran the last little bit, freezing against a boulder below and behind him. He must have heard her, because he spun about, looking straight at her. They stared at each other; then he turned and went back to sweeping the lower Rift, ignoring the flame jay's antics.

Safely past the sentry, Aria slipped through the last of the boulders, coming on a wide clear space with a spring-fed pool at the lower end. Two yurts and the sky-boat sat on a raised bank beyond the pond. She could see straight into their camp, except for a few spots hidden by the last of the rocks. There were no dogs, and only the horse lines were guarded. There was no guard at all on the sky-boat, which swayed slightly above the ground, held down by silken lines.

While she stood watching, two bowmen emerged from one of the yurts, carrying buckets, followed by a woman with a cloth bundle. Even from a distance, Aria could tell the woman was no Tartar, since she had a long blond braid and walked like a Markovite. Horse nomads were notoriously bowlegged. They went together down to the pond, where the men deposited their buckets on the bank, then headed back toward the yurt, leaving the woman to wash and draw water.

Aria waited until the men were in the yurt and the horse guards were looking the other way; then she walked calmly down to where the woman knelt by the pond, filling a bucket. Looking up, the blond woman started, nearly spilling her pail. Pretty but harried, the woman had keen blue eyes and Cupid's bow lips. "What are you doing here?"

Aria nodded toward the Tartar camp. "Spying on them."

"Good luck," the blonde laughed, and went back to filling her bucket. "Where did you come from?"

"Markov, from the royal palace. Prince Ivan himself sent me to see what these Tartars are up to." Since she had to claim some authority, it might as well be the highest.

"Four-year-old Prince Ivan?" Setting aside her full bucket, the woman sounded skeptical.

"That is him. I am his older sister." Aria proudly made herself a princess.

Scooping up another bucket, the woman began to fill it. "Forgive me, Your Highness, for not bowing. But as you see, I am already on my knees."

Letting the lèse-majesté pass, Aria asked, "Are you Markovite?"

"No, I am a Pole." Finishing that bucket, the Pole swiftly picked up the next. Even the presence of a princess did not tempt her to slow.

"You speak very well for a foreigner." Her own knight had a dreadful French accent, which Aria found charming.

"I have a good ear for languages." Seizing the final bucket, the blond woman started to fill it.

Aria asked, "What are you called?"

Watching her bucket fill, the Pole shrugged round strong shoulders. "Tartars call me Borte, which means 'Blue-Eyes.'"

"Charming." The young Pole did have big round blue eyes, which must have pleased the Tartars.

"Actually, my full name is Blue-Eyed Wolf Bitch," the blonde admitted, "but I usually leave off the 'bitch' part."

"But you must have a birth name."

Blue-Eyes shook her head. "If I hear it said, I may start to cry. Borte must do for now."

Men emerged from the nearby yurt, calling out in Tartar. Horse line guards looked her way, and Aria froze, whispering her spell. Tartars came striding over—the same two who led the woman to the pond—wearing leather armor and worried looks, glaring about with their bows strung.

One said a few curt words to Blue-Eyes, who looked around in surprise, then mumbled a reply in Tartar. Slinging their bows, the Tartars picked up the full buckets and carried them back to the yurt. When they reentered the yurt and the horse guards looked away, Aria relaxed and reappeared. Looking up from her washing, Blue-Eyes seemed more amused than shocked. "So, you are back."

Nodding toward the yurts, Aria asked, "What did they say?"

"They asked who I was talking to," replied the Pole, starting to pound her wash.

"What did you tell them?"

Chuckling, the blonde beat blue Tartar pants on a rock. "To myself, apparently."

"And they believed you?" Everything she had seen of the Tartars said they were lethally smart.

"They think I am a little crazy." Wringing out the pants, Blue-Eyes stared at her. "You are real, aren't you?"

"Oh, yes. Very real," Aria assured her. "You may touch me if you like."

Blue-Eyes went back to her washing. "Well, you come and go, claiming to be a princess spy. And I am a little crazy."

Studying the horse line guards, Aria asked, "What are the Tartars like?"

Without looking up from her washing, Blue-Eyes considered the question. "They are men, only more so. And smart, devilishly smart, smart enough to get along without women. Their women run the camps and herds at home, so their men can go where they please, taking what they want. If you are what they want, they treat you well—but give them the least trouble, and they will kill you, figuring there are more where you came from."

Aria shuddered. "That must be horrible."

"Very," Blue-Eyes agreed. "I was in a wedding party, a bridesmaid for my cousin, who was marrying a handsome Markovite landgraf. On the way to the wedding, we were ambushed by Tartars. All the men were killed, along with the bride's mother and grandmother. Then they went through the younger women, killing the ones they did not want. I was saved because I am blond and I speak several languages. Only the children were spared rape and murder. Tartars adore children immensely, doting on them when they can, and regularly raising their victims' offspring. Our mingghan commander began life as a Merkit."

"But only children?" Though still a virgin, she was no longer a little girl.

"Exactly." Blue-Eyes nodded. "You would do well to develop some useful talent, unless you mean to survive on sex alone."

"Besides turning invisible?" Aria asked, not particularly wanting to please the Tartars at all.

"Oh, no. They will love that." Blue-Eyes looked up to see if she was still there. "They like anything new and useful. They also like children, and women they can force—you are a bit of both. Tartars will see plenty of uses for you."

No doubt. Aria hoped the Tartars would never even see her.

"How long will they be here?"

"Not long," Blue-Eyes guessed, spreading out her wash on the rocks. "There is no grass for the ponies. They are only here to meet the sky-boat, which has something important aboard."

"What?" Aria looked at the sky-boat, tethered beyond the yurts, wondering what could bring Tartars to this forsaken place.

"Something—or someone—they took from your people. Tartars are incredibly smart." Blue-Eyes shook her head in weary resignation. "Way smarter than our men. Before going to war, they must know everything about their enemy—all his strengths, and weaknesses. What he wears, what he eats, what he fights with, how many warriors he has, how many horses. Where they can find water and pasture. Whatever might prove useful."

Aria understood, being here to spy herself—but most Markovites thought it a mortal sin to even learn a strange tongue, and were far more worried about avoiding foreign heresy than getting to know their neighbors, much less their enemies.

"And when Tartars come in earnest, they want people with them that know the land or speak the language: corrupt lordlings, disgruntled exiles, kidnapped peddlers, or just women who are good with languages." Laying out the last of her wash, Blue-Eyes bade her good-bye and went back to her yurt, leaving Aria standing by the pond, wondering what to do. So far she had neither food nor any real notion of why the Tartars were here.

At least there were no dogs. Headed for the sky-boat, Aria slipped between the yurts, playing hide-and-seek with the guards at the horse lines, vanishing if they looked her way. Men talked in the yurts, and Blue-Eyes sang as she worked. Horses snorted at her, but no men saw her, though a couple looked right through her, wondering what had spooked the horses. One of the Tartar horses was Prince Sergey's charger from the funeral procession, still wearing Sergey's silver-studded saddle. Hardly a good omen.

She finished up standing beneath the sky-boat, listening for signs of life in the wheeled hull swaying overhead.

Not a sound. Anyone aboard had to be asleep. Seeing a light silk ladder hanging from the stern, she guessed the last man off had left it hanging for when they returned. As soon as the horse guards were not looking, she swarmed up the ladder and slipped over the rail.

Freezing as she hit the deck, Aria saw no one, just a small silk and bamboo deckhouse. Thank goodness. Deck space was so limited, she would have landed in someone's lap. No one came out of the deckhouse to see who rocked the boat, so Aria put her ear to the paper door. Nothing. Just the strong smell of incense. Lifting the latch string, she slid back the door. Anyone inside must be asleep.

Or dead. Laid out on silk cushions was the corpse of Prince Sergey, looking very good for someone who had been dead for days. Dressed in a royal silver-and-blue robe, Prince Sergey seemed like he was sleeping, except for the puncture wounds on his neck where the wereleopard had bit down, snapping his spine. Someone had thoughtfully sewn the wounds closed, making the battered prince more presentable.

One look was all Aria needed. When the wereleopard clamped down on Prince Sergey's pompous neck, she had thought "good riddance"—never wanting to see His Highness again, alive or dead. Now here he was, where he had absolutely no right to be, aboard a Tartar sky-boat deep in the Rift. Not wanting to know what the Tartars meant to do with him, she slid the paper door closed and turned to go.

Too late. Aria felt the boat rock gently beneath her—someone was coming aboard. Resisting the impulse to freeze, she realized there was too little room on the tiny deck—anyone who boarded would be right on top of her. Corpse or no, she had to hide in the cabin.

Sliding back the paper door, Aria slipped inside, closing it behind her just as a man's hand topped the rail. Crawling around to the head of the corpse, she found a small space at the base of the silk cabin wall, between an empty pigeon coop and a couple of feather cushions. Hidden from sight and feel, she whispered her spell and waited.

First into the cabin was a Tartar shaman, looking like Death done up for a dance, with a necklace of monkey skulls, long wild hair, and a white smoke-stained robe—white being the color of death in Black Cathay. His face was painted like a woman's, and his cheeks were scarred to keep his beard from growing.

Sitting down cross-legged before the corpse, the shaman began a shrill keening chant, so high-pitched that he might really have been a woman. Or a castrato. But then what were the facial scars for, if not to curb his beard? Thankfully, her witch's rune kept the Tartar he-she from sniffing her out.

Behind the sexually ambiguous shaman came two hard-eyed Tartar officers wearing steel caps and leather breastplates, who seated themselves at either side of the door—the senior one wore a tunic trimmed with sable, showing he was a division commander, and the younger one wore the red fox trim of a regimental officer. Last of all came Blue-Eyes, who sat beside the shaman at the feet of the corpse, setting out a sheep's shoulder blade heaped with incense.

Heart hammering, but otherwise still, Aria lay watching the shaman burn yet more incense, going on with the shrill chant. From time to time, he would give falsetto instructions to Blue-Eyes, who anointed Prince Sergey's eyes, ears, and mouth with mare's milk, Cathayan spices, and fresh sheep's blood. Aria could smell the heady spices, even through the thick incense.

As the keening crescendoed, Aria's skin started to crawl—this was necromancy, blackest of the black arts, used to invite in ghosts, ghouls, and nightwalkers. She had seen the Bone Witch do it, hobnobbing with the dead and near dead on Halloween nights. Never her favorite sort of spellcraft.

What happened next made her like it even less. Prince Sergey's corpse responded to the chant, slowly lifting its head, as if trying to see who was wailing away at his toes. Having that badly chewed head rise up next to her nearly shocked Aria out of her spell. It took all her concentration to keep still as the dead grand duke bent at the middle and sat bolt upright.

With his neck bone severed, His Highness's head hung to one side, but that did not stop him from speaking, "What the devil are these demon apes doing stinking up my bedroom?"

Bowing their heads slightly, both Tartars politely introduced themselves, and Blue-Eyes translated, "This is Kaidu, noyan of the Forest Toman, and Mangku his van mingghan commander. I am called Borte."

Unable to do more than blink and breathe, Aria lay listening to the dead prince's reply: "Tell these unbaptized dogs they are squatting before Prince Sergey Mikhailovich, Grand Duke of Ikstra, Baron Suzdal, and uncle to Crown Prince Ivan."

Blue-Eyes said a few words to the noyan in Tartar, then turned back to the pompous corpse. "Kaidu wishes to know what could bring your august personage to these humble woodlands."

"Does he?" asked Prince Sergey. "Well, it is hardly his concern, is it? Damned impudent, even for a squint-eyed chimp in armor."

"Nonetheless, he must know. You are dead," Blue-Eyes reminded the prickly deceased. "And the dead speak only the truth."

Sergey glared, plainly irked by his makeshift resurrection. "Every dolt in Diymgorat knows I came to find the Firebird's Egg. Baron Boris bellowed it at my funeral."

After a few curt words in Tartar, Blue-Eyes asked, "Why is the Firebird's Egg so important?"

His Highness scoffed at their ignorance. "The Firebird's Egg is the luck of the Mikhailovich Kings, Markovy's greatest treasure. It is what makes us invincible, able to pummel you brainless fur-trimmed baboons whenever we like."

Blue-Eyes conferred with the Tartars, then asked, "So long as you have this Egg, you believe you cannot be beaten?"

"Whoever holds the Egg is invincible," declared the confident corpse. "Dare to come against us, and dogs will defecate on your graves."

Kaidu smiled and nodded, thanking Sergey for the warning; then he had Blue-Eyes ask, "Where is the Firebird's Egg now?"

"Stolen," Prince Sergey hissed, "taken by a traitorous heretic and a treacherous witch-girl."

Blue-Eyes asked, "Which traitorous heretic?"

"Sir Roye de Roye, Chevalier de l'Étoile and baron of France, the former Castellan of Byeli Zamak."

"And what treacherous witch-girl?"

"How would I know her name?" Such details were beneath a grand duke. "The one that goes invisible."

Aria saw the Pole's blue eyes go wide, but her voice did not falter. Hearing her translation, the Tartars leaned closer, asking soft questions. Blue-Eyes pretended ignorance. "What do you mean, 'invisible'?"

"Transparent, not there, gone as glass. I did not believe it myself until I saw her disappear."

Blue-Eyes dutifully translated, and the question came back, "Where are they now? The knight, the Egg, and the invisible witch-girl?"

"How should I know?" asked the indignant corpse. "These questions are tedious. Having monkeys for mothers does not make you amusing."

"You are dead, and need not be amused," Blue-Eyes replied. "You must merely answer truthfully." Despite his bluster, the princely corpse was clearly the shaman's puppet, called back to answer questions with no will of his own.

And the questions kept coming. Having failed to find the Firebird's Egg did not mean the Tartars were finished. They wanted to know all about young Prince Ivan. Was he well? Did the boy show promise? Which boyars were most likely to betray him? What was the strength of the royal horse guards? How many horsemen could each boyar muster? Which would be open to bribes? Did any have a weakness for women? Or pretty young eunuchs? Endless questions and caustic replies eventually put Aria to sleep, ending a day that began before dawn on the far side of the forest barricade.

She awoke with a start, instantly visible. Luckily she was alone, unless you counted the corpse. Prince Sergey's Tartar interrogators had left, taking Blue-Eyes with them.

Silk walls shone with dim pearl gray light, and Aria guessed she had slept through the short spring night, drugged by exhaustion and heavy incense. Prince Sergey looked none the worse for his interview—in fact, the act of sitting up and answering questions had infused him with a weird lifelike glow, putting color in his cheeks, though it had done nothing for his glazed eyes and severed spine. Easing past the prince, she opened the paper door a crack.

First light filtered into the cabin. Looking out, Aria found no one aboard, and the camp beyond asleep, aside from a pair of nodding guards on the horse lines. She slid down a silk line to the ground, keeping the sky-boat between her and the horse guards. As quickly as stealth allowed, Aria crossed the camp and skirted the pond.

Blue-Eyes had taken in her laundry, but lying by the pond was a bundle containing cooked millet, dried fish, and a jar of koumiss, fermented mare's milk. It must have been left for her at dusk, because wet pugmarks showed that during the night a female leopard had come down to drink, then sniffed the bundle before heading deeper into the Rift. Make that a wereleopard.

Clutching the gift from Blue-Eyes, Aria set out running back the way she came, only slowing to slip past the Tartar sentry, hoping her knight had waited for her. Gone far longer than she intended, she was returning with terrible news. Aria did not have to be a seeress to know these Tartars would soon be looking for them. Prince Sergey practically dared the nomads to find the Firebird's Egg, or face humiliating defeat.

Even before she reached the river, Aria began to feel she was being watched. Looking over her shoulder, she saw nothing, but that meant little. Hearing the firebird's warning behind her, she shifted direction, heading straight downwind. When she found the right rock, she froze against it and waited.

Within seconds, a lycanthrope slipped past her, his claws out and fangs bared. Unable to see or smell her, he quickly loped off, trying to catch up with his quarry. She let the wolfman get well ahead of her, then turned downstream again, running as fast as she could. When he realized he had lost her, the lycanthrope would cast about for her scent, and no doubt find it, but by then Aria meant to be with her knight.

She smelled his campfire first, then the horses. There was something so charming and artless about her knight's inability to take precautions. He naturally assumed a French baron would beat whatever the Rift sent his way, and was lounging about the campfire with his armor off and his sword within reach, wearing just his shirt, hose, and quilted arming jacket. Very fetching.

Such serene security was just what her jangled nerves needed, and he had barely said a happy *Bonjour* before Aria was in his arms, hugging him hard as she could. His welcoming kiss was as wonderful as she remembered, a brief bit of bliss after a wretched night.

When the kiss ended, she continued to hug him to her, grateful for his solid strength. Thank Heaven she did not have to face the Tartars alone. Her knight asked, "What has happened, Mademoiselle? Have you missed me so much?"

"More," she told him, "much more." How horrible to be in love—and on the run. All she wanted in the world was to be alone with him; instead, the whole world was after them. "I needed so much to be with you last night."

"And I hoped to be with you too," he assured her. His hand slid down to lift her linen shift, and she felt warm fingers on her thigh, making her want to melt into him—if only there were time. Sir Roye whispered, "What catastrophe kept us apart?"

"It was horrid." She buried her head in his shoulder. "There are at least two yurts of Tartars looking for us, probably more, with a he-she shaman and a talking corpse. And a lycanthrope too, though not with the Tartars." He just meant to murder and eat her.

Confused by this summation, Sir Roye stopped stroking her thigh. "What talking corpse?"

"Keep doing that," she told him, guiding his hand between her legs, where it felt solid and exciting. "You know him, Prince Sergey—the one bitten by the leopard."

Sir Roye was shocked. "He's back?"

"From the dead." She clamped her legs closed on his hand, wishing she could just keep it there. "Dead or alive, he does not scare me a tenth as much as the Tartars."

"So what must we do?" His hand started to move in a most amazing fashion.

"Flee, unfortunately." But not just yet. She could not bear to leave his embrace, even if it meant her death.

He kissed her again, and for a time they stood pressed together, exploring each other's mouths, while his hand worked wonders between her legs, and the world grew dangerously light around them. Finally, fear overcame passion, and she broke the kiss, whispering, "We must go."

"Must we?" asked her knight, who plainly enjoyed this as much as she did.

"It is that, or die in each other's arms," Aria warned.

"When you put it that way." He reluctantly released his grip, giving just one last squeeze, to show he would be back.

Aria smiled at that silent promise. Life was becoming more incredible by the moment, if only she lived to enjoy it. She told her love, "There was a woman too, a live woman. One you would like. Very blunt, but also caring. She gave me this." Aria showed him the food bundle Blue-Eyes left.

"Umm, millet." He looked over her shoulder into the bag. "I am almost hungry enough to eat it."

"There is fish as well," she told him, laying her head back on his chest, feeling on the verge of tears. Why could they not be left alone? Allowed to do what they willed.

"And what is in the jar?" asked Sir Roye, sniffing suspiciously.

"Wine," she answered weakly, afraid to tell him koumiss came from a horse.

"Wine? Really?" He grinned down at her. "Oh, wondrous wood sprite, what would I do without you."

That was what she most wanted to hear, that he needed her, because she so awfully needed him. She warned her love, "We are in desperate danger, and must make for the Iron Wood—before the Tartars discover we are here."

"*Absolument,*" Sir Roye agreed, trying the "wine" and then declaring it, "Sweet, but with a bite. Why is it so milky white? What grape does it come from?"

"You do not want to know." Aria pulled him toward the horses, saying, "Come, we must be going."

She had to get them out of the open Rift and into the relative safety of the Iron Wood, where they had only ghouls and werewolves to worry about. Her knight complied, donning his armor and saddling his charger, happy to have the spiked mare's milk, which made his kisses even more sweet and intoxicating.

Heading for the near bluffs, Aria kept looking back, expecting to see Tartars on their trail. But all she saw was the bare, bouldered Rift behind her, and a pair of wild rocs, circling between her and the sun—and to think she used to be afraid of them. Her knight told her, "I too missed you. And feared for you as well, when you did not return by nightfall."

She shivered at how she had spent the night. "I was safe enough. Safer than now, in fact." She glanced back over her shoulder, seeing nothing but sand and rock. "They did not know where to look for me."

Avoiding Baron Boris's hapless horde of serfs, Horse Guards, washer women, and charcoal burners was hard enough, but the Tartars were deadly efficient, flying through the air, grabbing up stray blondes, kidnapping Prince Sergey's corpse to use as a talking puppet. She told her knight how Prince Sergey had come back from the grave to botch things one last time by setting the Tartars on them.

"Mademoiselle needs fear nothing while I am at her side." His helmet off, Sir Roye smiled over at her, looking impossibly brave and sturdy. "Baron Roye de Roye, Chevalier de l'Étoile, is your champion. I have sworn to see you safe through this quest, pledging my life and honor for my lady's safety."

That was what Aria feared most, worse than her own death—that he would lose his life protecting her. She asked shyly, "Am I truly your lady?"

His grin widened. With his helmet off, Aria could see his stylish pudding-bowl haircut getting long in the back. Life on the run played havoc with your coiffure. "You are my lady, you are my love. How could you ever doubt it?"

"You are married to someone else," she reminded him, "your wife in France."

He laughed. "Having a wife in France has nothing to do with love. Marie married in order to be Baroness de Roye, not out of any fondness for me. Why should I love her for that? I love you for your beauty and your courage, and for your loving heart. I know no other woman who—"

She never found out what made her so singular. "Arr-ee-haa! Arr-ee-haa!" came from the firebird, and Aria looked back over her shoulder. This time they were there. Dire wolves, an entire pack, coming silently over the rocks behind them.

She told her knight, "Wolves mean Tartars. We must get up that draw ahead, before they catch us in the open."

Urging their horses to run, they sped for the notch in the bluffs, a steep bouldered side canyon leading up to the dense line of dark metal trees. Glancing back, Aria saw the first of the Tartars, a dozen men and three score horses, each rider having several remounts, letting them run down any quarry. When not at war, Tartars killed fast, fierce animals to stay in practice. At the rate they were gaining, the nomads would soon be in bow range. She shouted to her knight, "We have to get up that gully and into the Iron Wood." There the dense metal thicket would nullify Tartar arrows and numbers.

At the base of the gully, the first arrows arched toward them, falling short, but not by much. As the ground rose up, their horses slowed, while the Tartars raced over the rocky flats, firing as they came. Arrows began to land around them—long flight arrows, getting lift from their broad heads and big tail feathers. Aria dodged between boulders, leading the sumpter horse up the steep gully, while her knight brought up the rear, his armor being proof against the light flight arrows.

Suddenly the line in her hand snapped taut as the sumpter horse stumbled and went down. Reining in, Aria saw the palfrey had been hit in the hind leg.

Another arrow hit the fallen horse in the belly. A third shaft struck the pack saddle. And inside that pack saddle was the Firebird's Egg. She had to go back for it.

Turning her mare about, she urged the frightened horse back down the gully—meeting her knight, who was pounding up the draw, headed the other way. As they shot past each other, he twisted in the saddle, calling to her, "Aria, come back!"—the first time he had ever called her by name.

With her name ringing in her ears, she reined in beside the downed sumpter horse. Fortunately the horse had not fallen on the side holding the Firebird's Egg, since she never could have lifted the beast. Tearing at the packsaddle straps, Aria struggled to untie them and get at the Egg. As she tugged at the straps, an arrow buried itself in the leather saddle, inches from her hand, and another nicked her shoulder, tearing her shift without drawing blood.

Suddenly her black mare gave a horrible shriek. Hit in the neck, the horse collapsed almost on top of her, thrashing and struggling, kicking up dust and pebbles.

Panicked, Aria pulled harder on the straps, ripping open the packsaddle. Reaching inside, she seized the tapestry bundle, planning to snatch up the Egg and disappear.

Before she could, a mailed arm came down around her waist, lifting her into the air. Her knight had come back for her, reining in his armored charger next to her fallen mare, then scooping Aria up onto his saddle.

"Wait!" She gave a startled shout, clutching up the tapestry bundle. "We must have the Egg."

"Leave it," her knight shouted, choosing her over the magical Firebird's Egg. She refused to let go, clinging stubbornly to the bundle that had brought on all this trouble. Arrows rattled off his armor as Sir Roye turned again to head back up the gully, aiming for the iron trees at the top.

Aghast at almost losing the Egg, Aria clung hard to her precious bundle, shielded by Baron de Roye's armored body as they pounded up the rocky draw. By now Tartars at the base of the gully were firing heavy armor-piercing arrows, and in seconds the horse nomads would come swarming up the ravine after them. An arrow hit the charger's leather-armored rump, making the big warhorse squeal horribly.

Another arrow hit the horse, and another. Aria could not believe she had not been hit—the Bone Witch had to be watching over her.

At the top of the draw, the wounded stallion lurched and staggered, eyes aflame and nostrils flaring in agony. Ahead, Aria saw the first of the iron trees, but knew they would never make it. Hit repeatedly, the overloaded horse fell in an armored heap, flinging Aria into space, still clinging to the Egg.

Hard flinty earth slammed into her, scraping her skin and making her head ring. Aria rolled as she hit, tumbling butt over brainpan, curling herself into a protective ball around the tapestry bundle. She fetched up abruptly against a big boulder, banging horribly, but giving her some protection against arrows, or being trampled by overeager pursuers. Whispering her spell, she waited, her heart beating like a rabbit's.

Leaping to his feet, her knight turned to meet the nomad charge, swinging his hideous Lucerne hammer with both hands. Here at the top of the draw, the gully narrowed so much that only one rider could come at a time—nor could the nomads below get a clear shot at him, with their fellows in the way. Tartars had to take on Baron de Roye one by one, and hand to hand.

Which proved impossible. No lone Tartar stood a chance against the Swiss-forged blades of his saw-toothed Lucerne hammer. Curved steel sliced through scale armor and iron-studded leather like they were parchment and linen, inflicting gruesome wounds and pulling riders from the saddle. Light Tartar lances glanced off Sir Roye's armor, and the nomads never got close enough to use their short deadly scimitars and Khyber knives. Riderless horses bolted back down the gully or fell beneath the bright sharp hammer, landing in a thrashing pile atop their former masters.

More Tartars kept coming, until the top of the defile was jammed with dead and wounded, forcing the men struggling up from behind to dismount, and be hewn down on foot.

Aria saw a single arrow arch overhead, whistling as it went. At the top of its arc, the whistling arrow exploded in a bright flash, leaving a puff of black smoke hanging in the blue above.

As the feathered tail of the arrow fluttered down, the attack ceased. No more Tartars came scrambling over the gristly barricade of fresh corpses and dead horses. Eerie silence descended, broken only by high-pitched neighing from a wounded horse. Her knight looked anxiously about, until she moved and he saw her flattened against the boulder.

He grinned, and signed for her to stay down. Heavy armor-piercing arrows arched over the barricade, falling silently out of the sky like iron hail. Determined to be nearer her knight, Aria dashed to his side, sprinting through the deadly hail, covering the Firebird's Egg with her body. She dropped down behind Sir Roye de Roye's dead charger, using the high wooden saddle for cover.

Arrows continued to fall, most hitting the ground behind them, with a couple thudding ominously into the horse she was huddled against. So long as she kept her head down, Aria was hard to hit, and her knight's shoulder armor, and his crested houndskull helmet were designed to deflect arrows—but they would not be safe until they reached the iron trees.

Seeming to read her mind, Sir Roye lifted his pointed visor to say, "You must take the Egg into those trees. Where horses cannot follow."

"We can both go," she begged, knowing that was not nearly so practical—but love is never practical. "I swear I will lose them easily."

"No, my love, you must go, and I must stay." Plainly she had the best chance of escape, with her invisibility spell and knowledge of the Iron Wood. And her chances would be even better if he stayed to keep the Tartars at bay.

To emphasize his point, an arrow clanged off his upraised visor, showing it was dangerous to debate. "With the help of God, I can hold them off, while you get away."

She shook her head. "I must get you to the trees." Glancing up, she searched for a gap in the falling arrows, trying to gauge the right moment. He knelt down and pulled her hand to his lips, saying, "My love, you must live."

"We must live," she insisted.

Tears burned her eyes as he kissed her fingers, calling her Aria again. "Aria, sweet Aria, I love you so. I only held back from fear of hurting you—and now I have." He leaned down and kissed her on the lips, pleading with her, "Run my love, please run. Save yourself, for me."

Being French, he did not even mention Markovy's future, or the Firebird's Egg. All he wanted was for his love to be safe, and for that, he would give his life.

Unable to speak, Aria kissed him as hard as she could, more fervently than the Baron Roye de Roye had ever been kissed before. Then she turned and ran, holding tight to the Firebird's Egg, dodging through the falling arrows without looking back, not wanting to watch her love die.

5

the bishop and the witch-girl

Squirming between metal trunks, Aria heard arrows rattle the iron branches, but none found their way down to her. Safe for the moment, she hung her head and cried, holding the Egg tight to her heaving chest as she crawled on knees and elbows among the cold, unfeeling trees. She had lost her first and only love, her sweet, handsome, caring knight, Baron Sir Roye de Roye. Aria remembered Blue-Eyes' tale of the massacred wedding party, and how the Tartars casually crushed those people's lives, just for some useful captives and trivial informa- tion. Now these horse nomads had destroyed her life as well, treating everyone like boyars treated serfs, as dumb instruments to be used and discarded. That Tartars could only occasionally understand the pleas of their victims must have made the killing easier.

Hurt welled up inside her, as she kept thinking of all that her knight had done to cheer and sustain her. His jokes, his strange tales of the wide world be- yond the trees, his gentle touch, and passionate kisses that promised more. Now there was no more. No knight, no love, nothing. Life had become an empty husk of pain and loss.

And she could not even just lie down to die. If she did, the Tartars and their wolves would find her, and seize the Firebird's Egg—then things would get even worse. Her doomed idiotic quest kept her crawling ahead, though Aria ached for her simple life in the woods, where the Bone Witch had protected her. But the Bone Witch too was dead.

Hearing water ahead of her, Aria crawled toward it, hoping to hide her trail. Most Markovites had a superstitious fear of the Iron Wood, with its witches, ghouls, and werebeasts, but to Aria it was a second home, far less strange than the settled lands. Usually she much preferred the living wood—with its food, warmth, and hundreds of friendly eyes—though right now the metal wood's cold, bleak lifelessness matched her misery.

She found the stream, a small feeder headed down toward the Rift, and crawled along in it, adding her tears to water that would flow into the Zog. After a couple of hundred paces, the metal wood thinned, and Aria could stagger upright without getting spiked by low branches. Turning her apron into a sling, Aria tied the Firebird's Egg tight to her belly, to free her hands; then she sloshed along, searching for a good place to leave the water. Usually she relied on an overhanging tree, or a grassy bank that would not take prints, but here, the branches were knife blades, and the banks were rock or dirt.

Smelling a troll-bear's lair, she instinctively froze, feeling caught between Tartars trailing her and the troll-bear ahead. Cold water tumbled past Aria's ankles. Why was she even worried? The troll-bear would merely kill and eat her. Tartars would do worse, far worse—they would make evil use out of her, then kill her. Or let her live, seeing all the harm they did with the Firebird's Egg.

Put that way, there was only one choice, and she went straight on past the troll-bear's lair, not flinching at the gnawed ox bones scattered about, or the half-eaten leopard carcass hanging from a spiked branch. No dire wolf with half a brain would come within a whiff of this place.

And no troll-bear came rushing out to devour her. But as the lair's stench faded, so did her sense of purpose. Where to now? She had been running away from the Tartars—not towards anything. Aria no longer had her knight to aid her, or the Bone Witch's hut to go home to, so where was she headed? Downstream, apparently, following her fallen tears.

Iron trees thinned, becoming fewer and shorter. Soon she made out white bluffs between their trunks. Somewhere ahead of her, the stream followed a gully or ravine back down into the Rift. Did she want to go there? She stopped and considered. Was being in the Iron Wood better or worse than the open Rift? Were lycanthropes and wereleopards worse than Tartars and rocs? Tough choice.

"*Arr-ee-haa, arr-ee-haa, arr-ee-haa . . .*" The firebird's warning decided the matter for her; coming from close behind her, it was a sure sign she was being stalked.

Aria headed off at once, splashing downstream and crosswind, leaving the iron trees and making for the bouldered Rift below. Finding a spot to quit the stream, she headed upwind, stepping on rocks to leave as little of a trail as she could. Coming to a tall boulder, Aria went up its backside and lay down on top, looking back along her trail. She froze there, whispering her spell and clutching the Egg.

Minutes passed, and she wondered if the firebird was playing with her, trying to cheer her up by frightening her senseless—just the sort of trick the flame jay would enjoy. But not this time. As she lay still against the boulder, a lycanthrope came loping along, nostrils flaring, sniffing out her trail. She let the wolfman pass, then slid down the front of the rock and backtracked to the stream, putting the lycanthrope upwind of her, with no trail to follow. Eventually the man-beast would realize what happened and double back, but by then, she would be far away.

Finding another good spot to leave the stream, she stripped off her silk shift and sat down naked on a boulder, meticulously drying her feet to leave no wet prints. Then she dressed, reslung the Egg, and set off swiftly over the rocks, heading downwind, giving the lycanthrope no trail to follow. Aria kept looking over her shoulder, but she saw nothing, and that let her breathe easier—

Until she ran right into a loop of rope. Dropping silently over her head and shoulders, the lasso snapped tight around her torso. Horrified, she tried to twist free, but found her arms pinned tight, barely able to keep hold of the Egg.

Atop the nearest boulder stood a grinning Tartar, holding the other end of the taut rope. He had been hiding there, waiting for her, and had either seen her descending the draw, or just guessed that she would use the stream to hide her trail, and then double back into the Rift. Either way, he had her, so she stopped struggling, which was only tightening the lasso.

Leaping happily down off the rock, he coiled the rope to keep it tight, talking softly to her in Tartar, acting like she was a young mare he had lassoed and did not want to spook. Small chance. Aria was far beyond being spooked. Too crushed and heartsick to be frightened, Aria thoroughly hated this Tartar, hardly caring what happened to her so long as she saw him dead. He was a hideous stinking nomad who had come from beyond the Iron Wood to murder, rape, or enslave whoever struck his fancy. It would take more than a few kind words in Tartar to quell her anger—but he did not need to know that, so she shyly returned his smile.

Nor did he act like a murderer, grinning eagerly, plainly happy to have her, and trying to interest her in talk. He inspected the Firebird's Egg, feeling and poking it, joking with her in Tartar, and she nodded and smiled wider, as if she agreed. Blue-Eyes said the Tartars liked women and children, and this one was certainly pleased with the woman-child he had caught.

He led her down the bouldered draw toward the open Rift, heading downwind, while she kept looking back, working the lasso away from her elbows, up toward her shoulders, while keeping a firm grip on the Firebird's Egg. They recrossed the stream she had waded down, and ahead she saw a bend in the trail, where the path dipped down a bit, then turned sharply to circle three big boulders. With the wind at their backs, their scent was going straight toward the rocks, and the Tartar was making unnecessary amounts of noise, breathing heavy, and brushing things with his wide bowlegged gait. Like most born horsemen, he did not walk well. From above, the firebird sounded a warning.

Hanging back as they approached the three rocks, Aria kept the rope taut. When her captor disappeared around the turn ahead, she ran silently toward him, putting sudden slack in the line. Using that slack to loosen the lasso, she slipped swiftly out of the loop. Letting the line drop, she froze against the rocks, hugging the Egg and reciting her spell.

Surprised, the Tartar turned to see what had happened, stepping back into sight and staring straight at her, stupidly holding his limp rope. As he stared suspiciously through her, the lycanthrope leaped on him from behind. Leather armor was no match for the lycanthrope's superhuman strength, and the Tartar never even touched his scimitar. In seconds, the wolfman was feeding happily on the horse nomad—some parts of Markovy were just plain unsafe to invade.

Bloodlust dulled the werebeast's senses, and the wolfman did not look up as Aria quietly slipped away downwind, dodging between boulders to stay out of sight. What now? Her knight was gone, so was the Bone Witch, and she owed her freedom to one of her direst enemies.

Where should she go, besides away from here? Downriver to turn herself in to Baron Boris, and be burned for her troubles? Hardly likely. Home to the woods, where she had lived with the Bone Witch? Perhaps, but there was little left for her there, since Prince Sergey burned the Bone Witch's hut. And how could she ever complete her quest in hiding?

By now, Aria knew she needed people. She did not want to be a hermit in the woods, with only birds and squirrels to talk to, hoarding her precious

Egg—but which people? No one had been half so appealing as her lost knight. Except maybe Blue-Eyes, who had already been snatched up by the Tartars. Senses alert, Aria kept headed downwind, determined to be safe wherever she was going. At least the forest would feed her.

Following the stream until it flowed into the Upper Zog, Aria slipped back the way she had come, skirting the ravine, then waiting until dark to sneak past the booming ironworks, whose forges spewed sparks into the night sky. With civil war erupting, there were limitless orders for pike points and arrowheads, which Diymgorat eagerly strove to fill.

Once past the hideous stinking forges, with their insane pounding and choking smoke, Aria crawled into the brush and slept until morning, curled about the Firebird's Egg. So long as she had the Egg, her life still held some purpose, though she sorely doubted her ability to return the Egg alone.

Next morning she breakfasted on raw fish, fresh berries, and edible fungus, which made her feel somewhat better. Then she headed north, aiming to avoid the Rift, hoping to find a safer route through the Iron Wood to the nest on Burning Mountain. But Aria soon discovered that the settled lands had spread farther than she realized, for she ran smack into a fresh swath of felled timber. Threading through the stumps, she cautiously climbed the high barricade and descended into civilization.

Her first task was to hide the Egg, so she dug a hole beneath the inner edge of the barricade and buried the egg where no one was likely to dig. Then she looked about for the most prosperous farmstead she could find. No sense getting caught up by serf woodcutters, who could only think to turn you over to their betters. Seeing a likely place, Aria went straight to beg at the kitchen gate. Dogs gathered around her, barking in her face, but she stood her ground, determined to be fed.

These were clearly freeholders with dogs and servants, and many acres of cleared fields. Since they had cut down all the trees hereabouts, uprooted the berry bushes, and driven off the game, it was their obligation to feed her. Baking smells came from inside.

Presently a brawny serving woman in brown homespun appeared, a sharp-eyed serf's daughter with a round face and long braids, who called off the dogs, asking, "What do you want?"

"Alms for the Sisters of Suffering," Aria answered proudly, going down on her knees and holding out her hands.

"What suffering sisters?" The serving woman looked about suspiciously. "I do not see anyone but you."

"The most holy Sisters of Perpetual Suffering." By now Aria firmly believed in the sisters' existence, and she could not understand why this ignorant serf had not heard of them. Did the silly woman sleep through church? "I am a novice on my way to the White Sea, collecting money for the sacred sisters as I go. They dearly need salt and silver."

"Well, you will not even get squirrel skins here." The big serf woman laughed at Aria's presumption. "Best you can hope for here is pig slop."

Aria thanked her profusely, following the serf woman into the warm wood and stone kitchen. Pig slop was far better than Aria had expected. Pig slop was the best, mostly table scraps, vegetable cuttings, and cooked oats, covered in skimmed milk. A lot of people wished they could eat like pigs. When she begged as a child, Aria often got only a cuff and a crust of bread, or just a stern lecture. She told the serf woman, "The Sisters of Perpetual Suffering will remember you in their prayers."

Her hostess snorted. "My name is Natallya. See they get it right."

"Not-all-ya." Aria practiced the pronunciation. Prayers for pig slop seemed a fair exchange.

Presently the master of the house appeared, coming to give the serf woman a friendly pinch, and to get a look at the pretty beggar. He was a big red-necked man, with a misshapen face, who wore a long silk shirt without a collar, and he told Aria, "Stay for supper, and we will find you a bed."

Just what Aria feared. Worried that she might have to pay for her pig slop, Aria swore she was a holy novice and dared not delay her pilgrimage. "The Sisters of Perpetual Suffering are expecting me already."

"What sisters? Where?" The freeholder sensed she was making excuses.

"Their convent is far, far to the north, where the summer sun never sets." Aria wove in the Bone Witch's tales. "By the White Sea, near to Fair Isle, where no one ever dies, guarded by Sea Gate, the castle of Death."

"That seems very far and away," the big man declared. "A few nights' rest will never be missed."

"But I have a message," Aria insisted, "one that cannot be delayed."

"What message is that?"

Sadly Aria had to disappoint him. "Alas, it is for the holy sisters alone."

"Tell me," the master warned, "or you will be telling your tale to the boyar."

Knowing she had to say something, Aria decided to gamble on the truth. "Grave danger threatens all of Markovy with vast suffering, and the pious sisters must prepare. Even their distant convent is in deadly peril, and in need of my speedy warning."

"What deadly danger?"

"Tartars," Aria explained, "a terrible warlike people from the lands beyond Black Cathay, where the sun goes at night. They are on the march, driving lesser nomads before them. Already they have reached the edge of Markovy, where they are kidnapping Poles and plotting their next advance."

Her interrogator was unconvinced. "And you have seen these Tartars?"

"I only just escaped from them, though they tracked me with sky-boats and dire wolves."

"Sky-boats?" Markovites moved on foot, or horseback.

"Worse than rocs," Aria assured him. Then she added sadly, "These heathen fiends respect neither gender nor religion, and would have kept me from my holy mission. They might already be threatening the sisters, so I must get there swiftly."

"Not so speedy." He was not going to let her go. "If these Tartars are as terrible as you say, you must tell your story to the boyar."

Served her right for being honest. Betrayed by the truth, Aria fell back on lies, asking in awed tones, "Does my lord really know the boyar?"

"I do indeed." Thrusting out his chest, the freeholder boasted, "Baron Boris of Zazog is my lord, and I hold my land from him, paying my fees in person."

"Baron Boris, himself—how wonderful. Could I see him?" Aria begged. "His Highness could easily pay for my whole pilgrimage, and I would not have to beg. Would you please, please plead for me?"

His mouth broke into a crooked grin. "I will do more than that, pretty pilgrim."

Oh, goody. Smiling with feigned glee, Aria thanked the master, asking, "Let me stay the night, and I will make myself useful in any way that pleases you."

He patted her tangled black hair. "That you can easily do."

Still grinning, Aria dug back into her pig slop, determined to get something out of this visit. When she begged for more, the serf woman looked at her like she was daft, but said nothing, merely going back to baking her bread. Aria waited until the master called the hounds out for a hunt, then asked to use the outhouse. The serf woman went with her, to see she did not bolt now that she was fed.

As soon as she was inside, Aria said her spell and waited. Presently the serf woman pounded on the door, saying, "What is the matter? Did you fall in?"

Aria did not answer, and the serf woman beat harder, finally flinging open the door, and staring in disbelief. "Damn! Where did she go?"

Immediately the woman ran off to get her master, and Aria raced back the way she had come, grabbing a loaf of bread from the kitchen, knowing she did not have long before dogs were set on her. Humans were so much easier to fool.

To maximize human confusion, she carefully retraced her trail, dug up the Egg, filled in the hole, then climbed back atop the barricade, said her spell, and waited. When the dogs arrived, the freeholder was with them, armed with a bow and backed by serfs carrying staves, and a Kazakh to handle the dogs. The pack went straight to the base of the barrier and started furiously redigging her hole.

Men caught up and pulled the pack off, cursing the stupid hounds for looking for her in a hole. Since the hounds would not go left or right, the men were stymied, unable to get the pack over the barricade. The only trail led back to their farmstead, making it seem she had disappeared, when really the dogs had gone right to her.

Finally, they left, and Aria descended the barricade, heading north again, carefully avoiding the farmstead. When she was an urchin begging in the settled lands, no one had much wanted her. Growing up clearly changed that. Now everyone meant to grab her, for their harem, or for their boyar, or for the Tartars, or just for a bit of fun. Her quest was going to be harder than she had ever imagined.

With Byeli Zamak far behind her, she must ford the Dys farther north, near to the headwaters. Which would take days, but keep her out of the way of civilization, mostly. Ahead of her lay wooded hill country full of forest folk, where she could eventually find an upper fork of the Dys and follow it back to the Iron Wood, above the Rift, and away from the Tartars. Facing a long hike through strange country, she pushed on until noon, then stopped to rest by water, feasting on her stolen bread.

As Aria was getting up to go, she heard the dogs again, faint and far off, but unmistakable. Birds around her began giving warning. Hardly believing her ill luck, she stepped at once into the stream, following it down toward the Dys, using running water to hide her trail. They must have casted about and picked up her fresh scent, but so long as she stayed in the stream, they would not know which way she went. Barking faded behind her as the pack lost the scent.

From downstream came the firebird's shrill warning. Aria was alarmed to see stumps sprout up on either bank, as cleared land and a village emerged ahead, with its houses, mill, and onion-domed church. She froze, and behind her the barking began getting louder again. They were sending dogs downstream, looking for signs she had left the water.

Shit. She could neither backtrack nor hide from the dogs, so all she could do was forge ahead, holding tight to the Firebird's Egg.

She splashed on, and the stream became a mill race, shooting toward the mill and pond below. Which meant she must leave the water. At a low spot, she scrambled up the bank and sprinted off down a footpath, which took her straight through someone's barnyard. People yelled for her to stop.

Ignoring their cries, Aria ran faster, dodging between hovels, forced by the millpond to run right down the main street of town. More people appeared as families stuck puzzled heads out of painted doorways, and she heard horses' hooves behind her, beating on the wood plank street. Looking back, she saw riders, wearing Zazog green-and-black. Baron Boris's boys, whooping at the chase. And this time there was no knight to save her. What had she done to deserve this? Not much, beyond stealing a bit of bread.

She could not vanish, not with men and dogs almost on her, and she could not outrun their horses. Seeing the wooden street coming to an end, Aria redoubled her efforts, tucking the Firebird's Egg under her arm and dodging startled serfs. Mailed horsemen, pounding down the planks behind her, sent the crowd fleeing, and Aria saw the way open miraculously.

At the end of the plank road stood the town's ornate wooden church, crowned by its great shining dome covered in layers of gold leaf. Two white-robed priests stood by the church's painted door, looking wide-eyed at the tumult headed toward them, with knights, squires, huntsmen, hounds, and serfs, all chasing a witch-girl carrying a large leathery egg.

Bounding onto holy ground, Aria took the church steps two at a time, throwing herself past the shocked priests and into the polished wooden nave. Aria dropped to her knees and slid the last dozen feet to the altar, much to the horror of the onlooking monks and altar boys. From her knees, she reached out and placed the Egg on the altar, ringed by its towering icons. "Here is the hope of Markovy," she declared, "and I give it to the keeping of holy Mother Church."

She heard a huge commotion behind her as mailed knights tried to shove the priests aside, while monks and acolytes rushed to stop the sacrilege. Shouts and curses mixed with holy oaths, and a lot of pushing and shoving, but the boyar's men did not dare draw their swords. Halfway down the nave, the struggle came to a halt, and an out-of-breath ensign demanded their quarry, while an angry archpriest denied him, ordering the armed men out of his church. Neither had a hope of convincing the other.

Kneeling before the altar, hearing her fate debated in shrill tones, Aria decided this must be a moment to pray. She was hardly a fanatic about prayer. Heaven knows, her short life had seen moments that screamed for divine aid, but the Bone Witch had taught her to rely on her own wits and quickness. And at the worst moments, she was likely to be invisible, concentrating on her spell. But here she was, on her knees, in a church, with naught else to do.

Aria prayed first to Mother Mary, who looked down on her, and to Jesus, whose house this was, and then to the Bone Witch, who had taken her in when no one else would. She did not ask for anything specific. Things had gone way beyond that. Aria just asked for forgiveness, for having failed in her quest. She meant to get the Egg to Burning Mountain, but had brought it to this church instead. Nor was she giving up her quest. She would have gladly went on, but these men were not going to let her.

Trying not to sound like a complainer, she pointed out the basic unfairness of pitting her against all of Markovy, with its thousands of knights, dogs, huntsmen, armed felons, woodcutters, Kazakhs, and serfs. Could Mother Church at least be on her side? Or must she take them all on, and the Tartars too?

Finally she prayed for her knight, who surely deserved better than dying in a futile attempt to keep her free. Despite being a Catholic heretic, he had done her nothing but good, guarding her, comforting her, fondling her breasts, and teaching her how to kiss. She begged the Almighty to overlook his heresy and misguided worship of the wicked pope, and please, please find him a place in Heaven.

Aria whispered amen, and then looked up, finding herself flanked by two slient pillars of white cloth, taller and thicker than she. A voice from within one of the white cloth pillars whispered, "Rise up, daughter, and come with us."

She realized there were women inside the fabric. These were real nuns, wearing white head-to-floor veils. One reached a white-sleeved arm out to her, through a slit in the veil, saying, "Come, we shall see you safe."

That was hard to believe, but no one had a better offer. Aria obeyed, sad to leave her Egg, feeling that she had failed the Bone Witch, and her knight. When the great test came, wits and quickness were not enough. Though she had kicked the task up to Heaven, Aria was not expecting much help from there.

Her first disappointment was discovering that the nun's idea of seeing her "safe" was to lock her in a stone cell with a tiny barred window barely big enough for a sparrow. Food came through a slot in the door, and her chamber pot went out the same way, returning clean and rinsed. They would not let her out, not even for Mass, making her feel as safe as in a troll-bear's lair, waiting to become a late-night snack.

Despite such treatment, she prayed the church would not give her up. Anything was better than being given to the men and dogs who were after her. She knew they would hurt her, humiliate her, and then burn her alive. That was what men did to witches.

And Aria truly wanted to live, even though her knight was dead and she had failed in her quest.

Weeks went by in solitary confinement, which beat being burned, but not by much. When the lock finally turned, she was relieved to see nuns had come for her, wearing their long white trailing veils. Had she heard men coming, Aria would have gone invisible—but she was still willing to give the nuns a chance. After all, she was almost a novice with the Sisters of Suffering. They whispered to her from within the fabric, "Be strong, daughter. Be strong and obey."

That did not sound good. But it was reassuring to walk between cool protective pillars of white cloth that seemed to glide over the polished floors of the great wooden church. When Aria reached the nave, she shrank back between the nuns, wishing she had gone invisible.

Mailed men in green-and-black Zazog livery lined the walls, all of them eyeing her, the only figure not hidden in fabric. Aria kept her eyes downcast, knowing the Zazog retainers were here to see she got a death sentence, fearing the Church might find some absurd reason to spare a defenseless teenager who had harmed no one.

Bishop Cyrus of Zazog himself was here, filling the small forest church with his clerics and retainers. His Holiness was a gaunt, devout man of God, dressed in cloth-of-silver, and standing before the icons and the high altar, while servants held aloft his silver crosier as a sign for silence. Ignoring the armed onlookers, he asked Aria, "Daughter, do you understand the charges against you?"

"Not at all." This was the first she had heard of them.

"You are charged with witchcraft," the kindly old bishop informed her.

"Oh." Aria expected that, but it was always bad to hear.

"And participating in the murder of Prince Sergey," His Holiness added.

She had forgotten about that.

"Along with numerous members of his entourage . . ."

And them too. This was sounding worse than even Aria expected.

". . . as well as lesser counts of heresy, sacrilege, theft, consorting with foreigners, and impersonating a novice."

Hearing it said all together made her realize just what an evil creature she was, how completely damned, and deserving to burn.

"So, my child," asked the kindly bishop again, "do you understand these charges?"

She nodded. "Yes, Father. I do."

"Do you dispute them?"

It seemed small justification that they had hounded and attacked her, burning her home and riddling the Bone Witch with arrows, before she so much as lifted a finger against them. Aria shook her head sadly. "No."

"And do you fully submit to the judgment of Mother Church?" asked old Bishop Cyrus.

She nodded solemnly, vastly preferring Church judgment. Mother Church could not shed blood, though there were ways around the ban, particularly when secular justice would be worse. Fasting to death was a woman's favorite, a serene contemplative end, especially compared with being flogged naked through the streets to die on a breaking wheel. Whatever the Church devised for her was far better than being handed over to Baron Boris.

"Our judgment is that you will don the habit of a novice, and present yourself as the summer offering at Karadyevachka, the Shrine of the Black Maiden in Vyatichi."

Aria had heard all the scary childhood stories of upcountry Old Rite shrines that still performed virgin sacrifices. Dark grim temples to Death, where young girls were done away with in secret. Her serf foster mother had a mania for such tales, swearing they were true, often threatening to sacrifice her. Now Aria would find out for sure.

Nuns whispered, "Be brave. Submit to His Holiness." Not trusting her voice, Aria nodded silently.

Bishop Cyrus softened, saying, "Do you know you will be giving yourself up to Heaven?"

Justice required that she go knowingly to her doom. Nuns nudged her, and Aria answered as loud as she could, "I do."

Baron Zazog himself was there to hear her say it, a crafty-eyed boyar wearing half-armor even in a house of God. Sneaking a glance out the corner of her eye, Aria saw Baron Boris looking vastly irritated at her getting off so easily, sentenced to some vague far-off death in a northern shrine. His family had ruled Zazog longer than anyone could remember, and the baron could barely believe the Church was coddling a witch that he ached to burn with his own hand.

After pronouncing formal sentence, Bishop Cyrus blessed her, saying, "Despite your sins, you are both brave and obedient. May God have mercy on your soul."

Aria did not feel brave at all, being wretchedly frightened, but she gladly accepted the bishop's blessing, sure she would need it.

Nuns stepped up to take her away, surrounding her with quiet swishing fabric. As they led her off, Aria was startled to see the men's bearded faces had changed completely. When she was led in they were smirking, enjoying the sight of a witch-girl brought helpless and barefoot to her doom. Now their scorn and contempt had turned to pity—all they saw was a teenage girl being led away to a dark mysterious end, a death so secret, it could only be imagined.

Somewhat strange, since Aria was delighted with how things had gone, happy to stay in the care of nuns. If she had to be done to death, how much better that it be done at a later date, and in far-off Vyatichi, instead of here and now, at these men's hands. But men feared most what they could not see.

In fact, Aria enjoyed a sudden serenity, knowing her doom was moved to distant Vyatichi. She had lived most of her life a week's walk from this forest church. Now she had the bishop's word that they would kill her when they got her to Vyatichi, and not a moment sooner. For the first time in her life, no man—not even Baron Zazog—could harm her, not without striking a blow against Heaven. Miraculous, indeed. Prayer had paid off handsomely. Clasping her hands, she took a moment to silently thank the Almighty.

tales from far barbary

By Allah, O my father, how long shall this slaughter
of women endure?

—SHAHRAZAD, *THE TALE OF A THOUSAND NIGHTS
AND A NIGHT*

6

monsieur le baron and the tartars

Baron Roye de Roye watched Aria run, his aching heart lifting with every step she took, almighty glad she was getting away, even if it meant never seeing her again. He tried to fix every line of her in his memory, how her bare feet flashed in the sun, and how her strong young body curved beneath her wild black mane of hair.

Hold this notch against the Tartars, and she at least would live. Which was what mattered most. This wonderfully caring witch-girl, who had risked everything for him, and freely given her love, deserved a chance at life. He watched her disappear into the metal wood without ever once looking back.

Lowering the steel snout on his houndskull helm, Sir Roye de Roye turned to face his enemies with a light heart, hefting his Lucerne hammer. So long as his love was safe, what happened to him hardly mattered.

Arrows rained down around him, burying themselves in the dirt and corpses, or glancing off his armor. He could see Tartars crawling forward, covered by the storm of arrows, trying to get as close as they could without getting skewered. Baron de Roye got set to receive them.

This time the Tartars had something besides little sharp scimitars. As they crept closer, one Tartar reached behind his small iron shield and produced a mace with a shining glass head, hurling it at him. His attacker overthrew, and Sir Roye saw the mace sail past. When it hit behind him, the glass shattered, and its liquid contents burst into flames.

Fire maces. Sir Roye had heard of these flaming horrors, but this was the first time he had to duck them. The glass heads were filled with flammable naphtha and an igniter that caught fire when exposed to air.

Three more maces came flying at him from three different angles. He deflected one with his hammer, and the other two burst against the dead horse, splashing flames over the carcass, filling the air with smoke, and the stink of burnt horsemeat.

Baron de Roye stepped swiftly back, guessing what would come next. Arrows ceased falling, and Tartars scrambled forward, using the smoke and flames as cover, hoping to take him by surprise.

Only to run right into his bright, sharp Lucerne hammer. One tried to hit him with a fire mace, but his hammer sent the mace flying sideways, to burst against another attacker, setting him alight. Frustrated Tartars retreated back down the draw, dragging away their dead and wounded with braided lassos. So long as he could swing that horrid saw-toothed pole arm, they had no hope of getting past him, since they were merely obeying orders, while he was fighting for the life of his love.

Failure with the fire maces was followed by more arrows, falling at random, in hope of hitting a chink in his armor. Finally the arrows too stopped. And for a long while, Sir Roye stood and waited, wondering what the Tartars would try next.

What came next was a single rider wearing mirror-bright scale armor that flashed in the sun, trimmed with red fox fur. His horse was armored too, but the Tartar had no weapons, no sword, no lance, not even a quiver or bow case. Picking his way daintily through the corpses and dead horses, the armored horseman reined in before Sir Roye, smiling wide. His sharp, foxy beardless face, and steely eyes belied his jovial manner, and he stank of horse piss and sour yogurt.

Raising his empty right hand, the Tartar smiled wider, saying, *"Pax."*

"Pax?" Sir Roye thought he must have misheard the fellow. Heaven knew what that meant in Tartar.

Nodding eagerly, the shining horseman repeated himself: *"Pax!"*

For some unfathomable reason, this shiny nomad wanted peace. Or this could be some crude ruse, to get him to drop his guard, or lift his visor and get hit with an arrow. He raised the steel snout on his houndskull visor, just enough to say in Latin, "Yes, peace. Just so you do not come too close."

"Pax," agreed the Tartar, who apparently knew only one word of Latin.

Peace, indeed, we could all use a piece of that. Lowering his visor, Sir Roye waited to see what this peaceable Tartar would do. Every minute that this charade took gave Aria that much longer to get away.

Having exhausted his Latin vocabulary, the horseman did nothing, merely waved to his fellows below. Sir Roye looked to see if any were coming up. Peace was all well and good, but Tartar bows could puncture plate armor at point-blank range. However the Tartars stayed put, and instead a woman emerged from among the men below, a young blond woman wearing a peasant dress and a blue embroidered jacket, who walked slowly up the draw, lifting her dress to step over rocks and bodies.

Not at all what Sir Roye expected. As she got closer, he saw that the woman was once very pretty, but now seemed thin and worn. When she got near enough to speak, the blonde stopped, not wanting to come between the armored men, saying to Sir Roye in Latin, "They call me Borte. Who are you?"

He would not open his visor for the Tartars, but he would for her, raising it all the way to say, "Sir Roye de Roye, Chevalier de l'Étoile, et le Baron de Roye. At your service."

Blue-Eyes stared at him curiously, surprised to find a French baron so far from home, and so courteously disposed toward her. "I am a slave. No one serves me."

"I am sorry to hear of your condition." Sir Roye made a stiff armored bow, sincerely hurt by what the poor woman must have gone through. "My sword is at your service. If you wish, I will gladly kill this smelly fellow, and any other Tartar who has mistreated you, or holds you against your will."

Blue-Eyes smiled grimly, shaking her head. "That is not necessary."

Seeing he was being talked about, the Tartar spoke sharply to Blue-Eyes, who answered evenly. On hearing her reply, the horseman convulsed in laughter. Sir Roye asked Blue-Eyes, "What did he say?"

"He asked what you said, and I told him you offered to set me free with your sword." Blue-Eyes sounded somewhat put out, having to answer to two touchy warriors at once. "I added that I refused, since he has treated me honorably."

"Has he treated you honorably?" From what he had seen of the Tartars, Sir Roye could hardly believe that.

Blue-Eyes sighed, knowing the knight was trying to be helpful. Nobles never pretended to be practical. "Tartars have beaten me, and raped me, and slit the throats of my friends and kin before my own eyes—but none of that was done by him."

Sir Roye smiled up at the Tartar, saying, "A sterling recommendation."

Taking that as a good sign, the shining horseman dismounted, and Sir Roye de Roye did another awkward armored bow. "Any gentleman able to forgo assaulting helpless females has my utmost admiration."

Blue-Eyes translated, and the horse barbarian laughed even louder, then shot off a long string of Tartar. Waiting until he finished, Blue-Eyes turned to Sir Roye, saying, "This is Mangku, the van mingghan commander of the Forest Toman. He says that any warrior able to assault his helpless men so easily has his utmost admiration. Noyan Mangku would rather have you fighting for him than against him."

Until the last couple of days, Sir Roye had hardly known the Tartars existed, and he certainly had no desire to fight them—but he would not desert Aria, even if it meant his life. "Tell Noyan Mangku I would rather die than turn against the lady I serve."

Blue-Eyes exchanged some words with Mangku in Tartar, then asked Sir Roye, "Who is that lady?"

Sir Roye was not about to give them Aria's name, or any information that would help them hunt her down. "The girl he was chasing."

Hearing the translation amused Mangku immensely, and he made another long reply. Blue-Eyes told Sir Roye, "Noyan Mangku thinks that the vanishing witch-girl is far and away from here by now, and he hardly needs your help looking for her. Tartars are legendary hunters. He wants to know if you will accept life, to serve him in other ways."

If it did not aid Aria, it seemed silly to throw his life away. Aria would readily agree. "So long as I do not betray her."

"That is his offer," the Pole replied solemnly.

"What do you think I should do?" asked Sir Roye, figuring she knew the Tartars better than he.

Blue-Eyes smiled indulgently, as if wondering why he was suddenly asking her advice. "Have you ever met Tartars before?"

"Not until today." And this morning's introduction had been none too pleasant.

"You have done amazingly well so far." Blue-Eyes congratulated his amateur attempt at dealing with Tartars. "Had you given any other answer, Noyan Mangku would have had you killed. If you defied him, he would have his men kill you—but if you agreed to betray your lady, he would have poisoned you later. Tartars never trust a traitor, believing if you would betray your lady, you would certainly betray them."

How true. Sir Roye asked, "So what should I do?"

Blue-Eyes sighed again, hating to go over old ground. "I too stood where you stand. I could either die or serve the Tartars. I chose to serve, and I was raped, beaten, and forced to witness unspeakable cruelty. Other than that, I am alive, and tolerably healthy."

Sir Roye de Roye shook his armored head. "You hardly make slavery sound attractive."

"Meals are not much," Blue-Eyes confessed. "Otherwise, they will mistreat you only if they mean to kill you."

Dismal as that sounded, it was no worse than dying here and now. Grounding his pole arm, he lifted off his hot metal helmet, taking a deep breath of fresh air, knowing he might easily die in the next few minutes. There was also a chance he would live, and if he did, he might be able to find Aria again. With luck. "Tell Noyan Mangku I accept."

Blue-Eyes did not have to translate, since Noyan Mangku read the agreement on their faces. The van minghan commander singled to his men, who came briskly up the draw, leading numerous remounts and riderless chargers. Then Mangku turned back to Sir Roye, proudly repeating himself, "Pax!"

So peace it would be, for as long as this armed truce lasted. Sir Roye was given a big Persian charger to ride, most likely taken from the Turks. Tartars themselves preferred tough little mares that could carry a lightly armed man a long way. Only officers and heavy cavalry had big armored mounts. Blue-Eyes too had a mare to ride, tethered to the Sir Roye's saddle, so she would be there to translate. If any Tartars took it amiss that he killed their comrades, they were careful not to show it in front of the noyan. They all set out together, headed back up the Rift, trailed by the dire wolves.

Being the van mingghan commander, Mangku was eager to know all about his neighbors to the west, asking through Blue-Eyes about Sir Roye's service in Markovy. Having no reason to deceive, Baron de Roye told the noyan what everyone knew, that Markovy was in near anarchy, torn apart by the feuding great families. "I served King Demitri, and then his son Ivan, until I was betrayed by the late Prince Sergey."

On hearing the translation, Mangku merely said, "I spoke with Prince Sergey."

Sir Roye was surprised to hear the two had met. "I hope you found him as offensive as I did."

"Very offensive," Mangku agreed, "but delightfully honest."

"Honest? Truly?" Sir Roye wondered if something was lost in translation. "Not so I had noticed."

"I too was there," Blue-Eyes told him. "Prince Sergey spoke only the truth, and to a Tartar, honesty makes up for any amount of disrespect."

Sir Roye promised to remember that, grateful to have a friendly translator, who would keep him from tripping on his words. He wished he could do more for her.

Mangku barely believed such a mismanaged country as Markovy could survive, and he had Blue-Eyes ask, "What keeps the Cumans and Kipchaks from just carving it up?"

"Not to mention the Swedes and Germans. Markovy does not lack for enemies," Sir Roye admitted. "But the place has its strengths as well, with a national church, and a national identity. Much as they fight each other, they hate foreigners even more—believe me. Though the serfs are unarmed, and the nobility largely worthless, the northern cities have sturdy militias, and elect their own princes. When properly armed, they are stubborn fighters, afraid to surrender, and too unimaginative to retreat."

Mankgu was not impressed by civic militia. What use was an army that sat waiting in place? Blue-Eyes asked for him, "What horsemen do the Markovites have?"

"Kazakhs mostly, but they are as good as a Cuman or a Kipchak. And many of the boyars have Western armor and weapons." How they used them was another matter. In jousts, he had made good money off the Markovites, who held a lance like it was a bunch of lilies.

Mangku had just seen western armor and weapons turn back two arbans of light cavalry—while afoot. He wanted to know if more horsemen might come out of the west. Did Markovy have powerful allies that might come to its aid? Blue-Eyes smirked as she asked, knowing well what the answer would be.

"Allies? Markovy?" Sir Roye laughed. "Pope Pius thinks them hopeless heretics. Swedes and Germans would merely join in the plunder. No one from the west has the least reason to rush to their aid—just look how the Markovites treated me."

Mangku was pleased to hear the Markovites had no friends in the west. He asked through Blue-Eyes, "Is it true the king is an infant?"

"Ivan is merely Crown Prince, but he will soon be king." Markovy must rally around something, even if it was a crowned child.

Mangku looked disgusted, and Blue-Eyes explained, "Tartars adore children, even other people's. They think having children and making children are the most enjoyable things on earth. But they do not give children positions of command, thinking that adults do much better."

Most of the time. France had seen her share of insane kings and crowned infants, but Baron de Roye realized the Tartars had a totally new notion of government, where people won power by proven ability, and lost it by bungling their jobs. That was why these nomads were so scarily efficient. Making this a spectacularly bad moment for Markovy to be crowning a toddler. Yet no one wanted Baron de Roye's opinion, aside from Noyan Mangku, who was eager to know all about Europe. Blue-Eyes asked for him, "What is the most powerful nation in the West?"

"We are," Sir Roye replied proudly, happy to boast to a sympathetic blonde. Blue-Eyes was the only person in Mangku's entourage that Sir Roye cared for, or hoped to impress. He wanted her to know that he would defend her if he could. "France is the richest and greatest nation in Europe, though we are continually pushed about by smaller peoples, like the Swiss and the English."

Blue-Eyes offered Mangku's condolences, then asked, how many horsemen might the King of France muster?

"On a good day? That is hard to say." Arithmetic never much fascinated Baron de Roye, and it had not occurred to him to count the number of chevaliers in France. If Mangku wanted to know something useful, like the percentage of pretty women in Paris on a Sunday afternoon, the Frenchman might have made a more educated guess. "Chronicles claim we had twenty thousand knights at Crécy, for all the good that did us. A few thousand British bowmen turned the battle into a massacre."

"Were they horse archers?" Blue-Eyes explained that these were the only troops that much worried Mangku.

"No, they were afoot," Sir Roye admitted, "even their knights and lords."

"Two tomans of heavy cavalry routed by a few mingghans of footmen?" Noyan Mangku treated the greatest battle of the Hundred Years' War as though it were a stupidly arranged skirmish. He had Blue-Eyes ask, "Were you drunk?"

"I was not there," Sir Roye explained, "but the story is we blundered into an ambush at dusk. Since it was so late in the day, strong wine was certainly involved. King Philip did not want to fight, but he lost control of his knights, who kept pressing forward to be first on the field. Sometimes you can have too many horsemen."

"Very true." Mangku himself had just thrown two arbans of light cavalry at a single man, and they had merely gotten in each other's way, blocking the bowmen behind them, even setting themselves on fire. Then one woman easily took the pass.

Sir Roye sighed. "Crécy can hardly be blamed on the English, for they were badly outnumbered. And running away from us." Sir Roye knew his description of French chivalry charging blindly into a disastrous cross fire would not impress Mangku. Even Blue-Eyes' polite translation could not hide the nomad's bland contempt for aristocratic amateurs.

And the Tartar had every right to be overconfident. Not that the diligent brute was the least bit complacent—the smelly noyan took war seriously, even if his enemies did not. When it came to van commanders, there was a world of difference between keen, inquisitive Noyan Mangku, and the man leading King Philip's advance at Crécy, King John the Blind of Bohemia—who had to be led into battle on a leash. Put a blind man in the van, and you can count on being surprised. Back home in France, high birth and service to the crown meant far more than vision, foresight, or ability to avoid an ambush. It seemed like the Tartars had an unfair advantage, since they cared only about winning.

That night, Sir Roye de Roye, Chevalier de l'Étoile, *et le* Baron de Roye lay in the back of a stinking yurt, curled under furs crawling with lice. Heaven knew, Paris was pretty much a pigsty, but at least they had the decency to conceal it with fine wine and cheap perfume. Several snoring Tartars lay between him and the door, passed out on a few mugs of sour mare's milk. But it took far more than that for a Frenchman to forget his troubles.

He worried about Aria, and what the Tartars might do to him, and to his world. Europe had absolutely no idea what it was facing. The only good thing about the whole sorry business was that Markovy stood between civilization and the Tartar menace. Good for civilization anyway, bad news for Markovy.

Baron de Roye managed a fitful sleep, only to be awakened by a warm nude form sliding in next to him—the last thing he had expected from the enemy, though the body beside him did not feel or smell like a Tartar.

Sir Roye started to complain, but a slim hand covered his mouth, stopping his protest. Someone whispered softly to him in Latin, "Be still. I vow I will not hurt you."

He recognized his blond translator. "My lady, what are you doing here?"

"What do you think?" Blue-Eyes whispered back. Beneath the furs she was naked, and considerably cleaner than her owners.

"That this is an unexpected pleasure." Lest she take that the wrong way, Sir Roye added, "And an incredible compliment, considering our brief acquaintance—"

"Do not flatter youself." Blue-Eyes laughed lightly, not sounding in the least like a woman in love. "Noyan Mangku sent me."

So much for romance. Sir Roye slipped his arm around the woman's smooth bare shoulder, saying, "Remind me to thank the noyan."

"Naturally," Blue-Eyes replied. "I am under strict orders, and anything that passes between us must be reported to Noyan Mangku."

"Must it?" Baron de Roye did not try to hide his disappointment. Why did women feel they had to tell everything that went on when the lights went out? Demanding rings and giving tokens, so folks would know from a distance who belonged to whom. Just once he wished a woman would pass a pleasant night with him without needing to inform the whole world afterward.

"Sorry." Blue-Eyes apologized for her femininity. "Mangku's orders are clear. I must make love to you, teach you Tartar, and report everything you say. I am an indifferent liar, and I cannot abide torture, so please take care with what you say or do. Tartars will likely hear of it."

He found her fingers in the dark, and kissed them, saying softly, "Fear not, gentle lady. I will not burden you with anything you could not easily pass on to your noyan. Unless my lady wills it."

Giving a low sigh of relief, Blue-Eyes whispered, "You are a very strange man."

"Not really," Sir Roye objected, "just French."

"I myself am a Pole," Blue-Eyes informed him.

"United by Mother Church," Sir Roye declared, striving to find something in common with his naked bedmate.

"Actually, I am unmarried," Blue-Eyes replied primly, lest he get the wrong impression.

"I was married to a lady in France," Baron de Roye confessed, "but I meant united in a spiritual sense."

"So do I." She relaxed into his grip. "This is the first time I have so much as talked to another Catholic since coming to Markovy."

"Ave Maria," Sir Roye whispered, trying not to disturb any snoring Tartars, since the last thing he wanted at the moment was nomad accompaniment. He understood the Pole perfectly. Since Blue-Eyes had been ordered to sleep with him, chivalry commanded that he comply, courteously. Body and soul were one, and the object of bedding a woman was not to break her spirit, but to unite with her—even if in sin.

Blue-Eyes sighed, "I have been so horribly alone. Tartars can be incredibly kind and rational, tolerating every religion, giving scrupulous justice, and eliminating crime, unless they commit it. They do not care who you pray to, or what titles you have—all they care about is how useful you are to them. Please them, and they reward you; displease them, and you die."

Sir Roye swore solemnly, "May the Lord above be my witness, I would see you safely home if I could."

"I believe you would." Blue-Eyes knew he was not saying it just to have her, for her noyan had already given her to him. While translating Sir Roye's words into Tartar, Blue-Eyes had to think carefully about what the Frenchman said, and meant, listening to his words and his heart. "I wish you could free me. Otherwise, my only hope of seeing home is the off chance that the Tartars will invade Poland, dismal as that sounds."

"Only Markovy stands in their way." Sir Roye could not say if that was good or ill. He hoped the Markovites could keep out the Tartars, though it hardly looked likely from where he lay. "And they do not even know the Tartars are coming."

"What about the girl?" Blue-Eyes whispered.

"What girl?" Sir Roye felt a sudden stab of guilt, lying alongside a nude Pole when Aria was alone and on the run, hunted by the same Tartars who were wooing him with wine and naked women.

"You know what girl," Blue-Eyes replied tartly, unwilling to let him off so easily. "Do not dare deny her—the one who vanishes. She claimed she was sent by Prince Ivan to keep watch on the Tartars."

Sir Roye was trapped by that female mania to "know" everything, which would now force him to discuss the girl he loved with the woman in his bed. "I thought we were not going to talk about things Mangku might want to know?"

Blue-Eyes snorted contemptuously. "Mangku knows you were with her, since you were seen together. Mangku does not know that I know her—that is my secret. But you cannot betray me, because you do not speak Tartar."

Being French, Sir Roye had learned from an early age that women were decidedly different, and it did no good to argue with them. They were prone to worrying about what other women were getting, provoking weird fancies that got in the way of things. Absurd imaginings, which would not stop a man for a moment, put women totally out of the mood. Knowing he must flatter these fancies, he whispered, "She told me about you."

It was Blue-Eyes' turn to be surprised. "She did?"

"She said you were very blunt," Sir Roye recalled, "which is most surely true."

"Tartars drive all the subtlety out of you," Blue-Eyes warned. "To them, truth is absolute, making the most trivial concerns matters of life or death."

"And she said I would like you," Sir Roye added.

"Why so?" Blue-Eyes did not seem to believe him.

"Because you are so caring," he explained. "You left food for us—fish, millet, and some remarkable milky wine."

"Koumiss." Blue-Eyes sounded touched by how much he relished her gift. "It is made from mare's milk."

"Really?" Sir Roye was surprised, but not disgusted. "It was wonderful, even the millet. And our last meal together."

Even dried fish and cold millet could be a memorable meal, with the right company. Blue-Eyes asked, "Do you love her?"

Easy question. "She is sweet, and pure, and she saved my life. How could I not love her?"

"How, indeed?" Blue-Eyes sounded skeptical. "Yet you would make love to me?"

"Your noyan commands we do," he reminded her. They were prisoners, after all, captives of merciless nomads who insisted that they make love.

"My noyan knows only what I tell him," Blue-Eyes retorted proudly. "Mangku must take my word about your abilities in bed."

Sir Roye saw that his performance would be pure fiction. "Make me sound good."

"That would not be hard." Blue-Eyes smiled in the dark. "Though they are thoroughly adept at rape, Tartars can be incredibly unromantic. A dagger to the throat is their favorite form of foreplay."

"Believe me, Frenchmen are more refined." Most days, anyway.

"I will take your word for that," Blue-Eyes said. "And I will tell my noyan you are too in love with the witch-girl to sleep with another woman. Mangku will be touched by your loyalty."

"As Madame pleases." Sir Roye expressed polite disappointment, lest Blue-Eyes feel slighted. Women like to be wanted, even when they do not want you.

"Hannah." She kissed Baron de Roye lightly on the shoulder, happy to have found a man who would not just force himself on her, even when her lord commanded it. "My real name is Hannah."

"Also," Hannah added, "if we do not make love, Mangku cannot use me against you."

"Against me? How?"

"When a man resists the Tartars, they rape and torture his women in front of him," Hannah explained. "It makes the strongest man more amenable."

"Delightful." Noyan Mankgu already knew he had a weakness for women.

"I warned you that serving the Tartars was better than death—but not by much."

"You were more than honest," Sir Roye admitted.

Next morning, Blue-Eyes reported to the noyan and returned with water and rice, which she cooked, saying, "You may have some, but only if you name it."

"That is easy. Rice."

"In Tartar," Hannah added.

That was harder. "Then you must teach me Tartar."

"That is our noyan's plan. I am also not allowed to do anything that you cannot ask for in Tartar."

"Our noyan is not very subtle," Sir Roye observed.

"Tartars think subtlety a waste of time," she warned. "Any undue flattery means they probably plan to kill you."

"I swear to be worthy of any praise that comes my way," Sir Roye vowed.

"That is their intent." Hannah refused to so much as make tea for him unless he could ask for it in Tartar. Meaning he had to do his own fetching and carrying around the yurt, much to the amusement of the Tartars, who made a game out of his language lessons. They also laughed at him for helping Hannah cook the meals and water the horses. He in turn was glad to see they had given up searching for Aria.

Blue-Eyes was happy too. "At least one of us has gotten away."

Then the wind shifted around to the northwest, and the Tartars readied the sky-boat for flight, topping off the parasail with compressed gas from brass canisters. Hannah told him what was happening. "We are headed for Far Barbary."

"We are? How many?" Sir Roye guessed the sky-boat could hold four comfortably—any more would be a crowd.

Hannah put the morning rice water on the fire. "Just you and me, and a couple of Tartars to fly the sky-boat."

"Where are we going?" He watched the Tartars using kites to test the wind.

"Downwind." Sky-boats had limited ability to maneuver, and then only during ascent and descent—otherwise they flew at the will of the winds summoned up by Tartar shamans. She nodded toward the south and east, saying, "South of us is the Great Sea of Grass, then Kipchak country and the Inland Sea."

Far, far and away, that was for sure. So much for ever seeing Aria again. Noyan Mangku did not stop by to say good-bye, leaving his instructions with Hannah, who told Sir Roye, "You are to go to Balasaghun in Black Cathay, to serve the noyan of the Van Tuman—who is the eyes and ears of the Great Khan."

"And you?" Sir Roye did not want to be separated from the one person he could talk to.

Hannah smiled at his concern. "I must see you get there."

Liftoff was so smooth, the ground seemed to fall away. Standing at the port rail, Sir Roye saw the Tartar camp dwindle beneath him, and the bouldered Rift shrink into a rocky draw bordered by the Iron Wood. Then the metal treetops swallowed it up, and all Sir Roye could see was the black mass of the Iron Wood, merging with the surrounding boreal forest, a black-and-green treescape resembling the Zazog banner.

Since the Tartar crewmen preferred to sleep under the stars, their passengers had free use of the small cabin. Hannah brewed tea and fixed food, doing her sewing on the low bed that had previously held Prince Sergey. Aria had told Sir Roye about seeing the talkative corpse aboard the sky-boat, and he asked, "What became of Prince Sergey?"

"They buried him deep in the Rift, with his eyes, ears, mouth, and anus sewn shut, to keep his spirit from walking."

Baron de Roye grimaced. "Sounds ghastly."

"Hideous. I had to do the sewing." Blue-Eyes wiped off her needle and put it away, then added his mended shirt to the neatly folded clothes.

In the back of cabin was a little pigeon coop, but instead of birds, the pigeonholes held thin rice paper sheets covered with strange black characters. Sir Roye studied the sheets, unable to make any sense of them. "Did you not say the Tartars were illiterate?"

"They have no written language," Hannah told him, "so they use other people's. Those characters are Cathayan."

Sir Roye wondered what message they were carrying to Tartary. "Do you read Cathayan?"

"Only a few characters." Hannah studied the sheets, saying, "This is strange."

"Very strange," Sir Roye agreed. "Makes English look legible."

Hannah shook her head. "This is not normal. These are just lists of a few characters, repeating over and over."

"How can you tell?"

She showed him. "Here, see how these same characters keep reappearing."

They were indeed the same. "How do they get them to look so exactly alike?"

"It is called printing. They use carved blocks dipped in ink to make the characters."

One more Tartar wonder. Sir Roye asked, "Can you read any of it?"

"Oh, yes, though it does not do much good. That means 'horse' and those are 'pig,' 'snake,' 'ox'—"

"Lists of farm animals?" Sir Roye suggested.

"No, those are years in the Calendar of the Twelve Beasts. Tartars use them in casting horoscopes, and on astrology plaques I used to play with."

"So these are years?"

"No, just the characters, all out of order and mixed together." She pointed to the top of a sheet, saying, "Horse, ox, horse, pig, snake, ox, cock, pig . . ."

"And so on for pages and pages." Sir Roye flipped through the sheets. "It does not make sense."

Hannah agreed. "Not even for Tartars."

Sir Roye carefully replaced the sheets, in the exact order that he'd found them. "But whatever is being sent back aboard this boat is here for some reason."

"Including us." Hannah handed him his tea.

Exactly. They were useful property, and he had never seen the Tartars do anything without a reason. "What year is this?"

She told him in Latin and Tartar. "Capricorn, the goat." "Figures." Convinced the papers must mean something, he sipped his tea and had Hannah teach him the characters, and the Tartar names for them—imitating Mangku by studying his enemy.

For days they rode the prevailing westerlies south and east, passing over the Mother River, which made a huge turn in Bulgar country, to head for the Inland Sea. Below them, boreal forest gave way to rolling woodlands, broken by patches of steppe, reminding Hannah of Poland. Then came the Great Sea of Grass that ran from Hungary to the cold deserts of High Asia. On the far side of Kipchak country, hot winds off the Kyzil Kum, the Red Sands Desert, blew them north and east across the the Sarysu, a weird straggling river that arose in one bit of dry barrens and ended in another.

Beyond this lost river, the Tartar crew brought them down on the Hungersteppe, where they were greeted by riders for the local Turkish emir, Arslan the "Lion," who claimed to be both a Christian and friendly to the Tartars. Everybody in the Seven Rivers Country, from the lowest herdboy to Emir Arslan of the Qarlug Turks, plainly aimed to be on the Tartars' good side.

Deflating the parasail, the Turks found oxen to pull the sky-boat, and they wheeled south across the Hungersteppe, until they came on a great encampment, so many tents that Sir Roye thought it was a Tartar army—but it turned out to be a trade embassy to the Khwarezm Turks, headed for Bukhara by way of Otar on the Syr Darya. At the encampment, they were feasted by Arslan the Lion himself, a bald, brainy Turk, big and powerfully built, with cunning eyes and a ready smile, who enjoyed sparring in Tartar with Hannah while Sir Roye took in the opulent silk tent floored with Persian rugs and lit by gold lamps.

With them at the feast were the Tartars' ambassadors to the Khwarezm, pious merchants, Hammal of Maragha, Omar-Khoja of Otar, and Fakhr ed-Din of Bukhara, who abstained from wine and said their prayers, having five hundred fully laden camels to worry about, loaded with trade goods and presents for Shah Aladdin of Khwarezm, gold ingots, raw jade, ivory, silver, silks, sable, and white camel's wool. Sir Roye marveled at how the Tartars made use of anyone's talents, from sober Muslims to titled killers from France. Tartar bowmen even elected their own officers, showing the complete confidence they had in their leaders.

Emir Arslan himself escorted them south to Balasaghun, the capital of Black Cathay, giving Sir Roye de Roye a chance to practice his Tartar with a fellow Christian. Not a Catholic, of course—that would be too much to expect, this being the Hunger Steppe. But Emir Arslan had that supreme Christian forgiveness, letting him work cheerfully with Muslim merchants and godless nomads.

Sir Roye entertained the emir aboard the sky-boat as they rolled over short grass steppe. Since taking off from the Rift, Sir Roye de Roye had traveled more than a thousand miles, at least twice the length of France, in less than a week, first by air, then by land—without ever leaving his bedroom. Arslan noted that, "Before the Tartars, Black Cathay had a Christian Gur-Khan, and it was a disaster to the faith."

"How so?" Sir Roye had never known there were Christian nations in Far Barbary.

"Gur-Khan Gutchluk claimed to be a Christian, but he seized his throne by force, murdering the Christian emir of Almalyk. Worse yet, he oppressed the Muslims, crucifying the imam of Khotan, which made us roundly hated." Though not as popular as Islam, Christianity was seen as a peaceable people's religion, since local warlords were mostly Muslim or pagan. One Christian Gur-Khan had ruined the faith's reputation, undoing Christ's work—until the Tartars set things right.

"Was his name really Gut-chuck?" Sir Roye still had to rely on Hannah's translation.

"Gutchluk, with an *l.*" She corrected his vulgar pronunciation. "He was a Naiman, from far east of here."

"What happened to him?" Sir Roye asked, guessing it would be nothing good.

"When he murdered the emir of Almalyk, Gutchluk angered the Tartars." From the way Arslan said it, that was plainly fatal. "No one would stand by Gutchluk, since he had disgraced the Christians and angered the Muslims and Buddhists. Tartars hunted him with wolves, horsemen, and sky-boats, and though Gutchluk tried to escape over the Roof of the World, they caught him in a high valley, at the foot of a giant glacier, and brought his head back to Balasaghun."

South of the Hunger Steppe, they came on the wall that hemmed in Black Cathay, cutting across the steppe, a smaller version of the Great Wall, which separated Far Cathay from High Asia. Rising up out of clay pan and scrub brush, the forty-foot-tall stone barrier extending for as far as Sir Roye could see. Arslan said it went "All the way from Lake Balkhash in the east, to the river Chu in the west, where a connecting wall runs from the Chu to the Talas, then along the Talas to the base of the Tien Shan, the Far Mountains." Riding around was not a real option.

Beyond the wall, Sir Roye entered an oasis of peace and plenty sitting atop the Silk Road—fertile grasslands, shady woods, grain fields, and well-watered orchards where unbelievers and infidels lived side by side in peace. Here mullahs, lamas, and priests were all free to preach, and smiling kids came out to gawk at the nomad emir, offering up melons to quench the traveler's thirst, never fearing that the terrible Christian Turk would do them any harm.

Tartars called Balasaghun *Go-baligh*, which meant "Pretty City," and the place lived up to its name, standing foursquare within its walls, with gates opening to the north, south, east, and west. Wide boulevards shaded by elm trees and fronted with tall mosques and shining pagodas led straight to the center of town. Compared to Balasaghun, Markov was a squalid little settlement, while Paris and London were overgrown slums. Seeing no sign of a siege or sack, Sir Roye asked Arslan, "How did the Tartars take the city, with the walls so strong, and the place so well supplied?"

Arslan laughed, saying, "Walls will not stop the Tartars. Chepe the Arrow took Balasaghun by air. Sky-boats landed troops inside the walls, who surprised a gatehouse, letting the Tartars into the city. My own men made up the van mingghan," Arslan added modestly, "and were first through the newly seized gate. Chepe had leaflets scattered over the city from war kites, printed in Cathayan and warning that resistance would bring on a massacre. Right behind the leaflets came gliders dropped from balloons, which landed on the broad east–west boulevards."

"Gliders?" Another word Sir Roye had never heard.

"Winged craft made from wood, silk, and paper, able to carry an infantry arban," Arslan explained. "Cathayans designed them, and they are borne aloft by hot-air balloons, then released to land downwind."

"Sounds dangerous." Sir Roye preferred to fight from the saddle, or better yet from behind a stout parapet.

Arslan shrugged. "If you want a safe life, become a priest. Tartars will see no one molests you."

Noyan Chepe now sat in the Gur-Khan's palace, and he too wanted to know all about the west, its methods of fighting, and the numbers of its horsemen. Sir Roye was not much worried about betraying France, for if the Tartars got that far, Christendom was surely doomed, no matter what Baron de Roye had to say. Besides, they would have to go through the Germans first, which would be no end of trouble, even for the Tartars. "France," he warned, "is no easy place to invade. The English have been trying for a hundred years, with small sign of success."

Chepe the Arrow said France sounded too hilly and crowded for Tartars, "though I would like to visit Europe someday."

Hopefully Europe would take warning. His noyan rewarded Sir Roye with a silver plaque to be worn around the neck, showing he was the khan's man, entitled to regular rations and a free remount when riding for the khan. He was also given a pavilion with a rose arbor and peacocks, where Hannah could continue his Tartar lessons.

Arslan congratulated him: "Not bad, for a fellow who started out facing light cavalry alone, and afoot. Tartars can be outstandingly generous to the survivors. All Chepe the Arrow wanted from Black Cathay was a thousand white-nosed horses to give to his khan. Balasaghun still cannot believe its good fortune."

Hannah had seen the hard side of the Tartars, saying, "Balasaghun got off well because it gave in. Spread your legs and smile, and maybe they will spare you."

There was no arguing with that anger, and within the week, Hannah's words came back to Sir Roye. Shocking news came—the trade embassy to Khwarezm had been massacred; those pious merchants from Otar and Bukhara who had fed Sir Roye sweet lamb and green tea were all dead. "Was it bandits?" he asked. "Or Kipchaks?"

"Worse yet." Hannah shook her head. "It was Inalchiq Khan, Shah Aladdin's governor of Otar."

"Why in God's name?" This was an incredibly vicious slap at the Tartars.

"I can think of five hundred reasons." Hannah meant the camels loaded with treasure. "But Inalchiq Khan accused them of being Tartar spies."

So? Sir Roye wore the khan's silver plaque around his own neck. Tartars were insatiably curious. If Inalchiq meant to kill whomever the Tartars talked to, he had set himself a hard task, even for a Turk. "What will the Tartars do?"

"They will send another embassy, giving Khwarezm a chance to do right by returning the goods and punishing Inalchiq."

"And if Khwarezm does not?" Sir Roye realized that a lot rested on Shah Aladdin's good sense.

Hannah grimaced. "Then may Allah have mercy on them."

As Hannah predicted, a second embassy was sent out, again led by a friendly Muslim. After tense weeks of waiting, Shah Aladdin sent back the man's head. In a dismal attempt to curry cheap favor with the khan, the shah merely shaved the heads of the Tartars who escorted him. Hannah laughed mirthlessly when she heard that news, saying, "Shah Aladdin hopes to keep the Tartars at bay by killing only fellow Muslims."

Misplaced strategy, at best. "But the Tartars do not give a pressed grape whom you pray to," Sir Roye pointed out. It was their most endearing quality.

Hannah agreed. "Nor will it make them any happier to be robbed by an idiot."

"You are taking this hard," Sir Roye observed. Hannah had been through hell, which made her prone to see the worst in things, even when they had a tiled roof overhead and ate iced sherbet made from mountain snow, brought down by fast camel caravans.

"We will be going to war." Hannah rested her head on his shoulder, her eyes tearing up. "And in war, anything can happen."

Too true, but Sir Roye tried to reassure her, saying, "We are going to war with the Tartars." With a Christian army, he might be worried for his life, since every previous battle had ended with him running in panic at lance point. Tartars, however, had turned war from a mere pastime into a cut-and-dried business. "From what I have seen, there is not a Turk on earth who can stand up to them."

"Oh, yes, the Tartars will win." Hannah took that as given. "It is you I fear for."

Sir Roye pulled her closer, folding the weeping Pole in his arms. He had meant to make Hannah's bondage easier, not harder, treating her decently and trying mightily to please her. What else could a gentleman do? Was it his fault if women took that as love? He thought that by not sleeping together they could avoid romantic entanglements. Hannah clearly felt otherwise. All he could do was hold her tight, and whisper for her not to worry. He would come through this whole and hale, and all her tears would be for naught.

7

the killer of children

After spending half her life in the trackless woods, Aria's existence was suddenly swept up in travel. Her one and only look at the wide world beyond the trees began at once. Bishop Cyrus saw her off, sending her down the Dys to the Brovva in a bullock car, a little wooden bedroom on wheels, which she shared with a kindly young nun from Vyatichi named Sister Ida. The bullock driver and his boy rode on the roof, and they were escorted by three "lances" from Baron Zazog's household cavalry, a dozen armed riders, all ordered to see she got to the Shrine of the Black Maiden in Vyatichi before the first day of summer.

Serfs in roadside pastures and open fields touched their brows and bowed when they saw the curtained bullock wagon with its clattering escort of armed riders. Inside, Aria and Sister Ida enjoyed the luxury reserved for a sacrificial victim, reclining on cushions, or the big double bed, with its perfumed silk sheets, and cooking their meals on the small iron stove. Sister Ida said her prayers religiously, but otherwise they had no schedule to keep and no chores to do, leaving them free to talk, and loll, and watch the countryside roll by.

Despite her approaching doom, Aria mourned Sir Roye more than she mourned herself. Her knight was right: she loved too much, missing him with all her might. While Sister Ida prayed to Jesus, Aria silently begged Lady Death to look after her love, and hopefully reunite them in that cold northern Hell where the sun never shone in winter. She would happily keep him warm.

Pious and sympathetic, Sister Ida turned out to be from a landholding family in Vyatichi. Ida's father thought her too plain for marriage, putting her in a nunnery instead. "Best thing that could have happened to me," Ida declared, crossing herself enthusiastically. "Our Almighty's hand at work."

Aria's own pilgrimage to join the Sisters of Perpetual Suffering had taken a unexpectedly sinister turn. She tried to find out the fate of the Firebird's Egg, but Sister Ida said that it remained an object of contention. "Bishop Cyrus has kept Baron Zazog at bay—but His Holiness dares not remove the Egg from the church. As soon as they leave sacred ground, the baron's men will be waiting."

Heathen acts happened in the woods, and even a holy bishop did not have the same safe passage afforded a condemned criminal.

On the first night, camped by the Dys in their little traveling room, Aria could not sleep, haunted by images of her lost knight, who was facing the Tartars alone. And what might happen to her when they got to the shrine—everything from suttee to ritual strangulation. Finally she got up the courage to ask Sister Ida, "What do you know about the shrine at Karadyevachka?"

Heaving a sigh, Sister Ida said a swift prayer, then opened a jar of plum wine, pouring a healthy jolt into a wooden cup. Nuns naturally shared utensils, thinking it sinful to use two cups when one would do. Secure in their lamplit traveling room on a warm night, Ida had taken off her veil and habit, and now wore only a linen shift. With the wooden cup in her hands and her head and eyebrows shaved, Ida looked more like a starved Buddha than a young woman in her twenties. "I have never been there," Sister Ida admitted, solemnly handing Aria the cup, "but girls do go there. Not every year, but they do go."

Aria took a deep swallow of plum wine to steady herself, finding it sweet and heady, stronger than koumiss. "And they do not come back?"

Pouring more plum wine into the cup, Sister Ida stroked Aria's cheek, saying quietly, "Take another drink."

Surprised by the nun's touch, Aria obeyed, asking suspiciously, "Are you getting me drunk?"

"Yes." Sister Ida smiled good-naturedly. "It is part of the Old Rite. Some things are not not meant to be heard sober."

Taking another swallow, Aria thought of the girls who had gone before her, each getting drunk before she learned her fate. "Did you know any of them? The girls that went to the shrine?"

"Some." Sister Ida's smile vanished, and she took a sip herself, staring sadly into the carved wooden cup.

"Who were they?" Aria asked, already feeling like one of them. "What were they like?"

"Most had no choice." Sister Ida handed the cup back, resting her hand on Aria's knee. "Babies born badly deformed are offered to the shrine. And my best friend's little sister Katelyn was stricken with a wasting disease. When it was sure she would die, Katelyn offered herself at the shrine, not wanting her family to see her suffer. My last memory of Katelyn is her turning to wave to us before hobbling off, headed for the shrine, proud to have something to do with her lost life. Sometimes strangers from afar would offer themselves—infanticides, suicides, and the like. One spring I remember an older girl with a refined Markov accent coming to our home, politely asking my mother directions to the shrine, then thanking us and going on, without any word of explanation."

Thankful for the plum wine, Aria took a deep swallow, drinking to that unknown city girl. "What happened to them?"

"No one knows." Sister Ida shook her head, saying, "The secret name for the Black Maiden of Karadyevachka is the Killer of Children. Since the shrine is set against a high crag, some say the girls are taken to the top and thrown off. Or devoured there by wild rocs."

Some choice. Taking a swig, Aria told her, "I know which I would pick."

"At least you will not drown." Sister Ida patted Aria's knee, then poured more plum wine in the cup, asking gently, "Why are you offering yourself?"

Wine had gone to her head, making Aria unsure what to say, "For fear of what the Zazogs would do to me if I did not."

"But what was your crime?" Sister Ida asked, giving her hand a comforting squeeze.

"Witchcraft," Aria admitted warily, "and willful disobedience . . ."

Sister Ida looked askance. "What sort of witchcraft?"

Emboldened by the plum wine, Aria cuddled up to the friendly nun and told her whole sordid story, how she was abandoned by royalty as a baby, then apprenticed to beggars, then sold to the Bone Witch, only to be kidnapped by Prince Sergey, then menaced by Tartars, and finally captured by Zazogs. All she left out was Baron Roye de Roye, whom she resolutely refused to mention, lest he be tainted by her crimes.

Sister Ida shook her head in disbelief, tucking her drunken charge into the coverlet, saying, "And yet you are still alive."

No good nun could even know the half of it. "Temporarily."

"As are we all," Sister Ida reminded her, giving the drunken girl a long good-night kiss. Then the nun stripped off her own shift and slid under the coverlet, wrapping her naked body around the girl bound for sacrifice.

Aria drifted into blissful sleep, cuddled with Sister Ida, mildly surprised to find that nuns kissed like French gentlemen. Clearly she had a lot to learn about the clergy, for the Bone Witch had seriously neglected her religious education.

Waking next morning to the gentle sway of the wagon, amid sunlight falling through the small glass windows, Aria felt warm and hungover. They were still headed down the Dys toward the Brovva, and from her bed she could see shining green treetops rolling past, set against the bluest-ever sky. Lying tangled with a nude sleeping nun, Aria knew she was seeing a whole new world.

How new was apparent when they stopped to water the oxen, and Aria put on a dress to pee. As she squatted by a wagon wheel, a squire came up, asking if she wanted water from the river. This question nearly floored Aria, who had never had a man draw water for her, much less a boyar's squire. Flustered, she nodded her head, and he trotted off to oblige. Too bad she could not turn invisible to pee.

Then a Kazak bowman came up, offering her hot tea, followed by a groom with biscuits. In no time the squire was back with a bucket of water, and soap to go with it, scented soap, smelling of lavender.

Sitting by the wagon wheel, nibbling her biscuits and sipping tea, Aria had a steady trickle of men come up, to do her favors or just to watch her eat. Far from treating her as a witch and criminal, the men were caught up in the drama of her sacrifice; everything she did seemed to touch them deeply, no matter how simple or ordinary. Aria found she could walk freely among these strange armed men, drawing nothing but shy smiles, like she was a little sister or a secret sweetheart. No lewd come-ons, no attempts to fondle her or drag her into the brush, just ready helpfulness that would rapidly turn to lust—but only if she let it. Utterly amazing.

Within limits, she could have whatever she wanted. Aria had meant to bathe in the river, but when she asked for hot water, men stumbled over each other to obey. Sister Ida brought out a wooden tub, and Aria had a hot glorious bath in the spring air.

Squires and bowmen applauded when she doffed her dress and slip; then they lined up to lift heavy buckets, pouring heated water over her while she washed.

Standing under the warm cascade, Aria rubbed herself with scented soap, feeling her hangover magically melt away under the men's admiring gaze. Brought up among serfs and beggars, Aria had bathed in front of men since she was a little girl, and these fellows would have gotten the same show if she had washed in the river—only they would never have thought to work for it, or even to applaud.

Descending past the charred stump of Byeli Zamak, it saddened Aria to see the broken tower that her knight had commanded, another sign of her world's ruin. Her home destroyed, the Bone Witch dead, her love gone, the Egg lost— it had all started with the fall of this proud white tower.

Beyond Byeli Zamak, they crossed over to the Brovva, which Aria had never seen before. Each morning she awoke to a whole new world, another vast landscape that she would never see again. Black earth steppe stretched in all directions, grainfields so immense, it barely felt like the wagon was moving. Winding through this flat steppe south and east of the capital, the Brovva watered the heart of Markovy, fertile grainlands dotted with tiny hamlets and onion-domed churches. Here in central Markovy, tall luxuriant feather-grass had grown for untold millennia, storing nutrients in its matted roots, leaving deep black layers of humus so rich and thick that it was carted away for fertilizer on less fortunate plots.

Twice-walled towns loomed in the distance, but each time, they passed them by, headed for the highlands of Vyatichi. Finally, after days of travel, endless flats turned to rolling hill country carved by ancient glaciers, a low undulating landscape of marshy hollows, moraine ridges, and shallow lakes. Tiny islands of forest appeared, signs of the great sea of trees lying between here and the Iron Wood.

Each night Aria slept beside Sister Ida but dreamed about her baron. For a few golden moments in the night, he was alive and they were together, riding and talking, or kissing in bed. Each morning she awoke to find it was a dream, and life was hauling her to different fate. One night she told the nun, "It seems strange to die, never having been with a man."

"Why? I will die never knowing a man." Sister Ida raised the cup of plum wine in gratitude. "Thank Heaven I was not pretty enough."

"You are a nun," Aria pointed out. "You are expected not to." Being at best a honorary novice, but still never knowing a man seemed fundamentally unfair.

Sister Ida shrugged. "It is supposed to be a virgin sacrifice, but why stand blindly on tradition? None of these men will care. Get one of them alone—

whichever you fancy—you see how they look at you. Then you can tell me what it is like; but do it soon, for we are nearing the borders of Vyatichi."

Dire news. Nonetheless Aria hesitated, though she certainly had nothing to save herself for now that her knight was dead.

Next morning she had an unexpected reminder of the current civil war—the last D'Hay stronghold on the Brovva, Hebektahay Castle, the Bride of the D'Hays, was being beset by the Brovvniks and D'Medveds. Sited on a high outcropping above the far bank of the Brovva, Hebektahay was virtually impregnable, with three fortified wards ringing an inner keep, and further defended by a big bend in the river. Besiegers had taken the town, isolating the castle, then brought up catapults and trebuchets, erecting a huge earth platform on the landward side, to fire down into the outer ward. At the same time, miners brought by boats tunneled into the riverbank, trying to bring down one of the middle ward towers.

Miserable serf families turned out of the castle to conserve rations pleaded for food from passing boats. Their foes would not let them through the lines, hoping the castle would take them back, reducing the defender's larder. Destitute mothers knelt by the riverbank, holding up starving babies, begging passing boatmen to take them.

Two days later, they reached the final ford on the Brovva, and Sister Ida nodded at the dark wooded uplands across the river, saying, "That is Vyatichi."

Looking over the broad brown river, Aria saw the land of her doom, the ancient homeland of the Markovites, boreal hills that sheltered her people until they were brave enough to come down onto the plains, driving off the Kazakhs and Kipchaks, then pushing back the Finns and Poles, claiming the rich black earth as their own. On the far side, hamlets got fewer and farther apart, separated by high ridgelines and forest belts—but the people got friendlier. At their first stop in Vyatichi, women and children met the wagon, offering her flowers, spring berries, and fresh bread. When Aria took the gifts, people cheered, and she asked Sister Ida why. "Because you have offered yourself," the nun replied. "For the children."

"For the children?" Pleased but bemused, Aria clutched the flowers and smiled to the crowd.

"They are simple folks," Sister Ida explained. "To them the Black Maiden is a protector of children, and Karadyevachka is her shrine. Girls hereabouts who give themselves to the shrine do it to help keep children from harm—so they assume you are doing the same. It is a harmless folk heresy tolerated by the Church."

Aria saw loving gratitude in people's faces, knowing she was giving her life for their children, while they had only these poor offerings in return. This shy, worshipful look got stronger the deeper they went into Vyatichi. Mothers brought her smiling toddlers to bless and babies to kiss, calling out blessings to her in return. Little girls solemnly offered her their rag dolls, which she kissed but did not keep.

Having everyone always happy to see her, giving her greeting gifts, and taking every care for her comfort became like a narcotic. Hugs, kisses, and heartfelt tears of good-bye lifted Aria's spirits, making her feel she really was special, destined for some grand and mysterious purpose. These joyful, solicitous hill folk would have let her have whatever she wanted—except to turn back. Or to be alone long enough to vanish.

At night, when her solicitous nun was asleep, Aria felt overwhelmed by sadness at facing death alone, without her brave baron beside her. Not just death, but abject defeat as well, since she had lost the precious Egg, utterly failing in her quest. And now she could not even save herself. People watched her every waking moment. Her only privacy came in the little bedroom that was her moving prison. Disappearing did her small good, if it did not get her out of the moving box.

Maybe she deserved to die, like a forest creature that breaks cover and ends up making a meal for someone else. She remembered how the Bone Witch faced the bowmen's arrows, not flinching, or even seeming to care—but the Bone Witch was Death's own grandmother, and not afraid of anything.

Karadyevachka shrine sat at the base of a tall wooded crag, a black-timbered hall built in Markovite style, with low eaves and carved doorposts, set right up against the hill, blending into the ground and shaded by aged oaks. Veiled nuns filed out of the shrine to meet them, singing as they came, carrying a caged pigeon and a big two-handled silver cup. When Aria stepped out of the wagon door in her white sacrifical gown, flower-decked squires and bowmen went down on their knees, crying and kissing her hand. These former Zazog retainers had by now become her honor guard, fiercely loyal and heartbroken to lose her.

Aria was fairly heartbroken too. Finally seeing the dark, sinister shrine blew away all the good feeling from the happy throngs of well-wishers, sobering her up sharply.

But there was a ready remedy for that. Nuns from the shrine held out the cool silver cup they carried, telling her to drink. Aria did, sipping at first, finding it was sweet fruit wine, sugared to better please children. These were her last sober moments. The nuns meant to get her drunk, just as Sister Ida did that first night in the wagon. Old Rite ritual really did call for it. Saying a prayer for the girls who came before her, Aria drank deeply.

Giving her the caged pigeon, the nuns told her to set it free, which Aria did, to a chorus of cheers. Glad to get out of the tiny cage, the pigeon shot off, disappearing over the trees. *Good luck*, Aria thought, wishing she could fly off that easily.

Saying good-bye, Sister Ida threw her arms around Aria, kissing her repeatedly. Tears were pouring down the good sister's face. Already tipsy, Aria told the nun not to fret. "I am fine, totally fine, really."

Which was more than the nun could say. Clearly Sister Ida was in love with her charge, and she had a hard time letting go. Looking toward the oak-shaded shrine, Aria also had second thoughts, suggesting, "More wine?"

Sister Ida brought her the cup and held it while she drank. Feeling the wine go to her head, Aria signaled when she had had enough to send her on her way. Now she must make the walk to the shrine alone—everyone expected it. Throat tight, unable to speak, Aria nodded good-bye to the world.

Sister Ida kissed her again, deeply and passionately, then dropped to her knees, still sobbing and clutching the cup.

Frightened, giddy, and shocked at the force of that kiss, Aria set out up the path toward the dark shrine, drunken feet dragging. These were the last steps in her long journey, and in her life as well. How sad and strange, coming all this way and making all these new friends, only to die at the end—but none of these friendly worshipful folks gave her any choice. She thought of all the girls who had walked this path, drawing courage from their sacrifice, while her hand went inside her dress to stroke the straw doll tucked beside her pounding heart.

Built from ancient oiled timbers, stained black by time, Karadyevachka shrine had a fancifully carved front, with fiery salamanders climbing the doorposts, chasing brightly colored birds around the blue-painted door. Aria did not have to be drunk to feel like she had stepped into some faerie story from her girlhood—a scary one, for inside lived the Killer of Children.

She still had her invisibility spell, but it seemed a meager bit of magic to pit against this ancient mystery. Turning at the painted door, framed by the carved troll faces, she waved to the armed men and nuns, blowing them a kiss.

Folks cheered, and Aria went in, leaving the daylight behind. Darkness enveloped her, hot, wet, and smelling of sulfur, filled with the sound of water dripping on stone. Unable to see, much less turn invisible, she felt blind panic rising inside her, remembering Sister Ida saying, "At least you will not drown." Aria did not want to die gasping for breath with stinking sulfur water filling her face and nose—that hardly seemed fair.

Slowly her eyes adjusted to the dim light falling through the shrine's smoke-hole, and she saw that Karadyevachka shrine was built over a natural hot spring. Big rocks sat at odd angles embedded in the dirt floor, surrounding a warm simmering pool that smelled of brimstone. Seated on one of the rocks was an incredibly old woman with tangled white hair and a wrinkled toothless face. Lifting blind eyes, the old woman reached out a withered hand, whispering, "Come here, girl. Do not be afraid."

Since her one spell was utterly wasted on the blind, Aria obeyed, walking over and taking the crone's hand, wondering what would come next. Up close, she could see that the sightless old woman had parchment-thin skin stretched over fine, beautiful bones. When young, she must have been lovely. Feeling Aria's face, the crone asked, "What is your name?"

"Aria." She stood still, listening to water lap on stone, letting the blind old woman feel her.

"How old are you?" asked the crone.

"Seventeen at least, maybe more." No one kept accurate track of her birth date, least of all Aria.

"You are a brave girl," the crone informed her. "I feel it in your face. Do not worry—here you will merely be purified. Have you been with a man, or ever shed innocent blood?"

Saying no to both, Aria told enough of her story to explain how she got here. The crone asked if rebelling against Prince Sergey did not make her an accomplice in his death. Aria protested that she only acted in self-defense, "after the Prince attacked both me and the Bone Witch, and even then I did all His Highness asked, and told only the truth."

"Enough." The blind crone held up her hand. "I see well why they sent you here. Purify yourself in the pool."

No longer afraid of drowning, Aria stripped and bathed in the warm volcanic water, and when she was done and dressed, the crone had a goblet of wine waiting. Handing her the goblet, the crone told her, "Drink. We both sit on the brink of death—but you must face her today."

Taking a sip, Aria asked, "What will happen to me?"

"We will walk together to the top of the crag," the crone replied, "where I will leave you to await the Destroyer."

Aria took a hurried gulp, asking, "What destroyer?"

Laying a hand on Aria's head, the old woman ran fingers through her long dark hair, saying, "Be brave, my sweet. Though I have served this shrine for seventy years, I do not know what form the Killer of Children takes."

No longer as drunk as she wanted to be, Aria took another great gulp. "Will I see my knight? Baron Sir Roye de Roye."

"Is he dead?" asked the old woman, who had clearly never heard of the baron.

"I think so." Aria could not be sure—in fact, she hoped and prayed he had somehow cheated the Tartars.

"Then I would not know," the crone admitted. "There is much about death that remains a mystery, even when we sit at her door. Come, you can bring the cup."

With that, the old woman led Aria out the back of the dark shrine across a green banked stream and up the dusty path to the peak, a dizzying climb for a drunk girl and a blind crone. Aria saw huge swaths of Vyatichi through gaps in the trees, green forested hills cut by swift streams, with cottony clouds towering overhead. Halfway up, Aria finished off the wine. And a little farther along, she lost the goblet, but the old woman told her not to worry. So Aria did not, having other things on her mind.

Near the top, it struck her that she was still a virgin—a strange thought, but somehow apropos. Damn, she meant to do something about that. It certainly could not be helped now—one of life's great mysteries that was just going to remain one. Coming on a wide flat spot ending in a sheer drop, the old woman stopped, saying, "Here."

"Here?" Aria looked around, realizing this high grassy meadow was the last place she would ever see.

"Yes," the crone replied, giving her a withered kiss. "Say hello to Death for me, for I shall be seeing her soon." Turning away, the crone tottered back down the trail, feeling her way with a stick. Leaving Aria drunk and alone near the edge of the cliff, taking a last bleary look at the world.

Edging up to the drop, she glanced down, teetering alarmingly, seeing straight down to the steppe. If she did not like the look of this Killer of Children, she could always jump. Backing carefully away, she sat down on the grass, scared and lonely, wishing she had more wine to drink. Wishing even more she had Baron Roye de Roye with her. Why did she have to face this alone? Because her love was gone already.

Death did not seem so bad. What reason was there to live? Especially if her death might do little children some good. Even the smallest child's life seemed more useful than hers.

As she sat worrying, a shadow swept over her. Aria froze, whispering her spell. Whatever made the shadow had to be huge. Invisible—and immobile—she stared straight ahead, waiting. Again the shadow swept over her, moving more slowly as the bird of prey circled closer. It had to be a roc, a big one, a giant female dropping down on her.

All her carefully hoarded courage evaporated. Killer of Children? This monster could hunt tigers, with its saber-size talons and terrible curved beak. Of all the woodland hunters, Aria feared these tremendous raptors the most. They had uncanny eyesight, and this one knew right where she went to ground. If she stayed invisible, the roc would land on top of her, knocking her out of hiding, like a hawk flushing a grass vole.

Drunk or sober, Aria did not want to be ripped to pieces. Staggering to her feet, she tried to make it to the cliff, aiming to launch herself into space, preferring the stones below to being pecked apart by a giantic bird. But the roc was too quick, dropping down to land in a thundering flutter of wings, cutting her off from the edge. Shrinking back, Aria stared up at the huge raptor, petrified by its cruel curved beak.

Up close she saw that the fifteen-foot-tall hawk wore a leather hood with silk reins running to a saddle on the bird's back. Sitting in the saddle was a small blond teenager, looking very pretty and feminine in embroidered silk pants and a light leather flying jacket. Across her back was a silver bow shaped like the crescent moon and a quiver full of colorfully feathered arrows.

Aria knew she was looking into the shining face of Death. Neither her magic rune nor her invisiblity spell could protect her from this grim reaper on rocback.

Venom rings flashed in the sunlight on the bird woman's slim fingers, giving her the touch that killed. Looking levelly at Aria, the blond teenager told her, "I am the Destroyer, Persephone, Killer of Children. Who are you?"

8

the bride of the d'hays

"Aria," she replied meekly, amazed by the form the Killer of Children had taken.

"Very beautiful," Persephone declared. "What does it mean?"

"It means a song for a single voice." Or so her mother had said. Being told that story was one of the few solid memories Aria had of her mother.

Despite the friendly questions, Persephone was a fearful presence, with her silver moon bow, bird of prey, and flashing venom rings, but she was also a blond teenager, not much older than Aria, with a lovely serene face and alert blue eyes. That contrast was startling in Aria's drunken state, and all she could think to ask was a trite direct, "Have you come here to kill me?"

Persephone's lips curved up in a slight smile. "Did you come here to die?"

"Yes," Aria admitted, though she was not a fanatic about it, adding, "but I desperately want to live."

Persephone's smile widened, and she asked, "Then what are you doing here?"

What, indeed? Drunk as she was, Aria had no ready answer. What was she doing in this far-off corner of distant Vyatichi, talking to a scary blonde on a big bird? That did not even make sense sober. "I am not sure."

Cocking an eyebrow, Persephone asked, "Then you are not a jumper?"

"A jumper?" Aria looked nonplussed.

Persephone nodded at the drop behind her. "You were headed for the cliff when I landed."

"Only because your bird frightened me," Aria explained brightly—it still did, but not so much.

"Seems a thin excuse to commit suicide," Persephone sniffed. "You must have more reason than that. Are you perhaps fatally diseased? Or in intolerable pain?"

Aria was not feeling the least pain. "No, I am pretty happily drunk on fruit wine."

"All the more reason to live," Persephone laughed. "So why are you here?"

Aria told her story, or the highlights at least—being raised by the Bone Witch, finding her knight, and the Firebird's Egg, then losing both and being captured, followed by her choice of burning or sacrifice, then her long trip here and her brief inebriated stay at the shrine. Taking this last opportunity to confess, she cataloged her long list of crimes, ranging from being raised a witch-child, stealing bread and beer, and helping assassinate a prince, to drunkenly tongue-kissing a nun not half an hour ago. Aria was proud that she could get it out in her present state.

"And you loved this Baron Sir Roye de Roye?" Persephone asked, eyeing her carefully.

"With all my heart." It felt good to say it. Aria had never been in love before, and until now she had kept their love a secret, lest it be used against them. Now she could proclaim it to the world from atop this crag above the steppe, loud as she wanted, in the face of Death herself. "Baron Roye de Roye was my truest friend, and my dearest love, and I miss him mightily."

Persephone smirked at her enthusiasm. "Well, can you live without him?"

"If I have to, I suppose." It was not Aria's first choice, though if she must, she must. It seemed horribly unfair to finally proclaim her love, then have to give it up.

"Get on behind me," Persephone told her, nodding toward the back of her saddle.

"What?" Aria stared at Persephone's high perch, hardly believing what she was hearing.

"It is that or go over the edge." Persephone indicated the drop behind her.

"But I will never be able to get up there." Besides, she was afraid of the bird, but too scared to say so.

"Then choose the cliff," Persephone suggested. "Death is easy; life is hard."

And then some. Aria stepped gingerly up to the giant bird, grabbing the rear of the saddle. Why did she have to be drunk for this? Regretting each time she greedily begged more wine, Aria cleared her head with a deep breath, then hoisted herself aboard the bird.

Unbelievable. When she first saw this giant bird, not in her most drunken imagining did she think to end up on its back. She did not have much of a seat, just a small pad at the rear of the saddle, with her bent knees resting on Persephone's hips and her arms around the Killer of Children's waist. Close contact ended any doubts about Persephone being real, or anything but what she seemed: a blond teenager in harem pants and a flying jacket, a girl not much older or bigger than Aria. What else she was, Heaven only knew.

Leaning forward, Persephone urged the bird into the air. Spreading her wings, the roc obeyed, launching them off the cliff edge in a gut-wrenching dive to gain speed, then soaring outward, catching a thermal off a bare patch of fallow, spiraling upward. Aria got a dizzying view of Vyatichi, spread out below her, a big green-brown blanket of rumpled hills and patchwork fields, cut by loops of river. Hawks circled below them, hunting for mice on the fallow. Aria wondered if she was headed for the Land Beyond, without the messy business of dying—assuming she did not slip and spatter herself on the steppe. Summoning up her courage, she asked Persephone, "Where are we headed?"

"Home," Persephone replied, and the bird seemed to take it as a command, skimming off along a low ridgeline until she found a new updraft. Circling and rising, the roc climbed atop the thermal, then set out for the next one, headed for the black earth steppe. By coasting from thermal to thermal, the roc carried her double load southward out of Vyatichi, winging back toward the broad flat plain of the Brovva. Ahead of them, a black dot hung in the air, far out over the floodplain.

Aria saw the dot grow in size, becoming a huge silver gas-filled parasail, with a sky-ship hanging from it, a sleek ultralight craft pointed like a ship, with a big maneuvering fan on each side and a tiny aft cabin topped by a pigeon coop. Black grapples hung from the keel ballast tanks. Something else out of faerie stories, a sky-ship sailing along before a steady north wind, headed farther out over the flats. Persephone's roc flew straight through the control lines between the ship and the inflated parasail, landing on a tall perch directly amidships.

"Back so soon?" asked a cultured male voice below them. "What have you found this time?"

"Help her down and see," Persephone suggested, sliding her roc's hood closed so the bird could rest.

Aria found herself being plucked from the saddle by a man who had climbed the perch to get her. He was tall and blond and beautifully built, wearing a white page's uniform with gold hearts on his sleeve. His handsome face looked remarkably like Persephone's, but he was all man and handled her easily, setting her down but not letting go of her, asking, "Who is this beautiful catch?"

"Be nice, Eros," Persephone warned, swinging down out of her saddle. "She is merely a girl."

Eros shook his blond locks, laughing, "There is no such thing as 'merely a girl.' Look at her—young and tender, and already drunk—you should have sent me to collect her." Letting go of her arms, he bowed, saying, "I am Eros, God of Love. Welcome aboard the _Selene._ What is my lovely maid's name?"

"Aria," she replied shyly, still unsure on her feet, and glad to have this friendly God of Love ready to grab her—if needed. Eros was polite, affable, and plainly eager to put a smile on her face. Aria managed a drunken, "Delighted to meet you too."

Persephone took her by the arm, saying, "He is but a demigod, and much too busy running this ship. Come, I will show you our quarters."

Guiding her to the aft cabin, the Killer of Children pulled back a paper door, revealing a light airy room with cushioned window seats along each wall, and a curtained garderobe in the rear. Two caged pigeons stared back at her from behind slim wooden bars. Persephone apologized. "Sorry about Eros, but he is all boy, as well as semidivine. Still, he has his uses, and he is a cousin, my mother's sister's son."

"Are you human?" Aria asked, sitting down on a low cushion, since the skyship's little cabin hardly had headroom.

"Very much so," Persephone assured her, sounding proud of the fact, "the Killer of Children has to be human. Who else would do it?"

"What does it mean to be the Killer of Children?" This question had been hanging over her, unspoken, but always there.

"Watch and you will see," Persephone suggested. "For now, it is enough that you are mine. You gave yourself to me, and you owe me your life. In return, I will have need of you."

"For what?" Aria whispered, not sure she wanted to know.

Persephone studied her intently, weighing how much to tell, finally saying, "Nothing dishonorable, or deadly—I will do those things. Though it will certainly be difficult and dangerous. Life, as I said, is like that."

Taking out a stylus, Persephone made marks in a little strip of paper, then rolled the paper into a tiny tube. Opening the pigeon cage, the Killer of Children took out a bird, slipping the tube onto its leg, then releasing the pigeon out a window. Aria remembered the bird she released when she arrived at the shrine. One mystery was solved—she saw how the Killer of Children knew to come for her. So much of magic was merely misdirection.

Persephone smiled at her look of drunken recognition, saying, "Do make yourself comfortable. Play with Eros if you like, but only when you are sober—being a demigod, he has no morals, and will happily get you pregnant. And please, please do not leap or fall overboard, at least until I am done with you. Any questions?"

Only a million or so, but she was too drunk to frame them. Looking about the neat little cabin, with its wicker floor and cushioned window seats, she asked, "Do all girls from the shrine come here?"

"No." Persephone shook her blond head, opening a potion ring and pouring the white powder into a cup, then adding amber liquid from a silver flask. "Each girl has her own story and goes her own way; yours is to come here."

"Why make people think they will die?" After what she had gone through, that seemed incredibly cruel.

"To see I get the girls everyone else has given up on," Persephone explained, closing the potion ring, then jiggling the cup to mix the powder into the liquid. "And many do die—the base of that cliff is littered with small bones. Your case does not seem nearly so hopeless." Persephone handed her the cup, saying, "Here, drink this. It will put you to sleep."

Aria took it and drank without a qualm, finding it was sweet fruit nectar. Persephone might surely poison her, but she doubted the Killer of Children would stoop to lying about it. In seconds, she was sleeping soundly.

When Aria first awoke, it was dark, and she was lying on one of the window seats with a curtain drawn between her and the rest of the cabin. Stars shone through the glass onto her, but there was no feel of movement. Incredible. And she was no longer drunk, not even hungover. Aria burrowed deeper into the cushions and went back to sleep.

Next time she awoke, daylight filled her little curtained alcove, and she spotted clouds drifting below. Cautiously sliding back the curtain, she discovered breakfast laid out for her in the cabin, vinegared rice, smoked fish, and boiled pigeon eggs. Eating it all, she went out on deck, finding the sky-ship just as amazing sober as she did drunk. Persephone stood on the quarterdeck above the cabin, calling out orders to the crew forward, who worked the lines to the parasail. With the foot-pedaled manuvering fans at quarter speed, *Selene* crabbed crosswind, running "heavy" and relying on aerodynamic lift to give direction. To Aria, it was all more magic.

"Rested?" Persephone called down from the quarterdeck. When Aria nodded, the Killer of Children added, "Fed too, I hope, for I shall have need of you soon."

Somewhat alarming news. Aria nodded again, trying to look ready. Relaxing at the port rail, she gloried in the feel of flight, watching green woodlands roll beneath the sky-ship's keel, giving way to brown plowed fields and gleaming water meadows. Lazy loops of river curled and uncurled below, fanning out into silver marshland, full of weedy islands and bulrush channels. Wild ducks and herons rose up to greet them.

Running along the river was a ribbon of road, the same one she and Sister Ida had traveled in their bedroom on wheels. Somewhere down below, Sister Ida was probably praying for her, thinking she was in Heaven with her knight. Where Aria had expected to be.

"Landfall ahead!" shouted a sailor in the bow. Leaning far over the rail, searching for landmarks, Aria saw a column of smoke rising over a big bend in the Brovva. At the base of the smoke stood Hebektahay Castle—the Bride of the D'Hays—the D'Hays' last stronghold on the Brovva, ringed by besieging Brovvniks and D'Medveds. It had taken days to wind their way from here to Karadyevachka shrine by ox-house. Aided by the stiff north wind, *Selene* had covered the same distance in a day and a half.

"Come up," Persephone called to her. "We are going to land." Mounting to the quarterdeck, Aria found the Killer of Children standing with her embroidered pants pressed against the quarterdeck rail, feet planted on either side of the keel, sensing the balance of the sky-ship, feeling her way down. Persephone grinned at her, saying, "This is the fun part."

Eros shouted from the amidships rail, "Valkyries to starboard."

Looking to her right, Aria saw dark winged shapes spiraling downriver. "More likely vultures," Persephone declared. "Hard to tell at this distance."

"There's a difference?" Eros called back, looking as pretty as the god he was named for. Either way, a battle loomed ahead. Aria watched Eros arm himself. Brash, arrogant, though still in his teens, the demigod wore a silver doublet with angel-wing sleeves over green hose, to which Eros added a back-and-breast and an armored codpiece, just in case. His sallet helm and golden crossbow lay by the rail—even Love went armored into war.

But not Persephone, pressed against the quarterdeck rail, guiding the *Selene* down; her only protection was a green leather flying jacket.

Nor Aria, still wearing her sacrificial gown, which was no protection at all. She watched the sprawling triple-walled castle rush up toward them. Lines of tents stretched out from the base of the castle rock, covered by a blue haze of cook smoke, closing off the big river bend and bottling in the D'Hays. Closer to the castle rock, she could see catapults, tall siege towers, and war kites flying above the fortress. Fireballs arched over the walls, and a big breach had been pounded in the castle's outer bailey. Black flags flew from the besieger's towers, showing the Brovvniks would give no quarter.

Eros called out, "All hands aft. Bring up the bow."

Crew hurried aft, raising the bow. The huge gas-filled skysail overhead tilted back, slowing *Selene*'s fall. Persephone told Eros, "Take the helm," and then strode over to her roc sitting on the midship's perch. Picking up a grapple line and mounting her bird, Persephone called to Aria, "Come with me. Those are your people below."

Aria had trouble thinking of settled folk as "her" people, and doubted she knew any of them personally—still she obeyed, climbing up behind Persephone. They took off together, trailing the grapple line, diving for the middle ward of the castle.

Brovvnik ballistae on the packed-earth platform hurled spears up to greet them, great barbed shafts that the roc artfully avoided, setting them down on the onion-domed roof of the Basilica of the Black Virgin in the castle's middle ward. Aria found herself suddenly inside the walls of Hebektahay Castle, the same doomed keep she had seen from the far side of the river a few days ago, and never thought to see again. Arrows fired from war kites thudded into the roof around her.

Persephone sprang from the saddle, securing her grapple to the roof and signaling the oncoming *Selene*. War kites parted above them, unwilling to face the careening sky-ship coming in to land. Losing headway, *Selene* slewed about into the wind, and the line went taut as the windlass worked. Eros ordered the ground lines dropped, and grapples and anchors went over the side, catching on the basilica roof. *Selene* had made landfall without so much as a thump. Mews boys swarmed down a line to see to the roc, carrying clip-fed Cathayan repeating crossbows slung across their backs.

Giving Aria the saddlebags to carry, Persephone led her across the roof through a forest of carved stone spires, to a small door at the base of one of the onion domes. Nuns met them in an upper gallery, arrayed behind their Mother Superior, an unveiled stern-faced old nun, who could see sin in the crotch of a tree. Her Holiness asked frostily, "Why have you come here?"

"Your castle is doomed," Persephone replied, not wanting to give the D'Hays any false hope. "I have come for the children."

"This is our house, and these are our children," declared the aged nun, her wrinkled lips pursed, defying a teenaged demigoddess who could kill her with a touch. "You are not wanted here, with your poisoned weapons and pagan ways."

"Death is hardly ever welcomed," Persephone agreed amiably, "but this is my house too—there was a shrine here to the Dark Maiden long before there was ever a basilica or castle. And these children are marked for death, which makes them mine."

Mother Superior stiffened, insisting, "These children are under our protection." Between them lay the incredible chasm between Old Rite and Mother Church, between a girl who embraced death and a crone married to God.

"Tosh," Persephone told her. "You cannot even save yourselves. Have you not seen the black flags outside? When the Brovvniks come in, everyone not kept for rape or ransom will be put to death, even the little ones. Along with any nun who objects too loudly."

"We are a holy order," the Mother Superior protested grimly. "That is our protection."

Persephone snorted. "I could wait and deal with the Brovvniks when you are all dead—but children here are already dying."

"Why do you think that?" Mother Superior did not deny it.

Persephone smirked. "A bird told me. You know you can neither feed nor protect them—do I deal with you, or with the Brovvniks?"

Mother Superior sighed and signed to her nuns, saying, "With us."

What other choice was there? Nuns led them down to the main floor of the basilica, where homeless women and children huddled amid silk hangings and tall stern icons. Families sheltering in the nave shrank back as the Killer of Children walked among them, a sign of the terror to come. Nor did the witch-girl at her side inspire much confidence.

Looking into their frightened faces, Aria realized she was seeing the living dead. After the expense and loss of a siege, the Brovvniks would show no mercy, at least not on the weak and helpless. Starvation, followed by a massacre of the survivors pretty much summed up these people's future. Some faced death with bewildered indifference, others with cringing politeness.

Persephone went patiently from child to child, giving out candied fruit and honey cakes from the saddlebag, which the starved children wolfed down. As she did, Persephone quietly told the mothers she would take any child offered to her. Some mothers were aghast; others gave up their children immediately. To the women and girls who were pregnant, the Killer of Children offered an abortion potion, so they would not be forced to bring more innocent victims into the charnel house that Hebektahay had become. Some took it; some did not.

By the time they had gone through the entire nave, family by family, Aria felt numb, drained by the fearful doomed faces. Her own trip to be sacrificed was heaven compared with this, with warm morning baths, plenty to eat, and presents along the way. Her most primal heartfelt reaction was the same as Persephone's—at least get the children out, as many as they could.

Bad as things were in the Basilica of the Black Virgin, things were ten times worse in the outer ward. Rather than risk her roc, Persephone went on foot, with Aria right behind her, while Eros stood on the roof of the basilica, covering them with his golden crossbow. People in the middle ward had watched *Selene* land, but were still shocked to see the Killer of Children walking casually among them, with her silver bow and deadly touch. An absolutely abysmal omen. Already people walked only on the landward side of the ward, since trebuchet balls lobbed over the walls came crashing down on the river side, where they had smashed several homes and a brewery into kindling.

Whenever Persephone saw a child, she produced a sweet, telling her tale about taking children to safety. "Just have Mother bring you to the basilica." No one made a move to stop her. Guards at the inner gate took one look and ushered them through, lowering the drawbridge between the two baileys.

Beyond the bridge, the outer ward was a shambles, breached and burned, overshadowed by the huge mountain of earth the Brovvniks had erected to let their archers and catapults fire down into the bailey. Head-size stones came crashing down, more or less at random, and Brovvnik archers sniped at anyone who moved—being paid by the body. Into this hell were forced the better sort of townsfolk, who could not be just turned out of the castle like serfs. None of them seemed the better sort now, looking starved and scared, living in holes and basements.

Fortunately, most had already had the sense to give their children to the nuns, getting them into the middle ward. Persephone insisted on combing the smoking rubble in the outer ward, coming up with several cowering orphans and an abandoned baby that Aria now carried. But Aria's mind was on a skinny hollow-eyed boy who stubbornly insisted on staying with his dying mother. She gave him the last of her honey cakes.

Back at the Basilica of the Black Virgin, Eros had started a baby-lift, offloading rice and beans while taking on talkative children. "Where are we going?

"Does that big bird bite?"

"How come my mother cannot come?"

"I am still hungry."

"Yes, let's have more honey cakes."

"Where are they taking us?"

To which Eros patiently answered, "Home. Yes, keep away from her beak. Too old. There are berries and dates waiting in the cabin. Home, I told you."

Hearing the word *home* again, Aria asked, "Where are they going?"

"Somewhere safe." Persephone sounded purposefully vague. "So long as you do not know exactly where, the most hideous torture cannot wring it from you." Cheering thought. Aria wondered who Persephone's parents were. Who could have mothered the Killer of Children? Persephone must have family, aside from Eros, but all Aria knew of Old Rite religion came from faerie stories and ghost tales. She always pictured the Killer of Children as a horrible hag with bloody teeth. Grinning broadly, the blond young demigoddess asked, "Ready for more?"

"More?" Aria thought she had misheard her mistress.

"There is still the castle keep, and beyond the walls," Persephone reminded her.

"This is ghastly," she blurted out. After the outer ward, yet another round of carnage seemed too much.

Persephone cocked an inquiring eyebrow. "Did you think it was fun being the Killer of Children?"

"No." Aria had honestly never thought that. Nor had she ever wanted to hear these terrible stories and see people make gut-wrenching choices. "Whyever did you pick me for this?"

"Silly girl," Persephone scoffed at the notion, "I never picked you. You chose me, remember? Death makes do with whatever comes her way."

"Of course." How could she be so foolish? "I could have been burned at the stake instead."

"And a wise choice it was." Persephone gave Aria's hand a squeeze, kissing her on the forehead. "For which we are all very thankful."

"Really?" Aria felt fairly useless, carrying babies and handing out honey cakes to famished children, but it was nice to be appreciated.

"Certainly, have you not seen how Eros looks at you? And the mews boys too. I had to keep a lock on the cabin." Persephone rolled her eyes at all the trouble she had been put to, saying, "Buck up, girl. I will give you a treat. We will see to the castle keep next, saving the worst for last."

Something to look forward to. But she did feel better, knowing she had inadvertently chosen to do good. Should she die from a sniper's arrow or a stray catapult ball, it would literally be "for the children." As she promised the folks in Vyatichi.

Following her mistress to where their roc stood waiting, she looked at the mews boys in a new light. Did they really think her cute? One of them certainly was, standing by the roc, smiling broadly, his repeating crossbow held loosely at the end of a long brown arm. Mounting the giant bird, Aria put her arms around the Killer of Children and they took off, headed for the high stone heart of Hebektahay Castle, the towering keep overlooking the middle and outer wards.

As soon as she alighted in the inner ward, Aria was in another world, smelling bread baking and seeing chicken and ducks underfoot. Pigs guzzled milk from the buttery that could have fed babies in the middle ward—but boyars did not eat babies. Liveried servants met them as they landed, a steward and butler greeted them, while a groom and pages attended to the roc, all well-fed and wearing the D'Hay shock-of-wheat badge.

Persephone politely accepted the steward's invitation to meet with the castellan, then turned and knelt, ignoring the men and saying directly to the startled pages, "I assume you are fosterlings and have no parents here—if so, go straight to the Basilica of the Black Virgin. I am taking children out of here."

Before the shocked steward could stop them, one of the boys asked, "Will we go home to our mothers?"

"Not if you stay here," Persephone promised, then rose and followed the aghast retainers into the main hall to meet with the D'Hays.

All the castle leaders were assembled to greet them, a sign of desperate times—normally the Killer of Children was as welcome as spotted pox. Men in French hose and padded doublets sported fashionable slashed satin sleeves, while unveiled women wore long Viennese gowns. D'Hays affected Western ways, letting their women mix with men, not keeping them veiled and confined. With them was a boy in a silver-trimmed doublet who was introduced as Alexi D'Hay, eldest nephew to the baron.

From the tales the Bone Witch had told her, Aria realized that this boy was the D'Hay heir male, since handsome Baron Valad D'Hay was notoriously unmarried—the most eligible bachelor in Markovy. No wonder they had not given up Hebektahay. Alexi was worth a duke's ransom if the Brovvniks bothered to ransom him and did not just hold on to the boy, hoping the barony would come to them if dashing Baron Valad could be made to die childless.

Hovering over Alexi was his aunt, Lady Constance, merely a Tolstoy married into the family, making twelve-year-old Alexi the ranking noble present. Wearing royal blue trimmed in cloth-of-silver, he stood in sulky silence with a look of bored masculine condescension that seemed doubly alarming in one so young.

Lady Constance D'Hay spoke for him, welcoming them to Hebektahay Castle in the name of her nephew, introducing herself and the castellan, a blunt, swarthy professional soldier in half-armor. Begging Persephone's help, Lady Constance claimed the Brovvnik assault was an unprovoked breach of truce, aimed at seizing the heir. Cut off from reinforcement, and facing slow defeat through starvation, Lady D'Hay pleaded, "Will you take my Lord Alexi to safety with his mother in Markov?"

"You want me to fly him to the capital?" Persephone looked amused, patiently explaining she was not a semidivine delivery service. "I will take him, but to do with as I see fit."

Lady Constance blanched at the notion of the D'Hay heir being passed about like a serf with a limp, saying, "That is needlessly cruel."

"Cruel?" Persephone looked quizzically back at Lady D'Hay, as if unacquainted with the concept. "Has m'lady seen the black flags outside? To keep Alexi out of Brovvnik hands, you condemned every serf and servant in this castle to death. Merely giving him up to the Brovvniks could save dozens of children."

"Surely, you would not think of that!" Lady D'Hay's shock turned to horror.

"Think of it? I surely would." Persephone sounded sorely tempted. "Doing it is a different thing—but the decision will be mine and his to make. Who knows? I have seen children give themselves freely to save others from suffering."

"Blasphemous!" Lady D'Hay spat back, finding the notion of the D'Hay heir giving himself up to save starving serfs insultingly obscene.

Persephone nodded in agreement, adding, "Still it is his choice."

Stepping closer, the Killer of Children knelt before the surprised boy. Aria saw men's hands go to their swords, and the castellan looked to Lady D'Hay— but it was too late. As soon as Persephone got within reach, Alexi's life was in her hands. "I am taking children out of here," she told the D'Hay heir. "You can come with me. I cannot swear I will take you to your mother in Markov. But I will not lie, and I will listen to what you say, as I would any boy who offered himself to me."

Demigoddess and the D'Hay heir stared at each other. Lord Alexi said nothing, looking into that intent blond face, from close enough to smell the sandalwood soap on Persephone's soft white skin. He saw a beautiful but deadly teenager not much older than he, who flew through the air and killed with a touch—but promised to treat him like any other boy. "If you do not believe me, ask Aria," Persephone suggested, nodding toward the witch-girl and sometime novice nun. "She seemed utterly doomed when she came to me, and now is useful and much admired."

Aria smiled to show it was true, but Alexi looked dubious. Lady D'Hay tartly told them, "He is not just *any* boy."

Persephone rose to go, saying, "A day may come when he wishes he were." Aria followed the Killer of Children to the kitchens, where she told every turnspit and baker's boy what she had told Alexi D'Hay, that she was taking children out of Hebektahay Castle, and they were free to come too. Some put down their work at once, following her through the barns and living quarters, where she told the same story to stableboys and serving girls.

By the time they reached the inner wall walk, with its sweeping view of the three walled baileys, ringed by the river and the enemy lines, they had a dozen excited children trooping behind them, suddenly freed from their chores, sounding happy, scared, and eager. Hoping to be miraculously rescued.

Nor did Persephone disappoint them. Calling to her roc, she had the big bird fly up to perch on the battlements, introducing her to the awestruck children—then two by two, she flew them down to the basilica roof in the ward below. Then the Killer of Children came back for Aria, saying, "Now comes the worst part."

And it was. Dodging darts and fireballs flung at them by Brovvniks and D'Medveds, they flew down to the outer ward's riverbank postern, the tiny gate wedged between the bailey walls and the river's edge, where the Bride of the D'Hays dumped her refuse. Babies lay abandoned by the gate, and Persephone searched through them for signs of life, finding two she could save, and one so gone that the Killer of Children could only end his suffering. The others were already dead.

Aria took the two they could salvage and went searching for children among the people huddled at the river's edge—serfs and aged townsfolk living on belt leather and boiled grass. Brovvnik archers shot anyone attempting to leave the shadow of the walls, hoping the D'Hays would be forced to feed them. Emptying the food from her saddlebag so Aria could use it to carry the babies, Persephone found three emaciated children whose parents gladly gave them up.

Back atop the Basilica of the Black Virgin, smiling nuns took the abandoned babies, vowing to beg milk from the lords in the keep. Eros had returned with *Selene*, and he was taking on another load of noisy well-fed children while off-loading sacks of millet from the sky-ship. Aria sensed minute planning at work, and saw the urgent need for secrecy—for the first load of children could not have gone far. Somewhere close by, atop an unscalable rock or on an island in the Brovva, was a secret shrine, stockpiled with food beforehand under the unsuspecting noses of the Brovvniks. Now children were being swapped for food, with the *Selene* running full each way. More magical misdirection. So long as the children simply disappeared, no Brovvniks would come looking for them.

To adults in the doomed citadel, it seemed children were vanishing into thin air, replaced by their weight in beans and sweet cakes—making some of the younger nuns and novices giddy with excitement. Fear and hopelessness faded. Even families that did not give up their kids could at least feed them something. Eros met them at the sky-ship's ladder, saying, "Someone from the keep to see you."

Standing on the quarterdeck, between the pigeon coop and the ballast taps, still wearing royal blue-and-silver, was young Alexi D'Hay, looking very pleased with himself. Sunlight shone on the D'Hay shock of wheat, done in cloth-of-gold on his velvet jacket. He announced proudly, "I have come to offer myself."

Persephone smiled at his self-assurance, asking, "What did Lady D'Hay say?"

He replied loftily, "My aunt thinks I am having a geography lesson."

"Which you shall," Eros assured him. "The best place to learn geography is a quarter mile up."

"First let me speak with him." Persephone led Alexi into the aft cabin for a private interview, from which young D'Hay emerged looking more self-important than ever.

Before leaving *Selene*, Persephone took Aria aside, whispering, "Watch Alexi for me, and keep him happy. We may dearly have need of him, but he must be handled delicately."

Aria nodded, knowing that young Lord Alexi was all boy, and a boyar-to-be: nine parts ego, with a dash of devilment. Only someone as loving and ruthless as Persephone could hope to control him. Best Aria could do was to keep watch on him, making sure he did not climb the rigging lines or fall overboard.

Eros dumped water ballast and took off, using the increased lift and foot-powered fans to maneuver the *Selene* upwind, back the way they had come. Alexi *oohed* excitedly, asking innumerable questions, without awaiting answers, while hanging dangerously far over the quarterdeck rail to watch the ground go by below.

Weary of fielding wild questions, Aria asked one of her own. "Why did you come?" Alexi seemed alarmingly willful, and he showed scant desire to sacrifice for others.

"Because of her!" Alexi's eyes lit up at the thought of Persephone. "She is amazing, is she not?" Clearly Alexi was in love. Small wonder. Persephone was smashingly beautiful and utterly fearless, and being a boy, young Lord D'Hay was not the least turned off by her bow and poison arrows.

"And you too, Aria," Alexi assured her, not wanting his babysitter to feel bad. "You are nice, and let me do what I want. I like that much more than Aunt Constance, who is shrill and overbearing, and got us into this terrible mess. If you trust Persephone, so do I."

Aria thanked him, hoping love and trust did not get Alexi killed. Until now, Aria had been doing good, taking children out of a ghastly situation. But Alexi's situation had been anything but ghastly, living in luxury, with both sides wanting him alive and well—just under their control. Now Alexi had given himself to Persephone instead, following Aria's example, so whatever happened to him was in some sense her doing.

She thought the hiding place might be an island in the Brovva, or an unassailable rock, but it turned out to be both. Not far upstream, a tall flat rock outcropping rose right out of the river, dividing the tree-lined Brovva into a pair of white cataracts, making it nearly impossible to get to the rock by land or water. From above, Aria could see the hidden shrine, nestled in a low hollow atop the plateau, several small buildings surrounded by a drystone wall—already overrun with children. Releasing gas from the parasail, Eros glided down to a landing before the shrine, dropping grapples to a female ground crew.

Children helped reel them down to a jubilant reunion, and their enthusiasm turned the rescue operation into an impromptu party, as they reveled in their newfound freedom from fear, death, and parental discipline. No hunger, no war, no chores, just an incredible high-flying holiday. Aria watched Alexi take charge of the boys, selecting the games and assigning roles, which the others gladly accepted, happy to have a lordling leading them.

At the same time, adults piled food aboard the sky-ship to replace the newly arrived kids, comforting little ones who missed their mothers or who begged to return to homes that no longer existed. Upriver accents showed that the adults came from Norgraad, or even farther north. By now, Aria knew that Persephone and Eros came from way to the north, from the frigid white land of death, where winters were black hell and the summer sun shone at midnight.

Her window-bed had a white bearskin coverlet, and Eros trimmed his silk doublet with arctic fox fur.

When Persephone arrived on rocback, Aria attended her in the aft cabin, where the Killer of Children asked how things went with Alexi. "Well enough," Aria confessed—then added hesitantly, "Do you know Alexi is in love with you?"

"Yes, shamelessly so," Persephone agreed happily, "much to Lady Constance's dismay." Lady D'Hay must be having fits at the moment, facing thousands of angry Brovvniks without her lordly nephew and chief bargaining chip. Now Lady Constance was just another titled female in a doomed fortress, whose best hope was to disappear into a nunnery—or more likely, a Brovvnik harem. The Killer of Children's grin turned smug. "I know boys way better than Lady D'Hay. They are half my stock in trade."

Aria asked, "Will he now do whatever you want?"

"Apparently," Persephone replied. "Which is why we must be careful, for love is a terrible thing to abuse. And Alexi is a child under my care."

Aria nodded, thinking that so was she. How unfair that Alexi rated so much attention, merely for being an obstinate boy and a boyar. His feelings were catered to, and he got long personal meetings with Persephone while lording over the other children—whereas Aria dodged catapult darts and cared for starving babies.

Reading her mind, Persephone told her, "Do not be jealous. You have done wonderfully, bearing up better than I could ever have imagined. We are done here at Hebektahay, and you have more than discharged your debt to me."

"But I want to be with you," Aria blurted out. At the moment, she could not imagine life without Persephone, dirty starving babies and all. For the first time since losing her knight, Aria had someone she could believe in. "I gave myself to you."

Persephone smiled, taking Aria's face in hands and looking straight into her eyes, saying, "So you did. And for a good reason, though what that reason is, I do not yet know. But I am both pleased and happy that you chose me." The Killer of Children kissed her, then added, "Flattered, even."

"My other choice was being burned alive," Aria reminded her.

"Sometimes fate needs a helping hand," Persephone explained airily. "Still, you chose me sight unseen. Are you disapointed?"

"Not at all." Aria reveled in the demigoddess's touch, and in their eye-to-eye contact. Having this magical person to herself felt heavenly, even though the venom rings chilled her cheeks.

"Good." Lady Death's little sister grinned at her charge, reminding Aria, "We are all together only for a time, either long or short, and must make the most of it. I believe your fate lies with the Firebird's Egg. At least the Bone Witch thought so."

True, the Bone Witch chose her, but the world beyond the trees had turned out to be a much tougher place than Aria had expected. She no longer felt smart and strong enough to take on all of Markovy by herself.

From Hebektahay, the *Selene* sailed south, propelled by an uncannily steady north wind. Happily, Alexi bedded up forward, with Eros and the mews boys, learning manhood firsthand. Sailors slept on the fan-crank benches below, leaving the aft cabin to Aria and the Killer of Children. She and Persephone brewed tea together and ate rice from the common pot, seasoned with pickled fish and vegetables, enjoying lazy days aloft, leaving the Brovva behind and crossing over the Great Mother River, the huge stream that ran the length of Markovy, dividing the country in half. Aria sat in awe in the window seat, admitting the Mother River was bigger than she ever imagined.

"Mother Flood is the longest river in Europe," Persephone boasted, "longer than the Rhine and Danube combined, flowing for over two thousand miles, from the land of the Balts to the Great Sea of Grass."

Aria was impressed, though she had never heard of those other rivers, and knew the Balts only by reputation. "Where does the Mother River end?"

"She empties into the Inland Sea in Far Barbary."

Aria stared down at the strong brown flood swollen by the rains, spreading into the flats, and carrying away tree trunks and serf hovels. "That would be something to see."

"Oh, you will see it," Persephone assured her.

"What? The mouth of the Mother River in Far Barbary?"

Persephone nodded solemnly. "That is where we are headed, to the Inland Sea."

"Whatever for?" If Persephone had said the moon, Aria would not have been more amazed.

"We have business in Far Barbary," Persephone replied.

"We do? What business?" Aria could not believe the turn her life was taking.

Persephone raised a hand to still her. "For now, it is enough to know that you come willingly. Do you?"

"Most willingly." Aria was ready to go to the end of the earth, so long as it was with Persephone. Questing alone had totally lost any appeal.

Eros had not been lying about geography lessons, and that afternoon he took Aria, Alexi, and the mews boys into the prow to look at the land below. Aria quickly became Eros' prize pupil, learning to recite the Mother River's many names—like the Rua or Rha, the Atel or Itil, and the Bulga or Volga. "But always the Mother River is the fertile life-giver," Eros told her, "bringing water to the barrens and bearing people and trade on her broad back."

Alexi called her teacher's pet, and he wiggled his tongue obscenely when Eros was not looking.

Aria knew Eros wanted to make love to her—in fact considered it his divine duty, an indispensable part of her education. Without deigning to hide his interest, Eros never pressed the issue, being friendly but not familiar. Love would know when the time was right. Pretending not to notice, Aria felt secretly flattered each time he touched her to point out a landmark, or congratulate her answer.

Drifting south over the great Sea of Grass, Eros showed her how to spot herds of wild horses and steppe antelope, and how to tell a Kazakh from a Kipchak at a quarter mile up. When she was sent off to be sacrificed, Aria expected to see the world—but not nearly so much of it, and not with such a handsome guide. She eagerly anticipated each day's lesson, just for the chance to lie next to Love's long strong body and peer down from the prow, watching the world go by.

In the afternoon, Persephone gave her flying lessons, letting her ride up front on the roc, until Aria got a feel for guiding the bird. Then she soloed, just her and the huge raptor, coasting from thermal to thermal, exploring the sky together.

Persephone let her steer the *Selene* as well, standing Aria at the quarterdeck rail, straddling the keel, showing how to work the control lines and ballast taps. All the while, Aria strove to satisfy her curiosity about the Killer of Children, asking, "Who is your mother? What is she like?"

"Mother? My mother?" Persephone smiled at her question. "My dear mother is a most sainted woman, meek as a mouse, lives on a holy isle and never eats meat, the original earth mother. Looks nothing like me. Hard to think we are even related . . ."

Not liking the air low down, Persephone decided to go higher, searching for a more southerly wind. Drawing a knife, she emptied several bags of sand ballast over the aft rail.

"And your father?" asked Aria, following Persephone with her eyes, admiring how the demigoddess moved: bold and forward without seeming seductive—but not like a man either. More like a hawk. "Who is he?"

"Never met the man myself," Persephone admitted, "but Mother thought the world of him."

As *Selene* gained altitude, the Killer of Children showed Aria how to trim the rudder, and tilt the parasail, using their climb to crab southward.

Aria kept up her questions, learning that Persephone was born in a far-off northern castle on the icy shore of the Frozen Sea. Her sainted mother was Goddess-on-Earth, and lived in a sanctuary called Fair Isle, where they ate grain and cheese, and no one died except by natural causes. With Mother living the contemplative life, the family was led by Persephone's older sister, Lady Kore, the Dark Daughter, demigoddess of Death. Someday Persephone would succeed her sister as Lady Death, and Dark Daughter. "To start me out easy, Kore and Mother made me the Killer of Children." Persephone brought her back to the keel, standing behind her at the quarterdeck rail, where they could both feel the new tilt of the keel.

Using this as an excuse to bring their bodies together, the Killer of Children whispered in her ear, "Actually, I think Eros suggested it."

"Eros? Really?" Aria had no idea how this weird family worked, though she liked having Persephone pressed against her, full of that living warmth Aria had long missed.

"So he could get me alone." Persephone smiled at Aria's surprise. "Eros is all male. And since Kore spurned him, Eros has turned his considerable charm on me. He hopes to get one of us with child, so he may have an heir in the family."

"What do you think of that?" Aria asked cautiously.

Persephone made a face. "I am not ready to have anyone's baby, least of all a Love child. I never even asked to be Killer of Children. It was thrust on me by my family—big surprise there."

Having no family, Aria had to take her word.

"Now it is part of me. Something I must do." Persephone grimaced at her high-flying act. "Pretty much perfectly too."

"I understand." That is what she loved about Persephone. The Killer of Children had the same devil-may-care sense of honor as the late Baron de Roye.

"Good." Persephone grinned evilly, giving her waist a friendly squeeze. "For you are under a family obligation too."

Aria protested. "I have no family."

"You wish." The Killer of Children scoffed at Aria's naïveté, when it came to family matters. "Your foster mother was the Bone Witch, and she raised you to do big things."

"Like return the Firebird's Egg?" Which seemed absolutely impossible at the moment.

"Among other things." Persephone turned her about, so they could face each other, letting *Selene* drift downwind on her own.

"Other things?" As if returning the Firebird's Egg was not impossible enough. "There is more?"

"Much more." Persephone said it lightly, but with feeling. Clearly there were challenges ahead so daunting, it was better not to think of them. "Knowing everything now would only worry you. It is enough to know that you must visit the Inland Sea."

Aria shrugged. "If you say so."

Sensing her reluctance, Persephone whispered, "I will let you in on a family secret: the Bone Witch is my great-great-grandmother. Which makes us related."

"Really?" That barely seemed likely.

"You are my great-grand-foster-aunt." Persephone kissed her warmly on the lips, more warmly even than Sister Ida. "Welcome to the family."

"Great-grand-foster-aunt makes me sound old." Though it felt good to have a family, even one as weird as Persephone's.

"Good, for you are a senior family member, and will soon be making wise and important decisions." Persephone grinned wickedly, adding, "While I am merely the Killer of Children."

Said that way, it did sound frivolous. Aria did not suppose that she was really Persephone's superior in her new "family"—but for the first time since losing her knight, Aria felt that the Bone Witch's picking her was more blessing than curse.

Farther south, the great Sea of Grass thinned into short grass steppe mixed with desert scrub. Aria even saw huge drifting dunes below, crossed by camel tracks, a scene out of the *Arabian Nights* stories that the Bone Witch used to tell her. Then the land got greener again, as a great braided stream spilled over the wastes, enclosing long fertile islands cropped by herds of nomad cattle. She asked Eros, "What river is that?"

"It is called the Itil here," Eros told her, "but it is still the Mother River, which makes a great turn in the Sea of Grass, heading southeast instead of southwest, and emptying into the Inland Sea."

Again Aria marveled at the magnificent river, watching as the broad flood branched again, and again, becoming a gleaming maze of reed-choked channels. Finally the Inland Sea herself appeared, on the far side of the delta, swelled by the outflow from the two-thousand-mile-long river. Soon they were sailing over sea-green waters, and the low shore vanished behind them. For the first time ever, Aria found herself totally out of sight of land, suspended over a vast sheet of water running from horizon to horizon. Utterly uncanny.

Daily geography lessons came to an end, with nothing below but water. Aria found she missed the chance to be close to Eros, listening to him speak, smelling his scented sweat. On the second day at sea, she went up on the quarterdeck when Eros had the con, to check on the wave tops below and have a few words with the beautiful demigod.

This far south, noon heat was unnerving, even when the tilted parasail somewhat shaded the ship. Crewmen slept on their benches, while Alexi disappeared into his forecastle hammock, and Persephone retired to her cabin. When the mews boys went forward to see to the roc, Aria found herself alone on the quarterdeck with Eros. With the *Selene* drifting along at her pressure height, there was no maneuvering to be done, and Eros needed only to see they did not lose altitude.

Noontide gave way to sultry afternoon, and Aria languished in the stifling heat, stripping down to just a light top and loose harem pants, totally bored until Eros called to her from the port rail. "Here is something out of the *Arabian Nights*."

She rushed over to see, leaning close to look along Eros' strong broad arm. "What do you mean? Where?"

"That dot ahead of us." He pointed out a speck on the horizon.

"Yes, I see it." It was just a dot, but getting visibly bigger as she watched. "What is it?"

"Roc Island." Eros put his free hand around her shoulder.

Aria could barely believe that. The last story that the Bone Witch ever told her had been about Roc Island. She did not even know how Sindbad's story ended, because the Bone Witch never finished it. "This is the Roc Island that Sindbad visited?"

"Maybe not that one," Eros confessed. "Sindbad sailed from Basra, but there is doubtless more than one. Rocs like to nest on isolated islands, where their eggs and young will be safe."

Slowly the dot got larger, though it never got as big as the island in the Bone Witch's story, Shahrazad's island, which had high mountains and a pleasant harbor with broad sandy beaches, where Sindbad fell asleep. This Roc Island looked more like a tall boulder pile rising out of the Inland Sea.

Watching the rock pile grow, Aria was conscious of Eros' body beside her, holding her close, as his tanned arm directed her gaze. Love's loose white tunic sleeve was slit to the shoulder and decorated with gold hearts. By being alone with him, she was not too subtly offering herself, which both scared and excited Aria. Having someone so godlike so interested in her was like a narcotic. Aria knew she should not give in, but she could hardly help herself. Eros' friendly words and warm smile were incredibly reassuring. How could she be doing wrong when she was in Love's arms? He asked, "Do you want a closer look?"

She nodded shyly, not sure what he meant. When drifting downwind, the sky-ship had limited maneuvering ability, unless Eros woke up the crew and got the fans going—which neither of them wanted. They were both enjoying this moment alone, though neither said so aloud.

Reaching inside his gold-and-white tunic, Eros produced a farseeing tube, a long and narrow silver cylinder, with a glass lens at each end, like the ones Cathayans used for eyeglasses. Eros handed it to her, saying, "Here, look through this."

She took the tube and stared through it, but the miraculous cylinder only made things smaller, turning Roc Island into a pebble on the sea. "I cannot see a thing."

Eros laughed. "Try looking through the other end."

He reached around, helping her reverse the tube and steady it. Bracing her back against him, Aria looked through the tube again. Roc Island leaped into clear relief. Huge nests made from driftwood and tree trunks were perched atop the island's boulders, which were surrounded by a pebbled beach—not the sandy one Sindbad slept on. Though not Shahrazad's island, it was still utterly amazing. A giant mother roc came winging over the waves from the mainland with a dead steppe antelope in her claws, bringing food to her hungry young, who were already bigger than eagles. Her mate settled in as well, regurgitating right into his offspring's gaping mouths.

As Aria watched, Eros' chest and hips pressed hard against her back, and his arms enfolded her, helping support the metal tube. This felt alarmingly pleasant—so good, she could hardly keep from melting into his embrace—yet Aria kept her eye glued to the farseeing lens, studying the Roc Island rookeries intently. If she moved, Eros might let go, or worse yet, start to caress her.

She reminded herself that the beautiful demigod literally did this for a living, having seduced hundreds of girls like her. Heathens had no morals. He would love her, and leave her with child, thinking it merely a job well done.

All she did was slowly turn her head, following the island until it fell away to port. Only then did she lower the glass and look at Eros. His arms, which had been holding the tube, were now wrapped magically around her waist, overlapping just above her hips, fingers pressing lightly on her thighs. She could think of nothing to say, looking up into his cool blue eyes. So far, Aria had been in only one man's arms, and he was dead.

Eros smiled mischievously, saying, "It is hot, is it not?"

She could merely nod, not sure if he meant the day, or the warm way their bodies fit together.

"Come, I have something to cool you off." He ran his hands down her hips, thrilling her through the fabric, then let go, retreating to the quarterdeck awning, a thin patch of silk stretched to cover the side not shaded by the parasail. Which left Aria the option of staring at the vacant seascape—or accepting his invitation.

Naturally she accepted. Wary as she was, Aria knew in her heart moments like this never came again—so the Bone Witch had assured her. When she got to the awning, Eros was pouring from a silver flask into a pair of goblets. She sat down beside him, and Eros offered her a cup. "Here, try this."

She sniffed first, finding the fresh aroma heavenly. "What is this?"

"It is called nectar." He guided the cup to her lips. "It is what the gods drink."

One sip, and Aria saw why. Nectar tasted delicious, sweet but bracing, and unlike wine, it actually cleared her head, sending a tingling through her limbs, heightening her senses. Eros' skin suddenly smelled sweet as cinnamon, and the golden hairs on his hard muscled arms sparkled in the sun.

Eros took a sip of nectar, then passed the cup back, while casually stripping off his heart-studded tunic to relax against a cushion. Clothes were for mere mortals.

Amazed by the beauty of his long lean body, Aria took another drink of nectar. Worries and inhibitions fell away. Any fear of Eros utterly vanished, replaced by sharp sudden pangs of desire. Her skin actually itched for his touch.

Reading her mind, Eros reached over and pulled her to him, bringing their bodies together, then their lips. Love's first kiss was both tender and sensual, starting casually, lips just brushing, then building in intensity as Eros pressed her tighter to him. Saying a silent "sorry" to her lost knight, Aria opened her mouth and kissed back. His tongue tasted of nectar.

Maybe it was the nectar, but the wet contact seemed electric, sending shivers through her thighs. Sir Roye de Roye had shown her how to kiss, Eros aimed to show her why, slowly and artfully exploring her mouth while loosening the ties on her harem pants.

And Aria let him do it. Her knight was dead, so unless she really meant to be a nun, she must look for someone else. Why not start with Eros? He was beautiful, thoughtful, and bound to be good at what he did. True, she was his great-grand-foster-aunt, but that did not bother the demigod.

Despite the afternoon heat, Eros hardly seemed to sweat. Maybe it was the nectar, or just that he had done this hundreds of times, but his skin felt wonderfully smooth and dry, smelling of cinnamon, while her own body was getting wet with excitement. Without breaking the kiss, Eros rolled down her silk pants and spread her legs, his fingers tracing the pink folds of flesh between her thighs. Aria groaned and gripped him tighter, wrapping her bare leg around his calf.

Eros took that as assent, and rolled over on top of her, his large hands taking hold of her hips, his fingers reaching into the small of her back, tilting her up to take his long strong erection, already pressing hard and warm against her.

Aria lay wonderstruck in the love god's arms, feeling his eager hands on her, taking total control. She was about to make love for the first time with a demigod, in an airship under sail, flying far above the rocs and eagles, borne by the wind over the great Inland Sea of Far Barbary. Once she dreamed of being a princess, but being foster daughter to the Bone Witch and lover to a demigod was not so bad either.

"Pardon me," a cool voice coming from above interrupted her deflowering. "I must have my maiden back."

"Must you?" Eros sat up, still splendidly erect, but sounding peeved. "At this very moment?"

"Now will do admirably." Persephone had returned to the quarterdeck, looking all business, her blond hair done up in a ponytail, and the farseeing tube in her hand. Aria felt mortified, fearing she had endangered the airship by letting Eros molest her. What if the wind shifted, or they lost altitude? Neither of them would have cared.

Eros arched an eyebrow. "Is it part of your job to spoil my fun?"

"Not in the least." Persphone scoffed at that absurdity. "I am the Killer of Children. Seducing them is up to you."

"Then let me get on with my work," Eros suggested. Aria just wanted to disappear into the deck.

"Another time, perhaps." Persephone helped Aria up, and back into her pants, acting as if this happened every day at home. Which it probably did.

Aria expected to be scolded, though she had done nothing wrong—there had hardly been time. Instead, Persephone led her into the bow to have a look ahead through the farseeing tube. While studying the far horizon, Persephone wanted to know, "When you were with the Tartars, did you see any children?"

Aria was taken aback by the question, which had nothing to do with Eros. Nor did she ever think of herself as having been "with" the Tartars. "No, there were no children with them."

This was the first time the Killer of Children had bothered to ask about the Tartars, and as usual Persephone had only one concern. Without putting down the tube, Persephone asked, "What do you know about how they treat children?"

"Tartars adore children." Or so Blue-Eyes had told her. "Making children and rearing them are the favorite Tartar pastimes. They even kidnap other people's children and raise them as their own."

Persephone made no mention of catching her necking with Cousin Eros, acting as if that had been all perfectly natural. "Come," the Killer of Children told her, "we must get ready for landfall?"

"Landfall? Where?" Aria could see nothing but wavetops.

"At the fortress-palace on Abeskum Island." Persephone saw that Aria had never heard of the place. "The private preserve of Shah Aladdin of Khwarezm, built on an island in the Inner Sea because he fears the Tartars. Shah Aladdin has sent his whole harem there for safekeeping."

"And why are we going there?" Shah Aladdin was another name out of the *Arabian Nights*.

"Harems have children in them." To Persephone that was reason enough, and she released water ballast, using the resulting lift to steer toward her target.

Hours went by, then a dot appeared on the horizon, and Aria took the farseeing tube into the prow for a closer look. Through the glass she saw a small island topped by a walled palace, with a sheltered sea gate, where several ships rode at anchor behind an artificial breakwater. But the harbor entrance was closed off by a line of barges, and more barges were anchored upwind of the island, with sky-boats tethered to them, raining destruction down on the walls.

While Aria watched in awe, naphtha-filled glass balls dropped from the sky-boats, splashing liquid fire over the Turkish battlements. Black oily smoke blew over the alabaster palace and the harem's hanging gardens. At the highest point of the harem, a great Cathayan balloon supported a two-story bamboo pavilion, riding comfortably above the smoke.

Black flags flew from the Tartar barges, proclaiming they would give give no quarter. Having seen enough, Aria retired to Persephone's side, asking, "What is going on there?"

"Tartars have arrived," Persephone observed, without ever looking through the Cathayan tube.

With a bang. "But why are they attacking the Turks?"

Why, indeed? From the look on Persephone's face, Aria knew the Killer of Children saw no use in any of this. "Shah Aladdin beheaded a Tartar ambassador, and let his servants plunder their caravan."

"Whyever for?" Aria firmly believed in keeping clear of Tartars, and she had never been voluntarily visible in front of one, much less tried to ransack their merchandise—though under extreme duress, she did once feed one to a lycanthrope. "Is he totally insane?"

"Apparently," Persephone agreed. "But his people are the ones paying for it."

It did seem doubtful that anyone down there being showered in burning naphtha had gotten a single fig from that plundered caravan. Aria asked, "So why are we here?"

"There are children down there." Persephone acted like that was obvious.

Aria nodded. This time there was no question of these being "her" people—but there was no arguing with Persephone, who treated all children the same, noble or serf, baptized or pagan.

"Come, let's go," the Killer of Children told her. "I would not take you unless I thought you needed to go."

Aria needed to go invisible, but she had given herself to Persephone, for better or worse. Once more she climbed aboard the huge roc perched amidships, holding tight to the Killer of Children, as Eros brought the *Selene* down in a controlled glide, aiming for the palace below.

Which meant they must pass through a line of tethered sky-boats crewed by Tartar marksmen, much more deadly than the Brovvniks in war kites that they faced at Hebektahay. As the *Selene* approached, winches positioned the nearest sky-boats to pour arrow fire onto the *Selene*'s deck. Eros was in armor at the con, and the crewmen on the fan cranks were covered by the deck, but Aria's only protection was Persephone's slim body.

Persephone's power came from giving herself totally over to death, letting it take her at any time.

Aria held tight to the Killer of Children, wondering if her own death was fast approaching. She could see Tartars moving in the sky-boats, getting set to puncture her with merciless precision. Nor would going invisible help much, not amid the oncoming arrow storm.

Without warning, Eros ordered full ahead on the fans, and dropped water ballast. *Selene* shot upward, faster than any winch could unwind, and at that same moment, Persephone jerked the hood from her roc and urged the bird to fly. Aria's stomach heaved as they leaped into the sky, soaring high out of arrow range.

Glancing down, Aria saw Persephone's grapple line unwinding, and at the end of the line was *Selene*, sailing between them and the Tartars—with the mews boys plying their repeating crossbows through portholes in the forecastle, putting holes in Tartar parasails. All the Tartars could do was take arcing shots at Eros on the quarterdeck, which bounced off his armor.

Seconds later, they were through the line of tethered sky-boats with barely a scratch to the paintwork, while the hollow-core crossbow quarrels had riddled their opponents' parasails, causing the gas bags to sag. Both Tartar sky-boats were frantically dumping ballast, and in no shape to pursue them downwind. Aria had never seen Tartars so easily upended.

Looking down, she saw the rock breakwater and blue harbor flash beneath her. Ahead of her reared the harem heights: walled gardens topped by a white palace with golden domes, a huge gilded, windowless block, rising above the rooftops. Tethered to a harem tower was tall Cathayan balloon supporting a lovely little two-story pavilion. Behind her, on the Tartar barges closing off the harbor, catapults and giant crossbows continued to fling darts and stones at them.

Aria did not see the ballista fire, so the long steel crossbow dart seemed to come out of nowhere, hitting the roc beneath the right wing and shooting through the raptor's breast. Piercing the saddle as well, the steel shaft ripped through Aria's skirt, cut a long gash in her thigh, and shot upward, hitting Persephone in the back of the head. Blood splashed over Aria's face, some of it her own.

Blinded by the blood, she hung on to Persephone's limp form, feeling the roc buckle beneath them. They were going down, and there was nothing Aria could do. Falling into a flapping spin, the dying roc whirled earthward, while Aria held tight to Persephone, keeping the Killer of Children in the saddle. Legs locked in the saddle straps, Aria clung grimly to her mistress, praying to the Virgin as the world spun around her. Aria's last sight was green harem gardens whirling up to meet her; then she slammed into the ground.

9

the gilded cage

Aria awoke in darkness, with a horrible headache and a stabbing pain in her leg. Without opening her eyes, Aria knew she was back in the little traveling house that had taken her and Sister Ida to the Shrine of the Dark Maiden at Karadye-vachka. She could smell burnt lampblack and the familiar perfumed sheets, and feel Sister Ida's warm still body beside her. Though the little bedroom on wheels was stopped for the moment, Aria could hear morning birdsong, which meant they would soon be moving. Somewhere nearby a rooster crowed.

It seemed strange to be back in that little house, for so much had happened since she left it. But her whole time with the Killer of Children now seemed at best a blurry dream, full of blatantly impossible images, from blond, bold Persephone seated on her roc to the hell of Hebektahay Castle and Abeskum Island. Totally unbelievable, though her hurting leg and banged brain insisted it was all too true.

Sister Ida's long warm leg lay across Aria's bared hip, feeling familiar and comforting—but Aria was vaguely nauseated, and her own leg hurt. Moving slowly, so as not to rouse the sleeping nun, Aria slid out from under Sister Ida, propping herself up and opening her eyes.

Only her eyes did not open. No matter how hard Aria tried, she could not raise her lids. Weird—and scary. Panicking, she put her hands to her face, finding her eyes glued shut, caked with something splashed on her face. Wetting her fingers, she frantically unglued her lids, tasting blood.

Her eyes struggled open. Aria realized it was not as dark as she thought, nor was she in the traveling house at all, but instead lying on an ornate bed wrapped in silk sheets perfumed with musk. The bed's cloth-of-gold canopy was pulled back to reveal a sumptuous lamplit chamber, with windowless gold-inlaid walls and colorful Persian carpets. Had her body not hurt, Aria would have thought herself in Heaven. Her dress had been slit to the hip, and her thigh was bandaged where it hurt. Flies buzzed about in the dim closed space, and her nausea mounted alarmingly.

Surprised, Aria looked down and saw it was not Sister Ida lying next to her; it was Persephone, facedown and naked, the back of her blond head a mass of dried blood, drawing flies.

Everything came back to Aria in a hideous instant, the flight over the harem walls, the shaft hitting them, the helpless horror of falling—and now here. What covered her face and glued her lids shut was Persephone's blood. Gagging at the thought, Aria did finally throw up, onto the carpeted floor, just managing to miss the satin cushions.

Appalled at what had happened, she leaned her head back against the ivory bedstead, wiping her mouth with her arm, trying not to cry. The Turks must have them, since they had fallen inside the walls.

Glad not to be held by Tartars, Aria thanked Heaven that Persephone was alive. Her hand rested on the Killer of Children's bare rib cage, drawing strength from the deep steady breathing. So long as Persephone was with her, Aria had hope. Aside from her pounding headache and the wound in her thigh, she had survived the fall admirably. No snapped bones or sprained limbs—the roc must have broken her fall. Persephone was the one hurting.

Aria looked about, and saw a crystal pitcher of water waiting on a small sewing table. Taking a drink first, she washed her face, careful to keep the water clean for Persephone. Then she washed the wound at the back of Persephone's head, wiping off clotted blood and biting away hanks of hair with her teeth. It was a scalp wound, messy but not down to the bone.

Cleaning it as best she could, Aria finally did cry, softly while she worked, tears falling on Persephone's fine blond hair, and into the wound itself, helping to wash it. She thought about how she had done the same thing for her knight, on the day they first met, and now he was dead. Aria begged Lady Death not to take her little sister. Not yet, at least.

When she had the wound clear, Aria used needle and thread from the table to close it—not perfect, but not likely to fester either. She wished she had the north woods around her, with its vast stock of healing plants and antibiotic herbs.

Heaven knew what was going on inside Persephone's head; she had not stirred, even while Aria was sewing the wound closed. That was worrisome, but only if the Killer of Children did not wake up. For now, Persephone was getting dearly needed sleep.

Having seen to her mistress, Aria examined her own wound, finding a clean gash—already scabbed over, painful, but starting to heal. She mentally thanked the unknown woman who so diligently cleaned and dressed her wound. How many hours had she been out? It hurt her head to try to remember. Settling down, Aria went back to sleep herself.

When she awoke again, the lamp was out and daylight filtered from an air shaft through an ornately carved alabaster screen set high on one wall. Waiting on the bed table was salve for her temples, alcohol to clean their wounds, some cold herb tea, and a stoppered bottle of berry wine, along with sugar wafers and several lemons.

Invisible servants saw to her every need. Outstanding! That meant their captors wanted her and Persephone alive; otherwise, they would be in some filthy cell, awaiting slow dismemberment, not lodged in a plush apartments, rubbing salve on her aching head.

She cleaned Persephone's wound, but even pouring alcohol directly on the stitches did not wake the Killer of Children. Trying not to worry about her sleeping friend, Aria spiked her herb tea with berry wine and set out to explore the premises.

Clean clothes were laid out for them on the sewing table, including the clothes they came in, neatly washed and mended. Aria selected a silk chemise and a crimson robe, with cloth-of-silver flowers on the sleeves. She found they had three rooms, including an upper bedroom, trimmed in blue lapis and gold leaf, with a private tiled bath and a flush toilet, a wonder the Bone Witch had described but that Aria had never seen before. Downstairs she discovered a smaller bedroom and an attached dayroom with a fireplace, two overstuffed divans, the single locked door, and a half dozen songbirds living in silver cages. All the rooms were windowless and lit by white arabesque screens opening onto air shafts and an inner court. By pressing her ear against the screens, Aria could hear children playing.

Each time she came back to check, Sleeping Beauty was still there, cleaned and combed, and breathing softly, her golden hair shining in the lamplight.

Persephone slept through that day and into the next, thoroughly frightening Aria. Eunuchs fed her, slipping silently in at night to tidy up, leaving breakfast and clean linen behind, then coming again at dinner time to slide china bowls and silver filigree trays through a slot on in the single door. Warm bakery smells filled the dayroom at dawn, and each morning Aria heard the rooster crow.

Plush as it was, it was still a prison, walled away from people and sunlight. Every time the slot opened, Aria was there, trying to chat up the eunuch on the other side, keeping it light, since she did not know the language, thanking the fellow immensely for the food, while begging boiling water and more fennel for her tea—which she eventually got.

On the second morning, Persephone's eyes flipped open, taking a puzzled look around at the gold-and-lapis bedchamber; then her lips moved, asking, "Am I dreaming?"

"No," Aria told her, relieved to see the Killer of Children awake, but Persephone had already fallen back to sleep, her soft young face looking totally at peace. Aria went back to sewing, sipping tea, and watching her sleeping friend for signs of life.

Later that day, the blue eyes opened again, and Persephone asked, "Where am I?"

"We are prisoners in harem apartments," Aria replied excitedly, so glad to have Persephone awake again that she sounded far happier than the news warranted. "With caged birds, perfumed beds, and eunuchs you never see."

"What harem? Where?" Persephone glanced about, as though she might somehow recognize the place.

"On Abeskum Island, the harem of Shah Aladdin of Khwarezm."

"However did we get here? Persephone seemed completely puzzled by her surroundings. Slowly Aria coaxed the memories out of her, starting with their success at Hebektahay Castle, followed by their trip to Abeskum.

Persephone was impressed. "Amazing, and I do remember some of it." Tenderly examining her wound, the Killer of Children asked, "Who cleaned and sewed up my head?"

"That would be me," Aria admitted, wishing she had done a better job of stitching.

"Thank you so much." Persephone pulled Aria close, kissing her tenderly. "You are smart and brave, and I am sorry I have gotten you into this horrible place. I am sure I meant well, and must have had some plan ready if things went wrong. Only now I cannot remember what it was. . . ."

Aria said nothing, still recovering from being pressed to Persephone's naked breast and kissed so lovingly. Bad as things were, that was enough to put butterflies in Aria's stomach. She had wanted to be included in Persephone's world, and now that world had shrunk to this three-room harem apartment—until the Turks decided to let them out.

Persephone got up, still holding the back of her head, and prowled about the apartment, testing the walls and floor while working life back into her limbs. Aria saw that despite the fall and concussion, the demigoddess was still in control of her body, flesh and sinew trained since girlhood to be strong, graceful, and enduring. Wrapping herself in a blue robe trimmed with cloth-of-gold, which matched the lapis and gold tiles on the walls, Persephone decided, "We seem to be in the Gilded Cage."

"What is that?" Like Roc Island, the Gilded Cage was another name out of the Bone Witch's tales.

"Deep inside Shah Aladdin's harem there is a windowless walled-off section that no one ever sees," Persephone explained, "surrounding a barred court, called the Gilded Cage—used to hold women and children who need to be kept alive, but cannot be let out. Spare heiresses. Insane heirs. Children of executed enemies. Rich and difficult former wives. Some stay in the Gilded Cage their whole lives, or until menopause makes them safe to release. Or just until they are old enough to publicly execute. Outsiders see only the blank gilded walls of the cage rising above the surrounding harem apartments."

"How do you know about it?" Aria was amazed that Persephone could deduce all this just by examining their apartment.

"Serving women come here, so do eunuchs, and word goes out with them." And Persephone made it her business to know how children were treated. "I must take your word for how we got here, though, since all I clearly remember is seeing Abeskum from the air."

And now they were looking at it from the inside. Beyond their brightly painted walls was the harem proper, ringed by the fortress-palace, which was in turn surrounded by the Tartars. So even their captors were fellow prisoners, under sentence of execution. No wonder she and Persephone were being treated so well. Dinner was dried figs, fresh melon from the harem gardens, rice and beef jerky, washed down with green tea. Not much of a meal for two, but plainly Shah Aladdin did not mean to starve them into submission. Everyone must be on short rations.

When daylight faded, they curled up together on one of the scented beds, talking by lamplight. Aria gushed about how glad she was to have Peresphone awake, and with her, "Though you were an inspiration, even in your sleep."

"Really?" The Killer of Children was not used to such warm praise.

"So long as you were breathing, I did not despair." Aria had lost her parents, then the Bone Witch, followed by her black mare and her knight. Lady Death could at least leave her little sister. "But it is so much better to have you awake."

Persephone cocked an eyebrow, asking, "Whom do you love, me or your knight?"

The Killer of Children never spoke of Sir Roye de Roye as dead. Persephone hated to blame her sister Kore without positive proof. Aria objected, "It is not the same."

"Why?" Persephone demanded archly, enjoying Aria's discomfort. "Am I not desirable? Eros swears I am irresistible."

"He is a man," Aria replied, stubbornly hiding behind decorum. "It is different."

"So you say." The Killer of Children did not sound convinced. "But you like me, at least."

"I do, I do!" Aria meant it with all her being.

Persephone looked askance. "Even though I am the Killer of Children?"

"Because of it," Aria insisted. The good that Persephone did at Hebektahay had overcame all her initial fears.

Persephone put an arm around her, saying, "Do not worry, we will get out of all this. I like you a lot, and we work well together—despite current evidence to the contrary." Persephone did not sound the least worried by their predicament, trapped in a doomed fortress on an island ringed by bloodthirsty Tartars. "You chose me for a reason, though we do not fully know what it is yet. Nor will you always be a maiden under my care—time is the true killer of children."

With that, the demigoddess drifted off to sleep, still holding her close. For a time, Aria lay awake, wrapped in Persephone's arms, going over their problems in her head. None of her answers seemed hopeful, so she too went to sleep.

Only to be awakened by a woman with a lamp, who was standing over her like a white-robed apparition. One moment, Aria was deeply asleep, and the next, she was staring at the first person she had seen since arriving in the Gilded Cage: a dark-eyed woman wearing a half-veil and holding a brass lamp that looked like it belonged to Aladdin. If the woman had rubbed it and produced a genie, Aria could not be more amazed. Instead the woman said something in Persian that clearly meant, "Arise."

Before Aria could figure out what to do, Persephone was awake and answering the Persian woman in her own tongue. Sitting up, the Killer of Children coolly ordered the woman with the light to wait. Closing the bed curtains, she whispered to Aria, "We have visitors. Go invisible."

Which Aria immediately did, watching as Persephone pulled on harem pants and a pretty gold-embroidered jacket with green leaves twining along the sleeves. Then Persephone pulled back the bed curtains and stepped out, leaving them open so Aria could see, and not be seen.

By now, the bedroom was lit with brass lamps and jammed with women, all ringed around an old white-haired grande dame in yellow silk, with crafty eyes and a broad strong face. She looked to be Cuman or Kipchak. Her Highness sat in state on a small stool, attended by slaves, handmaids, and a pair of cute Cathayan manicurists. Standing before the khanum was a pretty blond Markovite teenager in a crimson dress, looking a bit bored. As soon as Persephone stepped out, the Markovite girl spoke up. "My serene mistress the Valide Sultana, Turkan Khatun, Queen Mother of Khwarezm, bids you prostrate yourself."

Persephone merely smiled at the blond girl, asking, "And who are you?"

"Me?" The young Markovite looked taken aback, being happy to speak for the sultana, but not sure she wanted to answer for herself.

"Yes." Persephone nodded encouragingly, to put the translator at ease. "What is your name? And how old are you?"

"Sonya D'Medved." The girl said it like everyone should know that name, then added evenly, "Sixteen, I think."

"Have you any children?" asked Persephone. Sonya did not look much like a virgin.

Sonya smirked, and did not answer.

"I thought not." Persephone's smile widened. "Which makes you still a child. Do you wish to leave here?"

"Who would not?" Sonya scoffed, clearly aware she was under a death sentence.

Her mistress spoke sharply, and Sonya added, "Her Majesty, Turkan Khatun, wants to know why you talk so much and do not prostrate yourself."

Persphone spoke blonde to blonde, saying, "Sorry, Sonya, but I may not. Tell your high and mighty mistress I am Persephone, the Destroyer, Killer of Children. Death's sister bows to no one."

Sonya rolled her eyes, and translated. The Queen Mother listened, then replied in a frosty tone, and Sonya D'Medved asked, "Does that mean you own the sky-ship that broke through the Tartar lines?"

Persephone shrugged. "It obeys me."

Hearing this, the shah's mother replied at length, pausing only to let Sonya translate. Turkhan Khatun began by apologizing: "I am sorry that your roc was killed, but that was done by the Tartars. When you fell among us, I saw that you were lodged and fed, and that your wounds were treated."

Persephone thanked her. "These lodgings are most pleasant."

Turkan Khatun went on, "You must understand that when Inalchiq Khan plundered the Tartar embassy, I told my son to give him to the Tartars. Now we have this tiresome war, and the Tartars have Inalchiq Khan anyway, trapped in a tower in his fortress at Otar, according to his last messenger pigeon. We all seem to be prisoners of the Tartars now, so we have great need of your sky-ship."

Persephone lifted an eyebrow at the translation. "Hopefully not to rescue Inalchiq Khan?"

Aria knew Persephone spoke Persian, and probably Cuman and Kipchak too, and was playing with the Valide Sultana. Turkan Khantun swiftly assured them that she cared not a whit for Inalchiq Khan, saying, "Tartars can skin him and boil him, and he would still not pay for all the harm he has done. We need your ship to escape on. You need take us only as far as Baku, where the King of Georgia will shelter us."

"I have come for children," Persephone explained patiently. "You must appeal to my sister, Lady Death. Or to the Tartars."

"Must I?" Turkan Khatun did not much like the translation. "If the Tartars come over the walls, they will likely slaughter us all."

Persephone refused to give a inch. "Which is why I am taking out the children."

"You are going nowhere," the Queen Mother declared. "Right now, Crown Prince Jal-Aladdin is gathering Kipchaks, Cumans, and Aral Turks to raise the siege, giving us hope of prompt rescue—but if your flying family wants you, they must come to us." With that, the durbar was over. Women rose, and escorted the Valide Sultana out, taking their brass lamps with them, going back into a bigger prison. Aria felt like one of those small dolls set inside a larger one, which was inside another even bigger, and so on. Too bad that outside the last doll was a bloodthirsty horde determined to break in and slaughter them.

Hearing the downstairs door click, Aria reappeared, asking, "Will your family trade for you?"

Persephone smiled mirthlessly. "Her Majesty is a horrible optimist, thinking to hold Death hostage. However much men might fear me, my older sister is ten times worse. I may be the Killer of Children, but Kore is Lady Death herself—if she comes south, it will make the Tartars seem meek."

"Is your sister really so terrible?" Aria had lived half her life with the Bone Witch, but was still impressed.

"Been feeding me snake venom since I was six," Persephone declared proudly. "It is what keeps us close."

"Will your sister come south?" Aria liked the idea of the Dark Daughter coming south to set them free.

Persephone laughed at her concern. "No, there is no need. Eros will come for us." The Killer of Children said it like an accomplished fact. "Turkan Khatun is a fool to think Jal-Aladdin and any number of Kipchaks can get through these Tartars—but Eros will. There are two women here he is interested in, and Eros will be back to get us as soon as he can. You will see."

Next morning, breakfast awaited as usual, and there was no sign of their midnight visitors. Even the eunuchs might not know that Turkan Khatun had been there, since this was the Gilded Cage, and harems kept secrets even from themselves.

To prove it, that noontide the door lock turned unexpectedly. Aria stepped into a corner and whispered her invisibility spell as the apartment's painted door swung open, letting in daylight for the first time.

Aria expected a eunuch, but in came a veiled woman carrying a tea tray. She set it silently on the floor—though this was all strictly forbidden. Closing and locking the door, the woman called out in Markovite, "Greetings, I have brought tea for Lady Persephone."

This had to be Sonya D'Medved, Turkan Khatun's translator. Aria stayed invisible, watching Persephone descend the stairs from the bedroom, asking, "And who are you?"

Sonya offered the Killer of Children some tea, humbly saying, "Merely a slave."

Persephone took the tea, noting, "Even a slave has a story."

There was no need to ask twice. Sonya gladly assumed the center of attention, a valuable trait for a translator. "My father was a half brother to Baron D'Medved, and his lands bordered on the D'Hays'. When our lord allied with Tolstoy's Brovvniks, Baron Valad D'Hay and his Kazakhs sacked our manor. Fortunately, my father was away, but I saw my brother killed and my aunt murdered. I was taken along with the serving girls and milkmaids, to be raped by Kazakhs, and then traded to Cumans for a pair of fine Arab mares. These Cumans presented me to Shah Aladdin, who likes young blondes in his harem."

And now he had yet another. Persephone asked, "How long ago was that?"

"It will be two years in the fall since I have seen my family." Sonya sounded wistful. "The Queen Mother made me learn Cuman to save her from having to learn Markovite; so I translate for the merchants and embassies. Last month, I learned my father died besieging Hebektahay on the Brovva, beheaded by the D'Hays."

"What about your mother?" asked the Killer of Children.

"She died when I was born." Sonya said it casually, but Aria felt the weight of her words. Beautiful, willful Sonya was an orphan just like her.

"Still you wish to go home," Persephone observed.

"Home would be a lot to hope for," Sonya replied ruefully. "I want to get out of here."

As did they all. Everyone in the harem, from Shah Aladdin and the Valide Sultana to the lowest eunuch and slave girl, wanted to somehow escape the place, since death by Tartars awaited whoever stayed.

"That is what we all want." Finishing her tea, Persephone nodded at the door. "Just getting out of these apartments would be a welcome change."

Sonya silently handed Persephone the key to the apartment, then announced, "I must return, before Turkan Khatun discovers I have come here."

Persephone took the key, saying, "Stay here with me. So long as you do, I can offer you protection. I fear what may happen to you when the Tartars come."

"So do I," Sonya admitted, letting her fear show for a moment. "But if Turkan Khatun catches me here, Her Serene Highness will have me tossed over the wall to the Tartars."

"Then come back as soon as you can," Persephone warned, loath to see even a grown child like Sonya get away.

Reluctantly, Sonya D'Medved bade Persephone good-bye, then turned and left, headed for the Golden Door. Aria watched the blond girl vanish, fearing Sonya was another one she would never see again. Thank the fates for giving her to the Bone Witch, and the Killer of Children—not to Kazakhs or Cumans. But sympathy for Sonya did keep Aria from rejoicing in getting out of the apartment and setting out with Persephone to explore the limits of the Gilded Cage.

Afternoon sunlight fell through steel bars covered in gold, splashing onto a fountained court. Aria saw that colonnades ran around the first two stories, letting air and light into the apartments, but the third story was blank white stone, all the way up to the gilt bars. Tucked under the colonnades were baths, kitchens, a bakery, hen coops, milk cows, and the rooster Aria had heard crowing. Women were washing in the fountain, and children played nearby, the children she had heard through the bedroom screen, several happy toddlers, two grave-eyed girls with black hair, and a sickly looking older boy.

Persephone immediately went down on one knee, introducing herself to one of the girls, who came solemnly over, saying in Bulgar, "You are new."

"So we are," the Killer of Children agreed, translating for Aria. "I am Persephone, and this is Aria. Who are you?"

"Khanum Sofia Popoff," the girl replied, then indicated her younger sister, saying, "This is Khanum Maria."

Both turned out to be Bulgar heiresses, with extensive lands on the middle Volga, which are now in the hands of the Cumans. Aria wondered how weird it must be to grow up under a barred sky, with this court and apartments as your whole world, never seeing anything that did not come through the Golden Door. Cumans meant for grown men to remain a total mystery to these two girls, since so long as the sisters were childless, the vast Popoff lands stayed in Cuman hands.

Happy to have two new souls in their world, Khanum Sofia and Khanum Maria introduced the other children, including a little lame Kipchak prince—slated to be strangled if he showed signs of reaching puberty.

Startled to see secret prisoners on the loose, eunuchs hurried over, telling them to return to their apartment. Persephone asked, "Do you know who I am?"

"We know," the chief eunuch spat back, glaring at both of them. "You are godless northern witches, who hate men and can kill with a touch."

"Then keep men out, and there will be no trouble," Persephone replied blandly.

"They are not always easy to keep out," retorted the head eunuch.

"Well, at least try to have them castrated first," Persephone suggested. "This is a harem, for Heaven's sake."

Rolling his eyes, the head eunuch replied, "Your mere being here puts everyone at risk. When Shah Aladdin first took power, he had every inmate in the Gilded Cage strangled—to make a fresh start. Eunuchs had to listen to their cries, and we do not want such terrible times to come again."

Who did? Persephone patiently explained, "I did not mean to be here; that too was the Tartars' doing. They are the ones who mean to kill you, not me. Keep men out of the harem, and I will not have to kill them."

That shut up the eunuchs. Aria and Persephone used their newfound freedom to visit the bathhouse built into one corner of the court, where conduits carried hot water down from the upstairs boiler and rooftop cistern. Entering steamy, perfumed darkness lit by shafts of sunlight coming through slits in the stone, Aria stripped before a hot foamy cascade, sponging away sweat and grime, carefully cleaning the pink flesh growing around the scab on her leg. As she washed, Aria stole glances at Persephone, whose body was so smooth and beautiful, it looked like it had been turned on a lathe. Aria thought of the first time she saw the demigoddess, so cold and dangerous aboard her bird of prey. Never did Aria think she would be so happy with the Killer of Children.

Slowly entering the water, Aria thought of Sonya, wondering if the blond girl could return in time. She asked, "Will Eros truly come?"

Persephone nodded. "Soon as he can. Eros is a wonder when he puts his mind to it. But the Tartars may come first, battering at the Golden Door. We must be ready."

"And what about Sonya—?"

Persephone stopped her lips with a finger, saying, "Shush, here we can be overheard. Talk about something light, like men."

Having been raised in the woods, this was not a subject on which Aria had a lot to say. She asked the Killer of Children, "Do you have much experience with men, I mean in bed?"

Persephone laughed as she splashed herself. "Only if you count Cousin Eros."

"You slept with Eros?" Her afternoon's heavy petting with the love god was clearly nothing special.

"Slept?" Persephone looked puzzled, saying, "Not that I recall, but he did show me several ingenious ways to bring a man to orgasm—the sort of instruction Mother was never any good at. He would have taught you one or two, had I not interrupted."

Aria blushed, embarrassed by her near brush with godhead. Persephone's memory was plainly returning.

"Sorry." The Killer of Children reached over and patted her. "I did not want you starting with Eros."

"Why?" Aria was worried she had done wrong.

"Eros is fun enough," Persephone explained, "but Eros does not count. He would do you out of divine duty. When you first make love to a man, I want it to mean something. Like with your knight."

If she still had her knight. Aria feared she would never find anyone as good as Sir Roye de Roye.

The Killer of Children put an arm around Aria, saying, "You are mine. You gave yourself to me. Like Alexi, you are a child in my care—let's just hope I did not wreck your chance to be with a man."

"I do not mean to stop." Except maybe with Eros, now that she was not on nectar.

"We are in a harem," Persephone pointed out. And besieged by Tartars, which greatly reduced the chances of meeting someone interesting. "You see how hard it is," the Killer of Children complained. "I keep my eyes open, but I never meet the right sort of man. Godhead is no problem for Eros, but it just does not work well for me—though being Lady Death's little sister has one great advantage: any man who lays hands on me must be brave, and in earnest."

"Alexi is in love with you," Aria reminded her.

"Another conquest." Persephone winced. "Why can I not do so well with grown men? Something about me makes men wary."

Too true. Boys might like the bow and attitude, but men saw Persephone as a menace. Their loss, so far as Aria was concerned, but she did not say so.

Lying back in the warm water, Persephone stared into the perfumed mist. "I envy you, and your knight."

"Why?" Their tragic history seemed pretty dismal—one of them slaughtered by Tartars, the other soon to be.

"You have found someone you truly love, and who loves you." Persephone shook her head in wonder. "Very rare, indeed."

"Suppose my knight is dead?" That was her greatest worry, more terrible than the Tartars.

"Then you will find someone new," Persephone assured her.

"How can you be so sure?" Aria felt like she had already lost her chance at true love.

"Do not worry. It is easier than it sounds." Persephone gave her shoulder a wet squeeze. "Harem or not, one day the right man will just be there. There are plenty of determined young men out there, eager to lay hold of you; that is why harems have guards and walls. And when your young man finds out he has a former Sister of Eternal Suffering in his hands, there will be no stopping him. Nothing excites a man more than a pretty young virgin who was supposed to go to God."

Aria hoped so. It was easy for Persephone to be nonchalant about men; even naked and a prisoner, the Killer of Children terrified the Turks, who left their care to women and eunuchs. Whoever took Persephone's bow and bloody clothes had not dared touch her venom rings.

Tartars came within the week, dropping silently out of the sky in the stillness of noon. Aria was in the courtyard with Khanum Sofia and Khanum Maria when swift dark shadows flashed overhead. Looking up, Aria expected to see rocs, but instead saw long high-wing biplane gliders falling from above, headed for the harem gardens. She leaped up and dashed to get Persephone, shouting, "Tartars are inside the walls!"

Persephone did not have to be told twice. Trading her robe for pants and a leather jacket, the Killer of Children went straight to the Golden Door, telling the eunuchs on guard, "Tartars are inside the harem, and we have to bar the door."

"Tartars? How?" Being inside, the eunuchs had seen nothing.

"They are falling out of the sky in big bird-shaped gliders." Aria pointed toward the shadows sweeping across the courtyard. "By now they are in the harem gardens."

Still the fools hesitated. "But we have no orders from the Head of the White Eunuchs."

"It is too late for orders," Persephone told them. "Bar the door, or you will be dead as well as gelded."

Caught between Tartars and the Killer of Children, the eunuchs began piling everything they could against the Golden Door. Men were already banging on the far side, angrily demanding entry—not Tartars, just desperate-sounding Turks. Eunuchs shouted back that they could not admit any intact men, not without written authority from Shah Aladdin.

Having only one door made the Cage into a natural fortress, with its barred courtyard and blank windowless third story rearing above the harem's rooftop gardens. As the pile of furniture against the door grew bigger, Aria thought of Sonya D'Medved, trapped on the far side as Tartars stormed through the harem. Exactly what she feared would happen. Aria silently asked the Bone Witch to watch over the blond D'Medved.

Someone pulled on her harem pants, and Aria glanced down to see Khanum Sofia looking up at her, saying something in excited Cuman. When she asked Persephone what the girl was saying, the Killer of Children replied, "She says there is a birdman in the courtyard."

Worried that Tartars might already be entering the Gilded Cage, they ran back to the courtyard and looked up at the barred sky. Eros was there, striding about atop their cage, wearing a light tunic and kilt, and hung like a demigod, his golden crossbow slung across his back. Aria gave a whoop of joy. *Selene* had arrived.

Eros had alighted on rocback onto the bars of the Gilded Cage, then dismounted to attach a grapple to the cage, letting *Selene* reel herself in. Children shouted and pointed as Eros unslung a silver moon bow and quiver, lowering them down three stories to Persephone, who seized them eagerly.

Fully armed again, the Killer of Children told Aria, "Collect all the children. I must see to the Golden Door." Persephone dashed off, while Aria did a swift head count, finding all the children were already together, gawking as crewmen swarmed down the sky-ship's grapple line, attacking the gilded bars with hardened steel saws.

Aria ran to tell Persephone the children were ready, and she found that the Turks on the far side had been replaced by Tartars, who were even more determined to get in. Tartars knew all about bringing down fortresses, and Aria heard the creak of wheels, followed by a bang that sent chairs and boxes flying off the barricade. They had somehow wheeled a battering ram into the harem, aiming to beat in the Golden Door.

Terrified by Tartar efficiency, Aria returned to the courtyard, shooing children to safety as the first gilded bar came crashing down. It was a race now—between the battering ram at the Golden Door and the crewmen cutting into the cage.

Even with only one bar down, the gap was wide enough for a child, and Alexi came sliding down on a sling. Eros had kept Persephone's promise to treat him like a regular boy—as D'Hay heir, he would never have gone down the line and into danger. Alexi reveled in it, helping load the smaller children one by one into the sling for the return trip.

Seeing she could leave the loading to others, Aria went to tell Persephone, "One bar is down, and Eros is lifting out the children."

"Good," Persephone told her, "because the Golden Door is coming down." As she said it, the barricade gave a great heave, and half of it tumbled aside. Another booming crash, and gilded splinters shot across the room. Eunuchs howled in anguish, knowing the Tartars were coming through.

Another bang, and Aria saw the Golden Door disintegrate in a cloud of splinters. Suddenly she could see into the chamber of beyond, where axmen chopped at what was left of the barricade, backed by archers and a noyan in scale armor. Behind them loomed the huge battering ram, tipped with a giant steel fist. Arrows zipped through the gap, scattering the horrified eunuchs.

Spinning about, the Killer of Children grabbed Aria by the collar, dragging her back into the courtyard, closing and locking the door behind them. And the door to the baths as well—though in minutes Tartars would break down the doors, or get in through the galleries. All the children were gone except for Alexi D'Hay—but the gap above was too small for anyone else. Aria and Persephone were still locked in the Gilded Cage.

Axmen beat at the doors as Aria looped the sling around Alexi and saw him hoisted aloft. Exceedingly proud to be the last boy out of the Cage, Alexi called down to her, "I will tell Eros to hurry."

No need. As Alexi went up, the second bar down came down, nearly braining him on the way. Now they could get through, but the sling was around Alexi's waist, and they had to wait for him to be hoisted up, and the line to come back down, all the time listening to axes beating on shattering wood.

When the sling came back, Persephone told Aria to put it on. Aria protested, but Persephone insisted, forcing it around her.

As they argued, the bathhouse door flew off its hinges, and Tartars burst into the courtyard. There would be no return trip. This was the last slingload out, and Peresphone meant to make sure her charge got away. Aria was equally determined, locking her arms around Persephone, then shouting, "Hold on!"

As she did, the sling suddenly took off, easily lifting both of them. Looking down, Aria saw shocked greasy faces staring openmouthed back at her. Archers raised their bows to fire, at a range where no Tartar could miss.

Without warning, water came cascading down in their faces, blinding the bowmen and spoiling their arrows. Eros had released the grapple lines and dumped *Selene*'s water ballast, making the sky-ship shoot upward, dragging the sling up with it.

In seconds, Aria was lifted up out of the Gilded Cage, like she was on a line headed straight to Heaven, seeing the harem's rooftop gardens recede beneath her. Even the big Cathayan balloon tethered to the highest point in the harem rapidly fell away below. Soon she could see all Abeskum Island—with its green-topped harem, blue harbor, and surrounding Tartar barges—all dwindling to doll-size below her. Sonya D'Medved was down there somewhere.

Slowly the sky-ship's windlass reeled them up; then Eros and the mews boys hauled her aboard. Aria found herself standing on *Selene*'s narrow deck, with Persephone beside her, while the sky-ship floated effortlessly at her pressure height. They were safe, and free. Moments before, she had thought escape was totally impossible; now she could start living again.

Children looked down from the quarterdeck rail, watching their prison-home drift away. Looking them over, Aria guessed that Alexi's days as an ordinary boy were numbered—but if he lived to be Lord D'Hay, hopefully his stay with the Killer of Children would not be forgotten. Seeing the children clustered together on the foredeck, ecstatic to be free and flying magically through the air, Aria found they seemed strangely small to her, so fragile and different—yet short years ago she had been so solidly one of them. Teetering on the edge of adulthood herself, Aria remembered Persephone's warning, that time was the true killer of children. Behind her, black smoke billowed upward from the fortress-palace.

10

the baron and the boyarinya

"Ready to die, round-eyes?" asked a smiling Tartar with stained teeth. By now, Baron Sir Roye de Roye understood enough Tartar to know he had been insulted, but he gave the man his best dumb barbarian grin. Tartars liked you to go happy into battle, greeting death with a grin; otherwise, why even go to war?

Sir Roye de Roye was sitting in full armor in the nose of a silk-and-bamboo Cathayan glider, hugging his mailed knees and hoping he did not go headfirst into the Inland Sea. He thought about Hannah back at Chepe's camp, and her tearful good-bye, begging him to come back safe. Which he absolutely intended to do, no matter what a woman might think.

Without warning, the deck fell away beneath him. His stomach heaved as they dropped free of the balloon holding the glider aloft. There were no windows, no way to look out, but Baron de Roye could clearly picture what was happening. The ultralight high-wing gliders were borne aloft by hot air balloons, and released upwind of the island. Right now they were gliding toward a landing in the harem gardens. Abeskum Island's fortress-palace was designed to defend in every direction, except above—the topmost section of the palace, and the highest point on the island, was given over to the harem's hanging gardens, where Shah Aladdin's women could lounge in the shade of fruit trees, safe from impious eyes.

But from where Sir Roye sat, staring at the silk nose of the glider, he could just as easily be aimed at the harbor, or at some unforgiving stone wall. Even if they made the harem gardens, there were trees to slam into and the huge blank third floor of the Gilded Cage. He could feel the wings bite the air, slowing their fall. Otherwise, Sir Roye had no feeling of movement—though he knew they were hurtling downwind, headed for a barely controlled crash.

Grinning Tartars in leather and iron patted his armored back. "See, round-eyes. Being white-faced does not make you a coward."

Sir Roye cheerfully gave his comrades the armored finger. Tartars did not care for foolhardy courage: witness their willingness to let him lead the charge. Sir Roye had the armor, so he should go first. Tartars fought to win, not to impress the enemy with suicidal heroics.

Baron de Roye had scant use for heroics himself, but he hated fighting people he did not even know. Tartars might despise the Turks for massacring their embassy, but Shah Aladdin of Khwarezm had done nothing to Sir Roye. As the Tartars saw it, they were totally in the right. Muslims had massacred a peaceful embassy, killing merchants and diplomats, along with some number of Tartar spies. But being in the right did not make the Tartars any less terrible—if anything, it made them more insanely ferocious, coldly determined to grind their foes to dust.

With a horrible crunch and a sickening lurch, the glider hit, slamming Sir Roye's teeth together. They were down, careening blindly along the ground, bursting through the shrubbery and bouncing over stone benches. Expecting the glider to fly apart, he held tight to a bamboo support, thinking of Aria.

An odd choice in such a desperate moment, since the girl had to be a thousand miles away by now—but it was to protect her that he had given himself to the Tartars. At terrible moments like this, it was good to remember that he was doing it all for Aria. She at least would live, no matter what happened to him.

Just as suddenly, the glider came to a crashing halt against a pear tree, throwing the Tartars into a heap. One began screaming in horror, stabbed by his own scimitar, making Sir Roye doubly happy to be in armor. Pulling himself out of the pile, he ignored the exit doors, which were jammed with Tartars, taking a swing at the silk wall with his Lucerne hammer.

His hammer's three-pronged saw blade sheared through silk and bamboo, and Sir Roye stepped out onto a garden path, scattering startled peacocks. A wide-eyed gazelle with gilded antlers took one look at him and bounded off.

Lifting up his visor to peer around, he saw another glider come crashing down the path he was on, breaking off treetops and raining leaves on him as it tore overhead, already spilling Tartars out of its split bottom. One unfortunate nomad landed a dozen feet in front of him. More gliders were coming behind that one, making this broad pebbled path no place to be.

Hefting his hammer, Sir Roye dodged frantically between fruit trees and flowered thickets, trying not to get crushed by the Tartar onslaught. Spotting steps leading to a sunken court, he dashed down them, holding his visor up with one hand so he could see where he put his feet. His last glimpse of the landing was seeing a Tartar glider slam into the gold-plated upper floor of the Gilded Cage.

At the bottom of the steps was a crystal pool full of darting silver fish, fed by a fountain and crossed by a wooden footbridge. On the far side of the bridge, Sir Roye was in another world, cool harem apartments shaded by hanging gardens. Male imagination could not help filling out the scene with scantily clad inmates.

Alas, no one was frolicking today, so he went in search of a passageway leading down into the fortress proper. Sir Roye de Roye felt silly striding hammer in hand through perfumed rooms filled with overstuffed pillows and caged songbirds. What was he afraid of? An enraged lapdog? Eunuchs armed with ostrich fans? This airborne surprise attack had already killed and maimed a fair number of Tartars, without meeting any opposition.

As he thought that, a full-grown tiger wearing a ruby collar burst out of the bedroom ahead of him, gave an angry growl, and bounded past him. Sir Roye was so shocked, he dropped his pole arm. Fortunately, the frightened tiger did not give him a second glance. Feeling even more silly, Sir Roye picked up his Lucerne hammer and went on.

All silliness vanished as soon as he saw the first body: a half-dressed young woman with skin the color of a fawn's and wide staring eyes. From the way her clothes were torn, he could tell she had been raped before her throat was slashed. Her small tawny feet had neat blue nail polish that exactly matched her blood-spattered gown. A nude body lay across the corridor, crumpled in a doorway, killed while trying to escape. Doves cooed in horrified distress.

Sickened, Sir Roye turned and retreated to the sunlit courtyard, and threw up into the crystal pool. Clearly the Tartars were turning the surprise assault into a massacre. For all he knew, they meant to kill everyone in the fortress-palace, just to teach the Turks a lesson—though most of these women must be Persian and Cathayan. Turks were not likely to let their own women lounge about in a harem, serving just one man.

He heard screams, and the slap of bare feet on marble. Several women ran past, one unveiled and wide-eyed with fear. Seeing his sawtooth blade, they shrieked in terror and fled down the courtyard colonnade, desperate to escape him.

Not the response a footloose French baron hoped for, but he could hardly blame them. Sir Roye also meant to get out of the harem *immediatement*. He would rather fight a fortress full of Turks than stand around and watch women being hunted down and murdered. More veiled women ran past, followed by an equally frightened monkey. Sir Roye very much wished to help them somehow, but he could not even speak their language, and they wanted nothing to do with him.

He started down an open white stairway that seemed to lead to the fortress proper, only to have a veiled woman come bounding up the steps, almost running into him. Confronted by an armored knight holding a huge sawtooth hammer, she came to a dead stop atop the stairs, shrieking, "Holy shit!"

Unable to believe his ears, Sir Roye grabbed the veiled woman's arm to keep her from disappearing down the stairs, asking her in Markovite, "Did you say *shit?*"

More Markovite came from beneath the veil. "Please forgive me, good sir. I did not mean to swear."

Without letting go of her silken arm, Sir Roye grounded his hammer and gently lifted her veil. Scared blue eyes were looking back at him. She was a blond teenager with trembling lips and tearstained mascara—somehow not the face he expected to find under a harem veil. He asked, "Who are you?"

"Sonya D'Medved," she replied politely, glad to see him put aside his pole arm, figuring she did not face immediate execution for profanity. "And you are?"

"Sir Roye de Roye, at your service," he answered automatically, acutely aware how absurd it sounded.

Two out-of-breath Tartars came racing up the stairs, crestfallen to see their prize already in the hands of a well-armed barbarian. As they turned back to the hunt, one called out in Tartar, "Be sure to kill her when you are through, Noyan's orders."

"Of course," Sir Roye called back, trying not to alarm the poor doomed girl.

Sonya asked suspiciously, "What did they say?"

"You really and truly do not wish to know." Sir Roye was scared, more than the girl in some ways, who obviously thought she had gained a protector. Showing how little she knew the Tartars.

Grimly, Sir Roye led Sonya back across the footbridge and up onto the rooftop gardens, which were now in a shambles, with trees pruned and fountains toppled by multiple glider landings. Bodies were strewn about, and fires had broken out, blowing smoke across the shattered gardenscape. Peacocks and pet monkeys cowered in the rubble.

He found his jagun commander alongside the remains of the lead glider. Commander Kado had broken a leg in the landing, which put him in an excellent mood, since he had served his khan, captured the fortress, and sustained a wound, without the indignity of having to fight on foot, something every horse nomad dreaded. Ushering Sonya forward, Sir Roye put on his most brainless barbarian smile, happily announcing in broken Tartar, "This is my pick of the loot."

Commander Kado laughed courteously at the big dumb Frenchman who clearly thought with his cock, saying, "Alas, all women in the harem are to be killed."

"Really?" Sir Roye could barely comprehend such an atrocity.

Kado shook his head sadly, obviously sorry to see a girl as pretty as Sonya going to waste. "Khan's orders."

"Let the noyan judge," Sir Roye demanded, since his silver plaque was equal to Kado's—only gold could overrule them. He hoped at least to gain some time, but it turned out that Chepe the Arrow was already on the scene, having landed by sky-boat right behind the gliders. With Sir Roye and Sonya looking on, Commander Kado courteously made his case to the noyan, saying, this brainless barbarian was insisting on having this woman despite the khan's clear orders.

Chepe agreed, "All the shah's women must die, lest they carry his seed." Under Turkish law, any son of Shah Aladdin could inherit his mantle, and the Tartars were taking no chances. "Besides, you already have a blonde in your yurt."

Sir Roye admitted that was so, sounding greedy even for a Frenchman.

"Fine," his noyan declared. "One is enough. Rape this one, and kill her. Then return to the blonde you have. If you cannot bring yourself to kill her, ask another to do it."

Of course. How stupid of him not to see such an obvious solution. Giving his best dumb smile, Sir Roye retreated from the audience, leading Sonya back the way they had come.

Sensing something wrong, Sonya asked, "What is happening?"

"Horrible things," he assured her, knowing that he would do her no favors by lying. "They say you must die."

"Are you sure?" Sonya did not look convinced. Everyone had been so friendly, and as a talented translator, she could not believe she had just heard her death sentence. "You do not seem to know the language that well. Have you studied it long?"

Long enough. He thought of Hannah and Aria, and all the other patient, willing young women who diligently tended wounds and learned the enemy's language, striving mightily to do as they were told. Must one be French to know it was wrong to kill them at whim? "Do not take it personally," Sir Roye told her. "All the Shah's women must die."

Sonya's steps did not falter; instead, the blond teenager looked seriously over at him, asking, "Do you mean to kill me?"

"No." Killing Sonya would solve his problems neatly, yet Baron Roye de Roye could not bring himself to do it—a serious mistake for which he would soon be punished. *C'est la vie.*

"So you mean to save me?" Sonya asked hopefully, wanting a firm commitment on this important point.

"I doubt if I can save myself," Sir Roye admitted, not wanting to get the doomed girl's hopes up.

"Then come!" Sonya commanded, suddenly all brisk business, lifting her skirts and dragging him along, though he was the one holding her.

With no notion how to get away, Sir Roye let Sonya lead him through the horrid harem gardens to a little door half-hidden by vines. She tried the lock, then stepped back, saying, "This door leads to the quarters of the White Eunuchs and the Khanum's tower."

Heaven knew what that meant, but Baron de Roye did not bother to ask. Using his Lucerne hammer as a lockpick, he brought it down in an overhand blow that shattered the brass bolt and splintered the door. His steel boot finished the job, and they were in, dodging through dark, deserted corridors and musk-scented bedrooms, until they emerged in a flowered court at the highest part of the harem.

Sir Roye saw the Gilded Cage rearing overhead, and next to it the tall, slender Khanum's tower. As he watched, an ivory sky-ship took off from atop the Gilded Cage, dropping white plumes of water ballast. Someone else was eager to leave Abeskum Island, and doing a far better job than he.

"Over there." Sonya pointed across the court to a door at the base of the Khanum's tower, thicker and stronger than the last. Sir Roye went to work with his Lucerne hammer, sending wood chips flying across the courtyard.

And attracting attention. Sonya screamed as a Tartar stuck his head out of the eunuch's quarters, curious at the commotion.

With no time to answer questions, Sir Roye took a swing at the fellow, and the startled Tartar jerked his head back. Sir Roye kicked the door shut, and Sonya slid the bar in place, but from the far side came the shrill wail of a Tartar bone whistle, calling for reinforcements.

Damning Tartar efficency, Sir Roye returned to hewing frantically at the tower door. Between blows, he heard Tartars hacking at the door behind him, making Sir Roye redouble his efforts. Finally his triple-pointed hammer smashed through the tower door, and Sonya reached inside, lifting the latch. At the same moment, the door to eunuch's quarters flew open, and Tartars spilled into the courtyard.

Sir Roye shoved Sonya into the Khanum's tower, keeping his armored body between her and the Tartar bows. As Sonya slammed the half-shattered door shut behind them, she pointed to the curving tower stairs, shouting, "Up!"

Stair climbing is the second hardest thing to do in armor, but Sir Roye threw everything into it, hauling himself up after Sonya. Behind him, Tartars burst through the broken tower door. Hearing that, he took the steps two at a time, trying to keep the curving stone between him and the Tartar bows. At the top of the stairs, Sonya held the door open for him, smiling encouragement.

He dived through, followed closely by a Tartar arrow, and then another. Sonya slammed the door shut, shooting home the bolt. Two more arrows thudded into the door, their points poking through the wood. It would take the Tartars another minute or two to get through the door.

Gasping for breath, Sir Roye glanced about, finding himself in a small room almost filled by a huge cable winch, whose thick cable disappeared up into a hole in the ceiling. Hanging from the cable was a wicker basket that could be reached by a rope ladder. Looking up through the hole and seeing only sunlight, he asked Sonya, "Where does that cable go?"

"To freedom," the excited blonde replied. "Can you climb the ladder?"

Quite a rope trick, but Sir Roye was not about to go back. Slinging the Lucerne hammer over his back, he planted his mailed foot on the rope ladder, hoping it would hold his armored weight.

"Up!" Sonya shouted, giving him a shove, then turning to the winch. Kneeling down, she jerked a release lever, freeing the cable. As she did, the door disintegrated, and Tartars burst into the room.

At the top of the ladder, Sir Roye heaved himself up into the big wicker basket just as the cable leaped upward, dragging him and the basket through the hole in the tower ceiling. He lay in the basket, looking up, while the winch whirled away below, playing out cable. Above him, he could see the giant Cathayan balloon, with its two-story pavilion hanging beneath. That was where the cable led, and as soon as the winch was released, the balloon carried cable and basket away downwind.

All Sir Roye could think about was Sonya. What had happened to her when she released the cable? He jumped up, tore off his helmet, and looked back down the cable at the rapidly receding Khanum's tower. The balloon was in free flight, rising toward pressure height, trailing its cable. Dangling from the last rungs of the ladder was Sonya D'Medved.

Sir Roye thanked Mary and all the saints—the girl was safe, hanging grimly to the last bit of rope ladder. Reaching down, he grabbed the lowest rung he could and started hauling the ladder into the basket.

Sonya came with it, tumbling into his lap. They lay together in the bottom of the basket, with Sonya clutching his armored body, sobbing quietly.

He stripped off his mailed gloves and stroked her golden hair, saying, "Do not cry. You are safe. You are free."

For the moment. Wiping tears from her blue eyes, Sonya stared at him, her soft cheeks streaked and stained, and her gold hair in frantic disarray, a wild child-woman who had plucked them both from the very teeth of the Tartars. Sir Roye thought of Hannah, waiting in Chepe's camp. He had truly meant to return to her, whole and happy, but the only way he could have done that was to kill the girl clinging to him, something he could never do. "Are we free?" Sonya whispered. "Really free?"

He nodded. Relatively, anyway. Heaven knows what fate had in store, but right now they were free to do what they willed—so long as they did not leave the balloon basket. "For a while, at least. When you have been through all the defeats I have, you learn not to cry over the latest disaster."

"I cannot help crying," Sonya confessed. "It does not mean I am not happy." To prove it, Sonya kissed him, tenderly at first, thanking him for her rescue, then swiftly turning the thank-you into a full-out harem-trained kiss—a sly tease and flutter, sure to delight the most discriminating French knight.

Startled to have the teenager he was comforting suddenly kissing like a courtesan, Sir Roye responded as best he could, his hand coming easily to rest on her rump, feeling the curve of her flesh through the silk. When their tongues untwined, Sonya looked him in the eye, asking solemnly, "Do you love me?"

"Mademoiselle, we have just met," Sir Roye protested. "We barely know each other."

Sonya reached around to press his hand harder against her rear. "We seem rather familiar already."

"I certainly find you appealing," Sir Roye admitted. What knight-errant would not? Besides, he was still in shock. Their chance meeting on the stairs had not only freed them both from the Tartars, but it had also sent him careening off in a totally new direction, with Sonya D'Medved as his traveling companion. Grabbing her rear had been purely reflexive, part of the kiss, though her rump felt very nice in his hand, round and firm, and pressing eagerly back against his fingers. "I risked my life to see you safe. Does that count?"

"That must do." Sonya D'Medved kissed him again, more hungrily than before, turning from courtesan to tigress. Her first kiss was a harem thank-you for saving her life, with frills that shocked a Frenchman. This kiss came from her heart, from an upcountry boyar's daughter, without a speck of education, except what she could glean from stud horses and stable boys, whose main religious instruction was being told all her life that she was a wanton, sinful vessel that must be filled by a man. Before entering the Shah's harem, the closest Sonya D'Medved had come to a formal date was being gang-raped on the open steppe by drunken Kazakhs.

Despite misgivings, Sir Roye kissed back. Sonya was brave and lovely, and in these circumstances, it was impossible for a French gentleman to do any less—though making love is the hardest thing to do in armor. Except perhaps for swimming.

When Sonya's kiss subsided, Sir Roye told her, "You are an amazingly willful young woman."

Sonya laughed. "That comes from always getting my way, ever since I was a little girl."

"You were a slave when we met," Sir Roye reminded her, doubting that harem life had gone all Sonya's way.

"Not anymore." Sonya shook her head in ecstasy, whipping blond hair all about. Clearly she meant to make the absolute most of her new freedom. "My great uncle is Lord D'Medved, and my last lover was Shah Aladdin of Khwarezm. And now you are my knight."

"Is that so?" He began to feel like he had let a genie out of her bottle—and was now her slave.

Sonya arched an eyebrow, asking, "What choice do you have?"

"Not much," he admitted. "Are you not at all afraid of me?" He was the one in armor, with a big nasty poleax in easy reach.

"When you have been savaged by Kazakhs and marked for death by Tartars, you do not have much left to fear." Sonya rolled over and sat up, resting her back against the wicker basket, and laying her shapely legs across his armored chest, casually claiming possession of her new champion—without a thought for who might have come before her. After all, she had made love to the Shah, and lived to tell, when so many others had not. "I am not afraid of any man unwilling to slit my throat."

"There are other ways of making you behave," Sir Roye warned, lest Sonya thought she could get away with anything.

Sonya scoffed. "What do you mean? Whip me? They tired of that at home."

With small sign of success. "Whipping seems a bit harsh. Perhaps a stern spanking. There must be something you fear."

Laughing, Sonya produced a knife from inside her robe, the type of slim sharp blade that killed through armor. Where it had been hidden, he had no idea. That is what you get for being a gentleman, for if he had felt her up more thoroughly, this would not have been such a surprise. She offered the knife to him, hilt first, at the same time raising her head, proudly baring her white throat. "Here's the knife I was saving for any Tartar who tried to rape me."

This should teach him not to tongue-wrestle with strange blondes. "Pray put the blade away," Sir Roye begged. "We can still be friends."

She shook her head sharply. "Friends is not enough. We are alone among enemies, and there can be no lies or evasions between us. The least bit of mistrust will kill us both. If we are not as one, you might as well kill me now."

What in the world would he do with her? Sir Roye sighed, saying, "Mademoiselle, I vow to protect you as best I am able." There was no lie or evasion about that.

"I know." Sonya primly put the knife back in its hidden sheath. "That is why you are my knight."

Sir Roye stared up at her in amazement, not sure what to say. Markovites always claimed their women must be kept under lock and key for safety—now he began to see why. He had assumed Aria's wildness came from being raised by a witch in the woods. Sonya D'Medved was raised by a boyar family, with serfs to nurse and serve her, and priests to pray over her. So far as Sir Roye could see, that had only made Sonya more sure of her desires.

"Do not take it so badly." Concerned for her new champion, Sonya leaned down and gave him a swift kiss, then added cheerfully, "If you must, you may beat me."

"Beat you?" That was the last thing he thought Sonya might suggest.

"But only with a strap, and only when I do something really dangerous or impertinent," Sonya warned, not wanting to be hit without reason.

Everything about Sonya was incredibly dangerous and impertinent; still, Sir Roye tried to be civilized. "Never fear, Mademoiselle, I will not need to beat you."

"Yes, you will," Sonya replied confidently, knowing herself far better than he.

"Knights do not hit women," Sir Roye de Roye explained, no matter how richly the damsel in distress deserved it.

Sonya looked shocked at such a senseless and unnatural suggestion. "You are protecting my body, and that makes it yours. How else will you ever command me?"

"I do not want to command you." Just escaping together intact would do nicely.

"You will." Sonya gave him another confident kiss, then added, "All men do. But I really do not mind, not with you."

"And only me?" How could he not feel flattered?

"Absolutely." Sonya D'Medved smiled down at him, saying, "We escaped because we trusted each other—if we did not, we would be dead. You are the first man I have trusted since Kazakhs seized me and sold me to the Cumans. Every single man since then, from Kazakhs to Tartars, to the Shah of Khwarezm, has been either brutal or indifferent to me—though I did them no harm, except for being overly slow to spread my legs."

"I am sorry to hear we have behaved so badly." Sir Roye really meant it. Sometimes his sex seemed awfully unfair.

Sonya snorted in contempt. "Even eunuchs treated me better."

He tried to apologize again, but she stopped his lips with a finger, saying, "All that changed when I ran into you on the harem stairs. You risked everything to save me, and asked nothing. I refuse to lose that bond between us, even if it means making love with you, and enduring a beating or two."

This blanket indictment of male brutality, wrapped in a ringing plea for love, trust, and corporal punishment, took Baron Roye de Roye totally aback. What an amazing creature!

"So, do you want to make love with me now?" Sonya asked, making no attempt to be seductive, just polite.

"Perhaps we could wait awhile." It had been a difficult day. Though he certainly deserved reward for his services, Sir Roye could not recall what the Code of Chivalry said about knife-wielding young blondes who begged for abuse.

"When you are ready, tell me." Sonya was not about to let him off. Currently she was in debt to him, and she wanted him in debt to her.

"*Absolument.*" Any other answer would have brought out the knife, but he knew that making love to this wayward boyarinya meant a serious commitment to a beautiful crazed young woman. Sonya already considered it done, aside from the physical act.

Sonya shifted her legs so he could get up, saying, "Then we should see who else is with us."

"Whom do you mean?" Until that moment, he had thought they were totally alone.

Sonya pointed up the balloon cable to where the wooden bottom to the little pavilion floated just beneath the balloon's big gas bag. Having been looking at Sonya the whole time, Sir Roye had barely noticed the balloon overhead, and totally forgotten the little pavilion. "How do you know there is anyone up there?"

His companion laughed. "During a Tartar attack? This was the only sure escape. That is why the tower door was bolted, to keep half the harem from crowding aboard this balloon."

Getting to his feet, Sir Roye stripped off his greaves and breastplate, leaving on his mail coat and hose, which would not hamper him much, unless he fell into the sea. He also left behind his Lucerne hammer, figuring his sword and

Sonya's knife ought to be enough for a casual call on fellow travelers. Sonya led the way up the rope ladder, giving Sir Roye a good look at her strong graceful legs.

Blue skies and blue sea seemed to stretch to infinity, and the only land in sight was the rumpled green hills of Hyrcania on the Persian shore of the Inland Sea. Close ahead of them was a white sky-ship under full sail, borne in the same direction as them by the light winds aloft. More escapees from Abeskum Island. Though he had no idea who was aboard the fleeing sky-ship, he wished them luck.

Halfway up the ladder, Sonya stopped to admire the sky-ship sailing ahead of them, saying, "That belongs to a demigoddess, the Killer of Children."

"What a grisly name for such a beautiful ship." Sir Roye could see children waving to them from the quarterdeck, watched over by a tall blonde with a silver bow. Then the sky-ship dropped a white plume of water ballast, pulling up and away from them, using its rising acceleration to turn southward, angling toward the Persian shore.

"She is not so bad," Sonya declared, watching the *Selene* slide off to the south. "I had tea with her once in the Golden Cage—it is good to see she got away." Tea with the Killer of Children? Sonya made harem life sound wilder than even Frenchmen imagined. Upwind was Abeskum Island, greatly obscured by smoke, as the whole fortress-palace seemed to be in flames.

They set out again, climbing the rope ladder. When Sonya reached the top, she rapped on the wooden pavilion bottom, and a trap opened. Women's arms reached down, drawing her up. Taking one last dizzying look down at the wave-tops below, Sir Roye climbed the final rungs and scrambled through the trap.

He was instantly back in a harem, surrounded by surprised women who were staring at him in various degrees of alarm. Sailing along, thousands of feet above the Inland Sea, the last thing they expected was for a man to suddenly pop out of the floor, wearing chain mail, with a broadsword slung across his back—like Richard the Lionhearted invading a sleepover. Worse, really, since Richard Lion Heart was notoriously gay, and would only have violated a harem to get makeup tips. Once again, Sir Roye did not speak the language. The only oriental tongue he knew was Tartar, which was hardly likely to calm these women.

Sonya did an immediate salaam before a tall lovely woman in her twenties wearing a yellow damask robe and henna on her hands, eyelids, hair, and nails.

She said, "This is Lady Fatima, the Kalfa, which means 'house mistress.' Please flatter her, or she will make everyone miserable."

He did an awkward armored salaam, saying, "Sir Roye de Roye, Chevalier de l'Étoile, *et le* Baron de Roye. At your service."

Lady Fatima was unimpressed, asking Sonya a couple of quick questions in Cuman, to which Sonya had ready answers that seemed to satisfy the Kalfa. Fatima made a short speech in Persian that put the women at ease. Sonya whispered in Markovite, "Fatima is happy. She did not like that you are armed, and obviously an infidel. But when I told her you were an eunuch—"

"Eunuch?" Is that what she thought of his kisses?

"Only because you are beardless." Sonya hurried to mend his hurt masculinity. "They assume that you are gelded. Which is much better, believe me."

"Why so?" Seeing the women's attitude go from alarm to nonchalance made him miss the original commotion.

"This is a harem, silly." Sonya snickered at his astounding naïveté. "If you are known as a man, it will bring trouble, and no women will come near you. If you are known as a eunuch . . ."

Anything was possible. All harems had their secrets, so how nice to know that this one's special surprise was his intact male organ, which might discreetly enjoy his stay. He bowed to Sonya's ingenuity. "I see my lady's point."

Sonya solemnly accepted his homage, saying, "I have told them you are a Western barbarian, trained as a lady's bodyguard, and they are very glad, having no other protection. Try not to openly abuse your position. This lower room is for the odalisques." Sonya indicated the half-dozen young women lounging on cushions and window seats. "These slave girls are the cream of the harem—the poets, musicians, and dancing girls most favored by Turkan Khatun."

"The Shah's mother?" Noyan Chepe had been eager to lay hands on her.

Sonya nodded. "Above us is the Valide Sultana's chamber, the most private part of the harem, where you do not go without me. Worry not—there is far more fun to be found down here."

Obviously. These young women were selected for their talent, beauty, and ability to entertain, and Sir Roye would not have exchanged their company for twenty sultanas. Sonya introduced him to Yasmi, a Persian poetess, and Zoe, a blond mandolin player from the Holy Land. Both of them were overjoyed to see Sonya, who was a lowly barbarian translator and had not rated a place in the sultana's pavilion. When they saw the harem burning, they assumed Sonya was ashes. Now they hugged and kissed her, calling Sonya "Roxelana."

"It is their name for me," Sonya explained. "In a harem, you always get a new name. I am the only Markovite, so I am Roxelana, which means 'the Russian.'"

"The Russ" was what people living along the Great Mother River called the restless fair-skinned Western strangers that came pushing eastward with their log houses, mail armor, and ringing axes—casually lumping Swedes, Danes, Kievans, and Markovites together, calling them "the Russians." Just like Markovites calling all Westerners "Germans."

Bad as it was to be thought a eunuch, at least no one mistook him for German. In fact, Sonya's friends immediately began asking Sir Roye about the world outside the harem walls, assuming that even half a man knew more about the outside than they did. "Where are we? And where we are headed?"

They knew they were over the Inland Sea, but that was all. He told them that the line of green hills to the south was Persia. "Hyrcania, actually. I talked to Tartar scouts who had gotten as far as the gates of Qazvin."

Yasmi and the other Persians got up to gaze at their homeland, gratefully praising Allah for delivering them from the infidels and letting them see his green lands again. Sonya translated her friends' joy, saying, "They cannot believe how green and lovely it looks."

"That was because they could not see the mosquitoes." Tartar scouts told him that the Hyrcanian jungles were a green hell during the summer. Tartars, who feared no human foes, had an absolute dread of malaria and typhus.

Unhealthy or not, Persia was home to most of them, and the women begged Allah for a north wind to blow them to this green shore. These Persians were Shi'a, who considered the Sunni Turks only a cut above the Tartars. According to Shi'ite belief, they were the true descendants of Muhammad through his daughter Fatima—a claim that so enraged the Sunnis that they periodically massacred and enslaved the Shi'a, just to show who were the true sons of the Prophet.

No wind came, and until Allah acted, all they could do was stay aloft, hoping to be blown to safety, while the impious pagan sky-ship used her superior mobility to tack southward across the Persian shore, leaving them steadily behind.

Sunset prayer found them drifting along in sight of shore, which got slowly closer as the coastline curved northward. Seeing the women washing out of a bucket as they prepared for prayer was not what Sir Roye imagined when he pictured a harem bath, though it was more touching. Frenchmen were firm believers in a Sunday Mass and a Sunday bath, while these women washed and thanked God several times a day.

After a simple supper, curtains went up for the night, and Sonya made him comfortable in the "eunuch's quarters" beneath the stairs leading to the Valide Sultana's chamber, where he could hear anyone trying to intrude on the queen mother. Sir Roye could even see a bit, where shafts of moonlight filtered through gaps in the curtains. Standing watch seemed silly, since they were thousands of feet above the open sea, reachable solely on rocback, and the only traffic was the light tread of slave girls going up and down, keeping the ladies upstairs fed and happy. Then even these visits ceased, and Sir Roye went to sleep.

He dreamed of Hannah, left alone among the Tartars, his sleeping mind confusing the drifting balloon with the sway of a sky-boat. What a godsend Hannah had been. Without her, he would never have survived the Tartars. Now he was free of them, and Hannah was still enslaved. How horribly sad. Yet in his dream, Hannah miraculously returned, and he felt her warm body beside him and her hand on his brow. Overjoyed, he started to get up, telling Hannah he had come back, just as he vowed.

That little movement jerked him awake. Suddenly he was no longer in the dark yurt, but back aboard the Cathayan balloon. Somehow, Hannah was still beside him, under the pavilion stairs, lying naked in the shadows by his bed, her blond hair shining in the moonlight. He asked in surprise, "Hannah, is that you?"

"No," the blonde replied, giving her a head a swift shake.

Completely awake by now, he knew it could not be Hannah, so he asked again, "Sonya?"

She laughed mischievously, sliding in beside him, pressing her body against him, whispering, "Yes."

Good, because he was running out of blondes. Sonya cuddled closer, asking, "Are you really the Baron de Roye?"

"*Absolument,*" he assured her, knowing he had no way to prove it here in Far Barbary. He barely believed it himself, feeling like a sultan lying in a perfumed bed, listening to a royal concubine tell her tale, providing light entertainment before being debauched.

Sonya did not ask for patents of nobility, sliding her leg over his, a wonderful smooth sensation. Turks shave their women from the neck down, so her flesh was as naked as a child's, making it hard to just casually take her. Hannah was a grown woman, and merely a traveling companion, yet her parting tears were heartbreaking. What was going to happen with this girl, so young and far from home? He told Sonya, "I fear for you."

"Why?" Sonya sounded surprised. "You saved me."

"For the moment." He had no idea where they would come down, and what would become of Sonya when they did.

"This moment is all I care about," Sonya insisted. "Now is all we have."

Too true. Sonya rose up on one elbow, looking calm and earnest in the moonlight, saying, "You worry too much over me. I have been raped, repeatedly, and have seen my family massacred. I have been sold into slavery, twice, and given to the Shah of Khwarezm because he prefers blondes. Being here with you is the by far best thing that has happened since leaving home."

Another victim of the international trade in blondes. Before coming to Far Barbary, Sir Roye had not realized this was such a problem, but here was another young woman torn from her family, then passed from nomad to nomad, all because of her hair color. His arm automatically curved around to comfort her. Being forced to learn Cuman and sleep with a philandering sultan was not the worst thing that could happen to a kidnapped girl, but it was bad enough.

"If I must die tomorrow, so be it," Sonya declared. "At least let me have tonight." She kissed him again, putting her whole body into the kiss, opening herself up to the first man who had cared for her, not for what she was worth. At the same time, her hand slipped down between his legs, bringing him to attention.

As the kiss subsided, Sonya sighed and rested her head on his shoulder, her hand keeping him aroused with minimal effort. For a teenager, Sonya was already marvelously adept at handling men, which showed her harem training: come naked in the dark, be under the covers without a word, speak when spoken to, but always concentrate on the task at hand.

Sir Roye was not that worried about the blonde in his arms. It was Aria who troubled him, though it hardly seemed likely he would ever see her again. Sonya whispered, "Trust means no secrets."

Clearly Sonya would not let a secret even get started between them. More harem training at work. Making love was literally both larceny and treason, since Sonya's body was not hers, but belonged instead to Shah Aladdin. Every time they kissed, they compounded the felony, using royal property for private pleasure. Baron de Roye was touched and impressed. When kissing and fondling were capital offenses, lovers held each other's lives in their hands—no woman had ever trusted him so much, except Aria. He told Sonya, "There is another."

"Who?" Sonya sounded more intrigued than surprised. She knew he was not a eunuch.

"I cannot tell you her name." As Sonya had said, the only openness came in secret. "She is your age, or thereabouts, and I met her in the woods near Byeli Zamak."

"What was she doing in the woods?" Sonya rightly guessed that Aria was up to no good.

"Gathering fungus." Among other things.

"Sounds like some runaway serf." Sonya laughed at his meager love life. "Where is the fair fungus gatherer now?"

"I do not know," he confessed, feeling a fool for having lost his true love.

Leaning closer, Sonya pressed warm, smooth perfumed breasts against him, saying, "I am here."

So she was. And incredibly hard to resist. Sonya was not only brave and beautiful, but utterly determined as well. A slim hand went to work again between his legs, going back and forth, showing off the Valide Sultana's training, employing techniques meant to please her son. Mother did know best. Fingers teased and stroked, squeezing low moans out of the supposed eunuch, moans that Sonya immediately stifled with her mouth. When their lips parted, she asked, "Have you made love to her?"

"No," Sir Roye admitted. Half a day with Sonya had involved more carnal relations that all his time with Aria.

"Good." She kissed him, more leisurely this time, letting him know that they had all night. Despite his reservations, Sir Roye kissed back, finding Sonya's mouth fresh and exciting, tasting like a clean cool spring. And a little like Aria's. He was going to make love to Sonya, since by now it was not possible to stop without doing damage to a major organ. Besides, Sonya had risked her life just by coming to him. Committing the crime together meant no one could be betrayed.

And what a delicious crime, committed on young willing flesh. From the moment he entered her, Sonya went utterly wild, making up for years of giving in by getting everything at once, now that her body was hers to enjoy. At times, she nearly cried aloud, forcing him to cover her mouth with his hand; at other times, she broke into silent giggles at the feel of him inside her. Which Sir Roye found both exciting and exhausting. Though Sonya had amazing energy, and a beautiful body that he fit into easily, this boyarinya was not who he wanted to be with. But even barons cannot be choosers, when it comes to love.

He certainly found it no hardship to feel the teenager beneath him shudder with joy, knowing he was the first man Sonya had freely chosen, the first one she truly wanted. An incredible compliment from the young boyarinya. When Sonya had spent herself completely, Sir Roye continued to hold the sleeping girl, stroking her fair hair and wondering what he had gotten himself into. Something wild, that was for sure, making his time with Aria seem absolutely tame.

Since giving in to the Tartars, Sir Roye de Roye had been deluged with female attention, more even than a French nobleman might desire. Which showed just how swiftly the Tartars had divined his weakness, getting Baron de Roye to betray France, and to fight for them, so long as Aria and Hannah did not suffer for it. Now he was free of the Tartars, thanks to Sonya D'Medved, and if things went badly with her, he had only himself to blame.

Dawn prayer found Sir Roye de Roye hors de combat, fast asleep while his bedmate cleansed herself for devotions and greeted the dawn purified in mind and body, affirming that prayer was better than sleep, for there was no god but God, and Muhammad is his prophet.

When the sinful infidel finally awoke, he found his morning tea waiting, along with hot water and a razor, so he shaved in the privacy of his little room, which reeked of musk and sex. Any continued attempt to play a eunuch should have been hopeless, but when he emerged, nothing was said about the night before. Sir Roye had to tell by looks and smiles who knew what had happened, and who merely guessed.

Daylight had revealed a bigger disaster than a man in their midst. The wind had died, leaving them becalmed high above the Inland Sea, no closer to the green coast than the night before—which the Persians sorely lamented, having hoped to wake up over their homeland. Sonya told him that as eunuch-in-residence, he was in charge of transportation. "How can we get to shore?"

Good question. As part of his "know your enemy" policy, Sir Roye had studied Tartar balloons and sky-boats. "Tartars control direction by going up and down to find favorable winds, and by tilting their parasails during ascent and descent. Our gasbag is a perfect ball, and cannot be tilted."

"Then we are stuck here within sight of land?" Sonya made it sound like a death sentence.

"Not necessarily." Sir Roye knew enough Tartar aerial technique to check the winds aloft. "But we have to get up to the control deck."

He climbed the outside ladder to the pavilion roof, which was ringed with sand-filled ballast bags and doubled as the balloon control deck, housing the gas lines and the water ballast valves. Sonya and Yasmi were right behind him, showing him they were the adventurous members of the harem. From the rooftop, he got a good look at their position, tantalizingly close to the Persian shore. Finding one of the black balloons used to test wind direction, Sir Roye filled the thin India-rubber sack from a gas tap. Then he tied off the balloon and released it, following the ascent through a Cathayan farseeing tube, watching the black dot rise, then veer northward before dwindling out of sight.

Not encouraging. Southernly winds aloft had carried the black balloon farther out to sea. Dropping ballast would just make their situation worse.

Taking a final look through the spyglass for the fading balloon, he saw the sky-ship again, sailing high above them, now headed north and out to sea. Sonya and Yasmi took turns ogling the sky-ship, which seemed to sail at will, while they were becalmed—another sign that the winds aloft were dead against them. Sonya shivered, saying, "The Killer of Children is headed for her icy home."

"Where is that?" Sir Roye asked.

"Death lives in a far-off castle at the edge of the frozen sea," Sonya declared. "That is where dead souls go, where it is always dark in winter and always bright in summer."

Yasmi muttered something in Persian, and Sonya translated. "She says a frozen hell is worse than Satan's fires. But Yasmi is an ignorant heathen. The Killer of Children is scary, but not Satan. She is Lady Death's little sister, a Valkyrie, a chooser of the slain, though she chooses children only."

"And you saw her?" The sky-ship looked very real, perhaps Death's sister was real as well.

Sonya nodded. "I talked to her when I translated for the sultana, in the Gilded Cage. Her true name is Persephone, the Destroyer, and she is very beautiful and fair spoken."

After seeing the Bone Witch, Sir Roye was ready to believe anything. "What was this Killer of Children doing on Abeskum?"

Sonya looked at him like he was a simpleton. "She was taking children. That is what the Killer of Children does."

"Taking them where?" He remembered the smiling children he had seen on board.

Sonya shrugged. "Who knows? Death's castle, perhaps. Or maybe Fair Isle."

Depending on if the kid was bad or good? It had the sound of a scary fairy tale. "Do any of the children ever come back?"

"None that I ever heard of," Sonya admitted, studying the sky-ship intently. "But I would have gone with her if I could."

"You would?" Sir Roye stared hard at Sonya D'Medved, noting how soft her lips were, how like a child's. Though those sweet lips had done unspeakable things to him in the night, he could not shake the feeling that Sonya was still a girl at heart.

"My other choice was being raped and murdered by Tartars," Sonya reminded him. "Whatever the Killer of Children wanted could hardly have been worse than that."

What a weird life this girl had, if her choices were death by Tartars, or being whisked off to the north pole. How did Sonya even stay sane in such a situation? But the young boyarinya willingly walked that knife edge, daring to live free rather than becoming another victim. No wonder the blond teenager was not the least afraid of him.

When they brought the bad news back, the Persians started wailing again, begging Allah to send a wind. Despite their prayers, the wind that blew up came from the south, pushing them farther out to sea. By dusk, they had lost sight of land, and they went to bed surrounded by endless dark water.

Rested and revived, Sir Roye hardly cared what direction they were headed, so long as it was not back toward the Tartars. He was imagining another night like the last, but the mood had totally changed—last night they had been headed for freedom, and now they were headed who knew where? And what would they find when they got there? Instead of slipping gaily into his bed, Sonya came and whispered, "We have much to do tonight. You are wanted upstairs. . . ."

"What for?" He had a hideous picture of having to perform for the Valide Sultana, who taught Sonya all those ingenious tricks.

"As a eunuch," Sonya hastened to assure him.

That sounded better. "What sort of eunuch?"

"One that can operate this balloon." Sonya reached out to take his hand, guiding him up the stairs. "All Turkan Khatun cares about is getting down, in the right spot. Do that, and you will be richly rewarded."

"Tell Turkan Khatun she has found her man." Having flown twice by sky-boat and once by glider, and having survived all three times, Sir Roye knew more about aerial navigation than anyone in Christendom.

"Her eunuch," Sonya reminded him.

"As you wish," Sir Roye replied, following her up the stairs to the Valide Sultana's chambers. Atop the steps was a small silken antechamber, which Sir Roye was happy to find empty. By now he had heard enough harem stories to know that such chambers were where unwelcome guests were met by the three-mutes-of-the-bowstring, brawny harem executioners who could not even hear a victim's pleas.

Sonya ushered him through the empty chamber, showing how to do the required prostration before the veiled Valide Sultana. While Sir Roye pressed his face against the carpet, Sonya and Turkan Khatun carried on a lively conversation in Cuman. Finally, Sonya told him to sit up, saying, "Her Majesty wants to know how much flying you have done."

Rising to his knees, he replied, "Tell her I have flown from Markovy to the Hungersteppe. And from the Red Sands Desert into the citadel at Otar, as well as into her own harem at Abeskum."

Turkan Khatun was surprised to hear he had been inside the citadel at Otar. Sonya asked, "How did you get there?"

"Not easily," he assured her. "That was a much smaller version of the attack at Abeskum, done with sky-boats because the citadel top was too small for glider landings. Which meant we had fewer men, facing a tower full of Turks fighting frantically for their lives."

Sonya translated, then turned back to him. "Her Majesty wishes to know what happened to Inalchiq Khan."

That would be the Turk whose cupidity started all these massacres. Sir Roye remembered Inalchiq Khan's end all too vividly. "Tartars took him alive, then melted down a great pot of the silver he stole, and they poured it in his eyes and ears."

Turkan Khatun chuckled gleefully at the translation, vastly amused by the fate of her former vassal. Then the Valide Sultana spoke to Sonya, and Sonya told Sir Roye, "Happy as that news was, it is no help in our current plight. His Most Merciful Highness, King George the Fourth of Georgia and his sister Princess Rusudan have offered us shelter. Can you bring us down in Baku?"

"Only if the winds carry us there." He could tell the Turkan Khatun did not know the least thing about ballooning, and it amused him that her choice of refuge was the nearest Christian kingdom. King George IV, the Light of the Georgians, and his sister Rusudan ran one of the most corrupt courts in the East, while managing to stay friends with everyone, from the Cumans to the pope— this harem on the run would fit right in with the loose morals of the premier Christian court in Far Barbary. "Tell her I can bring us down safely once we are over land, but I have scant control otherwise."

Sonya conferred with the Valide Sultana, then asked, "Where are the winds taking us?"

"Northward," he replied promptly, knowing that would please the Valide Sultana far more than it did her Persian slave girls. North of the Inland Sea was a huge arc of Kipchak country, on both sides of the Great Mother River, just the place that Turkan Khatun would want to come down.

He could hear the excitement in the Valide Sultana's reply, and Sonya asked him, "If we are blown all the way to Cuman lands, could you bring us down?"

"When it seems safe." He had never landed a balloon, but Turkan Khatun did not need to know that. Despite the veil and language barrier, he could tell the bloodthirsty old Cuman was ecstatic to have found a eunuch to take her home. And so long as Turkan Khatun needed him, things would stay free and easy in the slave quarters.

Afterward, beneath the stairs, Sonya was ecstatic, saying, "We are going home!"

"To Gascony?" Even if they made it to Cuman country, that was hardly home to him.

"Not your home, silly." Sonya kissed him to ease his disappointment. "My home. Turkan Khatun is frantic to find allies, and I told her that you were a

Markovite spy, sent to foil the Tartars. I told her you must return to Markov with a warning that the Tartars are on the march."

"And the Valide Sultana believed you?"

"Most of what Turkan Khatun knows about Markovy comes from me," Sonya noted proudly. "Moreover, I am a D'Medved, a boyar's niece. Who would know better?"

Who, indeed? Sir Roye asked, "Will you do that?"

"Do what?" Sonya asked.

"Warn your people about the Tartars." Someone should, for sure.

"Me?" Sonya looked surprised. "No one will listen to me. I am a wicked debauched girl, without parents or position. When I go home, I will be soundly whipped for getting stolen by Kazakhs."

Of course. Life among Tartars had accustomed Sir Roye to practical thinking. How wonderfully naïve that nomads took the world so seriously, and naturally expected civilized folks would do the same. No one in Markov cared what a Cuman thought, and few boyars had even heard of Khwarizm, much less the Tartars. Soon as Sonya got home, she would be clapped into a harem, or a nunnery, where any foreign influences could be beaten out of her.

Sir Roye wondered aloud, "Why do you want to go back?"

Sonya laid her head on his shoulder, saying, "Because it is home. Where my people are."

Sir Roye was struck by the sadness of this girl's existence. Aria at least had been brought up by the Bone Witch to believe in herself, and be wary of the world. Sonya saw herself as a sinful creature, fleeing one form of incarceration for another. However weird this airborne interlude might be to him, to Sonya it was all she would get of life. Running his hand down her thigh, he felt her flesh stir under his touch, aching to be free.

He asked her what the little golden bird tattooed on her hip meant. Sonya brighted up, saying, "That is the D'Medved golden martlet. My family crest."

For good or ill, the D'Medveds had long ago put their mark on Sonya, and his making love with her had not changed that.

Dawn found them completely at sea, and losing altitude. All day the wave tops got closer, with no sight of land ahead. Finally he told Sonya, "We must drop ballast or we will never make it through the night."

With Sonya's help, they dumped half a ton of sand into the Inland Sea, which brought them back up nicely—but next morning, they were back down at sea level, riding so low that the cable was dragging in the water, indicating a serious gas leak. Everyone else was excited because they could see land to the north—just as Sir Roye had predicted. Sonya asked, "What land is that? When will we get to it?"

"Kipchak country, I would guess. And we may never get there, not without getting wet." He could see a long snake of wet cable trailing behind them, threatening to drag them right down into the drink. "We have to release more ballast."

"There is still the water ballast." Sonya was learning how the balloon worked, and she knew the pavilion had a large trim tank, with release valves on the control deck.

"That land ahead is desert." Sir Roye nodded toward the northern horizon. "We need to drop something we cannot drink. Large pieces of furniture would do well. Surely Her Highness must have a couch or two upstairs that could easily go over the side, along with any ornamental woodwork not actually part of the pavilion."

Sonya D'Medved rolled her eyes at that suggestion, then marched upstairs to give the bad news to Turkan Khatun while Sir Roye descended to the basket to see about the cable. As he descended the rope ladder, a brightly striped ottoman went sailing past him to splash in the sea below. More overstuffed furniture followed. When he got to the wicker basket, which still contained his arms and armor, he found the basket was barely skimming the wave tops, with the long wet cable acting as a sea anchor. He hated to sacrifice the cable, which he had hoped would help bring them down, but there was no choice.

Sawing through the braided rope with his broadsword, he freed the balloon, which instantly shot upward, landing him in the bottom of the basket.

When he got up to look over the side, he saw the sea surface falling away, dotted with dwindling bits of furniture and some garish cushions. As he climbed back up the rope ladder, more fancy bric-a-brac came flying out of the pavilion, hurtling through the blue sky to impact on the waves below.

Land crawled closer. By afternoon, they were nearing the beach, with the basket back to dragging on the wave tops. Beyond the beach, scrub brush and claypan stretched in all directions. Though the women were overjoyed, Sir Roye did not much like the look of the pounding surf and surrounding desert. They were headed for a hard, wet landing in very inhospitable country. Trying to preserve their precious water, he told Sonya, "Everything must go. Curtains, throw rugs, pavilion paneling."

"It will hardly be a harem then." Sonya anticipated the protests.

"If we hit, we lose everything." Water and overhead cover were more important than modesty. As surf and sand got closer, he had no trouble convincing the women to part with enough weight to keep them aloft. Colorful swatches of fabric went fluttering down to land in the surf and carpet the beach.

Happy to survive their first brush with terra firma, the women kept asking, "Where are we? Who lives here? What is the nearest town?"

Having lived outside the harem did not make him a geographer, but obviously no one lived here. This was a desert. The nearest "town" would be a collection of nomad tents, which none of them wanted to visit. Eventually someone spied some goats, and everyone ran to look. Sonya suggested, "If there is a herdsman, we could set down and ask him directions."

Only a woman could think that was practical. "Once we are down, we are down. If we must ask our whereabouts, do it from the air."

"But we are too high up to talk," Sonya protested.

Sir Roye nodded absently. To him, that was a good thing. No one had so much as seen a herdsman, and he was certainly not going down to quiz the goats. There was a heavy three-pronged grapple attached to the basket, for use as a land anchor, but he would not attempt to use it until he was somewhere they might want to stay, and those goats turned out to be the only sign of civilization they saw all day.

At dusk, they tore down the last of the curtains and pavilion paneling. Even the garderobe went over the side. With the curtains and paneling gone, the lower floor of the pavilion felt like a ghostly flying veranda winging through the moonlit desert night. Without any privacy, everyone was on their best behavior, though Sonya curled up to sleep beside him, not caring what heathens might think.

He wondered what sort of dreams were going on inside the blond head on his breast. At home in France, girls and women went about their business in a free and easy way, be they milkmaids or shepherdesses, knowing they had royal protection to peddle cream or tend sheep. Pretty Parisian teenagers felt free to smile and look him boldly in the eye, since both Church and state stood between a girl and any man who meant her harm, be he baron or bishop.

Such freedom was unheard of in this part of Far Barbary. Here women were expected to live behind walls and veils, guarded by eunuchs. Since coming to Markovy, Sir Roye had resigned himself to never seeing a woman's face unless she was a serf or a whore. Fortunately there were many perfectly wonderful serfs and whores. Sonya was the first boyarinya that he had so much as talked to, and of course that conversation had led right to a night of sinful debauch, as everyone expected—but that would not happen if they would let their young women out occasionally.

Dawn showed a line of green in the distance, and by afternoon, they were passing low over the Great Mother River, nearly catching the trailing wicker basket on the high grassy northwest bank. Beyond the river was the steppe proper, grazed by cattle herds and small, tough nomad ponies. Sonya insisted on descending to the basket to see if she could ask directions. Sir Roye went with her to retrieve his armor and Lucerne hammer, which he might soon need.

Even in the barren Kazakh steppe, an immense Cathayan balloon barely grazing the grass tops attracted immediate attention. First to greet them was a dog or lone steppe wolf that started running in frantic circles.

Next came a small herd of cattle, drawn by the strange affinity that cows have for really big balloons. Trailing after the cows were a pair of amazed no-mads, whom Sonya called to in Cuman. Astounding them even more.

Mustering up their courage, the men claimed to be Kalmyks from south of the river, passing through with Cuman permission, planning to sell their cattle upriver, then see what they could steal. Sonya applauded their initiative, calling back, "Are there Cumans camped nearby?"

"Two, three days upriver." Or so the Kalmyks supposed. "Prince Yuri's peo-ple."

Sonya thanked the Kalmyks as the wind carried them away, saying to Sir Roye, "We should set down as soon as we spot Cumans, so they can send word to Prince Yuri."

"Good," he agreed, "because we are out of things to throw overboard." Sir Roye could clearly see individual grass tops below, which meant the basket would soon be dragging on the turf.

Presently they attracted still more attention from a dozen mounted bow-men riding down from the north. Through the spyglass, they looked like Kipchaks—wearing scale armor and tall conical helmets with brazen faces for visors. Maybe not Cumans, but close enough for Sir Roye.

He told Sonya, "We are going to land here, where the grass is soft." Hand-ing her the red rip-cord line that ran up to the reserve gas cell, he said, "Pull hard on this when you see me throw out the anchor."

Sonya nodded gravely, not saying anything, leaving everything totally up to him. Sonya D'Medved, boyarinya and the voice of Turkan Khatun, who demanded her way in bed and council, looked to him to lead—trusting his judgment better than hers. It was a bit of a surprise, and better than being a baron of France. He pulled her to him and kissed her, saying, "Ready to die, D'Medved?"

Sonya grinned back. "We will not die."

"Maybe." Not now, anyway—but he had already begun to miss this high-flying adventure. Down there, he was just another failed eunuch, afoot in Kipchak country. Sonya showed no such qualms. There was no waiting about with her. Whatever lay ahead, for good or ill, Sonya meant to dive right into it—taking him with her.

Sir Roye loosed the grapple, while Sonya called out to the Kipchaks. "Turkan Khatun has come from Khwarezm to call on Prince Yuri."

That got a long laugh out of the brazen-faced bowmen, which Sir Roye took as a good sign, and he heaved the heavy anchor overboard.

It hit, throwing up a cloud of dirt. Then the grapple bit, pulling up huge hunks of turf, which jerked the basket backward, and slowed it, but did not stop the balloon.

Being veteran herdsmen, the Kipchaks reacted immediately, loosening their lariats, lassoing the anchor flanges and the moving mass of turf, using their horses to slow it even more. At the same time, Sonya pulled the rip cord on the reserve gasbag, designed to bring the balloon down without deflating the main gasbag. Sir Roye could feel an immediate sag in the balloon's whole structure, since the gases holding them up were no longer as light—they were headed back to earth. His harem idyll was over.

Jarring to a stop, the basket spilled sideways, pitching Sir Roye out onto the steppe, with Sonya atop him. Lying bruised and hurt in the long grass, Sir Roye could see the balloon drifting downwind, still losing altitude.

Then the pavilion hit, splintering the lower floor, and making him immensely glad the slave girls were on the roof, aside from Sonya, who was on him. No longer having to support the pavilion, the balloon suddenly gained new life, standing up and tugging at its cables, trying to fly away downwind.

He helped Sonya to her feet, brushing off bits of the Kazakh steppe, saying, "Welcome back to earth."

They spent a week in that broken little house on the steppe, feasting on nomad beef, until Prince Yuri sent horses and men to take them to his camp by the banks of the Mother River. Here Sir Roye got to see the strength of the Kipchaks and Cumans, the immense horse herds, and the vast sea of nomad tents. Prince Yuri had more armored cavalry and mounted bowmen at his immediate command than the King of France, who had to call on quarrelsome vassals when war threatened.

But being barbarians, they had no notion how civilization worked, and stupidly believed Sonya D'Medved's story that the illustrious Baron de Roye had been sent by her boyar family to spy on the Tartars and form a grand anti-Tartar alliance stretching from Bordeaux to Baku. After all, it was what Europe ought to do. It never occurred to Prince Yuri that everyone to the west was totally unconcerned by the Tartar threat, and would laugh off any offer of help from a horde of horse nomads, no matter how numerous.

Prince Yuri gave Sir Roye a mounted escort and a string of ponies loaded with fine furs and stolen trinkets—as thanks for the return of Turkan Khatun, and to bribe the boyars back home. Sonya gleefully milked their terror of the Tartars, putting whatever words in Sir Roye's mouth would get the most out of the Cumans. As the august Baron de Roye's translator-cum-bedmate, Sonya dressed herself in splendid nomad style, wearing a tall felt hat and a long red jacket with gold clasps, over men's silk trousers and riding boots. Strapped to her saddle was a light rapid-fire bow and a quiver of arrows.

Yasmi and the other Persians said tearful good-byes, already being farther north than they ever wanted to go.

With Cumans for guides, the trip north took a couple of weeks, though they crossed hundreds of miles of steppe, staying on the east bank of the ancient Amazon, which Sonya called the Don. This was Kazakh country, but even steppe bandits feared Prince Yuri's Cumans and let them pass in peace. Riding steadily northward, Sir Roye felt the summer fading, and he knew they were headed into fall, which would soon be followed by a cold dark Markovite winter.

Sonya could tell by his kisses that something was amiss. In the hills south of Vyatichi, she insisted on practicing her mounted archery, letting the Cumans get ahead, then asking, "What is wrong?"

He had been retrieving her arrows, and handed her the spent shafts, saying, "Would you truly know?"

"No secrets," Sonya reminded him, taking the arrows.

He looked at her, sitting easily in the saddle, wearing her scarlet riding coat and cap, her bow bent, blond hair blowing free in the wind. He did not love Sonya as he had loved Aria, but he had hardly ever been with a woman who spoke so straight and knew him so well. "I feel that I am betraying you."

"Betraying me? How?" Sonya looked puzzled, since he was doing absolutely everything she wanted, from retrieving her arrows to pleasing her in bed.

Sir Roye sighed, then told her, "If I take you home, they will just put you in another harem."

"So?" Sonya had no idea where he was going.

"I would rather you were free," he explained, sensing the conversation would go nowhere.

"Free?" Sonya sounded like she had never heard of the concept. "Worth nothing? Free for the taking?"

"Not in a harem, free to go wherever you will." He waved his hand to indicate the world at large, which happened to be hilly grassland, cut by dark wooded draws.

Sonya looked about the landscape, which was too dry for farming but pleasant enough to ride through, asking, "Where I will?"

"You know what I mean." He could not believe that someone as forceful as Sonya had no better plan in life than going back to the family harem. Aria at least had her hopeless quest to return the Firebird's Egg.

"No, I do not know." Sonya was never afraid to admit she was at a loss.

He nodded back the way they had come. "Common sense says we should head south down the Amazon to the Sea of Azov and catch a ship for Venice, or Genoa if we can."

"Why would we do that?" Sonya made it sound like he had suggested a trip to Saturn.

"So we could sell Prince Yuri's presents to the highest bidder, then winter on the Italian Riviera." Alas, legal difficulties kept him from returning to France.

Sonya was not going for it. "What about the Tartars?"

"Let the Tartars take care of themselves." They would certainly do well enough without him.

"We must warn my people." Sonya said it so calmly and easily that it almost made sense—which only showed she had been with nomads way too long. Sonya had started to believe the bullshit that she fed Prince Yuri.

"Your people will ignore our warning and lock you away where I will never see you." That last was the worst part.

Sonya did not argue the point, riding for a while in silence, sliding her arrows one by one into her quiver. When she was done, Sonya asked coyly, "Will you really miss me so much?"

"Yes, indeed." Wild and difficult though she was, he had come to value Sonya, and thought she deserved better than to be locked up and beaten.

Sonya preened at the idea of being missed, saying, "Then you must make love to me now."

"And I do," he protested.

"I mean right now." Swinging out of the saddle, Sonya set down her bow and undid her riding pants.

Being a gentleman, Sir Roye had to comply, and he dismounted himself, spreading Sonya's shapely legs and taking her there in the long grass, with their horses watching and hawks circling overhead. Sonya locked her calves behind his as he rocked harder and harder inside her, pressing their flesh together until they felt like one. Sir Roye made sure the teenager climaxed twice before they were done, then asked afterward, "Is that what you wanted?"

Sonya stared dreamily into the deep blue cloudless sky, saying nothing. Sir Roye could tell she was storing up memories for when she was locked away from men. Finally Sonya rolled over and sat up, picking stalks of grass out of her hair, saying, "Yes, indeed, that was most wonderful."

"For me too," he admitted, fearing he would very much miss her.

She added thoughtfully, "Though you are always careful not to get me with child."

Being French, Sir Roye knew numerous means for prolonging pleasure while avoiding procreation, some of which Sonya certainly enjoyed. "This does not seem like the best moment to start a family."

Sonya smirked at his reply, pulling up her pants and remounting her horse, bow in hand. As she straightened in the saddle, the boyarinya told him primly, "It is nice knowing you will miss me, since it means that you do care for me, at least a little. But if you are not willing to throw a rope around me and drag me down the Don to this Italian Riviera, getting me pregnant along the way, then you do not really want me."

Sir Roye de Roye could hardly argue with that. He mounted as well, thinking of the little yellow bird on her hip. The D'Medveds were calling her home, and he did not love Sonya enough to stop her.

In Vyatichi they passed close by the shrine at Karadyevachka, and Sonya insisted on paying her respects to the Killer of Children. Sir Roye learned from the locals what the shrine was about, and he could not believe Sonya wanted to worship there. "Folks claim they sacrifice girls here, from teenagers to toddlers."

Sonya admitted that was so. "They are given to the Killer of Children."

"What on earth for?" This had to be the most senseless thing he had seen since coming to Markovy, and that was saying a lot.

"Karadyevachka is a shrine to the Black Maiden." Sonya acted like that was an answer.

Sir Roye stared down at her, kneeling in Cuman pants and a scarlet coat before the black wooden shrine. How could Sonya take child murder so calmly? Moments like this made him feel so separate from Sonya D'Medved, more even than from Aria, who was raised by a witch. He had been inside Sonya, repeatedly, as close as two people could be, but he never understood how her mind worked. That wild and willful Sonya could pray over putting little girls to death simply made no sense. "How can such a place be holy?"

"That is a woman's secret." Sonya had already told him more than he needed to know about the Killer of Children.

"And what about the girls who died here?" he demanded.

"That is who I came to honor." Sonya sounded determined to show patience, especially here, of all places. If these girls could give themselves up to death, Sonya D'Medved could surely endure male interrogation.

Seeing he was only feeding Sonya's insanity, Sir Roye de Roye shut up, glaring at the dark shrine with its grotesque carvings and brightly painted door. He too felt touched by the terror of the place, and by these girls' simple sacrifice. But it was just another example of how Markovite women took their immorality as a matter of course. Even little girls gave up their sinful lives without question.

From Karadyevachka, they crossed over to the far bank of the Brovva at Hebektahay, a burnt-out castle that used to belong to the D'Hays until it was seized by D'Medveds and Brovvniks. With her breached walls and burnt wards, Hebektahay smelled of death, and only the inner keep was in current use, leaving the once-busy castle ominously empty. Sonya dismounted and said a prayer for her father, who was captured and executed during a D'Hay sortie, showing that victories had their losses too.

Here Sir Roye's idyll ended, and he turned Sonya over to surprised D'Medveds, who were embarrassingly thankful to him, while treating Sonya like an annoying stray. Laughing at her Cuman bow and clothes, they asked, "Sure you have not caught a blond Kazakh?"

Sir Roye assured them that Sonya was one of theirs, and they hustled her off to the women's quarters. He did not even get a kiss good-bye, though later they returned Sonya's bow and arrows, as well as her pony, which they assumed was his. What need had Sonya for weapons or horses? Now he saw why the girl kept a knife strapped to her leg—so she would never again be naked among her enemies.

As a suspect foreigner, Sir Roye got small credit for bringing in one of their women—since it was generally assumed that he had debauched the girl once the Cumans and Kazakhs finished with her. But he made himself immediately popular by mentioning his involvement in Prince Sergey's death. Boyar families along the Brovva had no love for the court nobility, and Prince Sergey had been a particular bugbear of the D'Medveds', intent on pushing royal authority down the Brovva. Discovering that he had held Byeli Zamak against Prince Sergey—however unsuccessfully—made him a hero of sorts.

During the after-dinner drinking bouts, D'Medved men-at-arms wanted to hear over and again how Prince Ivan's uncle had been eaten by a leopard, something the Brovvniks found vastly amusing. Sir Roye complied, leaving out Aria, the Bone Witch, and the Firebird's Egg, which made his own role all the larger. Suddenly he was solely responsible for despatching Prince Sergey and several lances of the royal guard, aided by assorted woodland creatures. But even while being backslapped by drunken comrades, Sir Roye gazed at the room full of men, dearly missing the women—all locked safely away from his sight.

They headed upriver toward Brovvazamak and Markov, where Sonya would be put in the royal harem. She was taken there in a bullock car, like the one that carried Aria to Karadyevachka, and Sir Roye rode with the escort. That meant they shared private midday meals, with a maid acting as chaperone and doubling as a lookout when Sonya was in the mood. Her champion was horrified to find long red lash marks on the boyarinya's white skin, and he asked, "Were you beaten?"

"Not badly," Sonya declared, pleased by his concern. "For losing my virginity to Kazakhs."

Such senseless savagery still shocked him, for he could see what little good the whipping did. Here was Sonya D'Medved, still under heavy guard, lying naked beside the remains of her light lunch, about to make love to a foreigner, with the aid of her Kazakh slave girl. It would take more than a lash to make Sonya mend her evil ways.

Sir Roye left the bedroom on wheels delighted with his naked lunch, but angry at what was done to Sonya. He ignored the grins he got from the D'Medved escort, fed up with warriors who were too busy beating their women to care that the Tartar war machine was bearing down on them. Being feathered with nomad arrows seemed fitting punishment for such idiocy.

At Brovvazamak, he met Baron Tolstoy, the tall, balding, long-nosed head of the Brovvniks, who happily announced a key defection from the court faction. Prince Akavarr, Tolstoy's brother-in-law, aimed to wrest the regency from the hated D'Hays. With Prince Sergey dead, the court party no longer had an acceptable regent, so Prince Akavarr was marching on Markov, and the D'Medveds wanted to be there when the D'Hays were massacred and the treasury was thrown open.

Sir Roye told Baron Tolstoy all about the Tartars, and the man looked fairly alarmed, but that turned out to be just a sign of his caution. Baron Tolstoy meant to topple D'Hays and then worry about the Tartars. "We must have Markov," the baron explained, "for without the capital, we can do nothing."

Baron de Roye doubted they could do anything, with or without Markov. These Brovvniks and D'Medveds seemed most adept at drunken dwarf-tossing. They had managed to massacre helpless D'Hay retainers at Hebekta-hay, but taking the castle cost them dearly, and they were not aching for a fight—just an easy coup.

On the outskirts of the capital, Baron Tolstoy got the alarming news that the D'Hays had installed a regent of their own, Crown Princess Kataryna-Maria II, Prince Ivan's half sister, fetched from an arctic nunnery to rule for the infant prince. Every Brovvnik and D'Medved saw it as his duty to send this Crown Princess back to her northern nunnery—if only to profit off the anarchy that would ensue. However, Baron Tolstoy would not move on Markov until Prince Akavarr arrived, saying, "To enter the city alone would put my head in a D'Hay noose."

After what he had seen at Hebektahay, Sir Roye could well believe the

D'Hays would love to hang the man who murdered their spearmen and slaughtered their serfs. Baron Tolstoy did well to watch his back.

Sir Roye de Roye, however, was free to go on and deliver Sonya to the harem. How strange that he was the one who knew Markov middling well, while Sonya was seeing it for the first time. Topping a rise, they surveyed the wooden-walled Kremlin sitting above the Markov River, crowned by its golden domes and tall bell towers—it was Baron de Roye who pointed out All Saints' Cathedral, and the great wooden Church of the Annunciation, then the white turrets of the harem-palace.

Markov herself had no walls, since her citizens retreated into the Kremlin in times of troubles, and the town might have been a pleasant provincial capital in France, except for the poor food, worse wine, and the shabby oriental air. Under leaden skies, bowmen drove the bullock cart right through Red Square, and in the Kremlin's main gate. Sonya said her good-bye to him before the Red Stairs that led into the harem-palace. Sir Roye felt as gloomy as the day.

"Do not despair," Sonya told him, almost unrecognizable in her long gown and modest veil. Having survived Kazakhs, Cumans, Turks, and Tartars, Sonya had no qualms about entering the harem of the much-hated Kataryna-Maria II—while Baron Tolstoy feared to so much as set foot in the city. "Fate drew us together," she reminded him, "and trust kept us alive. We will meet again."

"If you ever have need of me, send word." For Sonya's sake, he would stick with Tolstoy and the D'Medveds—as long as he could stomach it.

"Worry not—I will send for you." If Sonya had the least need of him, she would let him know. Lifting her veil, Sonya D'Medved gave him a long shameless kiss good-bye. French-kissing foreigners in public, especially ones who were thought to have raped her, was just the sort of wildness that got the girl regularly whipped.

11

the old man of the mountains

As the *Selene* dumped more ballast, heading south and west away from Abeskum Island, searching for favorable winds aloft, Aria saw the Cathayan balloon, with its big two-story pavilion, falling farther and farther behind them. Unlike the *Selene*, the balloon could go only up and down, making the people in that pretty floating pavilion prisoners of the wind. Aria wished them well, praying they made it to dry land.

Anyone aboard was lucky to have escaped at all, because the fortress palace was engulfed in flames, a huge funeral pyre for Shah Aladdin, unless he had made it out on that balloon. She guessed the Tartars would leave nothing standing on the island, just a blackened reminder that even the rich and powerful could not steal with impunity—unless they were Tartars.

Aria found their cabin full of children chattering in Persian and Cuman, which Persphone understood perfectly. Here was the Killer of Children in her natural element, playing teenage mother to abandoned youngsters. Some had homes waiting to take them, like the two Bulgar heiresses, but others were now orphans who needed somewhere to go. Persephone already had a place for the Persians. "South and west of here is Alamut, and if this wind holds, we can be there by nightfall."

Long before dusk, they were over land, and the rock of Alamut hove into sight ahead, a white-walled fortress perched above a jade-green hidden valley.

By now, the Cathayan balloon was just a dot, far out over the water—they would have to find land another day.

Alamut Valley was walled off from the world, and the *Selene* entered the only way it could be entered: by air. Eros brought the sky-ship in low over a bare hill, and men grabbed the landing lines, showing the *Selene* had been there before. Persephone stood with Aria at the rail, saying, "Alamut is the valley of the Assassins, Death's best friends in Persia."

It made perfect sense that the Killer of Children's best friends should be Assassins, and people called out greetings in Persian, welcoming the lost children like their own. Though they were some sort of Muslims, the women were unveiled and bare-legged, wearing short kilts and no head covering but a white kerchief. Everyone was so relaxed and cheerful, Aria could hardly believe that this was the stronghold of the most feared killers in Far Barbary. Thinking that their reputation might be just an *Arabian Nights* tale, she asked Persephone, "Are they really assassins?"

"Absolutely the best," Persephone hastened to assure her. "If ever you need anyone killed, these are the people to see."

Aria would remember that. "Yet they seem so friendly."

"They have no reason to kill you," Persephone reminded her. "That is the secret of their success, the Assassins never kill without reason. They never kill women or children, or merchants and travelers, framers and tradesmen, or footloose foreigners. Ordinary people are safer in the Valley of the Assassins than in a cathedral sanctuary."

Having been condemned to death in a church, Aria could well believe her. "Whom do they kill?"

Persephone shrugged. "Caliphs, kings, grand viziers, and the like. Also wayward scholars and imams who preach hate, but mostly men of power and substance, and usually evil ones, at that. Assassins do not believe in wasting death. They kill only when they must, and willingly die with their victims."

"They die with their victims?" That seemed like a curious twist.

"Absolutely." To Persephone it made perfect sense. "You should not take life unless you are willing to give up yours. It makes you careful about whom you kill, and turns these people into unstoppable killers." Persephone was an expert on death, in all its forms—that being the family business. "They dress in whatever costume the occasion requires, and use poisoned daggers." Persephone herself always carried one on her person. "They need only get close enough to their victim, offering up a present, or a petition, and the deed is done."

Made sense. "But why kill people in the first place?"

Persephone smiled at her perceptiveness. "Why, indeed? These people are Shi'a, and according to Shi'ite doctrine, they are the true followers of Muhammad. Sunni Arabs and Turks take offense at that, and kill them when they can, massacring thousands of Shi'a women and children, and any Shi'ite clergy they can catch. Assassins strike back by killing the richest and most powerful Sunnis."

No wonder everyone here acted serenely happy. Their enemies were far away, though not far enough to escape retribution from those willing to pay the ultimate price.

In the upper citadel, Aria met with the sheik of the Assassins, the Old Man of the Mountains, who turned out to be an amiable old Persian offering sweet wine from Herat and small white cakes to his guests. Persephone translated his apology, saying, "He does not usually have women in his castle, or demigoddesses either."

Aria could tell. Though the shiek's audience chamber was clean and carpeted, it was spare as a monk's cell, without color or decoration, aside from a huge Koran, hand-lettered in gold ink. Persephone had Aria tell the sheik everything she had seen of the Tartars and their methods, from necromancy to air operations. "Normally, the sheik does not much care what happens among infidels, but the Tartars are a threat that he must know about. They have the discipline to defy his assassins, and the means to get to Alamut."

So Aria told the whole story, from when she first escaped the Tartars at the tree barricade, to when they killed her knight in the Rift, ending with the little she had seen of their glider assault on Abeskum, plus everything Blue-Eyes had told her about Tartar methods. As a reward, the sheik gave her a parting gift: a small brass lotion bottle with rings for attaching it to a belt. Removing the stopper, Persephone sniffed the perfumed lotion, then gave the bottle to Aria, thanking their host and bidding him good-bye.

They climbed back down the dizzying steps to the lush green valley floor, which Aria found much harder to do on a head full of Afghan wine. Persephone had to help her find the steps, and Aria complained, "I thought Muslims avoided strong drink."

"Most do," Persephone agreed, "and you did not see the sheik drinking.

Persians are an old people, far older than the Koran or the Bible, people who came to Alamut from the steppes of southern Markovy. Their speech is much closer to Markovite than to Arabic—which is why I speak it so easily. Even our name for *God* comes from ancient Persian, as does *demigoddess*. And like the old religions, this Shi'ite sect sees God in everyone: women and men, believer and infidel, killer and victim. For them, drinking wine and calling God by another name does not make you unclean." Even murder was permissible.

Back on the valley floor, shaded by fruit trees and flowering vines, Persephone suggested, "Take a closer look at that lotion bottle. It has a hidden catch. Release the catch, then pull on the neck."

Aria did it, and the brass bottle came apart, the neck becoming the handle of a small curved steel dagger, hidden in the bottle-shaped sheath. She stared at the bright keen blade that had suddenly appeared in her hand.

"Magic is mostly misdirection," Persephone reminded her. "Assassins can supposedly walk through walls and snatch daggers from thin air—now you know one of the ways they do those tricks. There is even a reservoir of lotion in the knife handle so the bottle looks and feels full."

Gingerly, Aria slid the dagger back in its brass sheath and closed the catch, somewhat aghast at her gift.

"This blade is not poisoned." Persephone was expert at such things. "And you do not have to wield it. This dagger is more symbolic. We have done his people an important service, so the Old Man of the Mountain owes you a life—preferably some suitably wicked infidel. Try not to use it frivolously."

Aria did not aim to use it at all. Leaving the Persian and Turkish children from the Gilded Cage, they headed north for home, along with Alexi D'Hay and the two Bulgar heiress—while the little lame Kipchak prince stayed with the Assassins, for the best he could expect at home was a bowstring around the neck. Borne aloft by a dawn wind from the south, the *Selene* made excellent time, over the flat blue Inland Sea.

Far below, Aria saw the Cathayan balloon, still aloft, but making so little headway that it seemed becalmed. Every time Aria spotted the balloon, her heart felt lighter, knowing those other harem survivors were still afloat. She prayed that Sonya D'Medved had made it aboard the balloon, and had passed a happy night in that pretty little pavilion. Though Aria knew the chances of that were no better than that of her knight having survived his own brush with the Tartars.

Eros' expert piloting soon left the drifting balloon far behind, as *Selene* sailed out over the Inland Sea, passing within sight of Baku, then crossing the coast, the desert, and the Kazakh steppe. They did not set her down until reaching Bulgar country, on the middle part of the Great Mother River, there called the Volga. There they returned Khanum Sofia and Khanum Maria, to the Popoff family, who were happy to get their valuable girls back.

Unfavorable west winds forced the *Selene* to get a tow from the Bulgars, who used row-barges to haul the sky-ship up the Great Mother River, past where it joined the Brovva, to the northeast edge of Markovy. Here, dense boreal forest again covered both banks of the river, and the *Selene* floated just above the pine tops, turned into the wind to give her maneuvering way, and keep the cable lines from fouling on the trees.

Persephone called Aria into the cabin, saying, "Time has come for us to part company."

Aria nodded sadly, having seen this coming, since the Firebird's Egg was somewhere to the south, while Persephone lived far to the north. "I will miss my lady."

"As I will miss you," the Killer of Children assured her. "But now you must turn south and retrieve the Firebird's Egg."

Aria still felt overwhelmed by the magnitude of the quest that she had so happily accepted from the Bone Witch. "I would not know where to even start looking."

"There is no need to search about." Persephone did not want Aria making the task worse than it was. "The Firebird's Egg has been claimed by the Crown, and returned to the Kremlin vaults in Markov, where King Demitri kept it before sending it to Byeli Zamak. How long it will remain there is anyone's guess, since the D'Medveds and Brovvaniks are threatening to march on Markov, and would likely seize the Egg if they take the capital—so the sooner you get there, the better."

Aria grimly agreed, though she had no idea how to get the egg out of the Kremlin vaults, much less back to Burning Mountain, with winter coming on and all of Markovy against her. Persephone sympathized, adding, "At least you do not have to do it alone."

"I do not?" Aria had been very much alone since Tartars took her knight.

"Not at all." The Killer of Children brightened, saying, "You shall have Alexi D'Hay with you."

Aria felt worse off, saddled with the vain and headstrong Alexi D'Hay. Not only must she save Markovy, but she must do while babysitting a petulant twelve-year-old. Why not blindfold her as well?

Seeing her disappointment, Persephone hastened to talk up Alexi's good points. "He is brave and agile, utterly determined, and totally loyal."

Only because he was hopelessly in love. Aria protested, "Alexi is but a boy—"

"And therefore easier to manage." Persephone arched an eyebrow. "Unless you are ready to give up demigods for grown men."

Aria had been doing well enough with a baron of France, before the Tartars took him, but she saw Persephone's point. Having age and height on Alexi was a definite advantage. Beatings and rape were out of the question, depriving Alexi D'Hay of the two main means of male control—that alone would make him more reasonable.

"More important, D'Hays hold the Kremlin. If you arrive in the capital with Alexi, they will naturally lodge you in the Kremlin palace." Persephone had clearly thought this all out, since doing the impossible was her forte. "Bulgars will see you to D'Hay lands near Markov, and Alexi's mother anxiously awaits him in the capital, along with his uncle, Baron D'Hay. None of whom know you are after the Firebird's Egg."

"And Alexi?" How much could he be trusted?

"He only knows I want you delivered to the harem-palace in the Kremlin, something he absolutely swears to do." If Persephone had asked for the crown jewels of Markovy, Alexi would have dashed off to fetch them. "The rest is up to you."

Too true. Aria was missing Persephone already, who had literally picked her up at the lowest point in her quest—drunk and alone atop the pinnacle at Karadyevachka, her knight lost, the Egg lost, and herself condemned to death.

As it turned out, Death was far friendlier than she had supposed. Aria was exceedingly grateful, but all she could say was, "I will miss you dearly."

Persephone reached out and ran her hand through Aria's black curls. "Everything comes at a price. Setting you back on your path means I must let you go."

"But we will see each other again." Somehow they had to meet again, maybe when her quest was done. Having lost her knight, there was no one Aria would rather be with.

"No, we will not." Tears appeared in Persephone's eyes, for the first time that Aria could remember, and the blond demigoddess held her tighter, saying, "You will grow up, like all ungrateful children do. It is not easy being the Killer of Children."

As Aria well knew. All she could do was hug the demigoddess to her, determined that this would not be good-bye forever. Persephone kissed her, saying, "Now go and grow."

Then they called in the men. Alexi was equally heartbroken at leaving Persephone, but manfully took his place as leader of the expedition. Eros gave her a good-bye embrace, coupled with a kiss that would have meant marriage in most countries. Aria could feel he was vexed, hating to see a virgin getting away. Everyone had something to regret.

Departing in a Bulgar boat, Aria wore her embroidered dress, now badly stained, while concealed on her person were her most prized possessions, the Bone Witch's protective rune, her straw doll, and the Assassin sheik's brass bottle. Saying good-bye to Persephone was not just painful, but terrifying as well, since Aria was again facing the civilized world alone, with nothing but her wits and luck to keep her alive.

Any grief Aria felt was overwhelmed by Alexi's longing for Persephone, which the boy insisted on proclaiming long after the *Selene* had disappeared around a river bend. Persephone was literally the first pretty thing Alexi D'Hay had seen but could not have. On the boy's ring finger was one of Persephone's pearl earrings, alongside a ruby ring bearing a bishop's crest.

That evening in the boat cabin, Alexi D'Hay got his second turn down when Aria refused to share his bed, even though the young boyar vowed he was fully able to "do his manly duty."

"Do your manly duty by yourself," Aria advised, curling up in a corner with the boat's dog, who was big, warm, and friendly, and not likely to molest her. Back among civilized people, Aria wished she could just stay invisible. Aided by a north wind, paid oarsmen rowed them relentlessly upstream, since by now the Mother River had twisted totally back on herself and was flowing north instead of south.

Days later, they docked at a D'Hay castle north of the capital, and Alexi immediately began ordering folks about, making sure the Bulgars were well paid, and that Aria had a harem car to carry her to Markov. Alexi himself commanded the cavalry escort, wearing boy's armor, while she rode in a little closed cab on wheels, horse-drawn, and far more jarring than her old traveling house, but mercifully quick. Alexi pressed the pace and arrived in Markov after night-fall, with torch bearers showing the way. Her horse car had carved screens, but all Aria saw of the capital was some narrow shadowy streets, followed by the market stalls in Red Square; then the huge black Kremlin gate blotted out everything.

Whatever she missed on the ride in was more than made up for by her torchlit reception she got stepping out of the horse car into the Kremlin Square, at the base of the Red Stairs leading into the harem-palace. Alexi was also arriving, so glittering underlings were rousted out of bed to receive the D'Hay heir, including butlers in silver-and-blue, royal stewards, and an honor guard of men-at-arms.

Baron D'Hay was waiting as well, with his most trusted Kazakhs, the men who burned Sonya D'Medved's home and introduced the teenager to group sex. If these were the sort of men hanging about Kremlin Square in the middle of the night, Aria was happy to be hustled straight from harem car to harem-palace. Valad D'Hay was twice as handsome as the tales told, and not at all cruel-looking for a boyar-cum-rapist. He had a short blond beard, neatly trimmed in the Western style, like the doomed men in the keep at Hebektahay. Wearing a full gown and a half-veil, Aria hardly got a glance. Alexi was already regaling his uncle with his wild adventures among the Valkyries.

If Baron Valad even half listened to his nephew, he would learn a lot, but Aria did not expect it. She was led up the Red Stairs, past the leering gargoyles that supported the stone balcony, and into the wooden heart of the harem-palace, where sleepy dwarfs peered out at her from behind doors, and nightin-gales sang in silver cages. Stewards led her through a series of presence chambers and to the Silken Door.

When Aria stepped through, she was in the harem proper, and veiled nuns took charge of her. Aria relaxed, amazed at all she had survived since last in the hands of nuns—her sacrifice at Karadyevachka, the hell at Hebektahay, Abeskum Island and the Gilded Cage—situations so fearsome that Bulgars and Assassins became brief interludes of sanity.

Aria expected to be given a straw matress and a crust of bread, or at worst a beating, for having been alone and unwatched in the hands of heathens. She was very much surprised when she was led by lamplight into the harem cloisters instead, past sleeping nuns and novices, to the Mother Superior's silver-lined chapel. There the Mother Superior herself waited before the candlelit altar, wearing a full veil, sitting beneath a blue cloud of incense smoke that shrouded a tall icon of the Weeping Virgin. Inviting Aria to kneel, the Mother Superior asked sweetly, "What is your name?"

"Aria," she answered, wondering where this was headed.

"Who are your parents?" asked the faceless nun.

She ran through her list of possible answers, from mysterious royalty, to the Bone Witch, and the Sisters of Suffering. None seemed to fit the occasion. "I do not have any."

"So you are an orphan, of unknown parents." Her Holiness did not make that sound bad; in fact, the Mother Superior seemed pleased and impressed by the news. And acted even friendlier, asking, "Are you with child, my dear?"

That was a question Aria had not expected, not from a nun, at least, especially when things were getting so friendly. Luckily, she could truthfully answer, "With child? No, not in the least."

Without changing her gentle tone, the head nun asked, "When were you last with a man?"

"Never." Did demigods count? Eros had never actually been in her, and Aria had Love's personal assurance that "all the way" was all that mattered.

Disbelief crept into the gentle tone. "Do you mean you have never had a man?"

"Not at all." This was the problem with the truth: no one was ever ready to believe it.

Hushed silence surrounded her, as if it were a miracle that a grown girl could be in heathen hands for more than a fortnight, and not already be nursing a toddler. Finally, the Mother Superior spoke, saying simply, "Bring the midwife."

Did everyone need to know this right now? Apparently, because a nun hurried off and returned with the midwife, a round, clever-looking woman with kindly eyes and gray in her hair, wearing a colorful kerchief and apron. Looking her over, the midwife asked gently, "What are you called?"

Again, not the question she had expected. "Aria."

Turning to the Mother Superior, the midwife asked, "May I see her alone?"

No one objected, so the midwife led her to a little curtained niche, just big enough for the both of them, and lit by a slotted brass lamp. Up close, she could tell that the midwife had been drinking, and Aria was immediately leery of what this cheery woman with beer on her breath wanted to do to her in that confined space. All the midwife did was look at her quizzically, at last asking, "Are you really Aria?"

"Yes," she replied cautiously—no one seemed ready to believe her, even about the simplest things.

Tears welled up in the woman's eyes, which seemed totally uncalled for, and the midwife whispered, "I think you might be."

Well, there was progress, someone who might believe her. Even if it hurt, perhaps the truth was not so hopeless after all.

Shaking her head in amazement, the woman asked, "Are you truly a virgin?"

"Yes." Aria wondered how many times she would have to say that.

With that, the midwife hugged her mightily, crying out, "Lord be praised."

Again, not what Aria expected, having thought a midwife might want some "proof" from her, maybe even make some godawful examination, looking between her legs for heaven knew what.

Beaming with delight, the midwife led her out from behind the curtain, saying, "She is Aria, and she is a virgin."

"Are you sure?" asked the veiled Mother Superior.

"Absolutely," declared the midwife, nodding, and smiling happily at Aria, who was astounded to have won the woman over so completely.

From behind the veil came a terse command. "Tell the bishop."

Tell the bishop what? Her virginity could not have that much ecclesiastical importance. Yet apparently it did, because nuns led her back out the Silken Door and through a covered way that led to the adjoining Arkhangelski Cathedral, where the Kings of Markovy were buried. There in a painted chamber, Aria was introduced to seventy-year-old Peter Petrovich, Bishop of Markov, seated in a low throne, wearing his purple-and-gold robes, but not his gold miter. His heavy crosier of office was held by a silent archpriest. Motioning Aria over, the friendly old prelate invited her to kneel, and tell him her story.

Which Aria did, so much as was fit for a bishop's ears. She was still a lost orphan raised in the woods, but the Bone Witch became a pious fungus gatherer, and her quest became a forlorn hope of joining the Sisters of Suffering, until she was waylaid along with Alexi D'Hay. She could safely assume Alexi had said next to nothing about her, and no one here seemed to know about her previous convictions, and her "sacrifice" at Karadyevachka. Baron Roye de Roye did not appear in this abridged version, nor did the Killer of Children;

instead, she laid heavy emphasis on the terror of the Tartars, and her miraculous return to Markovy.

That part of the tale did not interest the kindly prelate, who merely asked the midwife, "Is it her?"

Kneeling, the midwife nodded, saying, "Yes, Your Worship. I did not see her mother in her until we were close together. Look at her eyes, my lord."

Aria gaped at the midwife. "You knew my mother?"

"Child," the smiling woman replied, "you nursed at my breasts. Do you not remember?"

Aria did not. All she had were vague memories of a mother who sacrilegiously sang to her, calling her sweet little Aria.

"How about the straw doll I made you," asked the midwife, "you must remember that?"

Aria stood rooted, unable to move, staring at the midwife. Her whole world revolved around being an orphan, foster daughter to the Bone Witch, free to invent whatever mythical parents she wished. Now she must face the truth.

"Do you not remember the doll?" begged the midwife. "You loved it dearly, and kept it with you always."

Reaching inside her bodice, Aria brought out her tightly woven straw doll, showing the woman its happy painted face. "This doll?"

Again the midwife threw her arms around Aria, crying out, "This is her, this is our Aria."

Nuns fell to their knees, thanking Heaven above for her safe return. Even Aria found herself crying, knowing she was back in the arms of someone who held her as a baby, before she was lost to the world. Bishop Peter also seemed pleased, smiling at the women's enthusiasm.

Wiping tears from her eyes, Aria asked, "What about my parents? Who are they? Where are they?"

"Your mother is alive," the midwife replied. "She lives in a southern convent."

"We can even send for her if you wish," Bishop Peter offered. "Now that you are back, she has no reason to be in a nunnery."

Seeing her mother would be unbelievable. Aria asked hopefully, "What about my father?"

Bishop Peter's face saddened, and he simply said, "Your father is dead."

Aria's tears reappeared. All her life, she assumed her father was dead, and used that into a source of invention, making him a traveling prince, a noble knight, a Kazakh khan, or a straying priest, whatever the occasion demanded. Now that she knew he was really dead, she felt heartbroken. Her mother had been restored to her, but not her father—not now, and not ever.

Touched by her tears for a father she could not remember, Bishop Peter told her, "Your father is buried here in the Kremlin, if you wish say a prayer over him."

"Could I?" At least she would have a name, and a grave, to put in the place of nothing.

"Certainly," Bishop Peter declared. "That would indeed be best. Do your daughter's duty, and pray for him, for your father still has need of you."

Bowing to their bishop, the women led Aria back into the harem-palace, where the midwife went to fetch a boy and a light, saying, "I will show her."

When the midwife returned, she had a dark-haired boy of four or so with her, dressed in white and officiously carrying a slotted lamp with a candle inside. Aria followed them down stairs that got darker and narrower as they left the candlelit apartments above and descended into the harem vaults, an ancient warren of secret passages, hidden rooms, and dwarf tunnels. Arkhangelski Cathedral held generations of Markovite kings, but the harem vaults was where less saintly souls found their rest, according to the midwife, who claimed that, "Cranky old Queen Ivanovna the Second was bricked up alive somewhere down here, ages ago. When the wind blows right, you can still hear her screams."

Following the boy and his light, they wound their way deep into the heart of the labyrinth, where huge Romanesque vaults supported wood-and-stone floors above. Rats scurried out of their path, scared by the slotted lantern that cast swinging bars of light on bones stacked along the walls, long bones on one side, skulls on the other. Nobility lay mummified in stone niches, raised above floor level, but mostly the bones were mixed together, washerwomen and nuns, slaves and favorites, some in neat stacks, others in heaps and piles—only the small children's skulls stood out.

From deep within the charnel house, lights winked back at theirs, growing in the shadows, as they approached the heart of the harem ossuary.

There in a candlelit chamber lay a king's casket, done in the Western style with the dead king's likeness carved atop it, unhelmed, in plate armor, and holding his sword of state. Two empty spaces lay on either side of him, awaiting future entombments. Aria could tell by the crests on his armor that this was King Demitri himself, Baron Roye de Roye's former master, the king who had stolen the Firebird's Egg, then charged her knight with returning it.

Stopping before the casket, the boy lifted the lamp, proudly proclaiming, "My father."

Aria turned to the midwife, asking, "Truly?"

Nodding, the midwife replied, "This is his father."

Which made the boy Crown Prince Ivan, the heir to Markovy. Aria felt like she ought to be on her knees, but no one seemed to expect it, least of all the proud little boy, who merely wanted to show off his father the king. "How wonderful," she whispered to the young prince. "You have a great father, indeed."

Then Aria asked the midwife over the child's head, "Where is my father buried?"

"Right here." The midwife's smile widened. "He is your father too. By his first wife."

Aria shook her head, thinking the woman had gone completely mad. "That is impossible."

"This is he, Demitri the Fourth," the woman solemnly insisted, "and you are his true daughter Kataryna-Maria, called Aria by your mother, after the four last letters in your Latin name. She said it meant 'song' in a foreign tongue. I know because I brought you into the world, taking you from the royal womb."

Prince Ivan piped up, "Just like me!"

"You too, Your Highness," the midwife hastened to add.

Aria stood in stunned disbelief, betrayed by her name, by her whole nonexistent past, which had come suddenly back to haunt her in these grisly harem crypts. Her worst fears about civilization were shockingly confirmed. These people were not going to let her just slip in and steal the Firebird's Egg like a jay robbing a nest. They had found a far cleverer way to trap her, using flesh and family in place of chains and stone. She felt the midwife take her hand while resting another hand on her shoulder, saying in a soothing, almost familiar voice, "Come, children. Kneel for your father."

Ivan was on his knees at once, showing he knew the ritual even better than his big sister. As Aria knelt beside him, the midwife placed Ivan's hand in hers, his small fingers fitting easily into her palm. "Pray for your father," the midwife whispered. "Promise to be his true children, and loyal to each other, for you are all that is left of your faimly, the royal family."

"What about our mothers?" Already Aria felt compelled to speak for both of them.

"Yes, what of Mother?" echoed her little half brother.

"Both of your mothers have been put in convents for their safekeeping," the midwife explained.

"But we could send for them," Aria suggested. "That way the family could be together."

"It would not be safe for them." Looking fearfully about, the midwife shook her head. "Evil boyars plot to take the kingdom from Ivan. These men would not hesitate to harm your mothers."

Her whisper sank even lower. "Since only the dead are listening, I can tell you their names. Remember them, for you will not hear this by daylight—Prince Akavarr, and his brother-in-law Baron Tolstoy, along with all the Brovvniks, and the D'Medveds, and Baron Zazog. They want to divide you two, and take Ivan for their own."

Ivan's hand tightened in hers, and Aria answered for them, "We understand."

"Some you do, and some you will learn." The midwife smiled again, adding, "Do you know why your father is buried here, and not in Arkhangelski Cathedral?"

Aria shook her head, still getting used to even having a father.

"Being a foreigner, your mother could not be buried in the cathedral, and your royal father wanted his whole family together, for all eternity." Putting hands on both their shoulders, the midwife told them, "I am the woman who brought both of you into this world, drawing you from the womb, and giving you your first breaths. I am the only woman who has had both of you at her breasts. Now I charge you to carry out your royal father's wishes. You must honor each other, and your mothers. Aria, you must keep Ivan safe until he is of the age to rule, and Ivan you must be loyal to Aria, obeying her until you are of age, then protecting her when you are king. Swear you both, on the soul of your father."

Kneeling before the sculpted image of her father, Aria swore, and Ivan swore beside her. While the boy labored to complete his prayer, Aria added her own private vow to return the Firebird's Egg. Which, for all she knew, lay somewhere nearby.

When they finished, the midwife led them out of the crypts, past the piles of nameless bones, to an anointing chamber, where Aria was dressed all in silver, a shimmering gown that clung to her body—only it did not fit right, because it was made for someone else. Ivan was draped in cloth-of-gold and made to wear his child's gold coronet with rubies. Then they were both presented to Bishop Peter Petrovich, who in turn led them to the White Chamber, just above the Red Stairs, which was paneled in carved ivory, lit by mirrors and candelabras, and cut in half by a curtain.

Their half was empty, except for two unequal backless thrones, the type the Caesars sat on, and a small ornate ivory table supporting a glittering diamond tiara. Ivan automatically climbed over the smaller throne to sit in the higher, facing the curtain. Aria took the smaller throne, and he still only came to her shoulders. Bishop Peter stepped to the center of the room and lifted his hand, raising the curtain with just a gesture.

Aria saw that the rest of the room was filled with half the harem-palace, and the better half at that, headed by handsome Baron Valad D'Hay, and his nephew Alexi, plus the garrison and guard commanders, wearing blue-white surcoats over their armor. Seeing so many armed men made her want to disappear, but magically, they all sank to their knees—boyars, men-at-arms, ladies-in-waiting, nuns, priests, butlers, stewards, and dwarfs all bowed down to her. Everyone in the room except for old Bishop Peter.

What Bishop Peter did was even more alarming. He lifted the diamond tiara up over her head so that it shone in the candlelight, and then he brought it slowly down on her head, proclaiming her Kataryna-Maria II, Princess-Regent of Markovy. Aria could not tell what was more alarming, getting a new name, being expected to rule Markovy, or having a fortune in diamonds circling her brow. At least the tiara fit, and she already knew why. From what the nuns had said, it used to be her mother's.

markov tales

The Czar has no enemies, just dangerous friends.
—MARKOV PROVERB

12

the red stairs

Seamstresses raced death to sew Aria into her cloth-of-silver gown, the same one that had not fit right in her White Chamber coronation. Female dwarfs stitched the hems, while ladies-in-waiting did the sleeves and bodice. Pearl trim, silver pins, and ermine scraps lay scattered across the carpeted floor. Fingers and needles worked frantically over Aria's body—but not fast enough. She stood half-dressed when a flustered maidservant burst into her private presence chamber, announcing an armored visitor. "Lord D'Hay comes with dire warnings."

Small surprise there. Aria had been Princess-Regent barely a week, and already boyars were coming for her. She whispered a hurried prayer to the Bone Witch, knowing she must face angry men-at-arms in just a few minutes. Far too many people were watching for her to simply vanish.

Baron Valad himself came a heartbeat behind the serving woman, in armor and mail, violating the harem and giving Aria scant time to cover up. Clearly Valad D'Hay thought he could run things better than any teenage Princess-Regent. Aria strove to assume a superior air, ignoring his impropriety and instead glaring at her boyar's muddy boots.

Baron D'Hay stood and gawked. Dashing Valad D'Hay let his Kazakhs rape at will, but he had never been past the Silken Door before, plunging into the world of women, discovering that young princesses wore nothing under their closest fitting dresses.

Aria let him look, standing hip deep in dwarfs, draped in tangled black hair and cloth-of-silver, with one white thigh bared to the hip. But if she was timid with her body, men would think it was theirs to take—Eros taught her that. Better to be bold. Hopefully a bit of flesh would give Baron D'Hay courage.

Collecting himself, the startled blond lord dropped to one knee, assuming the self-important eagerness of a man with bad tidings. "Your Highness, I bring grave news."

"And ruin to my Barbary rugs." Which were brilliant pieces, brought by caravan over the Silk Road. To show he could not violate the harem with impunity, Aria motioned to her women. "Take off my lord's boots."

Serving women sprang to obey, happy to lay hands on handsome young Baron D'Hay. Nothing distracts a lord in armor like smiling females bending down and seizing his legs. D'Hay rose awkwardly, stammering out his message as her women lifted one leg, then the other, tugging off his heavy cavalry boots. "Prince Akavarr has come. With his boyars, and in armor."

"As are you," Aria reminded him tartly, tired of having to defer to men in iron. D'Hay wore the half-armor of her horse guards—gorget, cuirass, mail sleeves, and plate tassets on his thighs. His colors were blue and white, the same ones worn by Sir Roye de Roye. They were her colors now.

"And armed," Baron D'Hay added gravely.

"Naturally." He might as well have said they were wearing boots. No boyar would so much as stagger drunk to the privy without some sort of edged steel at hand—since weapons were what separated them from the serfs. Princes and boyars had swords, retainers, and the power of pit and gallows, and would right now be ruling the country if they were not so stark raving stupid. Very unnerving, but Aria had learned to live with it.

"Worse yet," D'Hay warned, "the guards at the Bishop's Gate have gone over to Akavarr and Tolstoy, who will be here within the hour."

Aria sighed in sincere exasperation, asking, "And I suppose they expect an audience?"

"Highness, Prince Akavarr means to take you." Hoping to salvage something out of the prince's defection, D'Hay offered her sanctuary on his lands. "We can still get away by the King's Gate, or by boat."

"Impossible." This harem-palace was her fortress, and it held the Firebird's Egg. Outside, she would be defenseless, and after what Aria had seen at Hebektahay, she had scant faith in D'Hay protection. Yet she hated to disappoint the eager baron, replying with the first excuse that came to mind. "Today is Saint Zelda's Day, devoted to prayer and repentance, so I may see no one. Please inform Prince Akavarr for me."

Dwarf seamstresses tittered, still sewing furiously. Baron D'Hay stared in disbelief as serving women handed him his boots. Cursing the idiocy of women, the young baron bowed and left, in clanking half-armor and stocking feet.

Aria turned to her women, saying with pretended seriousness, "I fear we must feed young Lord D'Hay to the horses."

Giggling broke the tension, and everyone worked all the faster for having someone to laugh at. Just getting dressed to die was horribly time consuming, since each piece of the gown now fit so perfectly, it must be sewn on. Such a gown came off the same way, one piece at a time. For a fashionable noblewoman to conduct an affair required more than bravery and a willing gallant; a successful liaison demanded the services of a clever maid, a discreet seamstress, and a dwarf to stand lookout.

Since becoming Princess Regent, Aria found that everything she did required a change of costume: a silk chemise to sleep in, a surcoat and sable mantle for the morning, a riding dress if she went out, a green-and-gold gown for supper, purple or cloth-of-silver for state occasions, red damask for evening wear. Almost overwhelming for a girl used to wearing the same dress, summer and winter, but a coup d'état was at least as important as a court reception, and Aria meant to look as good as she could.

If Prince Akavarr had her executed, that too meant another costume change, a black gown with crimson lining if it was a beheading, a plain linen shift if she was burned alive. Any informal strangling or suffocation would be come-as-you-are.

Ladies of the chamber placed the diamond tiara on her head just as Baron D'Hay returned—this time carrying his boots. "Your Highness, Prince Akavarr and his boyars are inside. The palace guards gave way to them."

Determined not to show fear before a boyar, Aria motioned her dwarfs aside, saying, "What do you think?"

D'Hay looked puzzled—not expecting to be consulted in a crisis. "Your Highness should call out any gendarmes of the guard that are still loyal, and come with me to D'Hay lands. Then we can hold off the Brovvniks and D'Medveds until..."

Aria smiled at Baron D'Hay's sincere concern while studying him in a serving girl's mirror. He was certainly brave, and able, and on her side. But after hearing what his Kazakhs did to Sonya D'Medved, Aria was loath to trust this handsome lord. She merely asked, "I mean what do you think of my gown?"

D'Hay gaped like a hooked sturgeon, his boots hanging limply at his side. "Stunning, Your Highness. Truly stunning."

Aria saw he meant it. How excellent—another handsome baron who liked the way she looked. "Good." She grinned into the mirror. "You may go."

Seeing he would get no serious answer, Baron D'Hay obeyed. Her women giggled again as he left, and Aria actually felt fortified, glad His Lordship approved of her gown. Male approval meant everything today—literally a life-or-death matter. And aside from her knight, men and demigods had so far cared only for her body, either to enjoy or rule through, never once wondering about her thoughts or feelings. Certainly no one wanted her opinion on ecclesiastical matters, the Tartar menace, or the uncertain future of Markovy. Prince Akavarr was just more honest than most, meaning to take such weighty matters entirely out of her inexperienced hands.

Her ladies pronounced her costume complete, and Aria felt ready to meet her foes, planning to face Prince Akavarr looking like she stepped off a cloud, not like she crawled from behind a couch.

She left her private apartments, followed by her handmaids. Shafts of morning sun filtered through the harem's narrow light wells, leaded windows, and arabesque screens. Live birds flitted through the halls and doorways, singing in alarm. Each hallway had its own color scheme, like royal blue, with sky-colored carpets and turquoise tapestries bordered with cornflowers; then the next chamber would be dark red, with burgundy hangings, alcove candles, and carpets dyed with dragon's blood.

Bishop Peter Petrovich of Markov waited at the Silken Door, dressed as befits a Prince of the Church in purple robes and golden miter, and armed with a gold-and-steel bishop's crosier heavy enough to use as a club. For all his age, Bishop Peter still had the divine fire, and would stand by the royal family to the death—for if noblewomen and children could be robbed with impunity, then the Church would be next. She bowed before him, feeling Bishop Peter's hand on her head and hearing him call her *daughter*—the only one who ever regularly did so. "Kneel before Heaven, daughter, and confess your sins."

Instantly she was a girl again—only the sins had changed. "Forgive me, Father, for I have sinned. I have not lied or blasphemed since my last confession. Nor have I fornicated, but I lusted after a man in my heart. And this morning a man saw my thigh. I skipped prayers two bedtimes in a row and listened to profane music, and was even moved to dance. Also I cursed Prince Akavarr several times in my heart, though only Heaven heard me."

Women whispered behind her while she waited for absolution, wondering whom she lusted after—not knowing that Tartars had taken him. Bishop Peter lifted his hand, signing in the air above her head. "Rise, my daughter, and be blessed. You face penance enough for your sins."

Perhaps. Chastity and prayer had not forestalled Prince Akavarr, but they let Aria face him with a lighter heart. No matter what she had done, no matter what lies were told about her, Aria did not feel sinful. Nor did she understand why music and dancing were mortal sins, while getting beastly drunk and whipping the clothes off serf girls or setting fire to a dwarf were harmless pastimes. The ways of the Almighty were ever a mystery—especially to Aria.

Still, she was grateful for confession, which always made her feel cleansed. Aria rose and kissed the bishop's bony hand, asking, "Is my brother here?"

Ivan was. Being a boy, and heir to the throne, his surcoat was cloth-of-gold. She took her half brother's hand. If the family must face death, they would do it together.

Bishop Peter walked before her, holding his crosier and swinging a censer, blessing the path ahead. Ivan clung to her hand, terrified, though he had the least to fear. Prince Akavarr would happily slaughter the lot of them just to lay hands on Ivan—but try to explain that to a frightened four-year-old.

Lord D'Hay appeared again, out of breath from going back and forth in armor. He knelt before the bishop, touching his forehead, then knelt again before Aria and Prince Ivan. "Highnesses, they are at the foot of the Red Stairs—the gendarmes of the guard have not stopped them."

Aria nodded. That is what came of not giving herself to her guard captain, despite the fellow's ardent advances. She thanked D'Hay, saying he should stand aside. She did not want young D'Hay throwing himself away in some futile attempt to defend her. "Wait for us here. Though I know that shall be hard for you."

D'Hay rose, looking like he might not do it, but then his gaze dropped and he stepped back. "As you say, m'lady, it will be hard."

M'lady? Here is a bold boy. What had become of *Your Highness?* Bare a bit of thigh in a crisis, and suddenly she was m'lady. At least he obeyed. Aria's worst terror was that her power of command would be taken away that after today people would not do as she said, and she would be whipped and ordered about instead, made to serve her captors, forced into marriage or a nunnery as occasion demanded. She would rather be dead.

Fear clutched her heart as she approached the Red Stairs. Some game idiot had called out her guard—D'Hay, perhaps. Small good that would do. Kazakh bowmen crowded the porch at the head of the stairs, smelling of sweat and spoiled butter, gripping their composite bows; unable to speak a civilized tongue, they would not know whom to shoot. The gendarmes of the guard were drawn up at the foot of the stairs in their silver-chased armor, but by now they were bound to be under Prince Akavarr's spell. Aria could not imagine them turning their poleaxes against a prince of the blood, backed by dozens of boyars, not unless she gave them some incredibly good reason.

Gargoyles crouched on the balcony rail, staring down at the open audience hall two full stories beneath them. Looking past their stone faces and into the hall below, all she saw at first was bared blades—the boyars' drawn swords, the gendarmes' poleaxes, and the guards' halberds. A hedge of edged steel seemed to fill the audience hall, bright and terrifying.

Her stomach gave a heave, and her hands clutched the rail. Kings had died on these stairs—including her great-grandfather, thrown over the balcony rail onto the pikes of rioting peasants. Legend said the steps were carpeted in red so they would not show blood.

Hisses rose from below, along with shouts of "witch" and "whore." It took a moment to realize they meant her. Standing still as a silver statue at the head of the Red Stairs, Aria fought to cast out fear. Fear eroded you, and Aria wanted to be as striking as she could—like the Killer of Children. That was why she stood before her enemies wearing a gown worth more than most Markovites saw in a lifetime, yet looking nearly naked, every curve exposed by cloth-of-silver. Beneath her silver, ermine, and pearls was her mortal body—a woman's body, weak and willful, but topped with a diamond tiara worth a queen's ransom.

Prince Akavarr stepped up on the stairs, wearing half-armor and a mail cowl. Blocked by Bishop Peter swinging his censer, the prince called up to her, "Come down, harlot."

Boyars began to chant, "Jez-e-bel, Jez-e-bel, Jez-e-bel . . ." Calling her by the name of the witch-queen in the Book of Kings. Aria stared hard at the harsh bearded faces. Akavarr was her uncle, her father's half brother, barred from the throne for being a bastard, but still an old-time prince of the blood—big, bearded, and unwashed, who ate with his hands, drank with his boyars, and hated her with all his heart. He had never reconciled himself to his half brother's foreign marriage—to a wife who had refused to hide in the harem, who dared bring minstrels and playacting to the palace. And he saw no need for a witchy niece who shared her mother's looks and disposition.

By now Aria had heard Prince Akavarr's tale many times over. After ten years of frivolous marriage produced only a daughter, Akavarr led the boyars in demanding that Aria's mother be set aside. Ailing King Demitri capitulated. Aria's mother was sent off with shaven head, to live on bread and water in a White Sea convent. "Let her dance and frolic to four stone walls," Akavarr had sneered.

Father then married a god-fearing girl from a good boyar family. And Aria herself had disappeared, either sent off to safety or kidnapped by king's enemies—no one seemed to know for sure. Finally Father's second marriage produced only a single living son, who currently cowered behind her.

Now, with Mother gone and Father dead, Prince Akavarr meant to complete the task, finishing off her family—if not by outright murder here on the Red Stairs, then by privation in some convent cell or walled up in a harem vault. Her mother's foreign blood made Aria hated, but her father's blood condemned her. Once he had Ivan in his hands, Akavarr could not risk her producing yet another heir.

She heard old Bishop Peter raising his reedy voice against the multitude, crying, "For shame! For shame!" He stood in front of the armed prince, shaking his censer. "Why have you violated the sanctity of the palace?"

Taken aback, Prince Akavarr had not expected the reverend bishop to side with Ivan's wicked half sister—but he quickly recovered, shouting even louder. "We have come to assure the safety of the heir!" He pointed a mailed finger at her. "She means to supplant Prince Ivan with a child of her vice."

Aria stared at the prince, thinking he must be entirely mad, since she had never even had a man, much less a child. Unable to help herself, she laughed aloud, a high musical laugh just like her voice. Scared as she was, Aria could not hide her amusement.

Atop the normal maidenly fears, Aria had the sure knowledge that her child would be a prize of state, immediately seized and used to replace her. Any heir of her body was vastly preferable to the Princess-Regent herself, being more easily manipulated and less tainted by foreign blood. Having a daughter would be dangerous; a boy would be her death sentence. Laughing high and long at Prince Akavarr's absurd suggestion, she could barely believe that her royal uncle had things so utterly wrong.

Her laughter was magical, shattering the tension, giving her sudden courage. Everyone stared at her—boyars, gendarmes, ladies and priests, guards and dwarfs, bewildered Kazakhs—all wondering what on earth she had to laugh at. "You think I mean to harm the heir?"

"You know you do," Akavarr shot back.

"Then ask him." She reached behind her and lifted up Ivan in his cloth-of-gold gown. Her tiny terrified half brother clung hard to her, blue eyes wide, horrified by the scene below.

Men stared back at her, nonplussed. The boyars' whole purpose had been to "protect" the heir, who now clung to his worst enemy, the scheming foreign half sister who plotted to put her ill-gotten seed upon the throne. And both of them were protected by the Bishop of Markov. What had seemed so simple when Prince Akavarr was marching on the palace turned out to be no easy task at all.

Tall, balding Baron Tolstoy stepped eagerly forward, being Akavarr's brother-in-law and chief supporter, married to the prince's sister. Leaning past the bishop, his armor rattling, Tolstoy asked, "How can we know that is really Prince Ivan?"

Aria laughed again. How could he know? Lord Tolstoy had seen the heir only from a distance, on state occasions like her father's funeral. She saw Ivan every day. Since his mother had been put away, Ivan had been brought up by the harem, and much of that bringing up had now fallen to Aria, his nearest female relation. What a ridiculous absurdity! After virtually ignoring him since birth, they were asking the evil stepsister, "Is this really our prince?"

Striding boldly down the stairs until she was close enough to smell the beer on Tolstoy's breath, she smiled triumphantly, holding the boy up so the whole hall could hear him. "Tell them your name."

Her boldness and laughter encouraged him. Hiding his tears, he grinned shyly, saying to her, "I am Prince Ivan."

Aria tickled him, making him laugh as well. "Say it louder. For them." She pointed at the men.

The boy looked quickly at Tolstoy, shouting, "I am Prince Ivan!" Then he hid back in Aria's arms. She stroked his head, telling the heir to Markovy he had done well.

Bishop Peter brought his crosier down, barring the steps, saying to Tolstoy, "Of course he is the heir. Just as I am patriarch of Markov. By the grace of God, whom did you expect to find in the palace?"

Tolstoy stepped back, stymied. Prince Akavarr pushed past his vacillating brother-in-law, saying, "The heir belongs in our hands."

Aria looked from him to the hesitant boyars behind him, then to the uneasy gendarmes of the guard. Behind her on the balcony, women in cloth-of-silver stood beside Kazakhs in skins and leather. Dwarfs perched on the gargoyles. All eyes were on them—which was her sole advantage. Prince Akavarr plotted his coup in secret, with just his creatures around him. It was wholly different to seize the heir to the throne in front of God and witnesses. She lifted Ivan up again. "Do you want to stay with me, or go with these men?"

Ivan shrank back, horrified, grabbing at her arms. "With you, Aria. With you." She took the frightened boy back to her breast, calming and comforting him.

She desperately hoped Akavarr would back down, announcing himself satisfied, then retreat to his lair to plot more mischief. Instead she saw him spin about to harangue the wavering boyars. Staring in wonder at his armored back, and listening to his shouts, Aria realized this was foolish of him. Tolstoy had been drinking, probably Akavarr had too, to fortify himself for the coup. He should either have given in or stormed past the helpless old bishop with his blade drawn. There are times when men must use either their feet or their swords. Talking for them can be fatal.

Everyone watched him castigate Tolstoy, upbraiding the reluctant baron, cursing his sister's husband as a coward and worse. Tolstoy then answered haughtily, unused to swallowing insults.

In an act of absolute lunacy, Akavarr shoved Baron Tolstoy scornfully, pushing him lightly on the breastplate with the gloved palm of his left hand. There was no flesh-to-flesh contact, but Aria saw at once it was a terrible mistake. Drunk and excited, Tolstoy instinctively clapped his hand to his sword, which he had sheathed while talking to Ivan, his legal sovereign.

Akavarr's sword was already out. Hitting his brother-in-law in the face with the hilt, he knocked Baron Tolstoy backward onto the stairs. Akavarr stood over the fallen baron, blade bared, staring down at Tolstoy, who lay bleeding from the lip. Aria knew her uncle had gone way too far, assaulting one of the Nine Barons, and his biggest backer. Did he really mean to kill Baron Tolstoy? Akavarr's own brother-in-law? On his back, with his hands empty? In front of the patriarch and the heir apparent? Even the boyars would be bound to call it murder.

Yet if he stepped back, Tolstoy would be up and at him, blade in hand. God alone knew what would come of that.

Giving him no time to think his way out of the impasse, she cried out at the top of her voice, "Treason! Treason! He means to kill Baron Tolstoy."

Her women took up the chant: "Treason. Treason. Treason . . ."

Even Ivan yelled it. "Treason. Treason." A terrible word to shout in that charged situation.

Akavarr gave ground, anxious to defuse the situation. Tolstoy bounded to his feet, drunkenly determined to get blood for blood. Drawing his sword, he slashed clumsily at Akavarr. Forced to defend himself, Prince Akavarr parried, trying to make himself heard above the chanting. He batted Tolstoy's sword aside, but dared not strike. Aria could see from his face that he wished none of this was happening.

Stumbling backward, Tolstoy tripped on the steps, going down on one knee, crying vigorously for help. Gendarmes suddenly remembered their duty, realizing that they could be called accomplices to Prince Akavarr's treason. Poleaxes lashed out. One clanged off the prince's gorget, slashing him across the jaw. Akavarr groaned and went down, his beard splattered with blood. More blades descended, hacking at his armored body. Once he was down, the gendarmes knew that it would be best for them if he never got up. Aria hugged Ivan to her, hiding his eyes so he would not see.

Bishop Peter weighed in with his silver crosier, forcing back the gendarmes. Too late. Prince Akavarr lay slashed and still at the base of the Red Stairs. Chants of "treason" subsided, replaced by shocked silence as brittle as Barbary glass. Saint Zelda's Day would be long remembered.

Aria turned and took Ivan back up, past the ladies and Kazakhs on the balcony, past the dwarfs on gargoyles, headed for the harem, putting distance between herself and what had happened. Prince Akavarr came looking for death and found it, but no good would come of this. When the boyars looked about for someone to blame, they were bound to remember her.

D'Hay stood waiting where she had told him to stay, shifting from foot to foot. Pleased at his impatient obedience, she released him, saying, "Take charge of the gendarmes—you are their new captain. See there is no more killing."

He bowed happily, bounding off to do her will. The lad showed promise, and she badly needed loyal young blades, having hardly anyone to trust—and enemies aplenty. Akavarr was only the most eager and bloodthirsty, but the most brainless drunken boyar could make the connection between the boy in her arms and the womb in her belly. Whoever laid hands on Ivan could rule Markovy in the boy's name, undisputed so long as Aria was childless. Or better yet, dead.

But if she married, or had a boy out of wedlock, the boyars would have to decide between the rights of a son by a second marriage, and any grandsons from a first marriage. And she had just seen how they settled things.

Tears welled up. The only sure way to save herself was to be as bloodthirsty as they were. To do as her uncle suggested—kill the child in her arms, making herself the sole heir, thoroughly hated, but absolutely indispensable. Whoever she gave herself to would then be King. Which is why she had learned to laugh at the notion of justice, literally laugh out loud. That spooked people, especially the boyars, seeing a female demon-child laughing at law and nobility. Totally untamed, and sitting on the throne.

13

the princess and the boyarinya

Harems often had to be built inside out and upside down with internal balconies and rooftop gardens, to best use limited sunlight while showing a blank face to the world. Aria's private bath and sauna were on the south side of the topmost floor, with thin columns supporting intricately carved alabaster screens that let in light and air. Heavy wooden shutters closed off the heated room in winter—but on a late summer afternoon, only the windward shutters were closed, and golden shafts of sunlight came slanting in. Wrapped in a silk bathrobe, her toes trailing in warm rose water, Aria lay on cushions embroidered with spring flowers, listening to a castrated choirboy sing in sweet contralto to amuse her.

He succeeded admirably, being cute as well as clever, with high Kazakh cheekbones, dark dreamy eyes, and black hair as untamed as a horse's mane falling down his smooth, strong back. His song thrilled Aria immensely, and his white robe trimmed in cloth-of-silver lay wide open at the throat. Seeing his sculpted neck shiver as he sang made her want to run hands over the boy's throbbing throat, feeling Jochi's singing with her fingers—but her reputation was bad enough already, without being caught molesting young eunuchs.

Girls came giggling in on bare feet, wearing light robes and carrying bowls of honeyed yogurt—Tasha, Marta, Anna Tolstoy, and Sonya D'Medved, whom Aria had not seen since escaping the Gilded Cage. She had been overjoyed to hear that Sonya was still alive, but not happy to have her in the harem. D'Medveds wanted her killed or overthrown, which made Sonya a spy.

Still, it was a thrill to see that this was the same smiling blond girl she left for dead on Abeskum Island. It was like getting someone back from Lady Death, someone young and happy, and full of hope. If Sonya had escaped the Tartars, there was hope even for Sir Roye de Roye. Too bad the young boyarinya was an enemy.

Clapping at the singing, they called to the boy, "Jochi, Jochi, play your balalaika for us. Play, and we will feed you."

Marta, a tall dark-haired harem favorite, waved her bowl of sweet yogurt. "You can lick it from our fingers."

"Or off our breasts, if you like," Tasha teased him, dripping yogurt down her open front, then wiping it up with her fingers, sticking them one by one in her mouth. Tasha was a Kipchak savage and Aria's slave, but ranked high in the harem's unofficial hierarchy by being intolerably beautiful and insufferablly sure of herself.

Jochi ignored them, still singing sweetly. Careful in his habits, the choirboy ate sparingly, knowing eunuchs ran to fat—it would take more than a bevy of teenagers to tempt him, no matter how they served the sweet yogurt. Seeing the boy would not give in, the girls set down their yogurt and swarmed over him, giggling and rubbing themselves against the singing boy, kissing his cheek, then sliding slim hands inside the silver trim on his robe.

His voice faltered, clearly distracted. Aria clapped for them to stop. "Sinful girls, why have you come to disturb this divine singing?"

"Your Highness." Tall, dark Marta made a teasing little curtsy. "We came to bathe."

"And sow trouble," Aria added. Being locked away completely from men, cooped up among widows, wives, nuns, children, dwarfs, and eunuchs could drive young girls utterly crazy—as Aria well knew. Much of Anna Tolstoy's reputation for wildness came from repeated attempts at escape.

"Do not make us bathe below," Sonya D'Medved pleaded. "It is dreadful."

"You do not know how we suffer," Marta complained, "with the noise, the steam, the closeness, the crowding—"

"With everyone talking at once," Tasha added.

"And all about us." Anna Tolstoy imagined herself the subject of limitless conversation.

"And wanting to wash you," Tasha complained.

"Or scourge you with willow switches." Marta shivered.

"All because we wish to be clean!" Anna Tolstoy, the bloody-minded baron's statuesque niece, sounded like the most put-upon soul in Markovy—a martyr to cleanliness, licking honey yogurt off slim fingers.

Aria shook her head, having seen the harem baths. Cleaner and better than any public bath in Markovy, they were tiled with marble and trimmed in gold, but still wet, steamy, sulfurously hot, and usually crowded with noisy naked women of all ages, washing, talking, and doing their hair—the very heart of the harem, where gossip circulated and girls' figures were judged. If you were cute and unwary, you could get groped in the sauna. Or be beaten with a willow switch. Why put up with that? These were the prettiest, and two of the noblest "virgins" in the harem. "That makes it hardly worth bathing at all?"

"No, no, m'lady!" They shook their cute heads in defense of cleanliness. "Not here! Not with you! This is paradise." Again that familiar *m'lady.* Her handmaids were as bad as Baron D'Hay, though they at least were all her age, and fellow prisoners, more entitled to be familiar.

Marta made another bobbing curtsy. "Please let us stay and bathe here, under m'lady's watchful eye."

Tasha ran her hand through Jochi's hair, nodding at a three-stringed instrument lying behind him. "And have the boy play the balalaika."

Everyone looked to Aria. Bathing was a harmless indulgence, even thought to be healthful, and a eunuch's voice was a gift of the Almighty—and the surgeon's knife—but musical instruments were tools of Satan. And the cute young eunuch they were tormenting was a choirboy dedicated to Heaven. Sonya D'Medved smiled wickedly. "M'lady may do whatever she wants."

Aria felt challenged. Here in the harem, that was nearly true. This was her private world, where she could have things as she wished. Freedom in hiding. It was the most fun thing about being Princess-Regent. Here, she and the lucky women who attended her could be cool in summer and warm in winter, free to sip strong coca and speak their minds, free to hear music and have hot saunas and cool sherbet. Free to make illicit love behind locked doors. A nagging voice told her it would not last.

She nodded, giving royal consent. With triumphant squeals, the girls slipped off their robes, smothered Jochi with parting kisses, then slid laughing into her great brass bathing basin, which was warmed from below. Youth and beauty won again over decorum and duty. Splashing playfully, they started washing each other's hair, standing up to let warm rosewater slide like liquid silk off their smooth young bodies.

Lying back on embroidered cushions, Aria watched the boy's reaction under her lashes. Anyone who thinks a eunuch cannot have an erection has never been in a harem. Embarrassed, Jochi put the rounded body of his balalaika in his lap to hide his condition. Jochi had the "kindest" cut, used for choirboys and ladies' companions, when only the testicles were taken, unlike the "clean cut" eunuch favored in Black Cathay. Jochi could copulate but not impregnate—a godsend to lonely harem inmates.

But not Aria, who admired the boy for his musical voice, not for his mutilated genitalia. She looked back at the girls, wondering which had gotten him so excited.

Clearly it was Sonya D'Medved, whose flowing curves could arouse the dead. Aria admired how easily Sonya's body moved, brimming with suppressed energy, reminding her of Persephone. She felt vaguely jealous, finding her enemy so desirable—easily the prettiest of her handmaids, and much more appealing than any eunuch. Sonya held up her long golden hair for Marta to wash, and Aria was aghast to see fresh red whip marks curving around the girl's back and thighs.

Immediately, she wanted to ask who had done this, and have them whipped as well. Being Crown Princess had its prerogatives, and this was one she ached to indulge. Though she had just been jealous of Sonya's beauty, it hurt her to see such loveliness marred. Then she realized Sonya's family must have done it. No doubt, they had their reasons. Aria's relations with the D'Medveds were bad enough, without having them publicly flogged.

"What does m'lady wish to hear?" Jochi asked, his balalaika tuned and ready. He no longer looked embarrassed.

"Something romantic," she confessed, not minding the familiar *m'lady* from him. "To take my mind off my troubles."

Jochi strummed his balalaika and sang a Kazakh love song, light and stirring, like a horse's canter, that tugged at Aria's heart, reminding her of the wild free life she used to live, flying over the open steppe with Eros and Persephone. Part of that life was standing just a few feet away, looking very fetching while getting her gold hair washed.

She envied Sonya's free and easy manner, and her blithe ability to please herself, invading the royal bath at the first opportunity. Aria knew that Sonya's maidenhead was but a distant memory, and most likely that was why she was punished. Yet at worst, Sonya faced merciless beatings or a forced marriage— no one would kill her for giving birth.

Seeing her sadness, Jochi stopped, asking, "What troubles, m'lady?"

"Everything." At this moment, her troubles were so immense, she could almost laugh at them. Her father was dead, along with the Bone Witch, and her first and only love. Her boyars meant to murder her, or force her into marriage—whichever best suited their needs. And she had no one to defend her, aside from D'Hay and the doubtful gendarmes, and perhaps his Kazakhs. Or maybe her dwarfs and eunuchs.

"Even me?" Jochi asked, clearly wanting to be no trouble. His obvious concern was touching. This ardent choirboy meant to be true to her.

Aria laughed. "You most of all." Love and loyalty were things she had started to fear.

"Why?" Jochi asked, taken aback, afraid he had offended.

"Because you give me hope." And love. Aria knew her boyars would not kill just her, but anyone close to her as well. Noblemen could be incredibly vindictive. When Baron Tolstoy caught his wife with a groom, he had the groom castrated and hanged outside his wife's window, alongside the stableboy who stood lookout. All winter, Baroness Tolstoy watched her lover twist in the icy wind beside the boy who helped bring them together. Aria did not want to see Jochi tortured to death by bullies in armor. Anyone who loved her must be able to defend himself.

"But, m'lady, I mean to give you hope," the young eunuch declared earnestly, "and to lighten your troubles."

When the girls were done with their hair, she gave them leave to go. Sonya D'Medved smirked at her as the teenagers toweled and dressed. The girl did not know her from the Gilded Cage, because Aria had been invisible, but being escapees from Aladdin's harem created an unspoken connection, even if only Aria knew the source.

Below her whip marks, the boyarinya had a little yellow bird tattooed on her hip, the D'Medved golden martlet. Tasha came over to whisper to Jochi in Kazakh before going giggling off with the others. As the girls swaggered out, Sonya gave her a impudent wink.

Girls' voices faded, replaced by the warm gurgle of water flowing into brass basins. "Does m'lady wish another song?" Jochi asked blandly, his balalaika still resting in his lap.

She shook her head. "Do not call me m'lady."

"Your Highness, I am sorry if—"

"Aria," she told him. "You need not be sorry. Just call me Aria."

"Aria, we all—"

"Say it again," she insisted, thrilling to the sound—to be surrounded by people and hardly ever hear your name can be incredibly lonely. Kataryna-Maria II sounded too cold, and Aria had a hard time thinking of herself as Her Royal Highness.

"Aria. Oh, Aria." Jochi laughed. "We all love you. My heart is yours to command."

She sighed, saying, "I do not want to command love. Sometimes I barely want to command at all—but no one gives me that luxury. Please, let love at least come free."

"Aria, I love you freely." Jochi turned suddenly serious, looking levelly at his mistress. "Everyone does."

"Everyone?" She thought of her hostile boyars and plain, and upright Markovites who hated her foreign blood and witchy looks. Or superstitious serfs who heard hedge priests' lurid sermons about her harem orgies—which had yet to happen. But Markovite opinion hardly counted to a nomad eunuch who played the balalaika and prayed to heathen gods.

"Everyone who matters," Jochi declared earnestly. "Prince Ivan, all the eunuchs, those pretty girls that just left, the best of the dwarfs, Bishop Peter, and what older women still have their wits. Some of them live in your grandfather's time."

And a fine time it had been—or so people said. If you could not use your imagination, what was the use of being locked away? But it was hard to believe she had the whole harem behind her. "Even Sonya D'Medved?"

"Sonya too," Jochi assured her.

"That is silly," Aria scoffed. "Sonya just met me."

"M'lady just met her," Jochi politely corrected his mistress. "Sonya has been hanging about the royal apartments, hoping for a private audience."

Aria arched an eyebrow. "So she could share my bath?"

Jochi smiled slyly. "If m'lady pleases."

"What does that mean?" Everything here was as the Princess-Regent pleased. She sensed her eunuch was laughing at her, and she resented the lèse-majesté. If her eunuchs could mock her, what would her boyars do?

Jochi did not answer, and his silence irked. Closing her eyes, she asked Jochi to play her that love song again. Which he dutifully did.

That night, when the harem was asleep, Aria slipped into a fur-trimmed robe and visited her treasury, located in a high tower that only she had the key to. Her father had died solvent, a remarkable achievement for kings of Markovy, and sacks of silver lined one wall, along with small iron chests of gold. Great jeweled cups and ruby coronets sat on velvet cushions, while the largest room was set aside for Markovy's greatest treasure, filled with bales of furs—sable, mink, fox, and otter. Safe amid the pile of furs sat the Firebird's Egg.

Aria ran her fingertips over the Egg, finding the leathery skin still warm to the touch, and vibrating with life. Though the windowless stone room was cold, it was not near as cold as the vaults—so the Egg was stirring, getting ready to hatch. Who knew what would happen then?

Time had come to move the Egg, for everyone's safety. Akavarr's attack had shaken her, showing the harem was no longer safe. Having the Egg here amid all this gold made Aria nervous, since this was the first place the boyars would head for if they seized the palace. Carefully lifting the Egg, she was shocked to find that it sat in a soft nest of extra-thick hair. Mink and sable pelts had started to grow more fur, despite being long dead, rejuvenated by the magic Egg.

She wrapped the Egg in a bearskin and carried it back to her private apartments, padding through silent colored halls. When she got to her apartments, Aria went to the rear wall of her bedchamber, pushing sideways on a piece of paneling that opened like a puzzle box, revealing hidden stairs. The harem-palace was full of such passages, and Aria had found this one during a thorough search of her chambers, which also revealed several peepholes and a secret cupboard big enough to hide in.

This passage led down into the harem vaults, where she had found the perfect hiding place for the Firebird's Egg, in a barred tomb, behind the mummy of a long-dead ancestor. Then Aria hid the tomb key beneath a pile of long bones in the ossuary, so only she would be able to get to the Egg.

As she retraced her steps, Aria was astonished to see a light ahead. Someone was emerging from the hidden stairs leading to her bedchamber, following in her footsteps. Who would dare stalk her, here in the harem vaults? Her first thought was boyar assassins. Direct assault had failed, so why not dispose of the pesky witch-princess in secret? This was a perfect chance.

Dousing her light, Aria stepped back into the shadow of an arch, whispering her spell. Silent and invisible, she watched the light get closer and brighter.

Sonya D'Medved appeared in the archway, wearing a plain black shift belted at the waist beneath a fur-lined cloak, and carrying a candle backed by a curved silver mirror that focused the light forward.

Seeing there was no one with Sonya, Aria stepped out of the shadows, asking, "What are you doing here?"

Sonya nearly dropped the candle in surprise. Then the boyarinya went down on one knee, bowing her blond head and saying, "Forgive me, m'lady, I came looking for you."

Again the familiar *m'lady.* "Whatever for?"

"To see that Your Highness is safe. Your bedchamber was empty, and the secret panel ajar. I feared something was amiss." So Sonya decided to discover what her mistress was doing.

"If I needed your assistance, I would send for you," Aria informed her. First her bath, now her bedchamber, and secret ways. Nothing was safe from the girl's prying.

Sonya kept her head down, asking with unaccustomed humility, "Does m'lady hate me?"

"No," Aria replied curtly. She did not hate the rebellious boyarinya; she just mistrusted her. It was an unpleasant shock to find Sonya familiar with the passageway in her bedchamber, since it made a perfect listening post. Now that D'Medveds knew about this passage, she must move the Egg yet again.

Setting down the lamp, Sonya nonchalantly drew a long thin knife from inside her cloak, though bringing edged weapons into Aria's apartments was forbidden—in fact, a flogging offense. But Sonya was a hopeless savage whose mother died in childbirth and whose father was disemboweled and beheaded by D'Hays. Aria wished she had stayed invisible.

Handing the knife hilt-first to Aria, Sonya pleaded, "Please, m'lady, if I have offended you in the least, take my life now."

"Nonsense!" Aria tried to hand knife back, exasperated by such impertinent theatrics.

Sonya would not take it, clasping her hands tightly behind her back. The boyarinya looked straight up at Aria, baring her white neck. "Your Highness, we are both fatherless and beset by enemies. So there must be total trust between us. After tonight, my life is in m'lady's hands. If m'lady means to kill me for being born a D'Medved, then I beg her to do it now. I would rather die here by your hand than be betrayed and have my own people burn me for treason."

"Burn you? Really?" D'Medveds were more barbaric than she had thought.

"Unless I betray you, they will," Sonya insisted. "Why do you suppose I was sent into your harem?"

Not what she expected to hear from the young boyarinya. Unlike her tame cousins, Sonya had seen the world outside a D'Medved harem, and it must have affected her. Intrigued, Aria asked, "Why not betray me? That is what your family wants."

"Because I love you." Sonya said it as plainly and simply as if it made sense.

"You love me?" Jochi's words came back to her.

Sonya nodded. "Ever since that day on the Red Stairs, when you stood up to Prince Akavarr and Tolstoy. I was watching on the balcony, and fell hopelessly in love. You alone can save us. You can make things right."

Feeling silly holding the knife, Aria told the blond girl at her feet, "Get up. I will not kill you."

Sonya shook her head. "If m'lady will not trust me, I would rather she did kill me. Then I will at least die by your hand."

Damning the girl's insufferable pride, Aria declared, "I do not care that you are a D'Medved."

"M'lady does care." Tears appeared in Sonya's sky-blue eyes. "Or she would not be so cold."

Aria stared down at the beautiful defiant girl, saying, "You are most remarkable."

"So I hope." Sonya smiled, wiping off tears on her shoulder while still holding her hands behind her. "When I was a motherless little girl, I gave myself to Lady Death, knowing I would never live my life as I willed, unless I was willing to die for it. Nothing I have seen since has swayed me, not a Kazakh kidnapping, a Tartar attack, or a shah's harem. Try to please others, and I will live under a husband's whip. Which means I must please myself."

Aria always knew Sonya D'Medved had airs above her station; now it seemed the boyarinya aspired to be free. "Is that so bad?" Sonya asked. "Will m'lady not forgive me?"

Lowering the knife, she reached out her left hand, the witch's hand, saying, "Aria."

Sonya looked dumbly up at her, the first time Aria had seen the Turkan Khatun's translator speechless. "*M'lady* is improper," she explained. "You must call me Aria."

Taking her outstretched hand, the young D'Medved pressed it to her tearstained cheek, murmuring, "Do I have m'lady Aria's trust?"

"You have my trust." Aria was happy and surprised to have Sonya D'Medved on her side, the first of the enemy to come over to her. Her first conquest—and a boyarinya, no less. D'Hay support hardly counted, since they had nowhere else to go. Sonya had chosen her freely. "I just did not know you loved me so."

"We all love you." Sonya stared up at Aria, looking like her mistress must be crazy. "You are the hope of the harem. Of those who still have hope—for without you, we are surely lost. We will end up prisoners for life, just like our mothers, those who have mothers."

With that, Sonya rose up, then kissed her mistress full on the mouth—a cool, thrilling sensation, surprisingly pleasant. The swift, easy way it happened told Aria that the boyarinya had done this a lot. For several heartbeats, they stood pressed together, breast to breast and hip to hip. Aria asked, "What was that for?"

"I told you, I loved you." Sonya relaxed, letting go of her mistress. "That was to show I meant it."

Aria smiled at the boyarinya, who now ranked as her most ardent supporter. Even Baron D'Hay had not dared go so far. This is what the D'Medveds got for letting Sonya run wild like a boy, consorting with Turks and Kazakhs. "I would have thought the knife was enough."

"Kissing is nicer than a knife." Sonya took back her blade, sliding it into the hidden sheath.

Aria led her presumptuous handmaid back to the royal bedchamber, where they shared the Princess-Regent's big curtained bed, lying on cushions, sipping berry wine brought by dwarfs. When the dwarfs were gone and the curtains were closed, Aria relaxed, mightily pleased with her new ally. She had liked Sonya ever since she first saw her in the Gilded Cage—only the D'Medved name had made Aria wary. Now, she suddenly had a new friend, and a spy in the enemy camp.

Sonya told what she knew of D'Medved plans. "They mean to depose you and rule in Ivan's name. Some want you murdered outright, while others want you married first." Sonya made it sound like death versus life in prison. "Baron Tolstoy is unhappy with his wife."

Aria made a face at the thought of marriage to the brutal, pot-valiant baron. Sonya nodded, adding, "With Prince Akavarr dead, there is even talk of Tolstoy marrying me." Sonya was not an heiress, but a few convenient deaths would make her one.

"Why not both?" Aria suggested. After all, Tolstoy had one wife already—unless she was poisoned as part of the prenup.

Sonya grinned mischievously above her cup. "Excellent, then we would be together."

And the country would be spared civil war, since Baron Tolstoy would be in bed with both the D'Medveds and the Crown Princess. There were certainly worse fates than marrying beautiful, daring Sonya D'Medved, with her wild restless energy. But this grand marriage alliance had one obvious problem. "Who would sleep with the baron?"

"That honor goes to the Crown Princess." As Sonya said it, she ran her bare foot along Aria's calf, showing which member of the troika attracted her.

"You would become a baroness," Aria reminded her, both alarmed and aroused by the smooth feel of flesh on flesh, even if it was only a foot. She was not repelled by Sonya's touch, just shocked by how enticing it felt. Friendly yet intimate, an exciting combination. Suddenly Aria did not feel so alone.

"I have already bedded a baron," Sonya boasted, continuing to stroke the royal calf. "As well as the Shah of Khwarezm." Cowardly, balding Baron Tolstoy would be a definite step down.

"I believe you have." Aria recognized harem training. Like the houris in the Bone Witch's tales, Sonya had not said a word about what was happening below the waist. Speak only when spoken to—offer yourself openly yet artfully, both seducing and submitting, without ever saying so.

Aside from Eros, no one had ever offered themselves so plainly. Taking another sip of wine, Aria thought of the sleek white curves beneath Sonya's black shift, and the yellow bird on her handmaid's hip. With Sonya, Aria knew what she was getting. Sonya had made sure of it, that first day in the bath. Aria asked, "What about women?"

"What do you suppose?" Sonya kissed her again, playfully, just brushing lips, chaste but sensual. Love had softened even Sonya, who could not be tamed by Turks or Tartars. "And you?"

Aria shook her head, embarrassed by her lack of experience with anyone. If she spent the night with Sonya, it would be her first time.

"What!" Sonya sounded delighted. "A virgin harlot? How incredible!"

Aria blushed and sipped more wine, mumbling, "There has been no chance—"

"Nonsense, a crown princess can always find love." Sonya rolled closer, eager to prove it, sliding her bare thigh into the hollow between Aria's legs, gently rocking back and forth. Another nicely shocking sensation. All the while, Sonya pretended to be perfectly at ease, her head propped on one arm, not touching Aria above the hips. "You have been kissed, at least?"

"By you," Aria pointed out, liking the warm feel of Sonya between her thighs. She clamped her legs together, forcing Sonya to rock harder. "Earlier this evening. Do you not remember?"

"But I cannot be the first." Sonya refused to believe her liege lady was so innocent. "You must have been kissed by a man?"

She nodded solemnly. "But he is dead."

"Then I am the only one living?" Sonya liked that idea.

"Well, I was drugged and assaulted by Eros himself, aboard the Killer of Children's sky-ship." She found herself trusting Sonya with some of her secrets—it was incredibly hard never to share the wonders she had seen.

Her handmaid was suitably impressed. "But I can give you something even Eros cannot." As Sonya said it, her hips moved harder and faster, pressing their thighs together.

"What is that?" Aria's hips began rocking almost on their own, in time to Sonya's.

"True love." Sonya kissed her again, at the same time undoing the royal robes and sliding up her own shift, saying, "Eros can never care about you the way I do."

Eros hardly cared for her at all, aside from his normal urge to protect and impregnate teenage virgins. Nor did Sonya seem at all like Eros, being smaller and female, and far more passionate. Sonya had a raw, unbridled urgency that went beyond harem training, or the artful dallying of a demigod, as if this were the first time for her as well.

Aria felt her handmaid's fingertips reaching down, tickling the tops of her pubic hair. She held her breath as the fingers probed deeper, massaged her with slow loving strokes that sent waves of pleasure surging through her thighs. This was nothing like Eros at all. More caring yet more urgent, it reminded Aria most of making love with Sir Roye de Roye on the trail into the Rift, with birds singing above. Shudders of pleasure turned to soft sobs.

Sonya stopped, asking, "Have I hurt you, my princess?"

"No, no." Not the way Sonya thought, though it was sweet of her to worry. "You were most wonderful."

"I was?" Most wonderful was plainly what Sonya wanted to be. "Then why are you crying?"

"For someone who died before I knew you." Aria felt ashamed of her tears. "For a knight who gave his life to save me."

Sonya had her own dead to mourn, and immediately understood, holding her mistress closer, letting the crying subside. Brushing damp curly hair out of Aria's eyes, Sonya whispered, "He must have been good to you, if you miss him so."

Aria nodded gravely. "Brave, and gentle, and true to me."

"Well, now you have me," Sonya declared, smugly ready to take any man's place.

Aria stared at her handmaid-cum-bedmate, asking, "Do you really love me?" Is that what this was truly about? Not some mad ploy by the D'Medveds.

"Of course, my princess." Sonya took Aria's hand, holding it to her breast. "Feel my heart. I have never loved anyone like I love you."

Aria felt the fast pulse beneath Sonya's cool clean skin. How weird to think she caused that. It made the Bone Witch's magic into mere parlor tricks. Aria did not love Sonya like that, but it was amazing to have this beautiful young boyarinya so terribly in love with her, just when she was most alone, and most in need of someone. She thought Sonya envied and despised her, but what the boyarinya wanted was her attention. Desperately.

"You are the love of my life." Sonya slid Aria's hand over to her erect nipple, letting her princess feel the full effect. "My miracle come true."

"Why me?" No one had ever loved her that much, except maybe Sir Roye.

Sonya smiled slyly, saying, "You truly do not know."

Her knight had said the same thing on the day they met. Aria still did not know the answer, and silently shook her head.

"I prayed night and day for someone like you, someone to stand up to the boyars and do what was right." As Sonya said it, her free hand slipped past the sable trim on Aria's robe, softly stroking a royal breast. "How wonderful to find that you are also brave and beautiful."

Not near as brave as Sonya thought. "I do not love you that way." Aria hated to say it, but for once she must be honest, especially with her hand on Sonya's heart.

Her handmaid laughed. "Believe me, my princess, I have more than enough love for both of us." Sonya proceeded to prove it, bringing their bare bodies together, in a fleshy explosion, showing her harem tricks Aria had never heard of. With Eros, Aria had been overwhelmed by the moment, and his tremendous male energy. Making love with her handmaid was totally different from being assaulted by a demigod; it was softer, smoother, more like coming home, finding that female love and comfort she had lost as a little girl. And unlike Eros, Sonya had no aim to get her pregnant.

As Aria climaxed, Sonya whispered, "We are each other's fate, want it or not. Together we can be free."

Just what she wanted to hear. How strange to have it come from Sonya D'Medved. Aria did not feel the same head-over-heels "have to have him" passion she had for Sir Roye—but to deny Sonya was like denying herself.

Afterward, Aria looked at Sonya across a pillow covered by long blond hair, which now smelled of sex. This was how her enemies imagined she spent her nights, so why disappoint them? She asked, "What will your family do if they find out?"

Sonya smirked at her family's reaction. "All my life, men have told me they will hurt me horribly if I did not do what they want. They would beat me, brand me, and if that did not work, burn me to death. You are my hope, and I will not give you up. How about you?" Sonya asked, "Who outside the harem do you truly trust?"

Alexi D'Hay, hardly. Bishop Peter maybe. Eros if she were desperate. "Just the Killer of Children."

Sonya's eyes went wide. "You know her! I spoke to her in the Gilded Cage."

Aria said she knew Persephone well, "But the last time I saw her she was headed into Nordling, on her sky-ship."

"I have someone closer," Sonya boasted, "a mercenary knight, fighting for the D'Medveds."

"And you trust him?" Aria asked.

"As much as any man. He got me off Abeskum Island, when the Tartars massacred Aladdin's harem," Sonya replied. "He is gallant and smart, but he is a stranger, and thinks I am crazy wild."

Imagine that. "Aren't you?"

"Some," Sonya admitted. "But if you had been through what I have, you would be too."

"Perhaps." Aria had been through plenty herself.

By noon the next day, the entire harem knew Crown Princess Kataryna-Maria had a new favorite, and few were surprised to hear it was Sonya D'Medved. When Aria asked Sonya if she had been boasting, the boyarinya just rolled her eyes. "I said nothing. Trust me, I do not betray your secrets to anyone, not even my knight on the outside." Sonya had not told her mistress the knight's name, showing the boyarinya could keep a secret.

"Then how did they know?" Aria had seen the eunuchs and younger women snickering, and got disapproving glances from pious old biddies who had not seen a man since her grandfather's day.

"Dwarfs, serving girls, the nuns who washed our sheets." Sonya scoffed at her innocence. "Everyone knew it would come to this. You had to bed me—or cut off my head."

How true. Sonya would not have it any other way. And for now, Aria was happy with her choice, feeling like she had found someone. If she could not have the man she loved, at least she had a woman who loved her.

Next day, Jochi played for the royal handmaids and harem favorites, who dined on yogurt, dried fruit, fresh loaves, and plump steppe larks in prune sauce, while Sonya described seeing the Killer of Children in the Gilded Cage. "Turkan Khatun begged help from a prisoner in her own harem, but all the Killer of Children cared about was me."

Aria kept silent about her own adventures in the Gilded Cage—not wanting to share everything with the harem. She did, however, admit to having met Persephone's cousin Eros. Anna Tolstoy asked, "Is he as beautiful as they say?"

"More so." Aria smiled at the memory. "He is strong and blond—looking like Persephone's male twin."

"More beautiful than me?" Jochi sounded jealous.

"Of course." Anna Tolstoy snorted in disbelief. "Love is a god—you are just a eunuch."

Haughty teenagers were a harem curse, but Aria did not have to put up with them. Instead of reprimanding Anna, she waved her to silence, saying she wanted to be alone for the evening. "Except for Jochi, who can play me to sleep."

Her handmaids rejected that, insisting she must have a woman to look over her. Tasha thought it was self-evident, since, "Jochi is a man—"

"Mostly," added Anna Tolstoy.

"He will be lost in his music," Tasha insisted. "Your Highness needs to be looked after, not just entertained."

"No man will do that," they assured her.

"Not even a eunuch."

"Enough." Aria let them speak their minds, but she would not let them run her life. Not totally. She chose Sonya to stay with her, to teach Anna Tolstoy not to be so proud, and because Sonya looked devastated at the thought of being dismissed with the others. Already Aria sensed a dangerous attachment— but these were dangerous times.

Tasha offered to keep watch outside, and Aria told her to get a trustworthy dwarf to help. Tasha and Jochi grinned to hear her telling a nomad to be wary.

Producing his balalaika, Jochi played Kazakh tunes that sounded like wind singing through the grass tops. In no mood to eat stewed songbirds, Aria picked at the fruit and dozed beneath a big down comforter, waking now and again to the music. Sonya was in and out of bed, making sure Aria was warm, and brewing strong black tea. Thankfully, the boyarinya behaved herself, and did not attempt to molest her mistress in front of a eunuch. Truth to tell, Sonya just wanted to be at the center of things, lying naked in bed and flirting with Jochi over her shoulder.

Suddenly, a terrified shriek came from down the hall, followed by running feet.

Aria looked up in time to see a dwarf in a feathered gown come dashing in. It was Pipit, one of her seamstresses, a smart girl from a serf family. Doing a swift bobbing curtsy, Pipit announced, "Men, m'lady. Boyars. My lord Tolstoy too."

Aghast, Aria sat bolt up in bed, pulling her robe tight around her, realizing that boyars had at last dared pass the Silken Door. Men were in the harem! Not just any men, but the men who most wanted to do her ill. Heaven help them all. Aria grabbed her lotion bottle from the side table, the brass flask given her by the Old Man of the Mountains.

She had no time to summon the guard—if she still had one—her only escape was into the harem vaults. Sonya leaped naked out of bed to open the secret panel, shouting, "Go, m'lady! Before they get here."

"What about you?" Aria hated to desert Sonya and the others.

Sonya rolled her eyes. "They care only about you."

How true. Aria stood clutching the brass bottle with the Assassins' knife inside, unsure of what to do. Pipit the dwarf was already headed for the door.

Anna Tolstoy raced in, nearly tripping over the dwarf, her face white as the Bone Witch's hair. "My uncle," the girl gasped. "He—"

Before Anna could say it, Aria was through the secret door and taking the secret stairs two at a time. Sonya was right. So long as she was not there, the boyars would not care about girls and eunuchs. By hesitating, she'd actually gotten Anna Tolstoy in trouble, leaving her with the guilty knowledge of which way the Princess-Regent went. If Aria had been a bit quicker, Anna would have nothing to keep from her uncle.

Behind her, the door slammed shut, and Aria was plunged into darkness, forced to feel for the steps with her feet, hands braced against the passageway walls. All she could do now was hide, or try to find one of the secret ways out of the harem, and somehow escape with the Firebird's Egg.

As her eyes adjusted, Aria realized she could see dimly, which meant there was a light somewhere ahead. She slowed, looking and listening. Luckily, there was no one charging down behind her, which meant that Sonya and Anna had managed to send pursuit in some other direction.

Nearing the bottom of the stairs, Aria clearly saw a light shining around the next corner. Someone must be waiting, but who? She gripped the neck of the brass lotion bottle, glad the Old Man of the Mountains had given her something to fight with.

When the steps ended, she peered around the corner, seeing a lamp sitting alone on the stone floor—like it had been left there for her. Aside from the lamp, all she could see was empty passageway and the vacant entrance to a side tunnel. Too good to be true, yet she could certainly use the light. Otherwise, how would she get to the Firebird's Egg?

Looking both ways, Aria stepped into the passageway, reaching for the lamp. As she did, a hand came out of the shadowy side tunnel, and cold metal fingers closed on her wrist.

Aria jerked her hand back—too late. She was caught, like a mink in a trap.

She could not get away, or go invisible. Her free hand was on the bottle hilt, but she could not free the blade. She shouted up the mailed sleeve, at the visored face of her captor, saying, "Let me go! I am Princess-Regent Kataryna-Maria, and you cannot touch my royal person."

Feeling his grip give, she flicked the catch on the bottle—one swift pull, and Aria would have the knife in her hand. What then? Anything had to be done quick.

Her captor reached up to lift his visor. This armored felon was the only one between her and freedom, between her and Firebird's Egg. Stab him, and she could disappear into the harem vaults. In the moment when his hand and visor hid his face, Aria pulled on the brass bottle.

Magically, there was a blade in her hand. Since her opponent was covered in steel, Aria had to strike at his face. As she did, her startled assailant cried, "Aria!"

14

monsieur le baron and the twelve beasts

Sir Roye de Roye had sadly watched Sonya disappear up the Red Stairs, but he was not there when Prince Akavarr tried to storm the Kremlin. He left such silliness to the Markovites, who made a characteristic botch of the whole business, killing Prince Akavarr instead of the hated princess Kataryna-Maria. D'Medved men-at-arms who had taken part in the carnage told him, "If you find our ways so distasteful, why not go home."

"Alas, I am an exile," Sir Roye explained, "barred from returning by sentence of death." Otherwise, he would have been long gone.

"That disaster on the Red Stairs was Prince Akavarr's idea," his hosts declared. "We can do better."

They could hardly do worse. Sir Roye lounged about a D'Medved estate downriver from Markov, fed and tolerated because the D'Medveds needed armed allies, now more than ever. Being their ally, Sir Roye felt compelled to advise them that they ought to patch up their relations with the Princess-Regent, then start to worry about the Tartars. They dismissed that as "ridiculous German folly."

"French folly," Sir Roye insisted.

"French folly." Whatever you called it, the D'Medveds habitually ignored any advice from the West. What could they know about the inhabitants of high Asia? "Princess Kataryna-Maria is here. These Tartars are far away. We will deal with the Princess-Regent first."

In Sir Roye's estimation, they would deal with neither, but he kept that opinion to himself—hoping that somehow, Sonya would send for him from Markov.

Which, indeed, she did. His summons came in the form of Tasha, who like him was a foreigner, free to leave the harem at will. Being hopelessly damned and corrupt gave the nomad serving girl a delicious sense of freedom that lay far beyond the dreams of any decent serf or boyarinya. Tasha could come and go in a covered horse litter, escorted by mounted bowmen, barely touching the ground between the harem and the lord's hall. Sir Roye accompanied her back to Markov, carrying sealed dispatches for Baron Tolstoy.

At the harem-palace, Sonya met him in a side chamber outside the Silken Door. It served as a robing room and concealed a secret entrance to the harem. There the blond boyarinya gave him a passionate kiss, promising much more later. "You will not believe what I have been up to!"

"No good," Sir Roye speculated.

She nodded enthusiastically. "Incredible things are happening in the harem."

"Really?" He was continually surprised by the wild young Markovite's enthusiasm for confinement. "Thought it might be a bit of a bore for a girl of your spirit."

"Oh, that too." Sonya kissed him again. "But soon we will be running the place."

Sir Roye smiled at Sonya's confidence. "I thought you already would be."

Sonya boasted, "I am the Princess-Regent's most trusted confidante."

"And the D'Medved spy in the harem," he pointed out.

"Exactly!" Sonya beamed at how quickly she had become indispensable. "Just watch." She took out the sealed papers he carried, setting them out on a table. The robing room doubled as a "black chamber," where visitors from the outside could secretly communicate with harem inmates, under the guise of changing into palace clothes. Here Sonya could both greet Sir Roye properly and inspect the papers he brought with him, without anyone in the harem or the palace knowing it. "Anything intended for Baron Tolstoy is interesting to us."

Using a heated knife, Sonya lifted off the seals and inspected the papers. Sir Roye saw her lips moving and realized Sonya understood the strange script. "You can read?"

Sonya nodded as she read. "Not just Markovite, but Cuman as well. I am a translator, in writing as well as speach." An impressive bit of magic in a land where most high ladies could not sign their own name. And a significant state secret. Once the dispatches were resealed, Baron Tolstoy would have no way of knowing his letters had been read.

"This is hopeless, though." Sonya handed him a sheet of characters. "Can you read Cathayan?"

Sir Roye stared in surprise at the familiar columns of characters, shaking his head and saying, "That is not Cathayan."

"How do you know?" Sonya glanced back at the characters, which surely looked Cathayan.

"Because, I have seen it before," Sir Roye explained, "aboard a Tartar sky-boat. This is a Tartar code. See, there are only a dozen characters, the twelve beasts of the Cathayan calendar, repeated over and over, in different ordered pairs. Rat and goat, tiger and monkey, dragon and cock—"

"Can you read it?" Sonya asked hopefully.

"Hardly." Sir Roye had repeatedly puzzled over these lists of paired characters. "But I have noticed some patterns. No character is paired with itself, and some characters are never paired. Rat is paired with horse, goat, monkey, cock, dog, and pig, but never with ox, tiger, hare, dragon, or snake."

"Rat? Ox? Snake?" Sonya snorted. "Sounds ridiculous."

"Only because we do not know the language. Suppose that language is Markovite." A good guess, since they were in the Kremlin. "How many letters are there in your alphabet?"

"Thirty-six," Sonya replied proudly, ready to use them all.

"What does that suggest to you?" Sir Roye ran his fingers down a list of characters, seeing the same pairings as on the Tartar sky-boat. "Twelve beasts and thirty-six letters."

"Not much." Sonya saw scant connection.

"To me, it suggests a chessboard." Sir Roye traced the board in midair. "If the twelve beasts were arranged to form a square, with six beasts on each side, how many squares would that enclose?"

Sonya thought for a moment. "Thirty-six."

"That is what I thought." The hardest part of this theory had been multiplying six times six, since Sir Roye de Roye did not have a cleric's head for figures. "Thirty-six letters in your language, and thirty-six squares, each defined by a distinct pair of characters. Thirty-six different pairs, and thirty-six letters, can hardly be coincidence. Each pair stands for a letter in your language."

"We still cannot read it." Being a woman, Sonya wanted to know what was said.

"True. But we know these are messages to the Tartars in Markovite. Why else go through all this trouble?" Baron Tolstoy's fearful response to Sir Roye's Tartar tales had been excellent acting, since the boyar had been talking to the Tartars all along.

Sonya mulled over the implications. "So Baron Tolstoy is getting coded messages from the Tartars."

"No." That did not sound right to Sir Roye. "I think it is the other way around. These messages are for the Tartars. They want to find out about doings in Markovy. Who is in charge here, and with what available forces? Believe me, there are whole lists of things the Tartars would like to know. And what would Tartars have to say to Tolstoy? Not a lot. I wager their replies come mostly in gold."

Sonya saw the sense in that. "Gold is what will best keep the messages coming." Tolstoy was more a fool than a traitor, thinking he had found a marvelous way to turn common knowledge into currency. Having been in Tartar pay himself, Sir Roye could understand the temptation. Sonya tapped the coded pages. "But why are these being sent to him?"

"That is the most worrisome part," Sir Roye admitted. "If I am right, it can only mean that Tartars are here in Markov, awaiting delivery. Or they are soon to arrive. Otherwise, why send for these coded papers?"

"Not a pleasant notion," Sonya agreed.

"We must be wary," he warned her, though Sonya was the one who lived in a fortress.

"Not too wary." Sonya knew her life was never going to be safe. "From what his other letters say, Baron Tolstoy will move against the Princess-Regent in a day or two. When he does, you must be with him."

"I must?" Sir Roye hoped to sit out the next demented attack on the government as well.

"Absolutely." Sonya kissed him to emphasize the point. "You will be the hero of the hour. So be serious—people's lives hang on this."

Sir Roye had never seen Sonya so concerned. This arrogant boyarinya, who shrugged off rape and calmly stared down death, was more worried than she'd been in Shah Aladdin's doomed harem. He stopped teasing and turned attentive. "Whatever my lady requires."

"It will be a lot," Sonya warned. "I want you to be here when the blow falls, but not with the others. When the time comes, enter the harem through a secret entrance that Tasha will show you, and wait at the base of the stairs leading to the Princess-Regent's apartments."

He nodded obediently. "Mademoiselle was right about this not being easy."

"There is more." Sonya was not letting him off that lightly. "I want you at that stair, because it is the way Kataryna-Maria will most likely flee. You are to hide there and wait for the princess, taking her alive."

"What, no giants to slay on the way?"

"No, silly." Sonya kissed him again. "But beware of the dwarfs—being small does not make them stupid."

Sonya resealed Baron Tolstoy's papers, then returned them to Sir Roye, saying, "Stay close to the baron, so you may be ready when he moves."

"I will be ready before he is," Sir Roye vowed.

"And watch out for Tartars," Sonya warned.

"I always do." He kissed her good-bye, and Sonya vanished back into the harem.

Staying close to Baron Tolstoy was not hard. As the time drew near, the chronically nervous baron became a magnet for armed drunken men who feasted in his hall and swaggered about Markov assaulting citizens, and fighting among themselves. When word went out on Sunday that there would be no carousing that night, Sir Roye knew to expect trouble. Why else would Sunday night be any different from Monday morning? Baron Tolstoy happily told him that the time had come to deal with Princess Kataryna-Maria. "After that, we can talk about the Tartars."

Such promises had a different ring now that he knew Tolstoy was "talking" with the Tartars. Sir Roye did not let any misgivings show, looking heartened by this false promise to take Markovy's problems seriously. He almost felt like he was doing Princess Kataryna-Maria a favor. With nobles like Tolstoy, what hope did she really have of running her country?

When the coup came, it was easy to slip away, since that was what many of the men-at-arms were doing. Only the most foolhardy blades were eager to follow Tolstoy and D'Medved into treason. He, however, was going to be the hero of the hour. After arming himself and getting a lamp, Sir Roye went straight to the secret entrance Tasha had shown him: a hidden doorway behind the harem stables. Here a narrow tunnel sloped down into the harem vaults, designed to give quick access to the stables during moments of dynastic crisis—for which this certainly qualified.

Rats scuttled ahead of him, and he heard water dripping in the dark. He had felt foolish, skulking through the stables in a back-and-breast and visored helm, hefting his Lucerne hammer; but in this dark tunnel, Sir Roye de Roye was happy to have plate and mail between him and the vermin.

Just as Sonya had said, the tunnel led straight to a passage ending in narrow stairs. Unwilling to wait in the dark, he set down the lamp where he could see it and then took position in a shadowy side passage, his Lucerne hammer in easy reach.

Being new to kidnapping princesses, Sir Roye was not sure what to do if Her Royal Highness Kataryna-Maria really appeared. He was supposed to see that Tolstoy took her alive. But what then? Turning Her Highness over to the boyars alive would not be doing her much good. Life in exile had left Sir Roye with scant concern for the worries of royalty, who never cared for those beneath their heel. Still, the idea of seizing some strange woman, then giving her over to her worst enemies was hardly appetizing. He hoped Her Highness would escape some other way.

So why was he doing this? For Sonya, obviously. Whom he cared for even though the girl was far too crazy, maddeningly unstable at times. He still wanted to see the willful boyarinya safe, something he had been doing since the first moment they met, on far-off Abeskum Island.

He sat, and dozed, and waited, wondering how long this snipe hunt would last. Then he heard a faint familiar sound coming his way.

Bare feet descended the stairs, stepping lightly but surely. Sir Roye did not have remarkable hearing, but he never missed a woman's step, not when he was cold and lonely. His body tensed as he watched to see who would appear.

For a long moment, all he saw was the brass lamp sitting in the passageway, like a lost bit of Aladdin's treasure that had somehow found its way to Markov, casting tall stark shadows deep within the harem vaults.

Then a slim hand reached out for the lamp, attached to a woman's arm sheathed in a silver sleeve, trimmed with white ermine. This was no handmaid off on a lark. Kataryna-Maria was coming down these hidden stairs, just as Sonya predicted. Being crazy did not keep the boyarinya from being right.

He lunged forward, seizing the royal arm just above the wrist, keeping the lamp between them so he could look at her face. Sir Roye had never seen the

Princess-Regent, so he did not know what to expect. What he saw made him stop—and need a better look.

Was this Aria? Dressed up like a crown princess, and slipping about the Kremlin vaults? Even as his eyes questioned what they saw, his heart was sure, and he started to say her name. At the same time, he instinctively lifted his visor. And got a knife in his face.

15

monsieur le baron and the princess

Hearing her name, Aria hesitated, just enough that her blade hit his mailed hand instead of his face. Her attacker's head jerked back, and his visor slammed down. As it did, he seized her dagger hand by the wrist, saying, "Why are Markovite women so ready with a knife?"

Aria stopped struggling and stared at her captor, hardly daring believe it was he. "Who are you?"

Her knight cautiously raised his visor again, saying with a grin, "Sir Roye de Roye, at your service."

"Thank heaven." She dropped her dagger and threw her arms around him, tears rolling down her cheeks. "You are alive!"

"Did you ever doubt it?" her knight asked. From his tone, Aria could tell that Sir Roye de Roye had no idea she had been mourning him for months, grieving horribly ever since she lost him in the Rift.

That only made her hold him tighter. So what if her love was a numbskull who did not understand her suffering, she had been given a second chance, and would not let go, reveling in his strong presence, feeling her world go from utter hopelessness to limitless wonder. Her love was alive, lifting an unbelievable weight from her soul. Without Sir Roye de Roye, all of Markovy seemed set against her, while with her knight at her side, anything was possible. She could only repeat over and again, "You are really and truly alive."

"Miraculously so," he declared. "And best of all, I still have my nose."

She might have managed that bit better. "I am so sorry. When a woman is seized by a man-at-arms, we often expect the worst."

He warily doffed his helmet. "No wonder they keep you in harems."

Aria shook her head vigorously, her black curls flashing in the lamplight. "That is not why they keep us in harems. This is why."

She kissed him, a deep enthusiastic kiss to show her French baron how much she had longed for him, and how much she had learned. Kissing him was as thrilling as Aria remembered, and for the first time, she caught a man totally unawares, surprising him with what she could do, with what she wanted. And not just any man—this was her own Sir Roye, whom she had almost lost forever.

Startled by this new fierce possessiveness, Sir Roye smiled when their lips parted. "Mademoiselle has certainly come up in the world."

"I told you I was a princess." She had only thought it was a lie.

"So you did," Sir Roye admitted, "and I was silly enough to doubt it."

"Now no one does." Not even the nobles currently hunting her down. "If they doubted for a moment that I was Demitri's lost daughter, they would not be after me."

"They will not get you." He folded his mailed arms around her. "I have you now."

His comforting embrace provoked another leisurely kiss, an extravagant indulgence when armed men were combing the Kremlin. Slowly Aria let reality intrude, if only to save them from immediate separation at the hands of her bloodthirsty boyars. Laying her head on his shoulder, she told him, "It is not just me they are looking for."

"Who else?" Sir Roye had what he wanted.

"I have a brother now." In fact, a whole royal family that she had not known about. "A four-year-old, named Ivan."

Sir Roye nodded soberly. "Crown Prince Ivan."

"And we must see to Sonya," Aria added.

"Sonya?" Sir Roye's eyes widened.

"Sonya D'Medved," Aria explained, not expecting he would know every blonde in her harem. "We have to find her too."

"Whatever Your Highness wishes," Sir Roye replied evenly, showing no special desire to run smack into Sonya D'Medved. Reaching down, he returned her knife, admiring how it fit into the brass bottle on her belt. "So why all the knives?"

"It is the law," Aria replied innocently.

"What law?"

"Women and serfs are not allowed any blade longer than their hand." Aria held up her fingers to show him. "So we must make do with knives."

Until now. Now she had her champion back, with his broadsword and bright triple-bladed Lucerne hammer. Aria stroked Sir Roye's steel-clad arm, mortally glad to have him standing between her and harm. "Though we much prefer it when men do the fighting for us."

Sir Roye shook his head. "And people dare call you uncivilized."

Hefting his sawtooth hammer, he followed her back up the stairs toward the royal apartments. Since no one had come down to seize her, Aria assumed her boyars had not found the hidden door. At the top, she motioned for Sir Roye cover the lamp, then looked through a peephole. He bedchamber was empty, and in no more disarray than normal.

"Come, we must see to Ivan." Aria opened the secret door and guided Sir Roye through her apartments to the back stairs leading up to Ivan's suite. Again she paused at the head of the carved wooden stairs, listening for trouble.

Nothing. No peaceful snores or child's cries. No clink of steel. Entering Ivan's apartments, she found them empty too. And in total disarray, as if they had been hurriedly searched. Hopefully that meant they did not have her brother, since what else would they be searching for in the nursery?

"Ivan is not here," she told Sir Roye. "I can only hope he is safe. I have hidden the Firebird's Egg in the harem vaults—but first we must look for Sonya."

"Must we?" he hissed back, looking more worried than when he faced the Tartars. "Every second, you risk discovery. We should get the Egg and go."

"Do not worry—I will use the secret ways." Aria was touched by his concern. "Besides, you will like Sonya."

"No doubt." Maybe a bit too much.

Aria grinned, adding, "She is even wilder than I am."

"Impossible." Sir Roye feared he would soon find out which young woman was wilder.

"Also Sonya knows a knight on the outside," Aria confided. And they certainly needed allies right now. For all Aria knew, young Valad D'Hay's handsome head already adorned a pike. "A knight who has never failed her, who plucked her from a Turkish harem beset by Tartars."

"Sounds like a stupendous fellow," Sir Roye agreed. "Cannot wait to meet him."

Aria could tell Sir Roye doubted that this new knight would be much of an addition—acting like he would end up having to do it all himself. She stroked his furrowed brow, saying, "Do not be jealous. He is Sonya's knight, not mine."

Easy for her to say. Sir Roye followed Aria up another secret stairway. This one connected the living quarters to the baths, a warm useful passage hidden behind the brick hearth that heated the sauna and bathing basins. Though the fires were banked for the night, the bricks still felt warm, and at the top of the stairs there was a virtual gallery of peepholes, as befitted a bathhouse. But still no sign of Sonya.

Aria retreated to her private apartments, finding them again empty, except for Pipit the dwarf, who bowed and asked, "Is there anything I can do for Your Highness?"

"Have you seen Prince Ivan?" Aria asked, hoping her half brother was not already in enemy hands.

"Not since supper," Pipit replied.

"And Sonya D'Medved?" Aria added.

Pipit looked surprised. "When I last saw Sonya, she was with Your Highness."

"Well, for now, it is just the two of us," Aria told her knight. Unless you counted Pipit.

Sir Roye looked relieved to hear it. "So should we go for the Firebird's Egg?"

That seemed right. It began with the two of them, that day in the woods; maybe that was how it must end. If they got the Egg, they could be out of the tunnel and to the stables before anyone knew she had left the harem. Let her boyars bicker over who was running Markov, while they returned the Egg to Burning Mountain—which was what the Bone Witch wanted.

Dismissing Pipit, Aria led her knight back down the secret stairs to the cool, dank harem vaults. Where she found the crypt niche empty, except for its corpse. The Firebird's Egg had vanished.

Stunned, Aria frantically felt about in the darkness behind a noble mummy. Nope, nothing. Just a warm blank space behind the decayed corpse.

When she stuck the lamp into the niche to look around, thinking the Egg might have rolled to the back, Aria got another shock. Where the Egg had rested against the mummy, the blackened flesh had turned warm and pink. Living skin was growing on a desiccated corpse.

Aria jerked the lamp back, amazed and horrified. When the Tartars resurrected Prince Sergey, he had been pretty freshly dead. This bony mummy was a century old at least, yet the skin had been as fresh and pink as a baby's. Such was the power of the Firebird's Egg.

And now someone else had it. But who? She did not think the boyars had found it. They would not know where to look. Only Sonya had caught her down here, but even Sonya had not seen where the Egg was hidden. Besides, the crypt key was where she left it, and Aria could not picture Baron Tolstoy just putting it neatly back after taking the Egg.

She had no idea what to do next. So long as she had the Egg, her duty was incredibly hard, but pretty plain—she must get the Egg to Burning Mountain. Without the Egg, she did not know what to do.

"Do not worry." Sir Roye wrapped his arm around her. "We are together, and that is all that counts."

"Really?" Aria feared that without the Firebird's Egg, and with everyone that mattered against them, all they could do was die together.

"Absolument." To prove it, Sir Roye de Roye turned her about and kissed her again, a long strong kiss that raised her right up on her toes, making Aria forget for the moment they were in a royal crypt. When he was done, he told her, "We have been apart far too long, Princess Wood Sprite."

How true. And no matter what she had lost, she had him back, reborn in her arms. Thrilled by how good it felt, she asked him, "Do you mind that your wood sprite is now a princess?"

"It is a shock," Sir Roye admitted, "but it will make loving you all the more exciting."

But not just yet, she told him. "We must get you out of here first."

Sir Roye clearly agreed, asking, "Where should we go?"

"Out of the Kremlin." Aria nodded toward the tunnel leading to the stables. "If we can get to D'Hay lands, they will shelter us." For a while, at least. Aria did not think the D'Hays would hold out long once the other boyars smelled blood.

Sir Roye led the way down the passage toward the royal stables, holding her hand and keeping his armored body between her and whatever was coming. Thank Heaven she had not slept with Eros. Her first time would be with the man she wanted. Sonya did not really count—that was something between girls. Sir Roye would surely understand, once she decided how to tell him.

Light appeared in the passage ahead, a faint glow that grew brighter as it got closer. Aria covered her lamp, and they waited, her hand on Sir Roye's mailed sleeve, his Lucerne hammer held at ready.

Soft footsteps approached, bringing the light with them. Aria whispered her spell, becoming an invisible presence at her knight's side, feeling his muscles tense beneath the iron mail.

Sonya came slipping down the passage, wrapped in one of her mistress's silver robes and carrying a twin-forked iron candlestick. Aria relaxed, glad to have finally found her blonde handmaid. Stepping past her knight, she greeted Sonya, saying, "We are saved. Look, my knight is here, alive and well!"

"So is mine," Sonya replied, giving Aria a kiss of greeting, then kissing Sir Roye as well.

Startled to see Sonya being so familiar, Aria asked her knight, "Do you know each other?"

"Intimately," Sir Roye admitted ruefully. From the way he said it, Aria knew that they had made love. Given Sonya's morals and attitude, anything else would be a major miracle.

"He is the knight I told you about. My knight," Sonya explained. "Yours too, it appears."

"Appearances are deceiving." It absolutely never occurred to Aria that her knight had been doing anything but trying to get back to her. He knew she was alive, and he had done a fine job of finding her, despite changes in name and occupation. One would think that left small time for anything else—but no, he was servicing her favorite handmaid as well. Aria had been flattered by his restraint toward her, which she took as a backward compliment. Sir Roye de Roye was so in love, he was loath to ravish her. Sonya D'Medved had no such worries, and had gleefully gotten what Sonya wanted, well ahead of her mistress.

Sir Roye heaved a sigh, saying, "Since we all know each other so awfully well, there is no question about what to do next." Lest either of the young women think it was her turn to speak her mind, he added loftily, "We need three good horses from the royal stables, and a head start into D'Hay country."

Sonya rolled her eyes, having had her fill of D'Hay hospitality.

Aria agreed, eager to get going. Her whole world had come crashing down, and she did not mean to die amid the ruins. Boyars had seized her palace, and her knight was dallying with Sonya D'Medved, who had deftly seduced her. Plus she had lost the Firebird's Egg, not to mention her new brother, Ivan. All this was far too much, and she mightily needed a horse to take her well away from here. Or better yet, a roc.

Emerging in the dark alley behind the stables, Aria took a deep breath of open air, practically her first whiff of the outdoors since arriving in Markov— it smelled of piss and manure. Heavenly. Sir Roye steered her toward the stables, where she hoped for a mount as hardy and docile as that black Kazakh mare that died under her in the Rift.

Instead she found Baron Tolstoy himself, waiting in full armor at the head of his thugs and retainers, greeting her with drawn swords and wicked grins on their faces.

Sickened by the sight, Aria ordered them out at once, pointing at the stable door and wishing she had on her crown. "Go immediately," she demanded, not thinking they would obey, just trying to give Sir Roye time to escape the way they had come. Not everyone had to die with her. "This is the harem," she declared, "forbidden to men—"

"We are in your royal stables," Baron Tolstoy reminded her.

So they were. "Even so, your being here is ungodly and indecent."

That got a nasty laugh from her boyars and their men-at-arms. Had Sonya known they were waiting here? Since finding her mistress in her knight's arms, Sonya had been oddly silent, just letting things happen. And Sonya had been coming from the stables. Why? To warn her? Or maybe to see her safely in D'Medved hands? Baron Tolstoy held out a steel glove, saying, "Her Highness had best come with me."

"Her Highness will do as she wishes," Sir Roye de Roye declared, hefting his Lucerne hammer. Sonya hung on his mailed sleeve, just where Aria had been when the boyarinya arrived. Aria could not tell if Sonya was giving support or holding her knight back, forcing Princess Kataryna-Maria to face her boyars alone.

Baron Tolstoy's malicious grin widened, and he warned the French nobleman, "You are a foreigner. We decide who reigns in the Kremlin, not you."

Baron de Roye stubbornly insisted, "I am sworn to serve your royal family, the true line of King Demitri."

Aria motioned Sir Roye to silence, saying to Tolstoy, "Give this knight safe conduct—then I will come with you."

Tolstoy sneered. "You have no choice but to come."

She shook her head. "Harm him, and I will make you kill me right here." Lady Death's little sister had taught her she always had a choice. "You will have done all this for a corpse."

Baron Tolstoy considered her offer. "So you will come peacefully, and do as I say?"

"So long as they are not harmed." She nodded significantly at Sonya and her knight, standing together, Sir Roye looking grim, Sonya smiling slightly. Was that a smile of triumph, or encouragement?

"Both of them?" Baron Tolstoy sounded peeved to be deprived of his just prey.

Here was her chance to throw Sonya to the wolves, giving Baron Tolstoy someone to blame and bully. Angry as she was, Aria could not do that. She had been abused and betrayed, but not by Sonya, who had no way of knowing Sir Roye was her knight. And there was a bond between her and the blond girl, more even than she had imagined. Besides, if Sonya was a spy, Aria would just be singling out Sir Roye. "Of course both of them," she scoffed. "We are bargaining for the crown of Markovy."

"So we are." Tolstoy's grin returned, and he motioned to his guard captain, saying, "Take her, but gently."

"Will you grant these two safe conduct?" she demanded.

"Her Highness has my word of honor." For whatever that was worth. Tolstoy's black-bearded captain advanced, and Aria motioned for her knight to be still. Her handmaid had her arms practically around Sir Roye, seeing he did nothing stupid. Neither of them wanted him cut down by the boyars, least of all Sonya, who was about to have Sir Roye to herself.

And that was the last Aria saw of her knight, safe in Sonya's arms, as the boyars closed in. Their blades were finally bared, snaring her in a net of steel. Ever since she was a baby, these men had hated her, despising her mother's foreign blood and strange ways. She and her mother had mocked their power, filling the Kremlin palace with music and dance. Now her mother was locked away, and she was at their mercy. Aria could feel their jubilant relief at finally having gotten this godless witch-princess, to do with as they willed.

16

the princess and the tartars

Aria found herself back in her old nursery, the very room where she was born, or so her old nurse had told her. Windowless as the Gilded Cage, the blue-white nursery had small decorative panels set at a child's eye level, and a gaily painted wooden door that locked on the outside. There were no secret entrances she knew of, and furnishings were equally meager—a pair of sleeping cushions, a fur coverlet, and a chamber pot—showing her stay was temporary. She lived by lamplight, never seeing day or night, walled in like old Queen Ivanova—all they needed do was to brick up the door.

Sitting on one of the cushions, the coverlet wrapped around her, Aria thought about her mother in a distant convent, a prisoner just like her. What was their crime? Loving music and beautiful things? Wanting to live free? She had harmed no one, and regularly confessed her sins to Mother Church—yet she was branded a witch and whore. How could men be so hateful?

Witch might be true—but whore was particularly unfair, since she was technically still a virgin, and the only man she ever loved was currently being comforted by her harlot of a handmaid. There was a lesson there, for sure.

Sleeping with Sonya seemed so right at the time. Aria thought she had been getting a lot for very little, finding a friend, ally, and confidante, and she just had to give a bit of herself. Sonya was so beautiful and so eager to please that making love had certainly been no hardship—in fact, entirely blissful—a mortal sin than had not hurt in the least, until now.

Nothing comes free, as the Bone Witch always said: "No life without death, no pleasure without pain, no love without heartache."

Sonya's eager affection was right now being lavished on her knight. If she could not resist Sonya, how could she ever expect Sir Roye to say no? Women were innately sinful, as this whole sorry episode showed. Sonya would be doing her utmost to comfort Sir Roye, and men were utterly helpless in the hands of a determined blonde.

Aria's only consolation was that she had already given herself up to Death, and the dead did not agonize over love and pain. All her life, these men had wanted to destroy her, and now they need only decide how. But even sitting at death's door, she still loved Sir Roye, and fervently wanted him to live—albeit with Sonya. Tolstoy had vowed to spare her knight, and Aria hoped her treacherous boyar would keep that promise. As for the others, Jochi and Tasha were valuable property, and the worst they could expect were new owners. Nor was she much worried about Anna Tolstoy. The dwarfs must look after themselves.

Anna Tolstoy's uncle appeared unannounced, not even giving her time to disappear. Silently unlocking her door, the bald boyar swaggered in, greeting her with a cheery, "Good morrow, Your Highness. Have you slept well?"

"Oh, how wonderful," Aria exclaimed, letting herself smile a bit. "Someone to change the chamber pot. You will find it in the corner by the door."

Baron Tolstoy laughed lightly. "As always, Your Highness has an excellent sense of humor."

Obviously. Otherwise, she would have gone utterly daft by now, ruling over such a gang of treacherous incompetents. "I merely hoped to get something out of your visit."

"Her Highness can indeed profit from my visit," Tolstoy beamed happily, "if you are cooperative."

"Cooperative?" Aria eyed him evenly. What could Tolstoy want now? "How?"

His voice dropped, becoming conspiratorially familiar, "Begin by telling me where you hid Prince Ivan."

Ivan gone? This was news to her, but it explained a lot. No wonder she was being treated so royally—giving a private audience to Baron Tolstoy, instead of two brawny eunuchs with a bowstring. Without Ivan, she alone had her father's blood and could produce an unquestioned heir. Aria dared not let Tolstoy know she had no idea what had happened to her half brother, saying stiffly, "Why should I tell you?"

"We are cousins," Baron Tolstoy reminded her, "sharing the blood royal—among other things."

"Distant cousins." Her blood was far more royal than his, but they were kin of a sort, both descended from Ivan the Idiot, but his was a bastard branch. Her paternal great-great-grandmother was half sister to Tolstoy's great-grandmother—and from what she heard, they had hated each other as only half sisters can.

"Precisely," Tolstoy declared warmly, "and cousins so distant could easily become closer."

This amazing clod was flirting with her. How ghastly. So what if they were kissing cousins—he was still married to the late Prince Akavarr's sister, Aria's own aunt. She told him pointedly, "Prince Ivan's safety means the most to me—he is the true heir to the throne."

"Of course," Tolstoy intoned piously. "And who better to watch over him than his loving cousins—we could be Ivan's foster parents."

"Yes, indeed." She smiled primly. "Too bad one of us is already married." Though not happily. Having his wife's lover hanging outside the window did hint at trouble in the boudoir.

Tolstoy smiled. "Wives can be put aside, as you well know."

Just what you hope to hear from a prospective bridegroom. Marriage was clearly a matter of convenience to Baron Tolstoy, and at the moment, he found it convenient to propose to her. Aria would be mad to accept, and a total dolt to turn him down directly. She flashed her sweetest smile, saying, "When you are free, come see me."

"Or we can wring Prince Ivan's location out of you with thumbscrews and burning irons," Baron Tolstoy suggested, "like some are loudly suggesting. That could amuse both of us."

Marrying Tolstoy or death by hideous torture—a hard call for any girl. How come she never got the easy picks? Worn down by a series of wrong choices, Aria wished she could just give in. Tolstoy seemed to think he could do a vastly better job of governing Markovy's absurd collection of murderous boyars, mad priests, impudent handmaids, and barbarous Kazakhs. Looking coolly back at her baron, Aria told him, "Torture will not make me give up my little brother."

"Really, Your Highness?" Tolstoy glared down his long nose at her. "Your loving boyars are still eager to try."

She shrugged, not knowing where Ivan was anyway. Having given herself up to Death made Aria far less fearful of torture. Lady Death offered a haven to all who had nowhere else to go. Or so Persephone promised. Seeing he was getting nowhere, Tolstoy departed, presumably to search for Prince Ivan.

Leaving Aria alone to think. Ivan was gone, so what could that mean? Ivan might just be dead, but she doubted it. Had Tolstoy secretly done away with Ivan, he would be pressing his suit much harder. Baron Tolstoy acted like he still hoped to get hold of Ivan, and might not need her at all. Yet if Ivan was alive, where was he? Aria almost did not want to guess, since what she did not know, they could not wring out of her.

So long as Ivan was missing, Tolstoy would not likely kill her, since that would mean a civil war, with a half-dozen claimants. Tolstoy wanted to be king, but he was merely a baron from a cadet branch of the family—Aria had bastard cousins with far better claims than he did. How terrible to think that all men wanted was her womb. Tolstoy would murder her, or make love to her, as needed, making her miss Sir Roye all the more. Yet she dared not ask about him, since the slightest sign of concern from her could easily get someone killed, or gruesomely tortured.

As she sat stewing in lonely misery, a wall panel popped out and a dwarf stuck his head into the room, saying, "Thought that huge nasty bigger would never leave." Remembering his manners, the dwarf asked, "Your Highness, have I leave to enter?"

"You have." She recognized Goliath, an especially tiny dwarf, barely two feet tall, but a perfectly formed man in miniature. Harem-bred, he was dressed by the women in yellow silk doll clothes, and was small enough to use the tiniest dwarf tunnels—those no "bigger" even knew about.

Stepping like a genie out of the wall, Goliath did a neat salaam, saying, "Please, Your Highness must come with me."

Even sitting on her cushion, Aria still had to look down at Goliath. "If I must, I must," she agreed, "but your tunnel is too tiny for me."

"Worry not, m'lady. You are small for a bigger. We will manage." Goliath produced a high-pitched bone whistle and blew on it. "When you were two, you used to use these tunnels all the time."

"I did?" Aria had no memory of it, unless as part of her girlhood fantasies of having royal parents.

"Absolutely," Goliath assured her. "Many of the royal children use these tunnels, before they grow up to become biggers. You just disappeared."

Goliath was one of the few harem inmates who dared speak of Aria's childhood, enjoying the free speech granted those under three feet tall. Dwarfs were prized in Markovy—some would say worshipped. What others called a deformity, Markovites counted a blessing, and any peasant or artisan family having a grown child less than three-feet-six never had to pay taxes again. Dwarfs born to serfs and slaves were automatically freed and made dependents of the Crown, living at royal expense among people their size, encouraged to find mates and multiply, in hope of raising the dwarf population.

Alas, most children of dwarfs grew to normal heights—but they too got good marriages or Crown jobs, encouraging their parents to try again.

Free from protocol, coming and going as they willed, dwarfs were the only "intact" males in the harem. They were often grossly mistreated—drunken boyars tossed dwarfs about, playing keep-away from the dogs, or just splashed them with brandy and set them alight. But dwarfs were never punished for not being "normal." They did not have to hold jobs, pay taxes, go to chapel, or bow to the Princess-Regent. Pipit was a seamstress because she liked to sew, and Goliath had good manners because he was harem bred—none of that was required. Growing up short was all that mattered. Hideous deaths awaited anyone who maimed normal children to pass off as dwarfs, both for mocking God and cheating the Crown.

An answering whistle sounded above; then a trap opened in the high carved ceiling and a rope dropped down to hang at her side. Neat trick, having her exit drop out of nowhere—though these tunnels in the wall and ceiling meant she was giving the dwarfs a peepshow whenever she washed or changed.

Goliath helped put her slippered foot in a loop at the end of the rope; then she held on while he whistled again. Slowly the rope withdrew into the ceiling, pulling her up with it. The opening above was just big enough for her shoulders, and the trap closed behind her as she was lifted into a smooth wooden shaft going straight up, then curving gradually, until she was being hauled along horizontally, her silk dress sliding silently over lacquered wood.

Negotiating several tight curves, she slid through tunnels too narrow for a grown man, and almost too small for her. Suddenly she came headfirst into a low closet-size room lit by an oil lamp and crammed with dwarfs, who had used counterweights and a windlass to pull her along.

Here she had room to stand, but all the tunnels leading out were at least as small as the one through which she came in. Pipit was there, along with four males who worked the windlass; Squinty, Gnat, Timothy, and Ezekiel. Aria thanked them enthusiastically. To be out of Tolstoy's hands was an amazing relief, saving her from being married or murdered—maybe both. Aria told them, "You have done the Crown an inestimable service."

Gnat stepped up, doffing his belled cap and bowing deep. "We thank m'lady for being so light, and delicately built—few biggers could have slid so easily through our tunnels."

"Beware, m'lady," Pipit warned. "He only wants to look up your dress."

She looked down at the dwarf, whose nose was practically in her silk crotch. "Really?"

"'Fraid so, m'lady," Gnat admitted. Being a dwarf, he did not fear punishment and answered honestly. Only dwarfs and boyars knew how it felt to be free.

"Ladies let him do it when he was young," Pipit explained, "and now he is sore addicted to it."

"So?" Gnat glared pointedly at Pipit. "There's skirts around here I would not look up, not for a pot o' gold."

Pipit snorted, telling him, "Throw back the trap." Gnat heaved open a trapdoor in the floor, and Pipit motioned to her, "M'lady, this is how you must leave."

Looking down, she saw light at the far end of a deep dark shaft that seemed to lead straight into the underworld. She put her foot in another loop of rope, then let them lower her into the heart of the harem vaults—not the charnel house this time, but into a walled-up stone chamber that could be reached only through dwarf tunnels.

As she alighted on the stone floor, she saw the dwarfs had turned it into a throne room. Ivan sat on an ornate dinner chair set up against one wall—the only piece of furniture aside from the royal doll bed and chamber pot. And in the far corner lay the Firebird's Egg.

Aria could barely believe the dwarfs had rescued not just her, but Ivan and the Egg as well. She had discounted them solely because of their size, merely hoping that they could avoid being trampled in the mayhem, never thinking they would succeed where she and her knight failed miserably.

Ivan beamed in the lamplight, plainly buoyed to see her. "Aria, Aria, this is so wonderful." Aside from Sir Roye and Jochi, Ivan was the only male who consistently called her Aria. "Oh, I so sorely feared you were dead."

"Not yet." She knelt before Ivan, feeling silly being the sole person over three feet tall. Suddenly a giantess, she asked, "What is this place?"

"My throne room," Ivan announced proudly, his feet swinging inches above the floor. "Dwarfs found it for me. They used to keep Queen Ivanova in here—but that was long ago."

Cranky old Queen Ivanova II had lost her private prison-crypt, ending up in the charnel house with everyone else. Even the horror of being walled up alive merely led to death, then the ossuary. "I am in charge now, Aria," Ivan told her solemnly, "so you must tell me what to do."

Aria reached out, saying, "First give your Princess-Regent a royal hug." Ivan hopped off his dining-chair throne and into her arms, sobbing with relief, while his dwarf court whistled and stomped.

When she was done comforting her prince, Aria asked the dwarfs what was happening in the harem. As she expected, Tolstoy's men were searching for Ivan, from the drains to the attic, much to the dwarfs' amusement. Biggers had scant hope of ever finding him, the room having been bricked up for over a century. "And they do not yet know that Your Highness is missing as well," the dwarfs added gleefully.

Aria asked, "Did anyone see the foreign knight I was taken with?"

"What foreign knight?" asked Goliath.

"The French one," Pipit replied, "that looks like a eunuch."

"That nervous knight who was lurking in the vaults by the base of the hidden stairs?"

"That's him." Aria recognized her hero.

"He is in the Kremlin dungeon," Goliath declared, "locked in a cell that we cannot get into."

So much for Baron Tolstoy's word of honor. Sir Roye de Roye and Sonya were not having the torrid time she pictured; in fact, her knight was in far more peril than she. "How do you know he is there, if you cannot get in?"

"There is a tunnel to the dungeon, but not to his cell," Goliath explained.

Aria asked, "What about my handmaids?"

"Making mischief as usual," Pipit replied, "except for the blond D'Medved. No one has seen her since Your Highness was taken."

Sonya too. Aria silently prayed to the Killer of Children, begging Persephone to look after her wayward handmaid. Then she asked if any of the dwarfs knew Lord Valad D'Hay—several did, remembering how he barged into the harem on the day Prince Akavarr died. "Most handsome for a bigger, but no one has seen him either."

No one that mattered, at least. Lord D'Hay was on his own. Aria asked, "Is anything else amiss?"

"There's a Tartar sky-boat on the harem roof," Goliath offered.

"My God!" Aria could hardly believe him. "How can that be?"

"They wheeled it in at night, while you were locked in the nursery," Pipit explained. "Then they inflated the sail in the north courtyard, raising it up to the roof."

"Are you sure?" Harem dwarfs lived a sheltered life, and had certainly never seen a sky-boat.

"It flies," Pipit assured her, "and has Tartars aboard."

"Smells awful." Goliath wrinkled his nose.

Pipit shivered. "Scares me."

That sounded like a sky-boat, getting set to fly. Winds had been from the south and west, not the best for reaching Far Barbary—but perfect for the Iron Wood and Burning Mountain. "Is it still there?"

Dwarfs assured her the sky-boat was still there, and promised to warn her if it moved.

Aria had herself hauled up to the windlass room, watching the progress of the search through peepholes. Seeing huge men-at-arms clanking about the silken rooms, slashing behind hangings with their swords, tripping over cushions, and ducking at the doorways gave her something of the dwarfs' contempt for biggers. Not better, not smarter, not nicer—just bigger.

But there was one bigger she could not do without. When Aria returned to the throne room, she asked Goliath, "Could we somehow break into Sir Roye's cell?"

"I could not," Goliath confessed, "but m'lady might."

"Me, really?" Aria did not see how.

"Your Highness can probably fit through the tunnel," Goliath estimated, "and the cell key is in a cabinet that I cannot reach."

After midnight, when the harem had quieted down, Aria dressed herself in black silk pajamas and had the dwarfs take her to the tunnel entrance, a narrow barred drain in the Kremlin sewers. Goliath led with a lamp, threading through the sewers, which emptied into the river, allowing the fortress to draw water under siege. Directly beneath the dungeon, dwarfs had loosened the bars so they could be lifted out. Aria was forced to hoist herself into the drain and inch her way along the narrow smelly shaft, guided by Goliath's lamp.

Worming up the wet horrid shaft, Aria felt like she was emerging from the primordial slime, struggling toward the light. Then, abruptly, the light vanished.

Aria fought not to panic, her eyes striving to pierce the blackness. Nothing. Though she could hear something scuttling toward her down the tunnel. It sounded like the world's largest rat, coming right at her.

Suddenly the beast was in her face, with wiry bristles brushing her cheek. Now she did panic, letting out a startled scream.

"Hush, Your Highness," hissed the beast, "someone will hear." It was Goliath, pushing a rope end toward her. "Take this."

She stopped behaving like a stupid bigger and grabbed the rope, hauling herself along. Presently she turned a tight corner, and the light reappeared as Aria emerged in a guardroom privy, at the lowest point in the dungeons. Both the privy and the guardroom were deserted, but propped against one wall was Sir Roye's Lucerne hammer, shining bright in the lamplight—an excellent sign.

Picking up the lamp, Goliath showed her the way to the cells, saying, "The doors above are locked, so there are no guards down here."

There were three cells, and only one of them was locked, making her choice pretty plain. Goliath showed her the high wooden cabinet that held the keys. It too was locked, but Aria went back to the guardroom and got the Lucerne hammer. One good swing, and she was picking keys out of the painted splinters. Sometimes it paid to be over three feet.

After a couple of tries, she found the right key and turned it in the lock. These lowest cells were windowless stone bottles that smelled worse than the sewers. Aria stuck Goliath's lamp into the dark hole and called softly, "Sir Roye, are you there?"

"If my lady needs me," came from within the black hole.

Her knight squirmed out the narrow entrance, no longer in armor, but looking fit and ready. He grabbed her up in strong loving arms that smelled no worse than she did. Forgetting Sonya, she just gloried in getting him back, even in the Kremlin dungeons. Sir Roye asked guiltily, "Are you mad at me?"

"How could I be?" she protested. "I have barely gotten you back." Her main concern was getting him out of here, then escaping with the Firebird's Egg. His romantic escapades would have to wait.

Sir Roye set her back down, still worried. "Did what happened with Sonya upset you?"

He did not know the half of it, unless Sonya had told him. But Aria was not going to talk love locked in the Kremlin basement, smelling of sewage, with a dwarf watching—which was as good as shouting her feelings from the harem rooftop. She handed her knight his war hammer, saying, "Get us out of here first."

Goliath went back the way they came, but it was plain that her knight would not fit down the drain. Aria tried keys until she found one that fit the outer door, and they entered the dark fortress above.

Everyone was asleep, from the guard at the dungeon door to the serfs and servants curled in odd corners for the night. One serving boy awoke as they passed by, seeing a woman in dirty silk pajamas leading a beardless warrior with a huge sawtooth ax. He must have thought he was dreaming, or seeing ghosts, for there was no outcry from the blackness behind them.

She led her knight to the paved foot tunnel connecting the fortress to the harem, used in winter when the Kremlin square was buried in snow. They did not meet an awake guard until they got to the Silken Door, where the startled eunuch on duty admitted his missing mistress and a smelly barbarian. After armed boyars had tramped through the harem, all attempt at decency was over.

There was no way to hide Sir Roye de Roye in the dwarf tunnels, so Aria led her knight up the warm dark stairs to the royal bath. A familiar odor wafted through the peepholes, a pungent mixture of sweat, decay, and sour mare's milk, which both of them instantly recognized. Sir Roye whispered, "Tartars."

Aria nodded. Climbing a small ladder to reach a rooftop trap, she cautiously lifted the lid and looked out. Blocking out the stars was the black shape of an inflated parasail. She shut the trap and descended the ladder, saying, "There is a Tartar sky-boat atop the harem."

Sir Roye nodded, having suspected something like this ever since Sonya showed him sheets of Cathayan characters in Baron Tolstoy's correspondence. "Be careful. They most like to sleep in the open, so the sky-boat's crew is probably lying just above us."

Tartars bathed but rarely, and only in the heat of the day, so Aria entered the bath to get a much-needed wash. She stripped silently by lamplight and washed in tepid water, glad to be done with the dungeon privy. As she finished with her hair, she looked over at Sir Roye, wanting him clean as well.

He sat naked at edge of the bath, just watching her, as if they had all the time in the world. "What is the matter?" she hissed.

He smiled and shook his head, saying, "You are incredibly beautiful."

What a moment for him to notice. Worried about the Tartars above and the boyars below, Aria wet a cloth and scooped some soap from the dish, then started to wash dirt and sweat off Sir Roye de Roye, finding her love cleaned up nicely. Working her way down his belly to the hips, she enjoyed the feel of his firm muscled body. Her knight liked the wash as well. Aria could tell by the way he started to move beneath her hands, another bit of women's magic she was just learning to control.

Suddenly, his arms were around her, pulling her nude body into his aroused lap. Her frantic hiss of protest was stifled by a long thrilling kiss, which she enjoyed far more than she should. *Control* might be an exaggeration.

In fact, it was incredibly liberating just to let go, and give in to his embrace, to think about nothing but how good his body felt. His hands slid down past her bare hips, and he whispered, "Aria, my angel, I love you so."

"You do?" She herself was hopelessly in love, caring for him more than anything, more than being Crown Princess, more than saving Markovy. She was just loath to say that to Sonya's new "champion."

"Since the moment Mademoiselle first found me in the woods." His hands pressed her hard against his groin, letting Aria feel how very much he wanted her.

And she wanted him too, more than she ever thought possible. The wet warm darkness of the deserted bath chamber reminded Aria of the shrine at Karadyevachka, and of her dream, back in the Bone Witch's hut, when she imagined him taking her in a harem bath. Which made it all the harder to whisper back, "We cannot do this now."

"Why?" Sir Roye stroked her cheek. "Because of Sonya?"

Sonya? Sonya who? Oh, yes, the beautiful boyarinya they were both sleeping with, the very last person Aria wanted to think of while sitting in his naked lap. "Forget Sonya."

"Gladly." Happy to hear that, Sir Roye took hold of her rear, starting a gentle rhythmic massage. "What worries you, then? The Tartars upstairs?"

"No." She laughed at his naïveté. Who cared about smelly old Tartars? "My dwarfs."

"Your dwarfs?" This was a novel feminine excuse, even to a well-traveled French nobleman.

"They are watching." To prove it, Aria spoke up, saying, "Gnat, are you there?"

"Of course," came from behind a peephole.

"Who else?" Aria asked.

"Timothy."

"Simon."

"Pipit."

Aria was surprised to hear her seamstress, asking, "What are you doing here?"

"Seeing things are decent," Pipit declared.

"No need," Aria told her. Royal decorum was the Princess-Regent's concern, along with maintaining national decency and revealed religion. Markovites wanted a godly government in return for their squirrel tax. "But we must have clean traveling clothes for both of us, and food for the road."

"I will see to it," the seamstress promised.

"And the Firebird's Egg," Aria added. Now was the time to make their escape, while her boyars were dumbfounded and the Tartars were asleep. "Bring it here, but be careful."

"At once, m'lady," Timothy dutifully chimed in.

Sir Roye was sorely let down, but it was good to know she aroused him, despite his recent debauch.

Twin pinholes of light appeared and then multiplied as dwarfs brought a lamp to the secret tunnel. Aria lifted her head, calling for them to enter, since there was nothing to see now except their bare bodies, which dwarfs had seen often enough. They brought in an odd collection of bigger clothes, including a mail shirt for her knight, monk's robes, riding pants, and elegant evening wear.

Aria selected a loose silk shirt, a black embroidered jacket, and the sturdiest pants that fit. Pipit had also thought to bring Aria's best boots. Kissing the dwarf in gratitude, Aria pulled them on, then looked to her knight, who wore an odd combination of a mail shirt and a embroidered green huntsman's jacket over cloth-of-silver hose, and big boots turned down at the knee. Prince Charming in seven-league boots. She told him, "Winds are fair for Burning Mountain. Can you pilot the Tartar sky-boat?"

Sir Roye snorted in amusement. "Sort of. I have flown hundreds of miles in such boats, and even helped handle them. With the aid of these dwarfs, I could get her aloft, but I cannot sail us to Burning Mountain."

Aria nodded. "I do not expect you to, just so we can come down safely. Even getting the Egg out of the Kremlin and headed east would be a blessing."

"So far, I have crashed in a balloon and a glider, but never in a sky-boat." He made that sound like a good sign.

"Splendid." She kissed him and the dwarfs applauded.

Then Aria opened the secret trap at the head of the stairs, emerging from a rooftop spider hole. Dark domes and spires dominated the Kremlin skyline, and the sky-boat was tethered between two pitched roofs, half-covering a harem courtyard. They were hidden from the citizens of Markov by the high Kremlin walls, and the great cathedral domes.

Goliath went out to look around, and came back to say the Tartars were asleep on a balcony by the bow of the sky-boat, snoring loudly. "I only had to follow my nose."

She dropped down to give Sir Roye a kiss, saying, "I will check out the sky-boat. Be ready to follow me with the Egg."

Sir Roye nodded grimly. "Take care, my princess."

Just what Sonya called her. She took his hand, getting courage from the physical contact, drawing on his steady sureness. "Always."

Her knight smiled. "When we first met, I told you that I was fighting for you. Now it is literally true."

"At the least sign of danger, I will vanish." She kissed his fingers, then let go. Whatever happened now would be between them. Sonya had already disappeared.

While her knight kept watch on the Egg, Goliath assigned reliable dwarfs with knives to each of the mooring lines. Aria took a deep breath, then went into the blackness, expecting to hear shouts of alarm, or feel an arrow striking out of the night.

Nothing happened. Aria clutched the rooftop beneath her, looking around, seeing no sign of the Tartars said to be sleeping nearby. Above her, the sky-boat strained in the west wind, wanting to take off but held down by her land lines. Slipping around to the stern ladder, Aria sniffed and listened. Again nothing, just the smell of incense and the west wind singing softly in the rigging. Encouraged, Aria climbed the stern ladder, finding no one on deck.

An excellent sign. Sliding back the paper door, she peered into the cabin, half-expecting Prince Sergey would be lying there in state. He was not, but in his place lay Prince Akavarr, looking so calm and peaceful, he might have been sleeping. There was no smell of death, and Aria saw that her royal uncle's armor was cut away around his wounds, which were neatly sewn shut, like Prince Sergey's had been.

As she stared at the stitches, the sky-boat rocked gently beneath her. Someone big was coming aboard. Leaving the corpse, Aria slipped back over to the paper door and whispered her spell.

Sir Roye came through the door, with the Firebird's Egg cradled under one arm, and his Lucerne hammer in the other hand. Seeing the dead prince, he stopped and stared, saying, "Aria, are you here?"

She stepped into sight and took the Egg, asking, "What has happened?"

"Tartars are up, and we need to get away." He spun about, aiming to see to the land lines.

Setting the Egg down in a safe spot, Aria followed him on deck, going straight for the stern ladder, while yelling to the dwarfs, "Cut the lines!"

She released the stern ladder, much to the dismay of a startled Tartar, who tumbled into the court below, still clutching the ladder.

Her dwarfs must have done their duty, for suddenly they were free, lurching off downwind, with Tartar arrows arching after them—some coming uncomfortably close. Carrying two people, an armored corpse, and the Firebird's Egg, the sky-boat was so slow to lift off that they were easy targets, and could never clear the cathedral domes. "We are too heavy," Sir Roye shouted. "Dump the sandbags."

She saw Sir Roye upend a bag of sand tied to the rail, spilling it out to lighten the ship. An arrow flew between them as Aria leaped to help, grabbing a bag and flipping it over the rail, then cutting it loose with her flask knife, sending the bag with the sand. Anything to get some altitude.

It worked. Dark domes dwindled beneath them as the west wind carried them over the Kremlin wall. Aria seized another bag, heaved it over the rail, and cut it free.

As she watched the bag fall away, an arrow burst through the light wicker bulwark, hitting her hard in the side, startling her into dropping the knife.

Shock washed over her, and Aria stepped back, staring at the feathered shaft sprouting from her side, barely a hand's span from her navel. There was no pain, and little blood, just a dark stain on her jacket, slowly growing bigger. It took her a second to realize that this wetness was her life oozing away.

17

the firebird's egg

"That should do it." Sir Roye sounded satisfied, emptying one last sandbag and then turning to her, happy to have escaped the Tartars. Seeing the arrow, Sir Roye's eyes went wide with horror, and he was instantly at her side, holding her up, warning, "Do not touch it!"

Not a chance—she had no intention of handling the arrow, which was starting to hurt alarmingly. Aria could see by the shaft that it was not a slim-pointed, armor-piercing arrow, but a broad-headed flight arrow that twisted and turned as it went in, tearing open your insides. She was good as dead already.

Gently Sir Roye laid her down on the deck, bending over her and saying, "My love, I can get the arrow out, but it will hurt horribly. Can you stand it?"

"Do I have a choice?" she asked weakly, staring up at the night sky, trying not to look at the arrow, which at best she could barely see.

"That's the spirit." Sir Roye kissed her, then gripped the base of the shaft and the silk shirt next to it. "I learned this from Tartars, who know all about arrow wounds."

He slowly pulled on the shirt, easing the silk out of the wound. "When an arrow hits loose silk, the point carries it into the wound. If you pull out the fabric, it will bring the point with it, retracing the arrow's path as the silk unwinds, doing no further damage."

Damage already done had Aria on the verge of fainting, and every tug on the fabric hurt like fire. Her hands clutched at the deck, nails digging into the thin wickerwork as she fought not to move. Closing her eyes, she tilted her head back, breathing in short, sharp gasps. Finally she did faint, slipping thankfully into a black void. If this was dying, so be it. By now she knew that Death could be a good friend.

Aria awoke smelling incense, lying in the lamplit cabin, right where her uncle's corpse had rested. Sir Roye was at her side, looking very concerned. Surprised to see him so worried, she asked, "What is happening?"

He smiled faintly. "I am sewing you up."

So he was, patiently pulling thread through her flesh. She remembered being shot, and passing out in pain on the deck, but the prick of a needle felt like nothing compared with the fire in her side. Her silk shirt was a mess, torn and matted with blood, mixed with yellow medicinal powder. She asked soberly, "What happened to Prince Akavarr?"

"I threw him overboard." Sir Roye tied the last stitch, then bit off the thread, asking, "Are you thirsty?"

"Parched." Aria's body cried for the fluids that had spilled out the hole in her side. Sir Roye propped her up, which hurt terribly, and held a sweet-smelling clay jar to her lips. She sipped and sputtered, expecting water but getting something startlingly tangy. "What is this?"

"Rice wine." Sir Roye encouraged her to drink some more. "It will help with the pain."

She did, drinking until her head got dizzy and her body felt numb. Then she lay back, and Sir Roye covered her with a blanket and a fur-lined Tartar flying jacket. Aria asked, "Where are we headed?"

"Downwind." Sir Roye did not sound like he much cared. "Almost due eastward, I would guess."

That was good. Burning Mountain lay east and north, deep within the Iron Wood, but it seemed silly to say that now, flat on her back and bleeding horribly. Instead she said, "Please give me the Firebird's Egg."

Sir Roye brought it to her, and Aria curled up around the Egg's warm, pulsing presence, then passed out again.

When she next awoke, it was daylight. This time Sir Roye had tea ready, warm and stirring, which went down better than the rice wine. He held the teacup, which seemed to weigh a ton, and stroked her sweetly while she drank.

Then he asked to see the wound, though her body clung tenaciously to the Egg even in her weakened state.

Gently, he separated her and the Egg enough to get a look at the wound. Aria saw a small slash of angry red flesh closed by Sir Roye's neat stitches. "Bleeding has stopped," he told her. "An excellent sign."

She lay back and looked up at him, asking, "Will I live?"

"You will if I have any say." He pushed aside wet black hair, stuck by sweat to her brow. "You are my heart, my love."

Aria smiled weakly, saying, "That is worth living for."

If she died now, it would be incredibly unfair. After having found each other despite impossible odds and immense dangers, they would never have time to be truly together. Not even a single night. Sonya D'Medved would be the only person she had ever been to bed with. What was the sense in that? Lady Death could be alarmingly arbitrary.

Hugging the Egg back to her, Aria said a silent prayer to the Bone Witch, begging her foster mother's help on this most perilous quest. *Preserve me for a little while, at least.*

Sir Roye boiled millet for her on the little charcoal stove, but Aria could not keep it down. When the Egg was not pressed against her belly, her insides hurt like fire. Her knight feared it might be infection, or poison. "Tartars are great poisoners. Which was why I was so set on getting the arrow out immediately, without tearing the silk."

Wiping vomit mixed with millet off her chin, she thanked him. "Without you, I would be dead already."

He kissed her tenderly. "You are all I have. My titles, my marriage, even my knighthood are mere mirages. You are all I care about."

So much for Sonya. Aria knew that if she died from this Tartar arrow, her favorite handmaid would soon be comforting Sir Roye in the nude—just like the last time her knight got lost. No oaths or vows could hope to keep them apart, since they would both have just lost the love of their life. Grief would bind them like lodestones. How strange to think that she was the love of Sonya's life as well. She remembered Sonya's eager smile and her golden hair spilling over the pillow. God, she hoped Tolstoy had not hurt her. Then one of them at least would live.

At midday, they passed over the Great Mother River, the only break in a vast sea of treetops. Sir Roye guessed the wind was from the south and west, and rather strong. "It is like we are being blown straight toward the Iron Wood."

Westerly winds were the most common, but Aria did not doubt that there was magic behind this stiff breeze. So long as the Tartars were trying to get home, the winds were hard from the south, but now the wind had veered around to the westward—which did not help the Tartars much, but was dead on for Burning Mountain. By dusk, Aria could see the dark line of the Iron Wood in the distance.

She suffered from night sweats, and then chills, while Sir Roye spooned rice wine down her throat. He was clearly worried about what sort of care he could give her in midair. "Once over the Iron Wood, it will be impossible to come down."

"I do not plan to," Aria replied wearily, starting to shake again.

He drew a comforter around her, asking, "What does my princess plan?"

"To get some sleep, then see how things appear in the morning." Assuming she survived the night.

He fixed her a pillow, and sang French love songs to her until she fell into a hot fitful sleep. As Aria lay curled around the Firebird's Egg, chilled and sweating at the same time, the Bone Witch entered her fever dreams, sorting through the fear and poison from her wound—discarding pain, horror, despair, hurt, and regret. Leaving only hope. And love.

Wakened by the weird dream, she asked her knight, "Where are we headed?"

He felt her forehead, then pulled the comforter tighter around her. "The Little Bear is still off the port bow, so the southwest wind must be holding. Maybe even blowing stronger."

"Good." Aria closed her weary eyes.

Sir Roye added, "There is a low red star almost dead ahead, very near the horizon, a strange one I have never seen before."

"That is Burning Mountain," she muttered, then went back to sleep. Clearly the Bone Witch was guiding the boat, and all Aria could do was attempt to mend a little. Tomorrow would be the true test.

Aria awoke to terrible nauseating pain, worse than when Sir Roye pulled out the arrow. All morning she lay hugging the Egg; unable to eat, or even stomach the smell of wine or boiling millet. Sir Roye made her tea and kept her as comfortable as he could, until noon, when he told her she needed to come on deck. "Forgive me, but you must see what lies ahead."

Gingerly, Aria tested her side, seeing if she could stand. It hurt horribly, but not enough to keep her off her feet. An anxious Sir Roye helped her pull on a rancid Tartar flying jacket and stagger out onto the tiny deck. Looming ahead of them downwind was a huge cone-shaped mountain, rising right in the sky-boat's path.

Wisps of white smoke billowed from the flat snow-clad peak, trailing away from them. Aria nodded. "Burning Mountain—it looks much bigger by daylight."

"So I see." Sir Roye eyed the volcano warily. "What are we going to do?"

"We must land on it," Aria explained. "Atop that mountain is the Firebird's Nest."

Sir Roye grimaced. "I feared you would say that. Why not wait until you are more mended?"

Why not? Despite the pain in her side, and the poison in her system, she could stand and talk, even think clearly—two nights alongside the Firebird's Egg did that. Who knew—given a few more nights, she might be fine. Aria was sorely tempted to give the Egg more time, for she desperately wanted to live, yet she shook her head, saying, "I will not make the same mistake that killed my father. We must return the Egg to the nest."

Sir Roye was unconvinced. "Can a few days matter so much?"

"Absolutely." Aria had no doubt. "My father stole the Egg, thinking he could use the magic for himself, but it killed him, and brought a fratricidal curse on my family. Certainly the Egg is healing me, but where did my wound come from? I used to live a charmed life in the woods—untouched by leopards or troll-bears—while you survived all those losing battles without a scratch. Since taking possession of the Egg, both of us have been wounded, the Bone Witch has been killed, and I have seen two of my uncles turn traitor and die."

"And a Tartar arrow has pierced my heart," Sir Roye added.

Aria hated to give up the Egg that was healing her, but she had to, saying, "Ivan and I must have a clean start."

Sir Roye gave in. "So you shall."

Exhausted from being away from the Egg, she asked, "Do you think you can land me on that mountain?"

Baron de Roye stared at the snow-clad volcano drifting toward them on the wind, looking as though he wished he had stayed in Bordeaux. "I do not see how we can miss it."

"Great," Aria whispered. By now the pain from standing was unbearable, and she felt her knees buckle. Sir Roye had to carry her back into the cabin, where he wrapped her up in the comforter, along with the Firebird's Egg.

Soon she was asleep again, drifting in and out of fever dreams, none of which included the Bone Witch.

Sir Roye woke her with a freshly brewed cup of tea, holding the cup for her.

He nodded at the aft end of the cabin, where she could see out the stern, through the caged-in pigeon coop. "We have company coming."

Her wound hurt worse than when she went to sleep. Peering through the coop, Aria saw what looked like a flock of rocs with thick black wings rising up out of the Rift.

"Tartars, a couple of arbans at least," Sir Roye estimated. "A half-dozen sky-boats, maybe more. They must have been warned by pigeon-post, maybe even one of the birds from that coop. Right now, they are accelerating as they climb, and gaining on us. I will dump ballast too, and try to stay ahead, making for a spirited downwind chase."

Pursuit at least gave her something to do. Even while lying curled in pain in the little cabin, Aria could look out the stern, watching the Tartar sky-boats grow bigger, gradually closing the gap between them. Sir Roye had the parasail angled to propel them forward as they dropped ballast and climbed, but he was just learning sky-sailing, while the Tartars had been flying all their lives.

As the Tartars crept closer, Sir Roye returned and tried to feed her some millet, which she promptly threw up.

Staring back out the stern coop, Sir Roye gauged distances, saying, "The Tartars are bound to catch us. In a flat-out chase, I might keep ahead of them until nightfall, then lose them in the dark, but we need to land this boat. As soon as I start to set down, they will be all over us."

With their deadly bows. She looked at him solemnly, saying, "The Egg must get to the Nest. We are too close to fail."

Sir Roye daubed vomit off her sweaty cheek with his silk handkerchief. "But we cannot just fly over and drop the Egg in."

"Why not?" Aria honestly hoped it might be that easy.

Sir Roye shook his head, having learned rudimentary aeronautics from the Tartars. "That huge plume of steam and sulfur rising from the mountaintop would send us whirling upward, probably even set the parasail gas afire. There is no way to make a pass low enough to drop the Egg in—best I can do is set us down on a snowfield upwind of the summit."

Summoning her strength, she told him, "Get me close enough, and I can take the Egg to the Nest."

Sir Roye was not so sure. "And the Tartars?"

She kissed him. "Alas, my love, you must deal with them."

Her knight's face brightened at the kiss. "So if I set you down by the summit, then I can take on the Tartars alone?"

Aria hated to leave him again, but it was their only hope. Back in the woods, when birds tried to hide their egg clutch, one of the parents would flutter helplessly away, hoping to draw off the hunters. "Forgive me for putting you in so much danger."

"What danger? A couple of dozen flying nomads." Sir Roye smiled at her concern. "So long as you are safe, I do not care how many Tartars I must face."

His cheerful certainty reassured her, and back on deck, her knight helped her into oversize Tartar boots and fur-lined leggings, stuffing cloth in the boots to make them fit. Then they strapped the Egg to her belly as though it were a baby, crossing a long length of cloth over Aria's shoulders and around her middle—the loose flying jacket went on over it all, making her feel like a pregnant Eskimo. Glancing back, Aria saw the nomad parasails were still gaining—so close, she could make out the boat hulls hanging beneath them, but not the men on board.

Slowly the mountain bore down on them, while her knight searched for a landing site, eventually selecting a broad tilted snowfield near to the peak. Which meant lightening the ship even more, and Sir Roye began pitching things over the aft rail, including bedding, wickerwork, cooking pots, and even the cabin door. Aria watched the Tartars do the same, dumping ballast and personal belongings in a determined attempt to catch up. Soon they were level with the snowfield, headed for a bumpy landing.

Up close, Aria saw that the flat-topped peak was a steaming volcanic caldera, ringed with frost and snow, looking like a vast ice-witch's cauldron. Boiling Mountain would have been a better name. Hugging the Egg to her belly, she drew strength from its pulsing warmth. With the Egg pressed against her wound, she might actually make it up the mountain, assuming the Tartars did not put more holes in her.

When it was time to take the leap, tears welled up in her sea-green eyes. Despite her determination to do right, Aria felt like she was giving up everything to return the Egg—her love, her life, her only hope of being healed.

Stuffing rice balls and jerky into the flying jacket, Sir Roye helped her over the aft rail, holding on to her arms to steady her. Face-to-face across the rail, he saw her tears and asked, "Do you really want to do this?"

No, not at all. She wanted to be with him—but no one was giving her that choice. Not the Bone Witch. And not the Tartars. "Yes," she lied. "This is the only way."

Looking down, she saw the first of the snowfield drifting beneath her, coming closer as the mountain tilted upward. Sir Roye leaned forward and kissed her on the lips, saying, "Until we meet again."

Aria replied with a teary smile, then braced herself for impact. The dark shadow of their parasail slid silently over the dirty snow.

Then they hit, bow-first. Plowing into the snow, the sky-boat jolted to a stop, and Sir Roye let go. Aria pushed off from the rail, falling backward to protect the Egg. She hit hard, rolling into the wet summer snow, finding it not near so soft as it looked—fortunately her big boots and Tartar jacket cushioned her fall. As soon as she let go, the lightened sky-boat lifted off again.

When she looked up, the boat was already drifting away over the snowfield, with Sir Roye at the stern rail, rapidly lightening ship some more, trying to make it over the mountain's white shoulder. Lying still in the snow, she said her spell.

On her back, staring straight up, hugging the Egg, Aria soon could not see the low-flying sky-boat, so she could not tell if Sir Roye had made it over the montain. Presently the nomad sky-boats appeared, drifting slowly across the sky. She counted five sails passing almost straight overhead. Where was the sixth? It was too much to hope that it had hit the mountain.

Suddenly the sixth one appeared right on top of her, coming in low to scan the snowfield, examining the spot where their prey had touched down. She saw Tartars leaning over the rail, their breath misting in the cold air, searching for her with dark alert eyes. All they saw was a hole in the snow.

Keeping still, she let her pursuers pass above, then float away downwind. She counted to nine hundred, slowly, giving them time to go and getting some much-needed rest. When it was safe, she looked up, seeing nothing: no Sir Roye, no Tartars, just white blinding snow blending into frosty sky. Somewhere above her, beyond the slanted snowfield, lay the Firebird's Nest.

She started out over the wet heavy snow, her big Tartar boots leaving deep hollow prints, a horribly obvious trail, easily seen from the air. Too bad. She was putting herself beyond such worries, climbing a snow-clad volcanic peak in the heart of the Iron Wood, hundreds of leagues from food and shelter, with nothing to sustain her but rice balls and jerky. Unless her knight came back for her, cold and hunger would find her long before the Tartars did.

Hugging the Egg tighter, she marveled at how it held her upright—without the Egg, she doubted she could even stand, much less slog through wet snow.

Yet slog she did, across the snowfield and over a gray, ash-covered glacier that groaned underfoot as Burning Mountain melted the ice from below. Great gaping cracks split the glacier, forcing her to cross unstable crevasses on tilted blocks of ice and cinder, tall dirty icebergs overlooking steaming craters and milky-blue acid lakes.

Eventually, gray glacier gave way to steep cinder slopes dusted with snow, leading up to the cone. She set out, finding it harder going, stumbling and sliding back, having to take long detours when the slopes got too steep or boulders blocked the path. And the higher Aria got, the harder she fought to breathe. Shooting pains pierced her lungs, and a sore rattle in her throat followed each ragged breath.

Finally, forcing her breath in and out was too much effort. Her lungs ached, and so did her legs, so much that the pain of her wound was a pleasant memory. Unable to go farther, she dropped to her knees, wrapping herself tightly around the Egg, hoping to draw as much strength as she could.

As she crouched there, eyes closed, breath misting in front of her, thinking of nothing but breathing, a voice in her head said, "You have done well, Daughter. Wonderfully well."

She recognized the cold, crisp voice of the Bone Witch. Aria told her foster mother, "I have tried my utmost."

"And almost succeeded." The Bone Witch applauded her efforts. "All you must do is get up and go on."

Aria opened her eyes and saw she was not talking to thin air. The Bone Witch stood in front of her, wearing her winding-sheet dress and child-bone necklace, white hair whipping in the wind. Aria smiled to see the woman who raised her, almost in the flesh. Straightening up, she asked, "Can I give you the Egg?"

The Bone Witch looked puzzled. "Give me the Egg?"

"Yes, give you the Egg, so you can return it." *And I can lie down here to die,* she thought. "The Nest is not far off."

"I cannot," her foster mother explained. "I am dead."

That seemed a thin excuse. She herself would be dead soon, and then who would deliver the Egg?

"There are some things that only the living can do," the witch insisted. "So you must get up and go on."

Aria shook her head miserably. "I cannot even get up."

"Yes, you can," the Bone Witch told her. "I cannot deliver the Egg, but I can get you to your feet."

Hard to believe, but the Bone Witch did it, extending a withered hand to her foster daughter. Aria took it, finding the freezing cold fingers sent energy coursing through her limbs. Pain faded and her knees straightened. Still clinging to the witch's icy skeletal hand, she set out again.

Together they tackled the slopes, one at a time, and Aria did not stop until she reached the crater top and looked down into the vast steamy cauldron, feeling Burning Mountain's hot sulfurous breath in her face. Below she could see her goal: a steaming acidic green lake bordered by clean white sand, and ringed by fiery wormholes, open vents in the basalt leading to the hot column of magma that made the mountain burn.

"It is all downhill from here," the Bone Witch promised.

Aria could well believe it. "Straight into hell, from the look of things."

"That's the spirit, Daughter," declared the Bone Witch. "It is good to see you have your confidence back."

Resignation was more like it. Aria no longer thought the task was impossible, just appallingly lethal. She no longer feared failing, but dying. And to the Bone Witch, that was nothing at all. With a jaunty "Farewell, my child," the Bone Witch vanished, leaving her alone on the mountain.

Hungry for the first time since being hit by the arrow, Aria sat down on a gray rock spattered with yellow crystals, to celebrate by eating one of her rice balls, washing it down with handfuls of snow. Snow, air, and rice ball all tasted of sulfur, and above her, the Tartar sky-boats were back, circling like vultures. By winding downward around the hot updraft, the sky-boats could maneuver almost at will, a very impressive bit of flying—but they had to come right into the volcano's fiery mouth if they meant to get her.

Seeing no sign of Sir Roye or his sky-boat, Aria begged the Bone Witch to watch over him. Then she descended into the steaming cauldron, negotiating slopes of slippery black grit and knee-deep volcanic ash threaded by hot streams of melted snow, bright green with algae—the first life she had seen on the mountain.

Fumaroles painted sulfur yellow and rust orange sent up roaring columns of searing toxic steam. Every so often, one of the bigger vents would belch suffocating ash and poison gas, forcing her to bury her face in her sleeve until she could breathe again. At the bottom lay three steep cinder terraces, each wider than the last, ending in the white beach of shining volcanic sand bordered by colorful heat-loving algae. Clouds of steam wafted off the simmering chlorine-green lake, stinging her eyes and making her head swim.

Kneeling down, Aria dug into the crystalline sand, hollowing out a warm hole. Then she untied the Firebird's Egg, kissed it good-bye, and for the final time slid it into the ground, saying a simple prayer and covering up the Egg with white sand.

She had done it, returned the Egg to the Nest, completing her impossible quest and making up for her father's terrible mistake. Hopefully the Bone Witch was happy.

Pain washed over her, nearly knocking Aria senseless. Collapsing into a heap on the sand, Aria lay groaning in agony, surprised at how much it hurt, since the wound itself was nearly healed. Without the Egg, she had no hope of climbing out of the crater and hiking down the frozen mountain, dodging Tartar sky-boats on the way. Aria could see them now and then through the steam, vulturelike shadows circling closer. No thanks—unless the mountain really erupted, she was staying right here.

Felled by pain and fatigue, Aria slipped into a stupor and dreamed she was back in the Bone Witch's hut, the way it was before Prince Sergey burned it, with doves cooing in cool eaves formed by long white mammoth bones. The Bone Witch was there with her rats and doves, saying, "Well done, Aria, well done. I knew you would do it."

Aria beamed in her sleep, happy to have done one thing right, despite horribly botching everything else, losing her knight and her life. "I tried."

"I will miss you terribly," the Bone Witch went on, looking fondly at her. "Though you were the death of me, you were a delight at the end of my much-too-long life."

Fearing the witch was leaving again, Aria asked, "What shall I do?"

"Why, take care, my child." The Bone Witch managed to sound kindly. "Always comfort the weak and dare to do right. Make me proud." With that, the Bone Witch did disappear, and Aria slept.

Warm sand shook as the mountain beneath stirred, jerking Aria awake. She could barely believe it. What a nightmare. Aria had finally gotten half-comfortable, sound asleep and barely in pain, and now Burning Mountain had started to erupt under her. Hardly fair.

Struggling awake, she rose painfully to all fours, as the chlorine-green lake began to boil over, throwing up a thin hot acid rain that burned as it fell. Tartar sky-boats were gone, racing off downwind, clearly having seen their fill.

Cinder slopes heaved around her, and sparks spewed upward, blowing away the acid rain. Glowing strands of lava flew through the air, trailing dark glassy threads that broke off and danced in the updraft. Glad to have her Tartar jacket, Aria shaded her eyes with her sleeve as a magnificent fireball shot into the sky, sending flames streaming in all directions.

At first she thought this was the mountain blowing its top, but then she saw it was the Firebird, not the little flame jay that guided her and gave warning, but the huge magical bird itself, born in fire, and brighter than a thousand suns. Spreading his shining wings, the Firebird kept Aria from harm as fire fell out of the sky like snow.

Slowly the mountain subsided, shaking stopped, and nature turned quiet as the newborn Firebird stood over her, already bigger than the biggest roc, his rainbow plumage the color of fire: crimson and ruby, blazing yellow, lava orange and lightning white, with electric blue plumes around his big golden eyes. His head was next to her, and his long red tongue licked her wound.

For a while she just lay there, marveling at the bright huge bird while his healing tongue licked her side. When he was done, the wound had healed and her pain was gone—so were the stitches, plucked out by the bird's sharp beak.

Rising to her feet, she looked the Firebird full in the face, and he bent down to greet her, begging for affection the way sparrow nestlings did when she held them in her hand, thinking she must be their mother. Reaching up, she stroked him softly, between his big golden eyes.

He liked that, nuzzling her, and licking her hand. Both she and the Firebird were parentless—not quite orphans, but plainly on their own. Yet from now on, they would have each other, and Aria told him so. "We will face the world side by side, since you are new to it, and I have been there. Together we can make the Bone Witch proud."

He nodded his great plumed head, showing he understood, and she saw her smiling self reflected in a gold saucer-size eye.

Climbing onto the Firebird's broad back, Aria found a spot where she could sit, sheltered by his plumage, with her legs straddling his neck. Leaning forward, she told the young bird to fly, and they took off, spiraling up into the great updraft rising from Burning Mountain. Below her, four black patches stained the snow—broken Tartar sky-boats crashed on the side of the peak, their parasails ignited by the brilliance of the Firebird's eruption. Aria and the newborn Firebird flew triumphantly over them, winging away downwind in search of her knight.

18

the princess and the firebird

Aria had never flown so high and fast before, and the sense of freedom she got was greater even than what being Princess-Regent allowed her. Having the giant bird beneath her really made her feel like the Bone Witch's foster daughter—mortal, for sure, but sitting in Heaven's hand. Sun shown down on her, and clouds stretched below, as the bird glided along, borne north and east by the breeze blowing off Burning Mountain. For the first time since leaving the woods, Aria felt like she could go wherever she willed, whenever she wished. So long as she and the Firebird were together.

What she wished most was to find Sir Roye, despite the huge plume of smoke spreading out downwind. Urging the Firebird upward, she climbed over the billowing smoke, searching the pure air above. Far downwind, hanging over the volcanic plume, were two Tartar sky-boats. She had seen four crashed on the mountain, so these were probably the two left over—but Aria decided to take a look.

She was glad she did. What looked like two boats from a distance turned out to be three. Two of the sky-boats were grappled together, while the third hung just upwind, firing arrows at the grappled boats. Her heart leaped, knowing her knight would surely be in the midst of that mess.

As the Firebird approached, arrows began to wing toward Aria as well. Sinking into the flame-colored feathers, she hugged the huge bird's neck as a Tartar arrow whizzed past her. More terrified than ever of their razor points, she could not help hiding behind her mount.

Another arrow struck the Firebird's wing, and Aria winced in fear, thinking of the poison that nearly killed her.

Her irritated companion answered with a breath of fire that ignited the sky-boat's gas cells. Flames turned the parasail into a black blotch in the sky while the boat fell whirling down, disappearing into the brown volcanic cloud below.

Horrified that he might do the same to her knight's boat, Aria told her mount, "No! No fire!"

He gave her a puzzled look, but complied. All that time spent guarding the Egg, and being healed by the Egg, had produced a primal bond between them. Aria doubted that the bird understood her words as much as read her mind. Still, it helped her to shout out the commands, if only to focus her thoughts.

As they flew nearer the grappled boats, she saw her knight defending against two attackers while dodging and deflecting arrows fired by a third. Aria pointed at the archer, telling her bird, "Grab the bowman."

Swooping down on the locked boats, the giant bird grabbed the surprised bowman from behind, holding the struggling Tartar in his talons, then looking back at her.

She smiled in approval, saying, "Perfect! Now let go."

Which the Firebird did, and the Tartar fell screaming from his grasp. Aria gave her mount a pat, and they circled back toward the boats, where the last two Tartars faced her knight across the locked boat rails. As they approached, an archer turned to face them, nocking an arrow.

Afraid he would make the Firebird flame the boats, she told the bird to swerve, throwing her whole body into the turn. Wheeling about, the Firebird threw off the man's aim, and the arrow went wide. The archer nocked another one.

Sir Roye de Roye took a swing at the Tartar in front of him, knocking the man off the rail. Then he leaped across the gap between the boats, scrambling onto the far rail, desperate to get at the bowman before he fired.

Just as the archer took aim, the Lucerne hammer came down, catching the bowman by surprise. But the blow rebounded against Sir Roye, and he lost his footing on the rail, stepping back into empty space, still clutching his blood-spattered pole arm.

"Catch him!" Aria screamed, pointing at the falling knight, and the Firebird went into a stoop, speeding after the flailing Sir Roye de Roye.

Aria watched in horror as her knight tumbled out of sight, vanishing into the volcanic cloud below. Plunging into the brown darkness, the Firebird did not hesitate for an instant, shooting straight through the choking mass, while Aria held her breath in fear. They had only seconds to find her knight before he hit the ground, and she could not even see the Firebird's wingtips.

Bursting back into the sunlight, Aria saw Sir Roye come falling out of the cloud straight in front of her. Without breaking his stoop, the Firebird plucked her knight right out of midair, seizing Sir Roye's armored body in his strong talons.

Delirious with joy, Aria shrieked her approval, then dug in her heels, ordering the bird, "Down."

Determined to see that Sir Roye was whole and alive, Aria guided the Firebird to a rocky clearing surrounded by dark metal trees. Here she had the huge bird set her stunned knight down; then she did a hurried dismount that ended in his arms.

Soon as he saw her, he cast aside his hammer, which he had held on to even while hurtling through ash and smoke. His arms went around her, and his voice wavered, saying through tears, "When I saw the mountain blow, I was sure you were gone."

And here she was, alive and whole, better even than when he left her. "We have got to stop giving each other up for dead."

He grinned, and wiped his eyes. "Since we are clearly fated to be together."

Hardly a hideous fate. He kissed her long and hard on the lips, making Aria wish they were not standing in a barren clearing, surrounded by the Iron Wood. His hand went inside her flight jacket, feeling for where the arrow had gone in, finding only a small scar. Sir Roye de Roye knelt down and kissed that scar as well.

Then he looked up at the huge flame-colored bird, saying, "So this is the Firebird?"

Aria beamed with pride. "Is he not magnificent?"

Her knight nodded, plainly amazed by the bird. "You did not say the bird would be born full-fledged and ready to fly."

"I did not know." Aria was having to feel this out, exploring the bond between her and the bird. Right now she just wanted to know if the Firebird would bear Sir Roye on his back as well as in his talons. So she introduced her knight to the bird, saying, "This is Baron Sir Roye de Roye, Chevalier de l'Étoile, my love and personal champion."

She wanted to be sure the bird did not drop her knight, or barbecue him by mistake. Then she tied Sir Roye's hammer across his back and showed him how to mount behind her. Glancing up at the iron branches with their blade-sharp leaves, Sir Roye shivered, saying, "My God, I am glad not to fall on those."

Aria agreed, guessing that the fallen Tartars had been pretty well shredded before they hit the ground. That's what they got for assaulting folks in the Iron Wood—a task best left to the local ghouls and lycanthropes. Wishing she had a proper saddle like Persphone's, Aria clung to the bird with her hands and knees, telling him to take them out of the Iron Wood.

Her bird did not hesitate, taking off with both of them, headed west. Aria guessed the Firebird was hungry, and had seen nothing edible in the metal forest. Black treetops gave way to green ones, and Aria brought the Firebird down at the head of Long Lake, the thoroughly familiar forest where she had spent much of her childhood.

By now the Firebird was so starved that he snagged an unwary swan on the way down and immediately made the big white bird his first meal. When the swan was reduced to blood and feathers, Aria sent the Firebird off to hunt some more while Sir Roye built a shelter for the night.

When dusk fell, the Firebird returned, bringing back half a deer for them to eat. Sir Roye cut up one haunch and used the spiked tip of his hammer to roast strips of venison. Aria had never eaten meat that tasted so sweet. Then she curled up and went to sleep between her knight and the fire.

Awaking to sunrise over tree-lined Long Lake, Aria felt her life coming full circle, lying within sight of the path she took to go fungus gathering the day she first found her knight. Staring up through the branches at blue bars of sky, she heard the flame jay call her name. *"Ahrr-ee-haa, ahrr-ee-haa, ahrr-ee-haa . . ."*

She spotted the trickster sitting on a tree branch, head cocked, staring smugly down at her—as if the flame jay had sprung some new joke and was about to enjoy its effect. Aside from the Bone Witch being gone, her world was back as it was; only she had changed. She had gone out into the world, and returned the Firebird's Egg. It hardly seemed possible her quest was over, and that Sir Roye lay at her side. She reached out and touched him, just to be sure.

Her touch woke him, and he grinned, pulling her closer. Aria went from musing about her past to having his hands on her flesh, pushing aside her blanket and feeling for her rear. When she started to resist, Sir Roye rolled firmly on top of her, naked and aroused, saying, "I have you now, my dear wood sprite."

"You do, indeed." Having him lying nude upon her, his bare body pinning her to the earth, felt incredibly exciting. For once, Aria was glad to be caught, relieved to be in the hands of someone else, someone she loved and trusted. Aside from family, like Persephone, Aria had hardly anyone on her side, unless you counted dwarfs and eunuchs. And Sonya. Her hips began to move beneath him in anticipation. "What will you do to me?"

His grin widened as he slowly spread her thighs. "What I have wanted to do from the first day we met in these woods."

Looking up at him from her bed of boughs, Aria opened her legs to let him in, excited by his stiff impatient arousal. Now it was about to happen, what the frogs sang about each spring, what eagles cried for on the wing, what every animal in the woods had done, except her. He kissed her tenderly, then whispered, "First, you must forgive me."

"Must I?" Whatever for? For what he had done? Or for what he was about to do? She had made it plain she wanted this, so there was nothing to forgive—except for his dallying with Sonya.

"For thinking I would never see you again." His grip tightened as he pressed her deeper into the bed of boughs. Princess or wood sprite, this time he meant to have her, before she got away.

"I thought you were dead," she reminded him, no longer caring about Sonya or Markovy, or anything but his strong, eager body, smelling of sweat and woodsmoke. As Persephone said, when the right man had hold of her, nothing else mattered.

"I was dead," he told her, "until you brought me back to life." As he said it, Sir Roye de Roye, Chevalier de l'Étoile, *et le* Baron de Roye thrust himself into her, sliding in with just a single stab of pain, followed by an intense wet friction that nearly drove Aria insane.

And not before time. Closing her eyes, she arched her naked body up to meet his thrusts, taking him in as deep as she could, giving herself totally to love. She had saved him, nursed him, pined for him, and loved him, from that first day when her knight came riding over the ridge above Byeli Zamak. Twice he had broken her heart, by pretending to die, then by consorting with Sonya.

And all the time he kept her at arm's length, treating her like a child and doing to others what he should have done to her. But not now, not ever again.

Her whole body convulsed in pleasure. Finally feeling like the wanton witch-princess that her pious enemies feared, Aria rocked back and forth, faster and faster, with Sir Roye de Roye firmly inside her, while sunlight streamed down from the branches above and the flame jay made mocking cries that Aria did not hear. Shutting out the world, she shuddered as she came repeatedly, her bare heels digging through the bed of boughs, making shallow dents in the cool dark forest floor.

Desire subsided by stages, and her body ceased to shake. Aria sank back into herself, staring up at the green forest canopy that had shielded her for half her life, listening to her heart beat harder than she could ever remember. Slowly the woods reawakened around her. Sir Roye asked, "Are you angry with me?"

"About what?" There was not an angry ounce in her body.

He whispered, "About Sonya."

Not at the moment. He had driven Sonya totally out of her head. All Aria could recall was her smiling handmaid rubbing happily against her, wearing nothing but whip marks and a yellow bird tattoo. She still liked Sonya, who had been so fiercely on her side, until they became rivals. "At least you have taste."

"Do I?" He leaned down and licked her nipple, turning it hard with his tongue.

Amazingly, she started to melt again, sliding her leg along his thigh. "Remarkably so."

"For finding the two women in Markovy who are most worth having?" He laughed at her innocence. "You forget, I am French."

What did that have to do with it? Aria still had a lot to learn about the world beyond the trees. He kissed her hardened nipple, asking, "Do you forgive me?"

"For sleeping with Sonya?" Aria sighed. "I fear I must, for I slept with her too."

That shocked him, almost as much as her outrageous opinions on domestic relations. "You made love with Sonya D'Medved?"

"Afraid so," she admitted cheerfully, thinking of their bodies twined together, coming all over the royal bedsheets. How good to have something that could still shock him.

Sir Roye stared at her with surprise, delight, and wonder playing across his face. "That really amazes me."

"Good," she declared. "I hate to be predictable."

Shaking his head, he assured her, "There is no danger of that."

To prove her unpredictability, Aria sat up, saying, "Much as I love this place, we must return to Markov."

"Must we?" Sir Roye looked askance. "I like my wood sprite just the way I have her."

How strange it was to be had. Until now, her life had been defined by having no one, and nothing. Suddenly she had vast responsibilities, and a lover as well, who took indecent liberties with her body, and must be consulted about everything. "My quest is finished, but I am still Princess-Regent, with a Crown Prince to protect and Markovy to rule." And Sonya to save. Fairly daunting, considering that getting this far had nearly killed her, several times.

He pulled her back down, pinning Aria against the boughs again. "And I fancied that if we returned this Firebird's Egg, and lived to tell, I would have you to myself, for a while at least."

Aria looked innocently up at him. "Living off berries and venison?"

"You make it sound delightful." He clearly cared only for her.

"Too delightful." Lovely as Long Lake might look now, teeming with fish and ringed by tall serene trees, life in the woods was no longer enough for Aria, even with her knight at her side. Winter was coming, and she had things to do in the world.

"So what does Princess Kataryna-Maria propose?" Sir Roye asked.

"Reclaiming my capital would be a start." Markov held the keys to the kingdom, the Crown Prince, the Patriarch, her most prominent boyars, most of the country's urban population, and the entire foreign community.

He reluctantly agreed, saying, "Since you are set on going back, there is something I should show you." Reaching into the padded arming doublet lying beneath his mail, he pulled out a sheaf of papers covered with printed characters. "I found these aboard the Tartar sky-boat. They are coded messages between Baron Tolstoy and the Tartars. I cannot read them, but I am guessing the Tartars are paying for information that will be useful if they invade."

Aria had seen the Bone Witch reading Cathayan, and recognized the characters. "If you cannot read them, how do you know the messages come from Tolstoy?"

"I carried them into the Kremlin for him," Sir Roye confessed.

Knowing no one was going to take a foreigner's word against Baron Tolstoy, Aria asked, "Has anyone else seen them?"

"Sonya." Here too her handmaid was ahead of her.

Aria doubted a teenage harlot's testimony would be any more convincing than Sir Roye's. Nonetheless, they had to start now if they meant to get to Markov before the boyars found Ivan, or some unforseen disaster occurred.

It took two days to get to the D'Hay lands north of the capital, and landing the huge Firebird in a manor courtyard created an incredible uproar, scattering serfs and servants. Sir Roye helped her down, then took possession of the master's suite, declaring nothing else would suit Princess Kataryna-Maria.

Slowly the serfs returned. First Aria heard children creep back into the courtyard to gawk at the giant bird, followed by their parents, scolding their boldness and warning them away from the Firebird. Eventually stewards stuck their heads in the master bedroom, where they found their recently deposed Princess-Regent and a brawny foreigner who told the startled retainers, "Inform Lord Valad D'Hay that his princess has returned, and means to be in Markov on the morrow."

They prostrated themselves, then leaped to obey. At dusk the next day, Aria and her knight landed the Firebird in the same harem court where the Tartars had moored their sky-boat. Surprised eunuchs admitted their wayward mistress, and Aria alerted the dwarfs, telling them to bring her Prince Ivan. Then she made a late-night call on Bishop Peter.

Morning dawned cold and dreary, bringing a brisk north wind smelling of snow. Summer was over, and fall promised to be brief and bleak. Dwarfs brought word that a breaking wheel and a pair of burning stakes had been set up in the square, opposite the Red Stairs. Determined to see for herself, Aria wormed her way through dwarf tunnels to a trap that opened above the King's Gallery, the marble balcony where kings of Markovy were proclaimed. Lifting the trap, she looked down on the Kremlin square two stories below her.

Between her harem-palace and the great wooden All Souls' Cathedral, the square was set for executions, with a breaking wheel, two burning stakes, and a great pile of brushwood. Aria said a swift prayer to Lady Death, whose day this clearly was, saying, "If I must die, so be it, but spare those whose only crime is to love me. May you dwell in darkness forever. Amen."

Then she crossed herself, and sent for Ivan. By the time dwarfs brought their little prince to where Aria waited atop the trapdoor, people were assembling below. Nothing brought out Markovites like a multiple execution. Bakers' boys hawked meat pies to the crowd, crying out, "Pirog, pirog, hot and meaty."

Trumpets blared, and she saw Tolstoy and his guards file out of the palace gate, leading a trio of prisoners—Jochi, Sonya, and Tasha. Anna Tolstoy was conspicuously absent.

So much for Sonya having betrayed them to Tolstoy. Jochi and Tasha were pagan nomads, with no rights whatsoever—but Sonya D'Medved would not be there unless she had done something to seriously annoy Baron Tolstoy.

Aria watched in horror as Jochi was bound to the breaking wheel, wearing only a loincloth and his broken balalaika hanging around his neck. Tolstoy's herald read off the charges, including treason, heresy, having illegal and unnatural relations with Princess Aria, and possessing a musical instrument.

Tasha and Sonya were led to the burning stakes, both accused of witchcraft. Only accused, since Tolstoy made no pretense of holding trials. Boyar law allowed lords to juggle the order of justice, and sentences could be carried out before conviction, or appeal. But this was not a real legal triple execution. This was a message to the harem, and to Aria most particularly—turn over Ivan, or else.

And it worked. Her boyars had discovered how to hurt her, even in hiding. Aria watched Tolstoy's guard captain turn her two handmaids over to the executioner—a big muscled brute called Magog, infamous for his skill and cruelty, who could flay a man to the spine with a blow of the knout. Or lightly carve his single initial in a woman's back with a whip.

As Magog bound her to the stake, Sonya D'Medved shouted a vulgar suggestion to the guard captain, who backhanded her across the mouth.

Hitting Sonya only made the boyarinya more mouthy. Which got the crowd on Sonya's side, cheering her retorts with cries of "Good for you, girl" and "Sass 'em, Sonya" mixed with the odd call to "Burn the bitch!" Jochi and Tasha were mere nomads, whose deaths mattered little. Folks had filled Kremlin Square to see how a D'Medved died, and Sonya did not mean to disappoint her public.

Tolstoy's guard captain raised his hand again, his mailed knuckles already flecked with the teenager's blood. "Hit me." Sonya goaded him as serfs piled wood at her feet. "I've known eunuchs more manly than you."

"You have known your last eunuch, Sonya." He nodded toward the nearby altar topped by flint and tinder. "In a few minutes, I will kindle your fire with my own hands."

Sonya smirked. "Finally found a way to warm a woman?"

Tolstoy's captain was at a serious disadvantage, mocked by a pretty girl half his size, with her hands tied, and about to die. He could not help but look silly threatening her.

Chanting rose up to drown out the catcalls as Bishop Peter emerged from All Souls' Cathedral in full regalia, followed by deacons, archpriests, acolytes, cantors, and singing choirboys dressed in white and trimmed with cloth-of-gold—a noisy glittered procession that parted the crowd, preceded by chanting curates swinging smoking censers. Backed by his white-robed flock, the Patriarch of Markovy marched straight up the Red Stairs to the King's Gallery, where he towered over Baron Tolstoy, who sat on horseback to be above the crowd.

Supported by his silver crook, Bishop Peter called down to the boyar, saying, "Cease and desist. What you do here goes against Heaven."

"Really?" Tolstoy sneered. "I thought sodomy, witchcraft, and stringed instruments went against Heaven. We are just carrying out the Almighty's will."

Old Bishop Peter shook his sliver shepherd's crook at the presumptuous baron, shouting, "Blasphemous sinner, Mother Church must judge these crimes! You have no right to say what Heaven wills. Satan has hold of your soul, and you stand on the very edge of the pit. Step back now, or vile death shall take you."

Tolstoy looked wholly taken aback, shocked by the Patriarch's vehemence. "Beware, old priest," Tolstoy warned, "meddle not in men's matters."

Vultures started to circle the square, sensing death below. Above them flew a giant roc, so big, she had to be female.

Seeing Tolstoy would not stop for Bishop Peter, Aria had to act. She swung her legs through the trapdoor, letting herself down into the shadows at the back of the balcony, while everyone's gaze was riveted on the stand-off between the boyar and the bishop. Whispering up to the dwarfs, she had them hand Ivan down to her. He clung hard to her, asking, "What is happening, Aria?"

"Nothing bad." Or so she hoped, her heart beating like a hare's. "We are just going to make an appearance—be a king."

Ivan nodded solemnly, his royal gaze fixed on her. Saying a short prayer to Lady Death and to the Killer of Children, Aria stepped up to the balcony rail to stand beside the bishop, shouting, "Cease, in the name of Prince Ivan."

"Yes! Cease," squeaked Ivan, "in my name."

Cheers erupted from the crowd, ecstatic at seeing their missing prince suddenly appear alive and unharmed on the King's Gallery. Aria saw Tolstoy retainers rush for the Red Stairs with misdirected enthusiasm, since the steps were blocked by monks and archpriests. Looking up in anger, Tolstoy called for Aria to come down. "And bring Prince Ivan with you."

"Prince Ivan is under Church protection," Aria declared. "And you stand accused of treason against the Church, Crown, and country."

As she spoke, a winged shadow swept across the upturned faces of the crowd, a gray feathery shape Aria recognized at once. People cried out in frightened wonder, "Dear Heaven! Look, it's Death's Shadow!"

Tolstoy alone seemed immune to the miracle, still calling to her, "Come down at once, harlot. Or see your creatures burnt."

Aria watched the shadow sweep by a second time, gliding over the sea of faces, like the gray cast that moves slowly over the visage of the dying. Common Markovites fell to their knees in prayer, or stood rooted in the square, stunned by what they were witnessing.

Annoyed with everyone's inaction, Tolstoy told his guard captain, "Kindle the fire." Which the captain did, lighting a pine-knot torch. "Will you come down now?" Tolstoy demanded.

When Aria did not answer, Tolstoy turned to the guard captain, saying, "Immolate one of the women."

Striding over to where Sonya waited, the guard captain held up the lit torch for the bound girl to see, letting her feel the heat. He grinned as the shadow swept past a third time. . . .

"Stop!" Aria cried out. "As your Princess-Regent, I will gladly come down and give justice."

Baron Tolstoy signaled his captain to hold, hoping to get his hands on Aria in trade for Sonya D'Medved and a pair of nomads.

Aria retreated from the balcony, going straight to the harem court, where the Firebird waited. Sir Roye was there as well, wearing a breastplate, mail, and a helmet, and holding his Lucerne hammer. Mounting together, they took off, spiraling up above the Kremlin domes into the sunlight, then coming down in a burst of fire, to land before the Red Stairs.

Tolstoy's retainers scattered, afraid of being burnt or crushed. Aria guided the bird down and urged him to aim high, lest he set the burning wood ablaze. Far from attempting any fancy aerobatics, Aria hoped to keep the half-wild bird on the ground, relying on his angry presence to overawe the crowd.

As the Firebird touched down, Sir Roye leaped off onto the wood piled by the burning stakes. Seeing him coming, the captain dropped his torch at Sonya's feet, then leaped back to draw his broadsword.

Bounding up onto the woodpile, Sir Roye flicked the torch aside with his blade, then spun about, catching the guard captain behind the heel, landing him in an armored heap. Sir Roye stepped down hard on the fallen man's sword, and raised his sawtooth blade. Helmetless, and wearing only mail, the bearded captain was at Sir Roye's mercy, and the Frenchman advised him, "Yield, and be quick about it."

Aria added the weight of law to his words. "Yield at once, or be judged a traitor."

Stubbornly, the captain said nothing, betting that Sir Roye would not decapitate him on the spot.

Tolstoy turned to his master-at-arms, saying, "Take ten men and bring me back that foreigner's head."

"Yes, m'lord," snapped the master-at-arms, who dismounted, motioning for the men around him to do the same. Which they did, though not very eagerly. Their swords were good enough for crowd control, but not much use against plate armor and a pole arm. Sir Roye turned happily to meet them, keeping between the swordsmen and Sonya, with the woodpile at his back.

Soon as Sir Roye turned his back, the silent captain scrambled upright and drew a knife, hoping to take Baron de Roye from behind. Sonya yelled out, "Beware, Sir Roye!"

As she spoke, a silver shaft struck the guard captain from above, a shining arrow that seemed to sprout suddenly from the back of his neck. Crumpling forward, he rolled down the woodpile to land at Sir Roye's feet. Thanking Sonya for the warning, Sir Roye turned back to face the timorous swordsmen, who were not the least encouraged by seeing their captain struck down from above.

Wings beat the air above the square, and a huge woman-carrying roc landed beside the burning stakes. Persephone sat on the bird's back, her silver moon bow in hand—people shrank back farther, giving Death's little sister room.

Tolstoy sat atop his silk-draped mount, staring in astonishment, unable to believe his seemingly simple plan could have gone so alarmingly wrong. Death's sister looked levelly at Magog, who had picked up the captain's fallen torch. "You trespass on my domain, for I am Persephone, Killer of Children, and Protector of Maidens."

Glancing anxiously about, Magog saw he was facing Death's sister alone. Sir Roye stood between Tolstoy's men and the stakes, while the Firebird had driven everyone else back. Magog lowered the torch, protesting, "They are not maidens, m'lady."

"Why?" Persephone asked. "Because you raped them?" Since it was unlucky to execute a virgin, the executioner had the duty to see that did not happen. "Do not think a man may unmake a maid so easily."

Tolstoy's anguished executioner asked, "M'lady, if I have somehow offended—"

Persephone raised a hand. "You have trespassed on my domain. Now you must enter it completely. Any preference how?" She nodded idly at the prone captain. "That was paralysis. He is not even dead yet."

Magog did not answer, watching in terror as Persephone flipped idly through the arrows in her quiver. "Plague? Too slow. Heart failure? Too swift. Stroke? Perfect, don't you think? Gives you time to remember your sins." Settling on the stroke arrow, she shot the horrified executioner with it, saying, "Welcome to our kingdom."

Aria was amazed by the arbitrariness of death, striking down an executioner in the midst of his labors. Startled gasps were followed by shouts of approval from the crowd, rising into a ragged cheer. Tolstoy's executioner had made a successful career of public killing and torturing—now Markovites were free to show their feelings.

Angered, Tolstoy ordered his shamefaced retainers to quiet the crowd, but no one moved. His men were unwilling to rush at Sir Roye's hammer or brave the Firebird's breath, not while Baron Tolstoy sat comfortably aboard his horse, shouting orders. Aria saw his control slipping. There were things loose in the Kremlin Square that people feared more than Baron Tolstoy—whose dreaded executioner had just been shot down by a blond demigod on a big bird.

Persephone told the angry boyar, "I am the Killer of Children, and Prince Ivan is under my authority—his life and death lie in my hands."

"How dare you?" Tolstoy demanded. "A heathen demon with blood on her hands has no rights to our prince royal."

"Really?" Persephone arched a blond eyebrow as she rummaged through her quiver. "What death do you desire?"

"Stop her," Tolstoy shouted to his men—but not a single retainer wanted to get between their lord and Persephone's deadly arrows.

Aria rose up in her perch atop the Firebird, asking Baron Tolstoy, "Do you wish to live?"

"What do you mean?" Tolstoy was a coward on the best of days, and found the question unnerving.

"Do you want to live any longer?" Aria repeated herself politely, as though dealing with a child. "If your answer is no, then you shall die, and things will go on without you. Please be quick—I am a busy woman with much else to do."

Tolstoy stared hard at her, finally saying plainly, "I wish to live."

Just what Aria expected. "Then you must set down your sword and submit to His Royal Highness, Prince Ivan. Anything else, and you are dead." As she said it, Kazakhs with heavy armor-piercing bows took up firing positions atop the harem palace, from which they could sweep the square; among them were men-at-arms wearing the D'Hay shock of wheat.

Aria almost felt sorry for Tolstoy, caught between priests, populace, and armor-piercing arrows. He had foolishly taken on the Church, Death, dwarfs, D'Hays, and her—when all he wanted to do was steal Ivan from the harem. She called to him, "Throw down your arms and submit. Only that will save you."

"Yes," Ivan added shrilly, emboldened by his sister's defiance. "Submit!"

Markovites packed into the Kremlin Square took up their Crown Prince's demand, turning it into a chant. "Submit, submit, submit . . ."

Voices grew in volume, rolling back through the crowd. All their lives, disarmed Markovites had lived in fear of the boyars and their overarmed retainers. Seeing that Death's sister and the heathen Kazakhs meant them no harm lifted that lifelong fear, replacing it with anger at what they had endured. Surging forward, the crowd called out even louder, shouting, "Submit! Submit! Submit! . . ."

One by one, the boyars did, bowing and dropping their weapons, going down on their knees before the child on the King's Gallery. Tolstoy too gave in, sinking to his knees in surrender, drawing an ironic cheer from the joyous crowd.

Jubilant, Aria ordered the prisoners freed, and Sir Roye led them over to her, with Jochi in just his loincloth and the girls in their burning smocks. Sonya gave her a sly lopsided grin, but their personal relations had to wait. Aria dismounted to greet Persephone with a kiss and hug, thanking Death's sister for coming to their aid, adding, "I feared I might never see you again."

Persephone scoffed at that notion, saying, "We are fated to keep finding each other, for you are in the middle of what is happening to Markovy."

Too terribly true. Aria asked, "Did you know all this would happen?"

"What? That you were a princess? And that the Egg would hatch into this magnificent bird?" Persephone admired the Firebird, which towered over the biggest roc, though he was a mere male. What must the females be like?

"No." Persephone shook her head, saying, "I am just the Killer of Children. No one tells me anything."

Aria knew how that felt. How strange it was to think that she and Persphone were just the latest generation in a wildly far-flung family that included kings, godlings, witches, and princesses, all expected to work miracles on command—while their elders sat back and pulled strings.

Persephone encouraged her to look on the bright side, nodding toward Sir Roye. "At least you have found your man."

Surprised and embarrassed, Aria asked, "How did you know?"

Persephone laughed. "By the way you look at him."

"This is my knight," Aria explained proudly, taking Sir Roye by his armored sleeve and drawing him away from Sonya, "who saved me from the Tartars, the one I thought was dead."

"Death does not always come when you think," Persephone reminded her. "Having her for my big sister taught me that right away."

Aria introduced her knight-errant, saying, "Persephone, this is Sir Roye de Roye, Chevalier de l'Étoile, et le Baron de Roye."

Sir Roye bowed and took the demigoddess's hand, finding a couple of fingers free from venom rings to kiss. Straightening up, he asked, "*Persephone* means 'destroyer'—does it not?"

"I am the Killer of Children," Persephone replied modestly, "younger sister to Lady Death."

"How charming to finally meet you." Sir Roye clearly appreciated the irony of being saved by Death. "I have seen your family's work from France to Far Barbary, but this is an unexpected honor."

Persephone thanked him for the compliment, saying to Aria, "I am glad to be leaving you in such good hands."

Then Persephone turned to the other blonde present, Sonya D'Medved, who managed to look fetching despite her bruised lip and burning smock. "How good to see you out of the Gilded Cage."

"Oh, that was all Sir Roye's doing," Sonya explained, stroking her savior's mailed shoulder.

"Really? You are a most handy man, indeed." Death's sister seemed sorry that Aria and Sonya had seen him first. "I hated leaving Sonya behind at Abeskum Island, but you saved her when I failed. Many thanks."

"While killing a slew of Tartars along the way," Sonya added proudly.

"There seems to be no end to your good deeds." Persephone was plainly impressed by Aria's choice in men. "You do my job better than I."

Sir Roye modestly demurred, insisting, "Mademoiselle D'Medved exaggerates."

"Not by much, I imagine." Persephone kissed Aria and Sonya good-bye, then mounted her waiting roc. In a great flutter of wings, Death's sister flew off, rising into the cold sky with her silver bow and poisoned quiver slung across her back, for the Killer of Children had much to keep her busy, and could ill afford to linger. Markovites cheered in happy relief, hoping Persephone would never return.

Ordering everyone to assemble for an audience in the throne room, Aria mounted the Firebird and flew back to the inner harem court. Changing into her skin-tight silver gown, and crown, Aria wrapped herself in a white ermine robe and went to meet her public, finding the throne room crammed to capacity, with the front row occupied by Bishop Peter and lesser patriarchs, plus Sir Roye de Roye, Valad D'Hay, Sonya D'Medved, various boyars, and of course, Baron Tolstoy, looking ridiculously truculent.

Backed by his Kazakhs, Valad D'Hay had disarmed Tolstoy's retainers, piling their weapons in a heap before the throne. Last of all, he tossed Tolstoy's sword on the pile of cutlery, then did a rattling armored bow, immensely pleased at his performance. "Please forgive me, Your Highness, in the absence of orders, I was forced to improvise."

Looking down at D'Hay, Aria decided that whatever his faults, he made a nice picture, kneeling in his shining armor before the gleaming pile of edged steel—a heap of weapons that would no longer be used against her. Not the total answer to her prayers, but a beginning. She bade young Lord D'Hay rise, saying, "Well done, my lord."

Tolstoy was predictably upset, swearing he had done nothing that rated being disarmed and insulted, insisting that Sonya D'Medved had picked up "foul and notorious practices during her horrid adventures in foreign hands."

Who could deny that? When all was said and done, Sonya had transgressed against law and religion with a happy smile on her lips. Aria meant to acquit her errant handmaid, but was not sure how, given that the girl was patently guilty. Sonya solved that by speaking up, saying, "That is not why he meant to burn me."

Tolstoy objected to having the condemned speak for herself, arguing that, "Any testimony from the defendant can only be self-serving."

"We shall hear her nonetheless," Aria announced, and nuns brought Sonya forward, still wearing her burning smock.

Everyone's attention turned to her, men and nuns all hoping to hear some suitably sinful secret from the notorious teenager who was sold into a shah's harem. Sonya pointed at Baron Tolstoy, saying, "He wanted me burned to silence me, because I know he is betraying Markovy to the Tartars."

Not at all what the court had expected. Instead of learning some steamy family secret, they were hearing an accusation of treason against the foremost baron in the land. Worse yet, Sonya had proof, saying, "Baron Tolstoy has been passing secret messages to the Tartars, using Cathayan characters."

Sir Roye de Roye reached inside his armor and produced a sample page. "This is one of many taken from a Tartar sky-boat."

Tolstoy scoffed at such evidence. "There is nothing to connect me to these scribblings but the word of a foreigner, and a whore."

"There is no need to take my word." Sir Roye held up the rice paper sheet for everyone to see. "These pages will speak for themselves. This is a simple checkerboard transformation, turning Markovite letters into specific pairs of characters. Right now, monks are counting and sorting these character pairs from scores of messages. Soon we will be able to read them as easily as the Tartars."

Tolstoy had nothing to say, staring at the paper as if it was his death warrant. When he finally started to protest, Aria silenced him, saying, "There is no need for you to defend yourself before we read the documents. Until a full text is ready, Baron Tolstoy will remain in protective custody."

Declaring this "protective custody" to be preposterous, Tolstoy demanded his freedom, "until real charges, backed by credible witnesses, are brought against me."

Aria patiently explained that that was impossible. "You stand accused of betraying the country to godless foreigners infamous for rape and murder. I fear if I let you go free, someone will take the law in their own hands. Remember what happened to Prince Akavarr, not fifty feet from here—no one wants that repeated."

Least of all Lord Tolstoy. Aria's message was plain: submit to arrest, or die on the Red Stairs. Valad D'Hay's retainers were the only armed men in the throne room, aside from Sir Roye de Roye and the Kazakhs—putting Baron Tolstoy entirely at their mercy. It would not take much urging for the D'Hays to drag the butcher of Hebektahay out to the stairs and do to Tolstoy what his men did to their helpless serfs and retainers. Sending Tolstoy out unarmed was indeed a death sentence.

Kneeling before Aria and putting his hands between hers, Baron Tolstoy begged Princess Kataryna-Maria's protection. Which she gladly granted, wanting him restrained, not martyred. Tolstoy's boyars and retainers would be obliged to obey him, while he was obeying her.

Later that day, Aria met in her private apartments with the other principal in the case, an unrepentant Sonya D'Medved, wearing a virginal white robe embroidered with yellow birds to match her tattoo. To show she had no hard feelings, Aria had fruit sherbet and sugar wafers for them to share—but as soon as they were alone, Sonya went down on her knees, her blond hair brushing the tiled floor. Aria told her to rise, and Sonya refused, saying to the tiles, "Does my princess trust me?"

With Sir Roye de Roye? No way and no how. Otherwise, of course. "That is a silly question."

"It is the only question," Sonya replied, still staring at the inlaid floor. "For without your trust, I am dead."

Aria had been through this before, and told Sonya, "Please, cease. You know I do not mean to kill you."

"Only my princess's trust keeps me alive," Sonya insisted, still talking to the tiles. "I am accused of hideous crimes, committed in your cause. If you reject me, then I am truly dead."

Suitably melodramatic, even if true. "Do you really believe you are being judged for my deeds?"

"We all are," Sonya swore, "the innocent along with the guilty."

And Sonya was both. Aria leaned forward, offering a bowl of sherbet, saying, "Sonya, I do not reject you."

Sonya looked up questioningly. "Really?"

"How could I," Aria asked, "after all we have done together?"

Sonya brightened, taking the bowl of sherbet. "So you do trust me, my princess?"

"With everything but Sir Roye de Roye," Aria answered.

"Good," Sonya declared, "for I will not let a man come between us. You are who I love."

"Do you really love me so?" That still surprised Aria, who thought she had done little to deserve such affection. Sonya's love for her had been by turns startling, exciting, and perplexing.

"Absolutely, I love you." Sonya dipped a sugar wafer in sherbet, then popped it in her mouth. "But if you must be with a man instead of me, I can swear that Sir Roye de Roye is by far the best."

No doubt. Aria meant to find out for herself. "And it does not bother you to see us together?"

Sonya shook her head, saying, "It never bothers me to see you, for you are the one I truly love. It only hurts not to be with you, or not to have your trust."

"Why does my trust mean so much to you?" More even than losing her princess to Sir Roye.

Sonya took another sugar wafer, dipping it in sherbet, and saying, "Do you know how my mother died?"

"You said she died in childbirth." Giving birth could be as dangerous as going into battle.

"That is the story." Sonya's usual smug confidence was replaced by a look of deep sadness that said this too would be the truth.

"My mother was a D'Hay, surprisingly enough, married to the D'Medveds as a peace offering. Had I been a boy, I could have inherited both baronies and united the bloodlines. My birth was easy and joyous, and came early in the

morning, in the Hour of the Wolf, with just a couple of handmaids in atten-
dance, and a serf wet nurse. My mother celebrated by inviting her handmaids
to share a light breakfast of sausage and quail eggs, which none of them
survived—they were all poisoned."

"My God, why?" Aria was horrified.

"Not everyone wanted peace with the D'Hays," Sonya pointed out. "And
they feared the next child would be a boy. Just the wet nurse and I lived, because
she was served bread and beer, and I got only breast milk. To keep peace in the
family, the story was put out that my mother died in childbirth, and her handmaids succumbed to grief. My nurse told me the true story when I was twelve."

And Aria had meant to bring her own mother here from her convent exile.
Her old nurse was right—anyone close to the throne was in danger. Tolstoy's
arrest would merely drive her enemies into hiding.

"That is what our foes will do to win," Sonya whispered. "How can we
hope to defeat them unless we are open and honest with each other? Without
your trust, I would not dare even eat this wafer." Sonya bit down on the wafer,
and swallowed.

Aria reached out and stroked Sonya's cheek, wishing she could take away the
hurt. Some things could not be done by royal decree. Sonya brightened at her
touch, adding affectionately, "And we must let no man come between us."

Not even loving and handsome Sir Roye. Aria wondered if that was even re-
motely possible. Sonya acted like men just did not count, though they owned
all of Markovy beyond the harem walls. Whatever their differences, she and
Sonya still needed each other, almost as much as when they were alone in the
harem. Aria told her, "Yes, you have my trust."

Sonya thanked her enthusiastically, adding, "And your forgiveness?"

"For what?" There was no end to her handmaid's demands.

"For sinfully giving myself to the knight who rescued me." Sonya made carnal intercourse sound like an overly warm thank-you.

"You are forgiven." After all, women were inherently wanton, and bound to
do wrong when not locked away from temptation. But any further sinning with
Sir Roye would be done by the Princess-Regent, not her harlot of a handmaid.

Princess Aria and her knight went flying to be alone, riding together atop the
Firebird, following the main branch of the Markova toward the Great Mother

River, until they came upon a secluded clearing, where they could relax while the bird hunted. Such times in the woods were precious bits of privacy for the Princess-Regent, who missed the freedom of her childhood in the forest.

Sir Roye de Roye set up camp, fashioning a lean-to, and starting a fire. When he was done, he asked, "So, what does Mademoiselle wish?"

"Me?" The question surprised her. "What do I want?"

"Yes, you." Lest there be no mistake whom he meant, Sir Roye leaned over and kissed her neck. "I know what you do not want—me bedding Sonya. But what do you want, not for me or Markovy, but for yourself?"

What a hard question. Even the Princess-Regent could not totally defy civilized opinion, especially when it was expressed with sword points and poison. She told him, "Most of all, I want to see my mother, as soon as it is safe."

"Very commendable," Sir Roye declared. "I too had a mother once, though she died some years ago."

"And I want to have children someday," Aria added. "With you."

"Really?" Sir Roye sounded pleased with the notion. So pleased, he pulled her closer and loosened her harem pants, as if planning to get started at once.

"But not right away," she warned. The Princess-Regent had plenty on her plate, and motherhood could wait. "I already have a little brother I must raise."

"And a brave bright boy he is." Ivan's standing up to Tolstoy's bullying had impressed Sir Roye.

Aria agreed. "One day Ivan will be ruling Markovy, and it is not too soon to pay attention to him. He needs a man to look up to, who will show him how to be a king. I was hoping that would be you."

Sir Roye smiled. "You seem to have big plans for me."

"Immense plans," Aria announced, enjoying the feel of his hands in her pants. "When Ivan is older, I will be free to do as I please. No one will care what children I have by you, since a heretic cannot father legitimate heirs."

Fire jays' cries interrupted them, saying the Firebird was returning. Settling into the clearing, the huge flame-colored bird had clearly eaten, having blood on his claws and beak. Sir Roye stopped molesting her to ask, "What plans do you have for this magnificent bird?"

"None," Aria replied, "but to live with him so long as we are together. Like Ivan, he is younger than me, and someday he will want to find a mate—until then, we can be the best of friends." Power was like Death: you could not defeat it, so you had to learn to live with it, or so the Bone Witch always said.

"And that is fine with him?" Sir Roye was clearly curious about her relationship with the giant raptor.

"He wants what we all want, to be free." To Aria that was as plain as snow in winter. "My father and uncles perished because they tried to bend power to their will, when nature demands you set it loose. But they feared freedom in all its forms, living off serfs, imprisoning their women, and keeping the Firebird's Egg unhatched. It is far too late for that—freedom is loose on the land, and nothing can hold it back. Not now, not ever."

Sir Roye stared at the determined young woman in his arms. "Do you truly believe that?"

"Yes, indeed," Aria assured him. "I was not raised in the woods for nothing. I was brought up to believe in myself, and to do what is needed. Necessity is the law of the wilds. Had I been raised in a harem, I would be as helpless before the Tartars as Turkan Khatun. Only freedom can defeat them."

"How so?" Having seen the Tartars, Sir Roye was sorely afraid that nothing could stop them.

Aria had seen them too, and knew what made them deadly. "The Tartars' strength comes from knowing what they want, and doing whatever they need to get it. They elect their leaders and do not oppress each other, or fight among themselves—finding it far more profitable to fight and oppress others. Anyone in their path who is foolish enough to disarm their people and lock up their women is doomed for sure. Tartars do not fight blindfolded, with one hand tied behind them, so why should we?"

He smiled at her, the frank admiring grin of a man who had found something to believe in. "When you say it, it sounds so right."

To a princess with Death's little sister for a friend, it made absolute sense. "Give them a free choice, and people will oppose the Tartars, but they must be given that choice. Only when we have our freedom will folks be able to say, 'They lived happily ever after.'"